POSEIDON'S GOLD

ALSO BY LINDSEY DAVIS

The Silver Pigs
Shadows in Bronze
Venus in Copper
The Iron Hand of Mars

POSEIDON'S GOLD

A MARCUS DIDIUS FALCO MYSTERY BY

Lindsey Davis

Crown Publishers, Inc.
New York

Published by Crown Publishers, Inc., 201 East 50th Street, New York, New York 10022. Member of the Crown Publishing Group.

Random House, Inc. New York, Toronto, London, Sydney, Auckland

CROWN is a trademark of Crown Publishers, Inc.

Originally published in Great Britain by Century, Random House UK Limited in 1992.

Manufactured in the United States of America

Library of Congress Cataloging-in-Publication Data
Davis, Lindsey.
Poseidon's gold : a Marcus Didius Falco mystery / by Lindsey Davis.—1st ed.
1. Falco, Marcus Didius (Fictitious character)—Fiction. 2. Rome—History—
Vespasian, 69–79—Fiction. 3. Private investigators—Rome—Fiction. I. Title
PR6054.A8925P67   1994   94–13060
823'.914–dc20   CIP

ISBN 0-517-59241-X

10 9 8 7 6 5 4 3 2 1

First American Edition

In memory of
Rosemary Sutcliff
who died while this was being written:
on behalf of all the children who know
how far it is from Venta to the mountains

Extract from the Family Tree

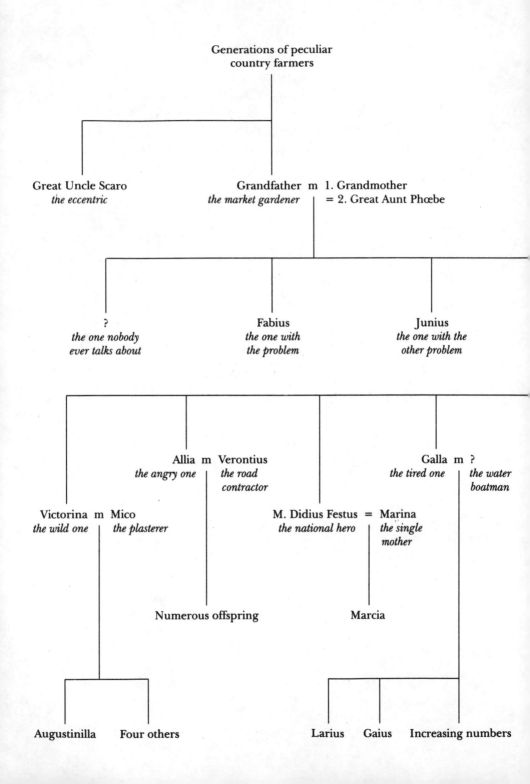

Generations of peculiar
country farmers

Great Uncle Scaro
the eccentric

Grandfather m 1. Grandmother
the market gardener = 2. Great Aunt Phœbe

?
*the one nobody
ever talks about*

Fabius
*the one with
the problem*

Junius
*the one with the
other problem*

Allia m Verontius
the angry one *the road
contractor*

Galla m ?
the tired one *the water
boatman*

Victorina m Mico
the wild one *the plasterer*

M. Didius Festus = Marina
the national hero *the single
mother*

Numerous offspring

Marcia

Augustinilla   Four others

Larius   Gaius   Increasing numbers

# of Marcus Didius Falco

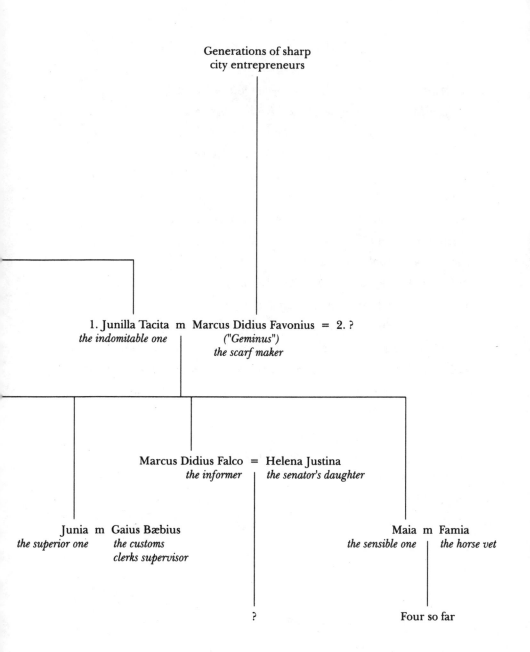

Generations of sharp
city entrepreneurs

1. Junilla Tacita m Marcus Didius Favonius = 2. ?
the indomitable one   *("Geminus")*
                             the scarf maker

Marcus Didius Falco = Helena Justina
        the informer | *the senator's daughter*

Junia m Gaius Bæbius   Maia m Famia
the superior one *the customs*   *the sensible one* | *the horse vet*
                    clerks supervisor

                    ?   Four so far

Key: 'm' = Married;
     '=' = Not exactly married;
     '?' = Unknown, never mentioned in public, or a matter of speculation.

Other Characters in the Story

T Censorinus Macer *a soldier who once believed a hot tip*

Laurentius *a centurion who knows that fortunes are there to be lost*

L Petronius Longus *a watch captain who does his best in trying circumstances*

Marponius *an encyclopaedia salesman: the trial judge to avoid*

D Camillus Verus & Julia Justa *nice parents with normal problems (their children)*

Lenia *a laundress with terrible taste in men*

Epimandos *a waiter who tries to please (on a hiding to nothing)*

Stringy *the cat at Flora's Caupona*

Flora *who probably does not exist*

Manlius & Varga *two painters with short memories*

Orontes Mediolanus *a much sought-after sculptor*

Rubinia *a model whose measurements are worth taking*

Apollonius *a geometry teacher who fails to get the measure of the real world*

A Cassius Carus & Ummidia Servia *discerning patrons of the (lost) arts*

The Aristedon Bros *shippers to the discerning (sailing in tricky waters)*

Cocceius *an 'honest' auctioneer*

Domitian Caesar *a ruler who claims he has to follow the rules*

Anacrites *a spy who maintains that it's not his fault*

Ajax *a dog with a criminal record*

Group of Jewish prisoners *building the Colosseum*

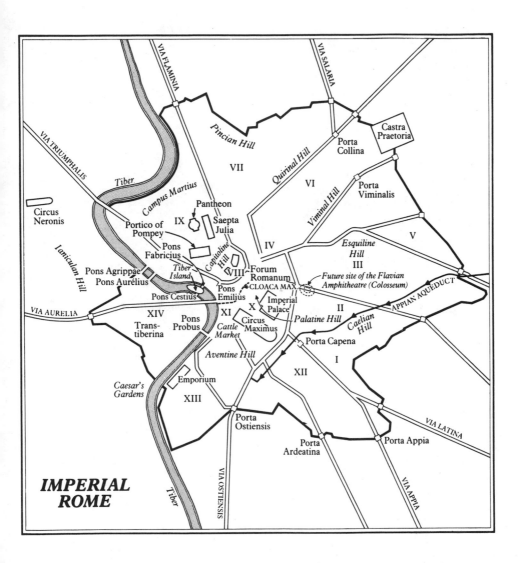

IMPERIAL
ROME

ROME; CAPUA; ROME

March–April, AD72

I

A dark and stormy night on the Via Aurelia: the omens were bad for our home-coming even before we entered Rome.

By that time we had covered a thousand miles, making our journey from Germany in February and March. The five or six hours on the last stint from Veii were the worst. Long after other travellers had tucked themselves up in wayside inns, we found ourselves alone on the road. Electing to press on and reach the city tonight had been a ridiculous option. Everyone in my party knew it, and everyone knew who was responsible: me, Marcus Didius Falco, the man in charge. The rest were probably expressing their views fractiously, but I couldn't hear. They were in the carriage, thoroughly damp and uncomfortable, but able to see that there were colder and wetter alternatives: I was on horseback, completely exposed to the driving wind and rain.

Without warning, the first dwellings appeared – the tall, crowded apartments that would line our way through the un-savoury slums of the Transtiberina district. Run-down buildings without balconies or pergolas stood pressed together, their grim ranks broken only by black alleys where robbers normally lay in wait for new arrivals to Rome. Maybe tonight they would prefer lurking safe and cosy in their beds. Or maybe they would be hoping the weather would put travellers off guard; I knew the last half-hour of a long journey can be the most dangerous. In the apparently deserted streets our hoofbeats and rattling carriage wheels announced our presence resonantly. Sensing threats all around us, I gripped my sword pommel and checked the knife hidden in my boot. Sodden thongs were trapping the blade against the swollen flesh of my calf, making it difficult to extricate.

I wound myself deeper into my waterlogged cloak, regretting it as the heavy folds constricted me clammily. A gutter collapsed overhead; an icy sluice doused me, frightened my horse and knocked my hat askew. Cursing, I fought to control the horse. I realised I had missed the turn that would have taken us to the

1

Probus Bridge, our quickest route home. My hat fell off. I abandoned it.

A single gleam of light down a side-street to my right marked what I knew to be the guard-post of a cohort of the Vigiles. There were no other signs of life.

We crossed the Tiber on the Pons Aurelia. In the darkness below I could hear the river at full surge. Its rushing water had an unpleasant energy. Upstream it had almost certainly overflowed its banks on to all the low ground around the foot of the Capitol, yet again turning the Campus Martius – which could be spongy at the best of times – into an unhealthy lake. Yet again turgid mud the colour and texture of sewage would be oozing into the basements of the expensive mansions whose middle-class owners jostled for the best waterfront views.

My own father was one of them. At least thinking of him having to bale filthy floodwater out of his entrance hall cheered me up.

A huge gust of wind stopped my horse dead in its tracks as we tried to turn into the Cattle Market Forum. Above, both the Citadel and Palatine Hill were invisible. The lamplit Palaces of the Caesars were drowned out of sight too, but I was now on familiar ground. I urged my horse past the Circus Maximus, the Temples of Ceres and Luna, the arches, fountains, baths and covered markets that were the glory of Rome. They could wait; all I wanted was my own bed. Rain cascaded down a statue of some ancient consul, using the bronze folds of his toga as gullies. Sheets of water swept off pantiled roofs whose gutters were quite unable to cope with this volume. Cataracts tumbled from porticoes. My horse struggled to press under the sheltered walkways against the shopfronts, while I pulled his head round to keep him on the road.

We forced a passage down the Street of the Armilustrium. Some of the undrained side-lanes at this lower level looked knee-deep in water and quite impassable, but as we turned off the high road we were going steeply uphill – not flooded, but treacherous underfoot. There had been so much rain sluicing the Aventine lanes today that not even the normal stinks rose to welcome me home; no doubt the customary reek of human waste and unneighbourly trades would be back tomorrow, steamier than ever after so much water had swilled around the half-composted depths of middens and rubbish tips.

2

A gloomy throb of the familiar told me that I had found Fountain Court.

My street. This sour dead end looked bleaker than ever to a stranger returning. Unlit, with shutters barred and awnings furled, the alley had no saving grace. Unpeopled even by its normal throng of degenerates, it still ached with human grief. The wind whooped into the cul-de-sac, then came straight back in our faces. On one side my apartment block reared like some faceless republican rampart built to withstand marauding barbarians. As I drew up, a heavy flowerpot crashed down, missing me by no more than a digit's width.

I dragged open the carriage door to shepherd out the exhausted souls for whom I was responsible. Swathed like mummies against the weather they stiffly descended, then discovered their legs as the gale hit them and fled into the quieter haven of the stairwell: my girlfriend Helena Justina, her waiting woman, my sister's young daughter, and our carriage-driver, a sturdy Celt who had been supposed to help guard us. Hand-picked by me, he had trembled with terror for most of the way. It turned out that he was as timid as a rabbit off his home ground. He had never been out of Bingium before; I wished I had left him there.

At least I had had Helena. She was a senator's daughter, with all that entails, naturally, and more spirited than most of them. She had outwitted any mansio-keepers who tried to withhold their most decent rooms from us and made short work of villains claiming illegal bridge tolls. Now her expressive dark eyes were informing me that after the last hours of today's journey she intended to deal with me. Meeting those eyes, I did not waste effort on a cajoling smile.

We were not home yet. My rooms were six floors up.

We tackled the stairs in silence and in the dark. After half a year in Germany where even two storeys were a rarity, my thigh muscles were protesting. Only the fit lived here. If invalids in financial straits ever hired an apartment over Fountain Court, they were either cured rapidly by the exercise or the stairs killed them. We had lost quite a few that way. Smaractus the landlord ran a profitable racket selling off his dead tenants' effects.

At the top, Helena pulled a tinder-box from under her cloak.

3

Desperation gave me a firm hand, so I soon struck a spark and even managed to light a taper before the spark died. On my doorpost the faded tile still announced that M. Didius Falco practised his trade here as a private informer. After a short, hot quarrel while I tried to remember where I had stowed my latch-lifter and failed to find it, I borrowed a dress pin from Helena, tied it to a piece of braid ripped from my own tunic, dropped the pin down the hole and waggled.

For once the trick worked. (Normally you just break the pin, earn a swipe from the girl and still have to borrow a ladder to climb in.) This time there was a reason for my success: the latch was broken. Dreading the outcome, I pushed open the door, held up my taper and surveyed my home.

Places always look smaller and scruffier than you remember them. Not normally this bad, though.

Leaving home had carried some risks. But the Fates, who love picking on a loser, had thrown every lousy trick at me. The first invaders had probably been insects and mice, but they had been followed by a particularly filthy set of nesting doves who must have pecked their way in through the roof. Their excrement spattered the floorboards, but it was nothing to the filth of the vile human scavengers who must have replaced the doves. Blatant clues, some several months old, told me none of the people to whom I had been giving houseroom had been nicely brought up citizens.

'Oh my poor Marcus!' Helena exclaimed in shock. She might be tired and annoyed, but faced with a man in complete despair she was a charitable girl.

I handed back her pin with a formal gesture. I gave her the taper to hold. Then I strode in and kicked the nearest bucket right across the room.

The bucket was empty. Whoever had broken in here had sometimes made an effort to throw their rubbish into the container I had provided, but they had had no aim; besides, sometimes they hadn't even tried. The rubbish that missed had stayed on the floor until decay welded it to the boards.

'Marcus, darling – '

'Hush, lass. Just don't speak to me until I've got used to it!'

I passed through the outer room, which had once served as my office. Beyond, in what was left of my bedroom, I found more evidence of the human trespassers. They must have fled only today when the old hole in the roof broke open anew to let in a spectacular deluge of pantiles and rainwater, most of which was still soaking my bed. A further inflow of dirty drips was joining the party. My poor old bed was beyond all help.

Helena came up behind me. 'Well!' I made a grim attempt to sound bright. 'I can sue the landlord if I want to give myself a *really* bad headache!'

I felt Helena's hand entwine in mine. 'Is anything stolen?'

I never leave pickings for thieves. 'All my movables were stowed with my relatives, so if anything's missing I know it's gone to family.'

'Such a comfort!' she agreed.

I loved that girl. She was inspecting the wreckage with her most refined distaste, yet her gravity was meant to make me burst into desperate laughter. She had a dry sense of humour that I found irresistible. I threw my arms around her and clung on to her for sanity.

She kissed me. She was looking rueful, but her kiss was full of tenderness. 'Welcome home, Marcus.' The first time I ever kissed Helena she had had a cold face and wet eyelashes, and then, too, it had been like waking from a deeply troubled sleep to find somebody feeding you honey cakes.

I sighed. Alone, I might just have cleared a space and curled up exhausted in the filth. But I knew I had to find a better roost. We would have to impose ourselves on relatives. Helena's parents' comfortable house lay on the other side of the Aventine – too far and much too risky. After dark Rome is a heartless, unethical city. That left either divine aid from Olympus – or my own family. Jupiter and all his associates were steadfastly chomping ambrosia in some other fellow's apartment; they ignored my pleas for help. We were stuck with my lot.

Somehow I chivvied everyone downstairs again. At least the night was so terrible the usual thieves had missed their chance; our horse and carriage still stood forlornly in Fountain Court.

We passed the shadow of the Emporium, which was bolted up but even on a night like this exuded a faint whiff of exotic imported timbers, hides, cured meats and spices. We reached another apartment block with fewer stairs and a less bleak exterior, but still one I could call home. Already encouraged by the expectation of hot food and dry beds, we scrambled up to the familiar brick-red door. It was never locked; no Aventine burglar was brave enough to invade this dwelling.

The rest were keen to be first inside, but I pushed ahead of them. I had territorial rights. I was a boy coming home to the place where he grew up. I was coming home – with an inevitable feeling of guilt – to the house where my little old mother lived.

The door opened straight into her kitchen. To my surprise an oil-lamp stood lit; Ma's habits were normally more frugal. Perhaps she had sensed we were coming. It was quite likely. I braced myself for her greeting, but she wasn't there.

I stepped inside, then stopped dead in astonishment.

A complete stranger was taking his ease with his boots up on the table. No one was allowed that luxury if my mother was in the vicinity. He eyed me blearily for a moment, then let out a deep and purposely offensive belch.

II

Like any self-respecting mother, mine had made her kitchen the
command post from which she aimed to supervise her children's
lives. We had other ideas. That turned Ma's kitchen into a lively
arena for people to eat themselves sick while complaining about
one another loudly in the vain hope of sidetracking Ma.

Some things here were fairly normal. There was a stone cooking
bench partly set into the outside wall with a view to spreading the
weight; in front of it the floor bowed disastrously. Ma lived three
floors up and her apartment had an attic, but my sisters used to
sleep up there as children, so by tradition the cooking smoke was
fanned out of a window downstairs by anybody who was hanging
about; the fan hung on a shutter catch.

Above the bench gleamed a row of copper pans, paterae and
frying skillets, some second-hand and bearing several lifetimes'
knocks. On one shelf stood bowls, beakers, pitchers, pestles, and
a motley batch of spoons in a cracked vase. Nails that would hang
half an ox carcass held ladles, graters, strainers and meat mallets.
A cranky row of hooks supported a set of giant cooking knives;
they had evil iron blades bound on to cracked bone hafts and each
was scratched with Ma's initials: *JT* for Junilla Tacita.

The highest shelf held four of those special pots for cooking
dormice. Don't misunderstand that: Ma says dormice are nasty
things with no meat on them, only fit for snobs with poor taste and
silly habits. But when it's Saturnalia, you are already half an hour
late for the family party and are desperately buying your mother a
present to excuse the last twelve months of neglecting her, those
dormice coddlers always look exactly what she needs. Ma
accepted each graciously from whichever offspring had fallen for
the sales pitch this time, then let her unused collection grow
reproachfully.

Bunches of dried herbs scented the room. Baskets of eggs and
flat platters heaped with pulses filled any empty space. An
abundance of besoms and buckets announced what kind of

7

spotless, scandal-free kitchen – and family – my mother wished spectators to believe she ran.

The effect was being spoiled tonight by the ill-mannered lout who had belched at me. I stared at him. Bushes of wiry grey hair sprang out either side of his head. Like his uncompromising face, the bald dome above was tanned to a deep mahogany gleam. He had the look of a man who had been in the Eastern desert; I had a nasty feeling I knew which bit of boiling desert it must have been. His bare arms and legs had the permanent leathery musculature that comes from long years of hard physical activity rather than the fake results of a training programme at the gymnasium.

'Who in Hades are you?' he had the nerve to demand.

Wild thoughts that my mother had taken a lover to brighten her old age flashed into my mind, then scuttled away sheepishly. 'Why don't you tell me first?' I answered, giving him an intimidating glare.

'Get lost!'

'Not yet, soldier.' I had guessed his profession. Though his tunic was faded to a thin pink, I was closely inspecting the two-inch-thick studded soles of military boots. I knew the type. I knew the garlic breath, the scars from barracks squabbles, the cocksure attitude.

His mean eyes narrowed warily but he made no attempt to remove those boots from my mother's hallowed work surface. I dropped the bundle I was carrying and pushed back the cloak from around my head. He must have recognised the wet tangle of the Didius family curls.

'You're the brother!' he accused me. So he had known Festus. That was bad news. And apparently he had heard of me.

Acting like a man visitors certainly ought to have heard about, I sought the upper hand. 'Things seem to have grown slack around here, soldier! You'd better clear the table and straighten up, before I kick the bench from under you.' This subtle psychology worked. He swung his boots to the ground. 'Slowly!' I added, in case he planned on jumping me. He eased himself upright. One good thing about my brother had been that people respected him. For at least five minutes (I knew from experience) associated respect would attach to me.

'So you're the brother!' he repeated slowly, as if it meant something.

8

'That's right. I'm Falco. And you?'

'Censorinus.'

'What's your legion?'

'Fifteenth Apollinaris.' It would be. My surly mood deepened. The Fifteenth were the unlucky outfit my brother had graced for several years – before he made himself famous by flinging his handsome carcass over a hot Judaean battlement into a thicket of rebels' spears.

'So that's how you knew Festus?'

'Agreed,' he sneered condescendingly.

While we talked I was aware of restless movements behind me from Helena and the others. They wanted their beds – and so did I. 'You won't find Festus here, and you know why.'

'Festus and I were good mates,' he declared.

'Festus always had a lot of friends.' I sounded calmer than I felt. Festus, rot his eyes, would enter into a drinking pact with any skunk which had mange and half its tail missing. Then, generous to the last, my brother would bring his new friend home to us.

'Is there a problem?' the legionary enquired. His air of innocence was suspicious in itself. 'Festus said any time I was in Rome – '

'You could stay at his mother's house?'

'That's what the boy promised!'

It was depressingly familiar. And I knew the Fifteenth Legion had been redeployed recently from the Judaean war zone back to Pannonia – so presumably large numbers of them would now be asking for a spell of leave in Rome.

'I'm sure he did. How long have you been here?'

'A few weeks . . .' That meant months.

'Well I'm glad the Fifteenth Apollinaris has been augmenting Junilla Tacita's budget!' I stared him out. We both knew he had made no contributions at all to my mother's housekeeping. What a home-coming. First my wrecked apartment, now this. It seemed that while I was away Rome had filled up with unscrupulous losers all looking for rent-free beds.

I wondered where my mother was hiding. I felt an odd nostalgia to hear her nagging me while she spooned hot broth into my favourite bowl and pulled me out of my sopping clothes like when I was a child. 'Right! Well, I'm afraid I shall have to unstick you

9

from your billet, Censorinus. It's needed by the family now.'

'Of course. I'll shift as soon as possible . . .'

I stopped smiling. Even my teeth were tired. I gestured to the pathetic band I had brought with me. They were standing in silence, too exhausted to join in. 'I'd be glad if you'd make your arrangements fairly briskly.'

His glance went to the shutters. Outside we could hear the rain splashing as hard as ever. 'You're not going to turn me out on a night like this, Falco!'

He was right, but I owed the world a few punches. I grinned evilly. 'You're a soldier. A bit of wet won't hurt you . . .' I might have gone on amusing myself, but just at that moment my mother came into the room. Her beady black eyes took in the scene.

'Oh you're back,' she said, as if I had just come in from weeding a carrot patch. A small, tidy, almost tireless woman, she brushed past me, went to kiss Helena, then busied herself prying free my sleepy niece.

'Nice to be missed,' I muttered.

Ma ignored the pathos. 'We had plenty you could have been doing.'

She did not mean picking ticks off a dog. I saw her glance at Helena, plainly warning that there was bad news for later. Unable to face whatever crises had befallen the Didius clan, I dealt with the problem I knew about. 'We need a refuge. I gather big brother's old bed has already been claimed?'

'Yes. I thought you might have something to say about that!'

I could see Censorinus starting to look nervous. My mother peered at me expectantly while I tried to work out what I was supposed to do. For some reason she seemed to be playing the helpless old soul whose big tough son had emerged from his warren to defend her. This was quite out of character. I handled the situation delicately. 'I was merely commenting on a fact, Ma –'

'Oh I knew he wouldn't like it!' Ma announced to no one in particular.

I was too tired to resist. I squared up to the legionary. He probably thought he was tough, but he was easier to tackle than a devious mother with complicated motives.

Censorinus had grasped that the game was over. Ma was now making it plain that she had simply let him lodge there while she

10

waited for someone else to argue about it. I was back: her agent for the dirty work. There was no point fighting my destiny.

'Listen, friend. I'm worn out and chilled to the bone, so I'll be blunt. I've travelled a thousand miles at the worst time of year to find my apartment wrecked by intruders and my own bed full of rubble from a leaking roof. In ten minutes' time I intend to be flat out in the alternative, and the fact that my alternative is where you've been making yourself at home is just fortune's way of warning you that the gods are fickle friends – '

'So much for hospitality to strangers!' Censorinus scoffed at me. 'And so much for comrades who tell you they're mates!'

Uneasily I noticed a threat in his tone. It had nothing to do with what we seemed to be discussing. 'Look, I want the spare room for me and my lady, but you're not being turned out into the night. There's a dry attic that's perfectly liveable – '

'Stuff your attic!' the legionary retorted; then added, 'And stuff Festus, and stuff you!'

'Whatever makes you feel better,' I replied, trying not to sound as if for this family, the one good aspect of Festus's death had been that we did not have to dole out free food and lodging to an endless succession of his colourful friends.

I saw Ma pat the legionary's shoulder. She muttered consolingly, 'I'm sorry, but I just can't have you here upsetting my son . . .'

'Oh Jupiter, Ma!' She was impossible.

To speed things up I helped Censorinus pack. As he left he gave me a malevolent glare, but I was too preoccupied with the joys of family life to wonder why.

11

III

Helena and Ma combined efforts to allocate space to my party. Our servants were briskly rushed off to the attic. My young niece Augustinilla was tucked up in Mother's own bed.

'How's Victorina?' I forced myself to ask. We had been looking after the child for my older sister whilst she was ill.

'Victorina died.' Mother gave the news matter-of-factly, but her voice was tense. 'I wasn't going to tell you tonight.'

'Victorina's gone?' I could hardly take it in.

'In December.'

'You could have written.'

'What would that have achieved?'

I dropped my spoon on to the table and sat cradling my bowl, taking comfort from the warmth that remained in the pottery. 'This is unbelievable . . .'

Wrong. Victorina had had an internal problem, which some quack Alexandrian doctor who specialised in prodding the female anatomy had convinced her was operable; his diagnosis must have been false, or more likely he bungled the surgery. It happens all the time. I had no business to be sitting there, feeling so surprised that she had died.

Victorina was the eldest in our family, tyrannising the other six of us who had somehow struggled alive through infancy. I had always stayed fairly remote from her, a matter of choice since I hated being bruised and terrorised. She was in her teens when I was born, and even then had a terrible reputation: an eye for the boys, a saucy green parasol, and the side-seams of her tunic always revealingly unstitched. When she visited the Circus, the men who held her parasol for her were always repugnant types. In the end she picked up a plasterer called Mico and married him. I finally stopped speaking to her at that point.

They had five surviving children. The baby must be not yet two. Still, childhood being what it was, he could well be joining his lost mother before he was three.

12

Helena was missing this conversation. She had fallen asleep, crushed against my shoulder. I half turned, easing her into a kinder position; one where I could gaze down at her. I needed to see her, to remind myself the Fates could spin a sound thread when they chose to. She was completely at rest. No one ever slept so deeply as Helena with my arm around her. At least I was some use to somebody.

Ma draped a blanket over both of us. 'So she's still with you?' Despite her contempt for my previous girlfriends, Ma reckoned Helena Justina was much too good for me. Most people thought that. Helena's own relatives were first in the queue. Perhaps they were right. Even in Rome, with its snobbery and tawdry values, she could certainly have done better for herself.

'Seems like it.' I caressed the soft hollow of Helena's right temple with my thumb. Utterly relaxed, she looked all sweetness and gentleness. I didn't fool myself that was her true nature, but it was a part of her – even if that part only showed when she was sleeping in my arms.

'I heard some tale she had run away.'

'She's here. So the tale's obviously wrong.'

Ma intended to find out the whole story. 'Was she trying to get away from you, or did you scram and she had to chase after you?' She had a good grasp of how we ran our lives. I ignored the question, so she launched off another: 'Are you any nearer settling things?'

Probably neither of us could answer that. Our relationship had its volatile moments. The fact that Helena Justina was the daughter of a millionaire senator while I was an impoverished informer did not improve our chances. I could never tell whether every day that I managed to hold on to her took us one step nearer our inevitable parting – or whether the time I was keeping us together would make us impossible to separate.

'I heard Titus Caesar had his eye on her,' Ma continued inexorably. That was best left unanswered too. Titus could pose a tough challenge. Helena maintained she had rebuffed his overtures. But who could really tell? She might privately welcome our return to Rome and the chance to impress further the Emperor's son. She would be a fool if she didn't. I should have kept her in the provinces.

To claim my fee for what I had done in Germany, I had had to come back and report to the Emperor; Helena had come with me. Life must go on. Titus was a risk I had to face. If he wanted trouble, I was prepared to put up a fight. 'Everyone says you'll let her down,' my mother assured me happily.

'I've avoided it so far!'

'There's no need to get snappy,' commented Ma.

It was late. Ma's apartment block hit one of the rare occasions when all its tenants had fallen quiet at once. In the silence she fiddled with the wick of the pottery oil-lamp, scowling at the crude bedroom scene embossed on the redware – one of my brother's joking household contributions. Being a present from Festus meant the item was impossible to throw out now. Besides, the lamp had a clean, steady burn despite the pornography.

The loss of my sister, even the one I had had least time for, brought my brother's absence to the surface again too.

'What was all that with the legionary, Ma? Plenty of people knew Festus, but not many of them turn up on the doorstep nowadays.'

'I can't be rude to your brother's friends.' No need, when she had me to do it for her. 'Maybe you shouldn't have evicted him like that, Marcus.'

My turning out Censorinus was what she had plainly intended from the moment I arrived; yet I was getting blamed for it. After knowing my mother for thirty years the contradiction was predictable. 'Why didn't you give him the twiggy end of a besom yourself?'

'I'm afraid he'll bear a grudge against you,' murmured Ma.

'I can handle that.' The silence carried ominous overtones. 'Is there a particular reason why he might?' My mother remained mute. 'There is!'

'It's nothing.' So it was serious.

'You'd better tell me.'

'Oh . . . there seems to be some trouble over something Festus is supposed to have done.'

All my life I had been hearing those fatal words. 'Oh here we go again. Stop being coy, Ma. I know Festus, I can recognise one of his disasters from a hippodrome's length away.'

14

'You're tired, son. I'll talk to you in the morning.'

I was so weary my head was still singing the rhythms of travelling, but with some doom-laden fraternal mystery hanging in the air there was little hope of sleep until I discovered what I had come home to – and probably no sleep then.

'Oh cobnuts, I'm tired all right. I'm tired of people dodging the issue. Talk to me now, Mother!'

IV

Festus was three years in the tomb. The writs had mainly dried up, but promissory notes from debtors and hopeful letters from abandoned women still trickled back to Rome from time to time. And now we had a military interest; that might prove harder to deflect.

'I don't expect he did anything,' Ma comforted herself.

'Oh he did it,' I assured her. 'Whatever it is! I can guarantee our Festus was right in there, beaming cheerfully as usual. Ma, the only question is, what am *I* going to have to do – or more likely, how much will it cost me – to get us all out of whatever trouble he's caused this time?' Ma managed to find a look that implied I was insulting her beloved boy. 'Tell me the truth. Why did you want me to kick out Censorinus the minute I came home?'

'He had started asking awkward questions.'

'What questions?'

'According to him, some soldiers in your brother's legion once put money into a venture which Festus organised. Censorinus has come to Rome to reclaim their cash.'

'There is no cash.' As my brother's executor I could vouch for it. When he died I received a letter from the will clerk in his legion that confirmed everything I could have guessed anyway: after paying his local debts and providing a funeral there was nothing for them to send home to me but the comfort of knowing I would have been his heir, had our hero been able to keep any cash in his arm-purse for more than two days. Festus had always spent his quarterly pay in advance. He had left nothing in Judaea. I could find nothing in Rome either, despite the labyrinthine complexity of his business schemes. He ran his life on a marvellous talent for bluff. I thought I knew him as closely as anyone, but even I had been deluded when he chose.

I sighed. 'Give me the full story. What was this sticky venture?'

'Some scheme to make a lot of money, apparently.' Just like my brother, always thinking he'd hit upon a fabulous idea to make his fortune. Just like him to involve everyone else who had ever shared his tent. Festus could charm investments from a dedicated miser whom he'd only met that morning; his own trusting pals had stood no chance.

'What scheme?'

'I'm not sure.' Ma looked confused. I wasn't fooled. My mother's grip on facts was as strong as an octopus entwining its future dinner. She undoubtedly knew what Festus stood accused of; she preferred me to find out the details for myself. That meant the story would make me angry. Ma wanted to be somewhere else when I blew up.

We had been talking with lowered voices, but my agitation must have made me tense; Helena stirred and woke, instantly alert. 'Marcus, what's wrong?'

I squirmed stiffly. 'Just family troubles. Don't worry; go back to sleep.' Immediately she forced herself awake.

'The soldier?' Helena correctly deduced. 'I was surprised you sent him packing like that. Was he a confidence trickster?'

I said nothing. I liked to keep my brother's indiscretions to myself. But Ma, who had been so wary of telling me the tale, was prepared to confide in Helena. 'The soldier is genuine enough. We are in some trouble with the army. I let him lodge here because at first he seemed to be just somebody my elder son had known in Syria, but once he got his boots under the table he began to pester me.'

'What about, Junilla Tacita?' Helena queried indignantly, sitting up. She often addressed my mother in this formal way. Oddly, it marked a greater intimacy between them than Mother had ever allowed my previous female friends, most of whom had had no acquaintance with polite speech.

'There is supposed to be a money problem with something poor Festus was involved in,' my mother told Helena. 'Marcus is going to look into it for us.'

I choked. 'I don't remember saying I'd do that.'

'No. Of course you're bound to be busy.' My mother changed tack adroitly. 'Will you have a lot of work waiting?'

I was not expecting an eager stream of clients. After six months away I would have lost any initiative. People always want to rush ahead with their foolish manoeuvres; my competitors would have

17

grabbed all the commissions for commercial surveillance, gathering court evidence and finding grounds for divorces. Clients have no concept of waiting patiently if the best operative happens to be busy in Europe for an indefinite period. How could I avoid it if the Emperor up on the Palatine expected his affairs to take priority? 'I doubt if I'll be stretched,' I admitted, since my womenfolk were likely to overrule me if I tried to fudge the issue.

'Of course you won't,' cried Helena. My heart sank. Helena had no idea she was taking the cart into a cul-de-sac. She had never known Festus; she could not possibly imagine how his schemes had so often ended.

'Who else is there to help us?' urged Ma. 'Oh Marcus, I did think you would have an interest in clearing your own poor brother's name . . .'

Just as I had known it would, the mission that I refused to accept transformed itself into a mission I could not refuse.

I must have muttered some grudging noise that sounded like assent. Next thing, Ma was declaring that she would not expect me to give my precious time for nothing, while Helena was mouthing at me that in no circumstances could I send my own mother a daily expenses sheet. I felt like a new length of cloth receiving a fuller's battering.

Being paid was not my worry. But I knew this was a case I could not win.

'All right!' I growled. 'If you ask me, the departed lodger was just playing on a slight acquaintance in order to clinch a free billet. Suggesting foul play was just a subtle lever, Ma.' My mother was not a person who gave in to leverage. I yawned, pointedly. 'Look, I'm not going to waste a lot of effort on something that happened so many years ago anyway, but if it will make you both happy, I'll have a word with Censorinus in the morning.' I knew where to find him; I had told him that Flora's, the local caupona, sometimes hired out rooms. He would not have travelled much further on a night like this.

My mother stroked my hair, while Helena smiled. None of their shameless attentions improved my pessimistic mood. I knew before I started that Festus, who had got me into trouble all my life, had now forced me to commit myself to the worst yet.

'Ma, I have to ask you a question – ' Her face did not alter,

18

though she must have seen what was coming. 'Do *you* think Festus did whatever his cronies are asserting?'

'How can you ask me that?' she exclaimed in great affront. With any other witness, in any other enquiry, that would have convinced me the woman was pretending to be offended because she was covering up for her son.

'That's all right then,' I responded loyally.

V

My brother Festus could walk into any tavern in any province of the Empire, and some wart in a spotty tunic would rise from a bench with open arms to greet him as an old and honoured friend. Don't ask me how he did it. It was a trick I could have used myself, but you need talent to exude such warmth. The fact that Festus still owed the wart a hundred in local currency from their last acquaintance would not diminish the welcome. What's more, if our lad then progressed into the back room where the cheap whores were entertaining, equally delighted shrieks would arise as girls who should have known better all rushed up adoringly.

When I walked into Flora's, where I had been drinking on a weekly basis for nearly ten years, not even the cat noticed.

Flora's Caupona made the average seedy snack shop look chic and hygienic. It squatted on the corner where a dingy lane down from the Aventine met a dirty track up from the wharves. It had the usual arrangement, with two counters set at right angles for people in the two streets to lean on reflectively while they waited to be poisoned. The counters were made from a rough patchwork of white and grey stone that a man might mistake for marble if his mind was on the elections and he was virtually blind. Each counter had three circular holes to take cauldrons of food. At Flora's most of the holes were left empty, out of respect for public health perhaps. What the full cauldrons held was even more disgusting than the usual brown sludge with funny specks in it that's ladled out to passers-by from rotten street food shops. Flora's cold potages were off-puttingly lukewarm, and their hot meats were dangerously cool. Word had it a fisherman once died at the counter after eating a portion of slushy peas; my brother maintained that to avoid a long legal dispute with his heirs, the man was hastily processed and served up as spicy halibut balls. Festus had always known such stories. Given the state of the kitchen behind the caupona, that one could be true.

20

The counters enclosed a cramped square space where really hardened regulars could sit down and have their ears knocked by the waiter's elbow as he went about his work. There were two sagging tables; one had benches, the other a set of folding camp-stools. Outside, blocking the street, lolled half a barrel; a feeble beggar permanently sat on it. He was there even today, with the remnants of the storm still producing showers. No one ever gave him alms because the waiter lifted anything he received.

I walked past the beggar, avoiding eye contact. Something about him had always looked vaguely familiar, and whatever it was always made me feel depressed. Perhaps I knew that one wrong move professionally could have me ending up sharing his barrel stump.

Indoors, I took a stool, bracing myself as it wobbled disastrously. Service would be slow. I shook today's rain out of my hair and looked around the familiar scene: the rack of amphorae, misty with spiders' webs; the shelf of brown beakers and flagons; a surprisingly attractive Greek-looking container with an octopus decoration; and the wine catalogue painted on the wall – pointlessly, because despite the impressive price list that claimed to be offering all styles of drink from house wines to Falernian, Flora's invariably served one dubious vintage whose ingredients were not more than second cousins to grapes.

Nobody knew if 'Flora' had ever existed. She could be missing or dead, but it wasn't a case I would volunteer to solve. Rumour reckoned she had been formidable; I thought she must be either a myth or a mouse. She had never put in an appearance. Maybe she knew what kind of vittles her lax caupona served. Maybe she knew how many customers wanted a word about diddled reckonings.

The waiter was called Epimandos. If he had ever met his employer he preferred not to mention it.

Epimandos was probably a runaway slave. If so he had hidden here, successfully evading pursuit, for years though he retained a permanently furtive look. Above a skinny body, his long face sunk slightly on the shoulders as if it were a theatrical mask. He was stronger than he looked, from heaving heavy pots about. He had stew stains down his tunic, and an indelible whiff of chopped garlic lurking under his fingernails.

The name of the cat who had ignored me was Stringy. Like the waiter, he was in fact quite sturdy, with a fat brindled tail and an unpleasant leer. Since he looked like an animal who expected friendly contact, I aimed a kick at him. Stringy dodged disdainfully; my foot made contact with Epimandos, who failed to utter a protest but asked, 'The usual?' He spoke as if I had only been away since Wednesday instead of so long I couldn't even remember what my usual used to be.

A bowl of vivid stew, and a very small wine jug, apparently. No wonder my brain had blotted it out.

'Good?' asked Epimandos. I knew he had a reputation for uselessness, though to me he had always seemed keen to please. Maybe Festus had something to do with it. He had made a habit of hanging around Flora's, and the waiter still remembered him with evident affection.

'Seems well up to standard!' I broke off a chunk of bread and plunged it into the bowl. A tide of froth menaced me. The meaty layer was much too brightly coloured; above it floated half a digit of transparent liquor, topped with sluggish blobs of oil where two shreds of onion and some tiny scraps of dark green foliage were wriggling like bugs in a water-butt. I took a bite, coating the roof of my mouth with grease. To cover the shock, I asked, 'Is there a military tyke called Censorinus lodging here since yesterday?' Epimandos gave me his normal vague stare. 'Tell him I'd like a word, would you?'

Epimandos ambled back to his pots, which he started poking with a bent ladle. The greyer potage glopped like a swamp that was about to swallow the waiter head first. An odour of overstrong crabmeat swam around the caupona. Epimandos gave no indication he intended to pass on my message, but I held back the urge to nag. Flora's was a dump that took its time. Its clients were in no hurry; a few had something they were supposed to do, but they were intending to avoid it. Most had nowhere to go and could barely remember why they had wandered in.

To disguise the flavour of the food I took a swig of wine. Whatever it tasted of wasn't wine. At least it gave me something different to think about.

For half an hour I sat pondering the brevity of life and the ghastliness of my drink. I never did see Epimandos make any effort to contact Censorinus, and he was soon busy with lunchtime customers who turned up to lean on the counters from the street. Then, when I was risking my second wine jug, the soldier abruptly appeared at my side. He must have come out from the back space where stairs ran up past the cooking bench to the tiny rooms that Flora's occasionally hired to people who didn't know anywhere more sensible to stay.

'So you're looking for trouble, are you?' he sneered nastily.

'Well, I'm looking for you,' I replied as best I could with my mouth full. The dainty I was toying with was too sinewy to be hurried; in fact I felt I might be chewing this gristle for the rest of my life. Eventually I reduced it to a lump of tasteless cartilage which I removed from my mouth with more relief than decorum, and placed on the rim of my bowl; it promptly fell in.

'Sit down, Censorinus. You're blocking the light.' The legionary was induced to plant himself on the edge of my table. I kept my tone fairly civilised. 'There's a nasty rumour flying about that you've been slandering my famous brother. Do you want to talk about your problem, or shall I just thump you in the teeth?'

'There's no problem,' he sneered. 'I've come to claim a debt. I'll get it too!'

'That sounds like a threat.' I abandoned the stew but carried on with my wine, not offering him any.

'The Fifteenth don't need to make threats,' he boasted.

'Not if their grudge is legal,' I agreed, applying an aggressive edge myself. 'Look, if something's bothering the legion, and if it involves my brother, I'm prepared to listen.'

'You'll have to do something about it!'

'So tell me straight out what's griping you – or else we'll both forget about it.'

Both Epimandos and Stringy were listening. The waiter was leaning on his pots and picking his nose while he stared at us quite openly, but the cat had enough delicacy to pretend to be licking a dropped bread roll under the table. Flora's was not a place to arrange your elopement with an heiress or buy a vial of poisonous green jollop to wipe out your business partner. This caupona had the nosiest staff in Rome.

'Some of us lads who knew Festus,' Censorinus informed me self-importantly, 'chipped in with him in a certain venture.'

23

I managed not to close my eyes and sigh; this sounded horribly familiar. 'Oh?'

'Well, what do you think? We want the profits – or we want our stakes back. Straight away!'

I ignored the heavy-handed bit. 'Well so far, I can't say I'm either interested or impressed. First, anybody who knew Festus will fully expect to hear that he didn't leave overflowing jars of coinage under every bed he slept in. If there was a pot there he pissed in it, that's all! I was his executor; he gave me a zero legacy. Second, even if this fabulous venture was legitimate, I would expect to see documentation for your debt. Festus was an airy beggar over most things, but I've got all his business chits, and they were immaculate.' At least, the set I found scratched on bone blocks at Mother's were. I was still waiting to discover other more dubious accounts hidden away somewhere.

Censorinus eyed me coldly. He seemed very tense. 'I don't like your tone, Falco!'

'And I don't like your attitude.'

'You'd better be prepared to pay.'

'Then you'd better explain.'

Something was not right. The soldier seemed strangely reluctant to come out with the facts – his only hope of persuading me to contribute. I could see his eyes dart, with more agitation than seemed called for.

'I mean it, Falco – we expect you to cough up!'

'Olympus!' I lost my temper. 'You haven't told me the date, the place, the scheme, the terms, the venture's outcome, or the amount! All I'm getting is bluster and blather.'

Epimandos came nearer, pretending to wipe down tables and flicking chewed olive stones about with the end of a mouldy rag.

'Get lost, garlic seed!' Censorinus shouted at him. He appeared to take note of the waiter for the first time, and Epimandos was overcome by one of his nervous fits. The waiter jumped back against a counter. Behind him other customers had started to peer in at us curiously.

Keeping an eye on Epimandos, Censorinus crouched nearer to me on a stool; he lowered his voice to a hoarse croak: 'Festus was running a ship.'

'Where from?' I tried not to sound alarmed. This was a new item in the canon of my brother's enterprises and I wanted to know all about it before any more debtors appeared.

'Caesarea.'

'And he cut some of you in?'

'We were a syndicate.'

The big word impressed him more than me. 'Shipping what?'

'Statues.'

'That fits.' Fine art was the family business on our father's side. 'Was the cargo from Judaea?'

'No. Greece.' That fitted too. There was a voracious appetite in Rome for Hellenic statuary.

'So what happened? And why are you only calling in your debt three years after his death?'

'There's been a damned war in the East, Falco – or hadn't you heard?'

'I heard,' I replied grimly, thinking of Festus.

Censorinus took more of a grip on himself. 'Your brother seemed to know what he was doing. We all put in with him to buy the stock. He promised us high percentages.'

'Then either the ship sank, in which case I feel sorry for both him and you but there's nothing I can do about it – or else you should have received your money long ago. Festus lived on the wild side, but I never saw him cheat.'

The soldier stared at the table. 'Festus said the ship did sink.'

'Hard luck. Then why in the name of the gods are you bothering me?'

He didn't believe it really had sunk; that was obvious. But he still had enough loyalty to Festus not to say so outright. 'Festus told us not to worry; he would see we didn't lose by it. He would get us the money back anyway.'

'That's impossible. If the load was lost – '

'It's what he said!'

'All right! Then he must have meant it. I'm not surprised that he was offering to make good; you were his mates. He wouldn't have let you down.'

'Better not!' Censorinus was incapable of keeping quiet, even when I sympathised.

'But whatever plan he had for recouping the loss must have involved further deals. I don't know about them, and I can't be responsible for arranging them at this stage. I'm surprised you're even trying it on.'

'He had a partner,' Censorinus grouched.

'It wasn't me.'

'I know.'

'Festus told you?'

'Your mother did.'

I knew about my brother's business connection. I didn't want anything to do with him, and more particularly neither did Ma. The partner was my father, who had abandoned his family years before. Festus had kept up with him, though Ma could hardly bring herself to mention his name. So why had she discussed him with Censorinus, a stranger? She must have been deeply concerned. That meant so was I.

'You've answered your own question, Censorinus. You need to negotiate with the partner. Have you seen him? What does *he* have to say for himself?'

'Not a lot!' That didn't surprise me. Pa had always been bad news.

'Well, that's it then. I can't improve on the story. Accept it. Festus is gone. His death's robbed us all of his joyful presence, and it's robbed you of your cash, I'm afraid.'

'That's no good, Falco!' Desperation had entered the soldier's voice. He leapt to his feet.

'Calm down!'

'We've got to have that money back!'

'I'm sorry, but that's fate. Even if Festus did produce a cargo to make a profit from, I'm his heir and I'd be the first in the queue – '

Censorinus grabbed my tunic to haul me from my seat. I had sensed trouble coming. I flung my bowl in his face, cracked his arm sideways, and broke free. As I sprang up I pushed the table back at him, clearing space to move. The waiter let out a bleat of protest; he was so surprised the elbow he was leaning on slipped and he lurched into a cauldron, armpit-deep in gravy. The cat fled, yowking.

Censorinus lashed out. I parried, more in annoyance than anything else since this all seemed so pointless. He went for me in earnest, so I fought back. Epimandos jumped up on the counter to avoid damage to his person; the other customers leaned in from the street, cheering raucously. We had a short, ungainly bout of fisticuffs. I won. I threw the soldier out into the lane; he picked himself up and slunk off muttering.

Peace resumed in the caupona. Epimandos was wiping his arm with his rag. 'What was that all about?'

'Jove only knows!' I flipped some coppers at him for the bill, then set off home.

As I left, Epimandos picked up the bread roll that Stringy had been licking earlier, and replaced it in the customers' bread basket.

VI

The following morning, I started re-establishing my normal life in Rome.

I stayed in bed long enough to prove that I wasn't a client who needed to leap out and grovel for favours at some rich patron's house. Then I showed myself to the eager populace in the Forum, though most were looking the other way. I dodged my banker, a girl I preferred not to recognise, and several of my brothers-in-law. Then I sauntered into the men's baths at the back of the Temple of Castor for a complete physical overhaul. After a fierce exercise and massage session with Glaucus my trainer, who was in one of his sarcastic moods, I bathed, invested in a shave and haircut, told some jokes, heard some gossip, lost a denarius in a bet about how many flea-bites were on some stranger's leg, and generally began to feel like a civilised Roman again.

I had been away six months. Nothing had changed in politics or at the racing stables, but everything cost more than when I left. The only people who seemed to have missed me were the ones I owed money.

I borrowed a toga from Glaucus and made my way up to the Palatine for an audience with the Emperor. My report made an adequate impression on the old man, though I should have remembered to leave it until after dinner when his mood would be more generous. But my mission in Germany had gone well; Vespasian liked to quibble, yet he always acknowledged success. He was fair. He sanctioned my fee and expenses. There was, however, no attempt to offer me another job. That is the risk with freelancing: the constant threat of unemployment and bankruptcy, then just when you've trained yourself to enjoy lots of free time, they offer you some mission even Hercules would baulk at.

Even so, I picked up a satisfactory bag of silver at the Palace, returned to the Forum, greeted my banker with a happy smile and watched him open my rather small bank box. The coins made a sweet chink as they were stowed. There was still not enough there to force me to make tricky investment decisions, let alone the huge amount I would require if I ever decided to approach Helena Justina's senatorial father in the role of hopeful son-in-law. Luckily the noble Camillus was not expecting it to happen, so never bothered me with pressing questions about my plans.

After that, I diddled away the rest of the afternoon making excuses not to look for private clients.

I ought to have known that while I was out taking the air so aimlessly, the spinning Fates would be preparing to snag my thread.

That morning Helena had shouted in my dozing ear that she and my mother were going to my old apartment to begin clearing up. Eventually I strolled along there. Around Fountain Court the streets all smelt of drains, because in that sector of the city they *were* the drains. The inhabitants looked as drab and despondent as ever. This was the hole I had found for myself six years ago, when I came home from the army and felt that unlike my brother who still lived at home with a mother, *I* was too big a boy for that. Festus had said I was crazy – which made me all the more stubborn.

Another reason for leaving home had been to avoid pressure to go into the family business – either breaking my back market- gardening out on the Campania, or auctioneering, which would involve getting even more dirt on my hands. I can earth up a leek or tell lies about an antique lamp. But I had thought myself a sociable, easygoing character, so, naturally, the solitary, cynical life of an informer had seemed ideal. Now I was thirty, fending off family responsibilities on all sides, and stuck with my disastrous choice.

Before I went upstairs I paused to pay my respects to Lenia, the haggard virago who owned and ran the laundry that occupied the ground floor. Thunder was still growling about, so not much was going on because nothing they bothered to wash would ever dry. A very tall man draped in a rather short toga was standing in silence while his wife harangued Lenia about sending back wrong laundry. Lenia was getting the worst of some tense issue about a stain, so when I popped my head indoors she left them at once and came to be rude to me.

'Falco, you half-arsed donkey-drover! Who let you back into Rome?'

'Public demand for my civilising influence.'

'Hah! Good trip?'

'Wish I had stayed there – my apartment's wrecked.'

'Oh really?' Lenia, who had connections with the snail slime I called my landlord, assumed an expression as though she would love to talk further, but must urgently dash to the pie shop before the ovens cooled.

'You know it is!' I retorted. In a dispute with the landlord there was no future; still, raising my voice eased the knot that was strangling my liver.

'Don't involve me. Speak to Smaractus . . .'

'I'm looking forward to the pleasure!'

'He's out of town.' That parasite Smaractus had probably heard I was back and arranged himself a six-month stay at his holiday home on Lake Volsena. Yachting would be a cold sport in March. 'So people got in, did they?' Lenia must have spotted the interlopers every time they took the stairs. In fact, they had probably stuffed a silver coin in her fist to find out where there was an empty roost. 'That's terrible!'

I gave up the struggle. 'Are my womenfolk here?'

'There's been some toing and froing. Your sister dropped in earlier.' That could have meant any one of five – no, four now. Victorina was gone.

'Maia?' Only Maia would put herself out for me.

Lenia nodded. 'Oh, and that bastard Petronius was looking for you.'

This was better news. Petronius Longus, captain of the Aventine Watch, was my closest friend. I was looking forward to swapping insults while regaling him with lurid lies about my foreign trip.

'How are the wedding plans?' I shouted at Lenia as I bounded for the stairs.

'Progressing!' That was bluff. Lenia and Smaractus were supposed to be linking fortunes, only somehow neither could bring themselves to the point of sharing their money bags. 'What about yours?' she retaliated.

'Oh, at about the same wonderful stage . . .'

I nipped for the stairs before this line of questioning bit too hard.

VII

I guessed that my rooms had reached the point of getting worse before they could be improved. On the landing outside there was hardly room to squeeze through the mounds of broken furniture and swag bags of jetsam in order to reach the front door.

Helena Justina met me coming out. She was carrying a heavy bale of rubbish, wrapped in what was left of a cloak with its corners knotted. She looked exhausted. Helena was stubborn and courageous about the squalor she had to live in alongside me, although she had been delicately reared. I could see her strength was failing. She knocked into the discarded frame of my bed, bruised herself badly, and spoke a word no senator's daughter should have known; she must have picked it up from me.

'Here – give me that!'

She edged away from my outstretched hand. 'I have to keep going. Don't upset my balance, or I'll drop.'

'Drop on me,' I murmured temptingly. Using my strength I took the bundle from her; Helena drooped against me, letting her full weight collapse while she held on around my neck.

Manfully I supported both my lass and the bundle of rubbish, pretending it was effortless. When she had made her point, she tickled my neck unfairly so I had to let go of the bundle. It crashed downstairs for a couple of landings. We watched, though with no interest in chasing after it.

'Ma gone?' I asked hopefully. She nodded. 'That's all right then!' I murmured, starting to kiss her while we still stood amidst the chaos on the landing. Mine was the only apartment on the sixth floor, so we were assured of privacy. Revived by a day in Rome, I didn't care who saw us anyway.

After a while I stopped, held Helena's hot, tired face between my hands and gazed into her eyes. I watched peace making itself at home in her soul. She smiled slightly, while she let me take the credit for calming her. Then her eyes half closed; she hated me to know the effect I had. I hugged her and laughed.

31

We went into the apartment holding hands. The place was virtually empty, but now clean. 'You can sit on the balcony,' Helena told me. 'We washed it out – and scrubbed the bench.'

I took her with me. It was nearly dark and pretty cool, but that made a good excuse for huddling close. 'The apartment has never been so clean. It's not worth it. Don't wear yourself out over this dump, fruit.'

'You won't want to stay long at your mother's.' Helena knew me.

'I can bear living at Ma's if I have you to protect me.' That was surprisingly true.

I kept her there, looking at the view while she rested. Ahead of us an aggressive wind was driving clouds at a fast pace above the Tiber and a dull threat of rain darkened our normal vista across to the Ianiculan. Rome lay below, sullen and muted, like a disloyal slave whose sins had been found out.

'Marcus, you never told me properly what happened when you saw the soldier yesterday.' That's the trouble with gazing at views; once people start feeling bored, gluey issues may be raised.

My attention lingered on the winter scenery. 'I didn't want to worry Ma.'

'She's not here; worry me.'

'I wanted to avoid that too.'

'Keeping things to yourself is what worries me most.'

I gave in. She was badgering, but I like being badgered by Helena. 'I saw Censorinus at the caupona, but we got nowhere. He told me some of my brother's cronies in the legion lost money on importing Greek statues.'

'So what's their point?'

'Our Festus gaily assured them all he would see them right for the loss.'

'He failed though?'

'He promptly dropped off a battlement. Now they want me to square matters, but Censorinus refused to come clean about the original deal . . .'

As I tailed off Helen's interest sharpened. 'What happened?' She knew I was hiding something. 'Was there trouble at the caupona?'

'It ended in fisticuffs.'

'Oh Marcus!'

'He started it.'

'I hope so! But I bet you were digging your heels in?'

'Why not? Nothing else they can expect if they choose to be secretive.'

Helena had to agree. She thought for a moment, then asked, 'Tell me about your brother. I used to have the impression everyone approved of him. Now I can't decide *what* your feelings are.'

'That's it. Neither can I sometimes.' He had been eight years older than me. Distant enough for an element of hero worship – or for the other thing. Part of me hated him; though the rest loved him much more. 'He could be a trial. Yet I couldn't bear losing him. That sums him up.'

'Was he like you?'

'No.' Probably not.

'So are you taking this any further?'

'I'm waiting to see.'

'That means you want to give up.' It was a reasonable comment. But she didn't know Festus. I doubted if I could escape; even if I tried doing nothing, the situation was out of control.

Helena was starting to hunch against the cold. I said, 'We need some dinner.'

'We can't keep imposing on your mother.'

'How right – let's go and see *your* parents!'

'I thought you might say that. I brought a change of clothes. I ought to bathe first . . .'

I surveyed her; she looked filthy, but full of fight. Even a layer of grime could not smother her resourceful character. Being covered with dust enhanced the brightness of her great dark eyes, and when her hair was slipping out of its pins I only wanted to help dismantle it . . . If there had been a bed, we would have gone no further that evening. There was no bed, and no reasonable substitute. I grinned ruefully. 'My darling, it may not be a bright idea to bring you to your parents looking as if you've spent all day working like a slave in a furnace-house. On the other hand, bad treatment is all your noble relatives expect from me, so let's go and use your papa's private bathhouse for free.'

I had a double motive in this. If Helena's parents were about to

33

reveal that Titus Caesar had been sniffing around while we were abroad, the worse Helena looked on arrival, the easier it would be for them to accept that I had won her first. It had been pure chance, but as the one piece of luck in my sordid life I intended clinging on to it. Once Helena threw herself at me, no one could expect me to refuse the gift – any more than they ought to hope the son of a deeply conservative emperor would take her on after me.

That was *my* hope, anyway.

The Camillus family lived in one half of a private two-house block just off the Via Appia near the Capena Gate. The next-door house was empty, though they owned that too. It was deteriorating while it stood unoccupied. Theirs was no worse than the last time I saw it, a modest spread that bore the marks of a permanent cash shortage. Poor paint in the interior had faded badly since the house was built; mean fittings in the gardens failed to match the standards of grandeur originally set by the rest of the house. But it was comfortably furnished. Among senators they were an un-usually civilised family – respectful to the gods, kind to children, generous to their slaves, and even gracious with underprivileged hangers-on like me.

There was a small bath suite, served by water from the Claudian Aqueduct, which on winter evenings they kept fairly hot. Struggling or not, they had the right domestic priorities. I scraped Helena down, enjoying the delicate bits. 'Hmm, I've never yet made love to a senator's daughter in the senator's own bath-house . . .'

'You're versatile; you'll come to it!'

Not then, however. Noises off announced company. As her father turned up for his pre-dinner soak, Helena threw a towel across my lap and disappeared. I sat on the side of the plunge bath trying to look more respectful than I felt.

'Leave us alone, please,' Decimus Camillus commanded the slaves who came in with him. They went, but made it clear that giving instructions was no business of the master of the house.

Decimus Camillus Verus was a friend of Vespasian's and therefore on the up at present. He was tall, with uncontrollable hair and vivid eyebrows. Relaxing in the steam, he had a slight stoop; I knew he made an effort to exercise but he preferred to lurk in his study with a pile of scrolls.

Camillus had taken to me – within limits, of course. I hated his rank, but liked him. Affection for his daughter had partly bridged the social abyss between us.

But he was in a tetchy mood. 'When are you and Helena Justina planning to make yourselves legitimate?' So much for thinking he wasn't expecting it. An extra load of pressure descended on me. It was measured in sesterces, and its exact weight was four hundred thousand of them – the cost of my joining the middle rank so that marrying me would not entirely disgrace Helena. I was making little progress in collecting so much money.

'You don't need an exact date? Quite soon, I should think,' I lied. He always saw through me.

'Her mother asked me to enquire.' From what I knew of Julia Justa, 'asked' was putting it mildly. We let the subject drop like a hot boiled egg.

'How are you, sir? What's the news?'

'Vespasian is summoning Justinus home from the army.' Justinus was his son.

'Ah! I may have had a hand in that.'

'So I gather. What have you been telling the Emperor?'

'Only to recognise talent.'

'Oh that!' scoffed the Senator, in his wry way. A shy man's mischievous wit sometimes broke through his diffident manner. Helena's sense of humour came from him, though she threw her insults about more lavishly.

Camillus Justinus was the younger of Helena's two brothers; we had been living with him in Germany. 'Justinus has been building a fine reputation,' I encouraged his father. 'He deserves the Emperor's favour, and Rome needs men like him. That's all I told Vespasian. His commanding officer should have put in a good report, but I don't rely on legates.'

Camillus groaned. I knew his problem; it was the same as my own, though on a much grander scale: lack of capital. As a senator Camillus was a millionaire. Yet there was no slack in his bank account. Providing the trappings of public life -- all those Games and public dinners for the greedy electorate – could easily wipe him out financially. Having already promised a career in the

Senate to his elder son, he now discovered his younger boy had rather unexpectedly fixed himself a notable reputation. Poor Decimus was dreading the expense.

'You should be proud of him, Senator.'

'Oh I am!' he said glumly.

I reached for a strigil and started to scrape the oil off him. 'Is anything else on your mind?' I was probing in case there were developments on the Titus front.

'Nothing unusual: modern youth, the state of trade, the decline in social standards, horrors of the public works programme . . .' he said self-mockingly. Then he confided, 'I'm having trouble disposing of my brother's estate.' So that was it.

I was not the only Roman whose sibling had caused him embarrassment. Camillus had had a brother, now disgraced, whose political plotting had blighted the whole family. That was why the house next door still stood empty, and apparently why Decimus looked tired. I knew the brother was dead – but as I also knew, things don't end there.

'Did you approach the auctioneer I recommended?'

'Yes. Geminus is very helpful.' That meant very undemanding about provenance and probate.

'Oh he's a good auctioneer,' I agreed wryly. Geminus was my absentee father. Apart from his habit of running off with redheads, he could pass for an excellent citizen.

The Senator smiled. 'Yes. The whole family seems to have an eye for quality!' That was a gentle poke at me. He pulled himself out of his gloom. 'That's enough about my troubles. How are you? And how is Helena?'

'I'm alive. Can't ask for more. Helena is herself.'

'Ah!'

'I'm afraid I brought her back fractious and full of foul language. It hardly fits the decent upbringing you and Julia Justa have given her.'

'Helena always managed to rise above that.'

I smiled. Helena's father enjoyed a quiet joke.

Women are supposed to behave demurely. They can be manipulating tyrants in private, so long as the good Roman myth of female subservience is sustained. The trouble with Helena Justina was that she refused to compromise. She said what she

36

wanted, and did it too. That sort of perverse behaviour makes it extremely difficult for a man who has been brought up expecting deceit and inconsistency to be sure where he stands.

I liked it. I liked to be kept jumping. I liked to be shocked and astonished at every turn, even though it was hard work.

Her father, who had had no choice in the matter, often looked amazed that I had volunteered to take her on. And there was no doubt, he enjoyed seeing some other victim on the jump.

When we went into dinner we found Helena glittering in white, with golden hems on elaborate swags of drapery; oiled; scented; necklaced and braceleted. Her mother's maids had as usual conspired to make their young mistress look twice my rank – which she was – and twenty times my worth.

For a moment I felt as if I had tripped over my boot-thong and fallen headlong on the floor mosaic. But one of the necklaces was a string of Baltic amber that her mother had not seen before. When the noble Julia asked about it in the course of her scratchy small talk, Helena Justina announced in her own brisk fashion, 'That was my birthday gift from Marcus.'

I served Helena's mother to the best delicacies from the appetisers with rock-steady decorum. Julia Justa accepted with a politeness she had honed like a paring knife. 'So some good did come out of your trip to the River Rhenus, Marcus Didius?'

Helena spoke up for me quietly. 'You mean some good in addition to securing peace in that region, rooting out fraud, rallying the legions – and providing the opportunity for a member of this family to make his name as a diplomat?'

Her mother waived her sarcastic objection with a tilt of the head. Then the Senator's daughter gave me a smile whose sweetness was as rich as the summer stars.

The food was good, for winter fare. It was a friendly meal, if you like your friendship of the formal, surface kind. We all knew how to be tolerant. We all knew how to make it plain we had rather a lot to tolerate.

I had to do something about it. Somehow, for Helena's sake, I had to scramble into the position of a legitimate son-in-law.

37

Somehow I had to find four hundred thousand sesterces – and I had to find them fast.

VIII

Petronius Longus caught up with us that same evening.

We had been on the verge of turning in. Ma usually went to bed early, because at her age she needed to build up her stamina for the next day of furiously organising the family. She had waited up for our return – one of the restrictive practices that made me prefer to live elsewhere. After dinner at the Senator's I had chosen to come home, partly to reassure Ma but also because I knew if I stayed, as Helena's father offered (though her mother was markedly cooler), the Capena Gate house steward would give Helena and me separate rooms and I could not face a night of creeping along strange corridors trying to find my lass. I told Helena she could stay behind in comfort. 'They'll give you a softer pillow – '

She thumped my shoulder. 'That's the pillow I want.' So we both came back, which made two mothers happy – or as happy as mothers ever like to feel.

When they saw Petro shambling into the kitchen even Ma and Helena decided to stay up longer. Women took to him. If they had known as much about him as I did they might have been more disapproving; then again, they would probably have blamed me for the wild episodes in his past. For some reason Petro was a man whose indiscretions women excused. For some other reason, I was not.

He was thirty years old. He arrived dressed in various shapeless brown woollen garments, his usual unobtrusive working uniform, plus winter additions of fur in his boots and a hooded cloak so voluminous he could have been hiding three loose women and their pet duck under it. Stuck through his belt he carried a thick cudgel for encouraging quiet behaviour on the streets; these he supervised with a light, reasonable hand, backed up by well-aimed bodyweight. A twisted headband rumpled the straight brown hair on his broad head. He had a placid mentality he certainly needed when picking through the grime and greed at the low end of

Roman society. He looked solid and tough, and good at his job –
all of which he was. He was also a deeply sentimental family man
–a thoroughly decent type.

I grinned widely. 'Now I know I'm really back in Rome!'

Petronius slowly lowered his large frame on to a bench. His
expression was sheepish – presumably because he had a wine
amphora under one arm, the usual credential he offered when
visiting me.

'You look tired out,' Helena commented.

'I am.' He never wasted words. I cracked the wax of his
amphora to save him the effort, then Ma produced winecups. He
poured. He sloshed the liquor into the beakers with careless
desperation, paused briefly to chink his cup on mine, then drank
fast. He had trouble written all over him.

'Problems?' I asked.

'Nothing unusual.' Ma topped him up, then found a loaf and
some olives to cosset him with. Petro was another friend of mine
who was reckoned to be a cut above what I deserved. He rubbed
his forehead wearily. 'Some tourist who managed to get himself
slashed to ribbons by a maniac, or several, in a hired room . . . I
can't say he should have used the door-bolt, because in that flea-
pit so much luxury wasn't available.'

'What was the motive? Robbery?'

'Could be.' Petro sounded terse.

In winter the rate of muggings among strangers usually fell.
Professional thieves were too busy counting their winnings from
the summer season. Actually killing the victim was a rare event. It
attracted attention, and was normally unnecessary; there were
pickings enough from idiots who came to see Rome, their pouches
bursting with spending money, and then stood around the Via
Sacra like curly little lambs waiting to be fleeced.

'Any clues?' I asked, trying to encourage him.

'Not sure. If there are, I don't like them. They made a disgusting
mess. Blood everywhere.' He fell silent, as if he could not bear to
talk about it.

Helena and Ma came to a mystical decision. They both yawned,
patted Petro on the shoulder, ignored me, and made themselves
scarce.

Petronius and I drank some more. The mood relaxed – or I assumed it did. We had known each other a long time. We had been best friends throughout our army careers; those had both been short (we helped each other fake reasons for leaving), but the province we had been allocated to was Britain, during a fairly lively period. Not something to forget.

'So how was the famous German trip, Falco?'

I told him something about it, though saved the best; his mind was clearly unreceptive to anecdotes. I saw no point in enduring the mishaps of travel and the trials of dealing with foreigners unless I could entertain my friends with them afterwards. 'Gaul seems as lousy as we remember it.'

'So when did you get back to Rome?'

'Day before yesterday.'

'I must have missed you around – been busy?'

'Nothing special.'

'I was looking for you earlier today.'

'Lenia told me.'

'So where were you?' Petro had a stolid insistence when he wanted to exert himself.

'I told you – nowhere special!' I was laughing at him cheerfully. 'Listen, you curious bastard, this conversation seems to be taking an odd tone. If I was a provincial sightseer you had stopped on the Via Ostiana, I'd be frightened you were going to demand a peek at my docket of citizenship on pain of five hours in your lock up . . . What's the game, Petro?'

'I wondered what you were up to this morning.'

I was still grinning. 'That sounds as if I need to consider it carefully. Jupiter, I hope I'm not being asked to produce an alibi.'

'Just tell me,' Petronius insisted.

'Bumming about. What else would I be doing? I've just come home after a foreign trip. I need to assert my effervescent presence on the streets of home.'

'Who saw you?' he asked quietly.

That was when I first realised the inquisition must be serious.

'What's up, Petro?' I heard my own voice drop several tones.

'Just answer the question.'

'There's no way I'm going to co-operate with a legal officer – any officer, Petro – unless I know why he's latched on to me.'

'It's better if you answer first.'

'Oh rot!'

'Not at all!' Petro was growing heated now. 'Listen, Falco, you've placed me between Scylla and Charybdis – and I'm in a very flimsy boat! I'm trying to help you; that ought to be obvious. Tell me where in Hades you were all morning, and make it good. You need to satisfy Marponius as well as me.' Marponius was a judge on the murder panel whose aegis included the Aventine. He was an interfering halfwit whom Petro could hardly tolerate; that was usual with officialdom.

'Right!' Anxiety made me speak angrily. 'Try this. This evening Helena and I gorged ourselves with luxury at the home of the most excellent Camillus. Presumably His Honour's word will be acceptable? You know Glaucus; Glaucus is straight. I was in the Forum; I saw my banker and Sattoria, not to mention Famia and Gaius Baebius, but I made sure they didn't see me, so that's no help. Perhaps they noticed me skulking behind a pillar, trying to avoid them,' I added with increased restraint, since Petro was looking at me mournfully.

'Who's Sattoria?' he asked, having recognised the other names.

'No one you know. No one *I* know any longer.' Not now I had a respectable girlfriend who took a sombre view of my bachelor past. Nice to have somebody bother about you. Nice, but occasionally things grew tense.

'Oh her!' Petro commented matter-of-factly. Sometimes I wondered about him. He looked henpecked, but occasionally gave the impression that he led a double life.

'You're bluffing, you beggar. You've no connection with Sattoria . . . After that I was up at the Palace for an hour or two, so surely even Marponius will say I'm in the clear for that period – '

'Skip the Palace. I've already covered that angle.' I was amazed. The sneaky bug must have been sleuthing round Rome as tenaciously as a clerk after promotion. 'I want your whereabouts earlier on.'

'Can't help you. I was tired out after travelling. Helena and Ma went to clean up my apartment. They left me here in bed. I was asleep, so I wasn't up to anything, but don't ask me to prove it – the classic useless excuse . . . Petro, I can't stand this! What in the name of the Capitoline Triad is fretting your tiny worried mind?'

Petronius Longus stared at the table. I could tell we had reached the crunch. He looked as lonely as a gold piece in a miser's pocket. 'Try this. The corpse I had to look at this morning', he informed me in an unsteady voice, 'was a centurion called Titus Censorinus Macer. He was done in at Flora's Caupona – and every time I ask if he had upset anybody recently, people rush at me with lurid tales of some blazing row he had with you.'

IX

I groaned. Not too loudly; a murder suspect needs to beware of bad acting.

'Lucius Petronius, I can hardly believe I'm hearing this . . .' I believed it all too easily. From the moment my brother's business life had become an issue yet again, I had expected deep trouble on the next throw of the dice. This was the worst yet, however.

'Believe it!' Petronius advised.

'Oh gods, Petro, I'm standing on a real midden heap of shit. You know Marponius hates informers. Now my name's written on a tablet in the denouncing jar! Just the chance he needs to interfere with my free movement and slander me at Pincian Hill dinner parties. Still!' I cheered up. 'Since you're the investigating officer, Marponius doesn't need to know.'

'Wrong, Falco!'

'Don't worry about it. I'll help you track the killer down.'

Petro sighed. 'Marponius knows already. He's having one of his "social responsibility" fits. Every five minutes he wants me to show him round a brothel or introduce him to a professional gambling cheat. I was with him discussing another case when they turned up to fetch me to Flora's. Coming along to have a squint at a genuine body was the highlight of the judge's year. Well,' he added reminiscently, 'it was until he actually set eyes on the mess.'

'I get it.' I had gathered this was a murder that would deeply affect a judge's shockable mind. 'Having seen the gore, and thrown up his breakfast on the doorstep of the action, His Honour feels personally involved in the whole damned enquiry? You'd better tell me everything. I suppose all the hangers-on at Flora's who normally wouldn't pass the time of day with their own lice, couldn't wait to talk with the great man?'

'Exactly. Your name took about three seconds to surface. We hadn't even forced a passage through the throng. I was still trying to get upstairs to inspect the remains.'

'This looks bad.'

'Smart, Falco!'

I knew Marponius was the impetuous type who would expect the first suspect he heard about to be condemned. Much neater than complicating life with other possibilities. He was probably already drawing up a jury list for my trial in the Basilica. Assuming he reckoned I rated the Basilica.

'So what's the situation, Petro? I'm a wanted man; Marponius thinks you're looking for me. Have you found me now, or do I get leeway to search for evidence myself?'

Petronius Longus gave me the straight look he normally kept for women; it meant he had no intention of being straight. 'Marponius wants this tied up speedily. I told him I couldn't find you at your apartment. I may have forgotten to mention I might be seeing you later on here.'

'How much to go on forgetting?'

'I'm sure you'll manage to persuade me!' There was nothing corrupt in Petronius. On the other hand, he would reckon any favours he notched up voluntarily ought to be accounted for in kind at a later date.

'Thanks.'

'You'll have to move fast. I can't keep it up for ever.'

'How long?'

'I can probably bluff for a day.' I thought I would be able to stretch him to three. We were pretty close friends. Besides, Petro hated Marponius too much to give an inch to his requests for speed. Watch captains are elected by the populace; Petronius took his authority from the plebeian electorate.

That said, he liked the work, he enjoyed his local status, and with a smart wife and three young daughters to keep he needed his public salary. Upsetting a judge would be a bad idea. Not even I could expect that of him; if it came to dilemma-time, I wouldn't even ask.

Petronius excused himself; discord always went to his bladder. While he was otherwise occupied I spotted his note tablet lying alongside his cloak on the table. Like everything he owned, it was solid and heavy, four or five reusable waxed boards bound with a criss-cross of leather thongs between two square wooden protectors. I had seen him use it on numerous occasions, unobtrusively scratching details about some luckless suspect, often at the

45

same time as he talked to them. The tablet had a substantial, well-aged look that made it appear reliable. Produced in court, to be read from in his sombre tones, Petro's memory-jogger had secured many a conviction. I had never expected to be listed there myself among the reprobates. It gave me a feeling I didn't like.

I flipped the top cover and found he had been assembling a timetable of my own movements that day. Suppressing my indignation, I inserted the missing events for him in a neat, bitter script.

X

When he came back he immediately recaptured his notes. He noticed my additions but said nothing.

I moved the amphora aside, then set Petro's winecup well out of his reach.

'Sobriety-time. You'd better go over all you've found out so far.'

I saw an uneasy look on his face. Maybe telling the chief suspect exactly what evidence had been amassed against him struck a wrong note, even when I was the suspect. But habit won. He opened up. 'All we have is an extremely bloody corpse.'

'When was he done?'

'Marponius thinks last night, but Marponius just likes the idea of unspeakable crime at midnight. It could have been early this morning.'

'It would be!' The one period for which I had no alibi. 'I'll have to dodge Marponius while I try to prove what really happened. Let's cover every possibility. Any chance of suicide?'

Petro guffawed. 'Not with those wounds. Self-infliction can be ruled out. Besides,' he informed me reasonably, 'the victim had paid in advance for his room rent.'

'Yes, that would be stupid, if he knew he was depressed! And he was badly hacked, you say? Was some villain trying to prove a point?'

'Could well be. Are you going to suggest what? Or tell me *who* is trying to make their mark?'

I had no idea.

Together we considered alternatives. Censorinus could have picked up a bedmate – of either sex – who had turned spiteful at some point. 'If so, no one at Flora's saw the paramour,' Petro said. 'And you know Flora's!' A curious hovel, as I was remarking earlier.

'Had he been robbed?'

'Probably not. All his kit appeared to be present and correct.' I made a private note to try and get a look at it some time.

47

'What about a disappointed debtor?' Even as I said it, I could hear the false note. Censorinus was *collecting* debts. Petro stared at me. The details of my quarrel must have whistled all along the Tiber's southern bank. Petronius certainly knew at least as much as I did about why the soldier had been in Rome, and what he had wanted here.

'I met him a couple of times when I came over to see your mother while you were away. I had already formed the impression he might be leaning on your family for more than a free bed. Would I be right in assuming your wonderful brother was at the back of it?' I did not reply. 'With the greatest respect, Marcus Didius,' Petro began, employing only slight reproach, 'there do seem to be one or two aspects which you could help clarify!' He said it as if he were loath to embarrass me. That meant nothing. He was tough; which meant tough on his friends too. If my foolish behaviour made an arm lock or a knee in the groin necessary, Petro would not flinch from it. And he was bigger than me.

'Sorry.' I forced myself to unwrap the parcel from him. 'Whatever you want. Yes, there is some problem over a project Festus was involved with. No, I don't know what it was. Yes, I did try to extract details from Censorinus. No, he wouldn't tell me. And most certainly, no, I don't want to be involved if I can help it – but yes, as sure as the little goddess likes pomegranates, I'll get to the bottom of this mystery rather than let myself be sent to the public strangler for something my fabled brother failed to square!'

'I'm rather assuming,' said Petronius, smiling slightly, 'someone else killed the soldier at Flora's. I presume even you would have had more common sense than to quarrel with him so publically first.'

'True, but with Marponius on your back you'd better keep me on your list of suspects until I'm formally cleared.' Marponius would agree eventually with Petro's view of my innocence; he would appropriate Petro's verdict and claim it as his own. Until that happened life for me could be extremely difficult. 'If the dead man's grouse against Festus was legitimate, I might have had a motive for removing him.'

'Everyone who saw you fighting at Flora's was quick to admit that Censorinus never explained to you what his bugbear was.'

'Good of them! But he did walk part of the way along the sandy

48

track. He was telling me that Festus had owed money to a gang of his old pals for some galley that foundered.'

'If I know you,' Petro argued loyally, 'they only had to prove it and you would have robbed your own savings coffer to put the golden Festus in the clear.' Petro never shrank from swimming against the tide of public opinion; my brother, whom so many people adored, had not been wildly popular with my old friend. They were different types.

Petro and I were different too, but in another, complementary way that made us friends.

'I do use a knife.'

'Neatly!'

Petronius had seen me use my knife.

I knew now that Petronius Longus must have stood up to the judge Marponius and insisted that the soldier's killing lacked my personal style. Even so, I could see they had no choice but to harry me until something else turned up.

'Just for routine,' Petronius asked me levelly, 'where is your knife at present?'

I produced it from my boot. I tried not to feel harassed. He examined it, carefully looking for blood. Of course he found none. We both knew that proved nothing; if I had killed someone I would have cleaned my weapon scrupulously after the event. Even if the occasion had been legitimate, that was my normal good housekeeping routine.

After a time he returned it, then warned me, 'You're liable to be stopped and searched on sight. I presume I can trust you not to carry an offensive blade inside the city boundary?' Going armed in Rome is illegal, a neat trick which means that the law-abiding have to walk down dark alleys undefended, just waiting to have their throats cut by wicked types who ignore the rules. I said nothing. Petro went on insultingly, 'And Falco, don't take your ugly hide *beyond* the city boundary – or any temporary amnesty is cancelled at your first step.'

'Oh that's rich!' I was highly annoyed with him. He could become extremely irritating when he exerted his official role.

'No, it's fair!' he retorted. 'It's not my fault if you start throwing punches at an off-duty legionary who next minute gets himself

49

sliced up. Think yourself lucky I'm not measuring you for manacles. I'm freeing your reins, Falco, but I want a return. I need to know what this business with your brother was, and you stand more chance of discovering the details than anyone, including me.' That was probably right. And I was going to start digging in any case; I was now irresistibly curious about the statues scam.

'Petro, if the body is all we have to go on, I'd like to take a look at it. Is the carcass still at Flora's?'

Petronius looked prim. 'The body's off limits. And keep away from Flora's, if you don't mind.'

There were moments in this conversation when our old friendship started coming under too much strain. 'Oh cobnuts! Holding a public post goes to your head sometimes. Stop treating me like a tired husband whose nagging wife has just been found laid out lifeless on a public compost heap.'

'Then you stop giving me orders as if the whole bloody Aventine was yours under private lease!'

'Try being a mite less officious!'

'Just try growing up, Falco!'

Petronius rose to his feet. The lamp guttered nervously. I refused to make an apology; so did he. It didn't matter. Our friendship was too close to be blown apart by this condescending exchange of personal views.

At least I hoped it was. Because without his help, my witless implication in the murder of Censorinus could have fatal results for me.

He was stomping off in a huff, but turned back from the doorway.

'Sorry about your sister, by the way.'

With so much else on my mind, I had forgotten about Victorina. I had to think hard to realise what he was saying.

I opened my mouth to remark that he must be more sorry than I was, then stopped. I did pity her children, left to the mercy of their feeble father the plasterer. Besides, I had never been quite sure about relations between Victorina and Petronius. But one thing was certain: when women were involved, Lucius Petronius Longus had never been as shy as he appeared.

XI

After he left I sat where I was. I had a lot to think about. It was the proverbial case with no easy solutions. In fact, as was normal for me, no solutions at all.

Helena Justina came to see what I was doing (or how much I was drinking). Perhaps she had heard me quarrelling with Petronius. Anyway, she must have guessed there was a problem and that the problem might be serious. At first she tried to pull me gently by the arm, attempting to lure me to bed, but when I resisted she gave way abruptly and sat down alongside.

I went on thinking, though not for long. Helena knew how to handle me. She said nothing. For several moments she simply stayed with me, holding my right hand between both of hers. Her stillness and silence were comforting. As normal, I was completely disarmed. I had been intending to keep the situation from her, but pretty soon I heard myself saying despondently, 'You had better know. I'm a suspect in a murder case.'

'Thank you for telling me,' Helena remarked politely.

Immediately my mother popped out from somewhere near at hand. She has always been shameless about listening in.

'You'll need something to keep your strength up then!' exclaimed Ma, banging a patera of broth on to the embers of her cooking bench.

Neither of them seemed the least surprised – or at all indignant – that I had been subjected to such a charge.

So much for loyalty.

XII

Next day the weather continued to be abysmal, and so did my own mood. I was faced with far more than investigating my shady brother's past for family reasons, a hard enough task. But if I was to escape a murder charge, within the next day or so I had to find out why Censorinus had died and name the real murderer. Otherwise the best I could hope for was exile to the ends of the Empire, and if I came up before a judge who hated informers – as most of them did – there might even be the threat of crucifixion beside a highway like any common criminal or being turned into bait for an arena lion.

Only my own family seemed likely to offer any clues as to what Festus and his army pals had been about. Forcing my relatives to sit still and answer questions like witnesses was a dire prospect. I tried my sister Maia first. Maia was my favourite, but as soon as I spread myself out on a couch she upset me by commenting, 'I'm the last person you should be asking. Festus and I never got on.'

She was the youngest surviving child in our family, and in my opinion had the best looks and character. We had barely a year between us, while a gap three times as long divided me from our next sister, Junia. Maia and I had stuck together ever since we shared a nursery beaker and took turns learning to stagger about in a little walking-frame on wheels. In most ways she was easygoing. We rarely squabbled, either when we were children or later on.

Most women on the Aventine look like hags from the moment they have their first baby; Maia, with four behind her, still appeared younger than her thirty years. She had dark, extremely curly hair, wonderful eyes, and a round, cheerful face. She had picked up a good dress sense when she worked for a tailor, and had kept up her standards even after she married Famia, a sozzled horse vet with a bulbous nose and minimal character. Famia was attached to the Green faction, so sporting discernment was not his gift; his brains seemed to have run out once he latched on to my sister. Luckily she had enough apples in the basket for both of them.

'Give me some help, Maia. The last time Festus came home on leave, did he say anything to you about being in partnership with some people from his unit importing art from the East?'

'No. Marcus, Festus would never have talked about anything important in front of me. Festus was like you were in those days. He thought women were just for being rammed from behind while they were bent over a cooking bench preparing dinner for him.'

'That's disgusting.' I felt upset.

'That's men!' she retorted.

One reason Maia disapproved of Festus was the effect he had had on me. He had undeniably brought out my own worst side, and she had hated having to watch it. 'Maia, don't do him down. Festus had a sunny nature and a golden heart – '

'You mean he always wanted his own way.' Maia remained implacable. She was normally a treasure to deal with. On the rare occasions when she took against someone she enjoyed letting rip. Excess was our family's strong point. 'There's one obvious person you ought to talk to, Marcus.'

'You mean Geminus?' Geminus, our father. Maia and I shared views on the subject of Father. They were not complimentary.

'Actually,' she scoffed, 'I was thinking of ways you could avoid trouble, not walk right into it! Marina, I meant.' Marina had been my brother's girlfriend. For various highly emotional reasons I did not want to go and see Marina either.

'I suppose there's no escaping it,' I agreed gloomily. 'I'll need to have things out with her.' Talking to Marina about the last time we both saw Festus was something I dreaded.

Maia misinterpreted. 'What's the problem? She's dim, but if Festus ever said anything that her soppy brain actually remembers, she'll tell you. And Juno, Marcus, she certainly owes you some favours!' After Festus died I had made an effort to keep Marina and her young daughter from starving while Marina was out enjoying herself with the fellows who eventually replaced Festus in her disordered life. 'Do you want me to come with you?' Maia demanded, still trying to push me into it. 'I can make sense of Marina – '

'Marina's no problem.'

53

My sister seemed to have no idea why I wanted to steer clear. That was unusual, because the scandal was no secret. My brother's girlfriend had made sure the entire family knew that she and I had a sordid connection. The last time Festus was home on leave in Rome, in fact the night before he departed back to Judaea, he had left her and me together, with results I preferred to forget.

The last thing I wanted nowadays, especially while I was living with Helena at my mother's, was to have that old story raked up again. Helena Justina had high moral standards. A link between me and my brother's girlfriend was something Helena would not even want to understand.

Knowing my family, Helena was probably being told all about it even as I sat glumly in my sister's house trying to put the saga out of my mind.

XIII

Maia lived on the Aventine, not two streets from Mother. Not far away was another group of my relatives whom I needed to visit; my dead sister Victorina's household. It was unlikely to help my enquiries, but as nominal head of our family it was my duty to pay my respects. With a murder sentence hanging over me, I went along as soon as possible, feeling like a man who might soon be arrested and deprived of the chance.

Victorina and her depressing husband Mico had made their nest on one side of the Temple of Diana. Victorina, with her long career of dirty assignations at the back of the Temple of Isis, had never appeared to realise that living next to the chaste huntress might be inappropriate.

As addresses go, it occupied a glamorous site, but had few other selling-points. They existed in two rooms among a warren of dingy apartments at the back of a large copper shop. The constant clanging of mallets on metalware had left the whole family slightly deaf. The tenement they rented had slanting floors, frail walls, a rotten ceiling and a strong odour from the giant vat of urine in the stairwell which the landlord never emptied. This polluting dollium leaked slowly, which at least made room for refills. Hardly any light could penetrate to the apartments – an advantage, since seeing their homes too clearly might have led to a long queue of suicides on the Probus Bridge.

It was some time since I had needed to pay a visit to my sister's place. I could not remember exactly where she lived. Treading gingerly because of the leaky dollium, I made a couple of false attempts before I identified the right apartment. Hastily avoiding the neighbours' curses and lewd propositions, I dived through what remained of a coarsely woven curtain and found my destination. There could have been no greater contrast than that between the neat apartment where Maia was successfully bringing up her children and the humid hole, with its fragrance of cabbage and children's damp tunics, in which this other feckless family lived.

Mico was at home. Inevitably, he was out of work. As a plasterer my brother-in-law had no skill. The only reason he was allowed to remain in the Plasterers' Guild was pity. Even when contractors were desperate for labour, Mico was the last man they called in.

I found him attempting to wipe honey from the chin of his youngest but one. His eldest daughter, Augustinilla, the one we had been looking after in Germany, glared at me as if the loss of her mama was all my fault, and stalked from the house. The six-year-old boy was systematically hitting the four-year-old with a small clay goat. I prised the baby off a distinctly grubby rug. He was an antisocial tyke who clung to his perch like a kitten putting out its claws. He burped, with the evil relief of a child who was choosing his moment to throw up now that a visitor had provided a respectable cloak for him to throw up on.

In another corner of the room a slack bundle of flab clothed in unappealing rags cackled at me amiably: Mico's mother. She must have slid in like fish oil the minute Victorina died. She was eating half a loaf but not bothering to help Mico. The women in my own family despised this placid old dame, but I saluted her without rancour. My own relations were born interferers, but some folks have the tact to sit by and merely act as parasites. I liked her style. We all knew where we were with Mico's mother, and it wasn't being harried out of doors by a broom or having our guilty consciences probed.

'Marcus!' Mico greeted me, with his usual effusive gratitude. I felt my teeth set.

Mico was small and swarthy. He had a pasty face and a few black teeth. He would do anyone a favour, provided they were prepared to accept that he would do it very badly and drive them wild with incessant chat.

'Mico!' I cried, slapping him on the shoulder. I reckoned he needed stiffening. Once his balance was upset for any reason, depression set in. He had been a long river of gloom even before he acquired the excuse of five motherless children, his mother at home, no work, no hope, and no luck. The bad luck was his real tragedy. If Mico tripped over a bag of gold bits on his way to the baker's, the bag would split open, the aurei would scatter – and he would watch every one of them drop down a manhole into a sewer at full flood.

My heart fell as he drew me aside with a purposeful air. 'Marcus Didius, I hope you don't mind, but we held the funeral without you . . .'

Dear gods, he was a worrier. How Victorina ever stood him I don't know. 'Well of course I was sorry to miss the formalities . . .' I tried to look cheerful since I knew children are sensitive to atmosphere. Luckily Mico's tribe were all too busy pulling at each other's ears.

'I felt terrible about not allowing you a chance to do the eulogy . . .' Apart from the fact I was delighted to be spared it, this idiot was her husband. The day they married, Victorina had become his charge in life and death; it was Mico's duty to dredge up something polite to declaim at her funeral. The last thing I would have wanted was for him to step aside in my favour as some misplaced compliment to me as head of the Didius family. Besides, Victorina had had a father living; we all did. I was just the unhappy soul who had had to shoulder the responsibility when our shirking, self-seeking father chose to do a moonlight flit.

Mico invited me to a stool. I sat, squashing something soft. 'I'm really happy to have this chance for a chat, Marcus Didius . . .' With his normal unerring judgement he had chosen as a confidant a person who could hardly bear to listen to five words from him.

'Pleased to help . . .'

Things went from bad to worse. Mico assumed I had come to hear a full commentary on the funeral. 'A really good crowd turned out for her – ' Must have been a quiet day at the racecourse. 'Victorina had so many friends . . .' Men, mostly. I can never understand why fellows who have tangled with a good-time girl acquire such peculiar curiosity if she passes on. As Victorina's brother I would have resented it.

'Your friend Petronius was there!' Mico sounded surprised. I wanted to be surprised myself. 'Such a decent fellow. Good of him to represent you like that . . .'

'Lay off, Mico. Petronius Longus is on the verge of locking me up in jail!' Mico looked concerned. I felt a renewed surge of my own anxiety about Censorinus and my deadly predicament. 'How are you managing?' I changed the subject abruptly. Mico's nasty-tempered baby was kicking my left kidney. 'Is there anything you need?' My brother-in-law was too disorganised to know. 'I've some New Year presents from Germany for the children. They're still packed, but I'll bring them round as soon as I can get at them. My apartment's wrecked – '

Mico showed a genuine interest. 'Yes, I heard about your rooms!' Great. Everyone seemed to know what had happened, yet not one of them had tried to do anything about it. 'Do you want a hand putting things straight?' Not from him, I didn't. I wanted my old place to be liveable, and by next week not next Saturnalia.

'Thanks, but you have enough to think about. Make your ma look after the children while you get out a bit. You need some company – you need some *work*, Mico!'

'Oh something will come up.' He was full of misplaced optimism.

I gazed around the sordid room. There was no sense of absence, no silence left by Victorina's loss. It was hardly surprising. Even in life she had always been off somewhere else having her own idea of a good time.

'I see you're missing her!' Mico remarked in a low voice.

I sighed. But at least his attempts to comfort me seemed to cheer him up.

Since I was there I decided to get a few questions in: 'Look, I'm sorry if this is not the right time, but I'm making some enquiries for Mother and I'm seeing everyone about it. Did Festus ever say anything to you about a scheme he was involved in – Greek statuary, ships from Caesarea, that sort of thing?'

Mico shook his head. 'No. Festus never talked to me.' I knew why that was. He would have had more luck trying to dispute the philosophy that life is a bunch of whirling atoms with a half-naked, barely sober garland girl. 'He was always a pal, though,' Mico insisted, as though he thought he might have given the wrong impression. I knew it was true. Festus could always be relied on to throw crumbs to a stranded fledgling or pat a three-legged dog.

'Just thought I'd ask. I'm trying to find out what he was up to on his last trip to Rome.'

'Afraid I can't help you, Marcus. We had a few drinks, and he arranged a couple of jobs for me, but that's all I saw of him.'

'Anything special about the jobs?' It was a forlorn hope.

'Just normal business. Plastering over brickwork . . .' I lost interest. Then Mico kindly informed me, 'Marina probably knows what deals he had on. You ought to ask her.'

I thanked him patiently, as if the thought of speaking about Festus to his girlfriend had never occurred to me.

XIV

If I was ever to solve the soldier's murder I needed to take a more
direct hand. Petronius Longus had warned me to keep away from
Flora's. I had no intention of obeying him. It was lunch-time, so I
turned my feet straight towards the caupona.

Wrong move: I was compelled to go past. One of Petro's troopers
was sitting outside on a bench beside the beggar on the barrel. The
trooper had a pitcher and a dish of soggy stuffed vine leaves, but I
knew what he was really doing there: Petro had told him to make
sure I didn't get in. The man had the nerve to grin at me as I passed
by, faking a nonchalant expression, on the far side of the street.

I went home to Ma's house. My second mistake.

'Oh Juno, look what's straggled in!'

'Allia! What have you come for – a bodkin or a pound of
plums?'

Allia was my second-eldest sister; she had always been
Victorina's closest ally, so I was as low in Allia's affections as the
grit in an empty amphora, and she had never featured at all in
mine. She must have been here to borrow something – her normal
occupation – but luckily she was leaving just as I arrived.

'Before you start on about Festus – don't!' she informed me with
her regular brand of truculence. 'I know nothing about it, and I
really can't be bothered.'

'Thanks,' I said.

There was no point in attempting to argue. We parted company
on the threshold. Allia lurched off, big-boned and slightly
ungainly, as if she had been mishandled during the birth process.

Helena and Ma were sitting at the table, both fairly straight-
backed. I threw myself on to a coffer, ready for the worst.

'Allia has been telling us some interesting stories,' Helena
announced bluntly. That would be the Marina incident. It had
been useless to hope she would never find out.

I said nothing, but saw Helena lock her teeth on the left-hand side with an angry overlap. I was angry myself. Encountering Allia always felt like reliving several hours of childhood – the dreariest part that normal memory sensibly wipes out.

Looking tired, Mother left me alone with Helena.

'Stop looking so shifty!' At least she was speaking.

I drew a long breath, surreptitiously. 'You had better ask me.'

'Ask you about what, Marcus?'

I wanted a chance to explain things away. 'Ask about whatever poisoned thistle Allia planted in the melon field.'

'I'll find you some lunch,' said Helena Justina, pretending she had not heard this magnanimous offer.

She knew how to punish me.

XV

The lunch Helena provided was adequate, though no more. I shuffled off afterwards, looking as if I had useful work to do. In fact I spent the afternoon exercising at the baths. I wanted a chance to brood over the Censorinus killing – and to get myself in shape for whatever problems lay ahead of me.

When I first appeared at the palaestra Glaucus gave me a sideways look. He said nothing, but I guessed he had been interviewed about me by Petronius.

I was in no hurry to return to Mother's house. As I dawdled along the Ostia Road the rain finally stopped. A pale sun forced itself through the clouds, touching roof finials and awning-poles with a cheerful gleam. I risked pushing my cloak back from my head. When I breathed, the air smelt cold but no longer full of storms. It was simply winter in Rome.

The city half slept. The streets felt lonely. A few people who had no option scuttled here and there, but it was hardly the glad place I knew in warmer days. No one walked for pleasure in Caesar's gardens, no one sat out on balconies shouting across to their neighbours, no one drowsed on stools in doorways, no one went to the theatre and filled the evening air with distant rumbles of applause. I heard no music. I saw no partygoers. The acrid smell of bathhouse smoke crawled sluggishly on the still air.

Lights began to be lit. It was time to be going somewhere positive, even if the somewhere was not home. Wandering aimlessly could attract the wrong attention. Besides, it makes a man depressed.

With nothing to lose, I had another go at Flora's.

This time there were no visible representatives of the watch. I had to be careful, since Petronius sometimes dropped in on his way home to dinner. I won't say he needed to strengthen his resolve before he faced his wife and their three raucous children, but Petro was a man of habit, and Flora's was one of his habitual haunts. I had a swift look round both outside and in before I let my feet come to a halt.

I had timed it just right. Petro's operative had done his job and reported back to the guardhouse. There were no other customers. The day's wastrels had drifted off. It was just too early for the evening trade. Flora's was all mine.

I leaned on the counter. Epimandos, the shabby waiter, had been scraping out bowls, but the minute he saw me he dropped his spatula.

'The usual?' he let out before he could stop himself, but then he froze in panic.

'Skip the food. I only have time for a half jug of house red.' I was keeping him on tenterhooks. For once he leapt into action. The jug appeared so rapidly I nearly put my palm in it as I turned back from a quick survey of the street behind. Still no sign of Petronius.

Epimandos was staring at me. He must be well aware I was chief suspect in the Censorinus case. He must have been amazed even to see me when the whole Aventine was waiting to hear I had been arrested.

Still stringing him along, I took a huge swig of wine like a man intent on getting horribly drunk. Epimandos was bursting to ask questions, yet petrified what I might say or do. I amused myself bitterly wondering how he would react if I had actually done the deed; if I did get drunk; if I sobbed on his welcoming shoulder and confessed my crime like an idiot. He ought to be grateful I was here, providing a scene to thrill the customers with when he told them about it afterwards. Mind you, saying 'Falco came in, drank a half-pitcher, then left quietly,' would hardly grab their attention.

I paid up, then made sure I had finished the wine, in case Petro appeared and I had to abscond hastily.

Fear that I might be leaving without providing any gossip must have helped the waiter find his tongue. 'People are saying you're going to be arrested.'

'People love to see someone else in trouble. I've done nothing.'

'The men from the watch told me you'll have a hard time getting out of it.'

'Then I'll be serving some slander writs.'

Epimandos tugged at my tunic urgently. 'But you're an investigator! You can prove you're innocent – ' he had a touching faith in my skills.

I interrupted his agitated mutterings. 'Epimandos, how much to let me have a look at the room upstairs?'

'What room?' he gasped feebly.

'Why, just how many nasty secrets are you hiding at Flora's?' The waiter blenched. This place had certainly been used by antisocial characters more than once. 'Settle down. I'm not prying into the caupona's murky past.' He still looked terrified. 'I mean the room where your lodger signed off from the legions before his time.' Epimandos did not move or speak. I began more sternly: 'Epimandos, I want you to take me up to the room Censorinus hired.' I thought he was going to pass out. He had always been easily unnerved. It was one of the reasons I summed him up as a runaway slave.

'I can't!' he finally whispered desperately. 'They've roped it up. There was a guard here until ten minutes ago . . .' He seemed to be thinking up excuses.

'Oh Hercules! You're not telling me the body's still in your pigeon loft?' I glanced up expressively. 'That's a bit inconvenient. You'll be losing trade if blood starts dripping through the ceiling.' The waiter looked more and more uncomfortable. 'Why can't they drag the corpse away on a cart?'

'It's because he was a soldier,' Epimandos croaked. 'Petronius Longus said the army had to be notified.'

That was rubbish. Most unlike my disrespectful friend Petronius. I frowned. Petro would always override what others regarded as proper formalities. I even wondered for a wild moment if he was stalling on the removal order so as to give me a chance for a squint . . .

'Got any oysters tonight?' I asked Epimandos.

'No.'

'I think I'll have some.'

He found a slight increase in confidence now I had stopped talking about corpses. 'We never have oysters, Falco.' He was used to dealing with people who were deaf or drunk or both. 'You'll get oysters at the Valerian.' The Valerian was the caupona on the opposite corner. It was neat and clean, but always empty. For no obvious reason the locals had decided to ignore the Valerian as steadfastly as they patronised Flora's, even though Flora's was overpriced and gave you gut-ache.

64

'I can't be bothered to shift. Epimandos, run over and get me a bowlful, will you?'

Whether he grasped the idea or not, Epimandos let himself be bullied into running over the road. I hoped he had the sense to dally for a long chat with the Valerian's waiter.

I nipped through the kitchen area and up the back stairs. I knew where lodgers were installed, because when Ma's Campania relations descended we sometimes bedded them out here. There were three rooms – two tiny cubicles over the kitchen and a larger one above the bar. Censorinus had had the biggest. I knew because its door was tied up.

Petronius had returned my knife after his inspection, so I already had it out to slice through the rope, which had been wound on to two large nails by his men. Their efforts were pretty feeble, however. The web of heavily stranded hemp looked impressive at first glance, but a pantomime dancer could have made a forced entry without breaking a fingernail. I managed to drag one knot right off, which meant I would be able to replace it intact when I left. If I was fast, I might be able to come and go undetected.

Without pausing to wonder any further about the pathetic attempt to deter entry, I opened the door gently on the room where the soldier's murder had taken place.

XVI

Don't ask me to describe it.

You never expect what you find. Sometimes – the lucky times – any evidence that a violent crime has occurred seems hardly noticeable. So little shows that quite a few crimes must entirely escape discovery. At other times, the violence is horrendously clear. You reel back, amazed that anyone could wreak such savagery on another human being. This was one of those.

This murder had been committed in a frenzy. Even my warning from Petronius had failed to prepare me. Petronius apparently believed in Greek understatement.

We had talked about villains 'making their mark', as if Censorinus's death might have been a syndicated killing ordered by some magnate in the underworld. As soon as I saw the room I gave up the idea. Whoever killed Censorinus Macer was acting under devastating stress.

It had to have been a man. Impassioned women can achieve vindictive damage, but this act had taken brute strength. Blow after crazy blow, long after death had occurred. The face, when I forced myself to look at it, was difficult to recognise. Petro was right: there was blood everywhere. Even the ceiling was splashed. To clean the room properly would entail dismantling the furniture and swabbing the surfaces several times. Olympus knows what the killer must have looked like when he left.

I felt reluctant to move around even now, after the gore had dried.

But there was no point in having come unless I used the opportunity. I forced myself into routine activity.

The place was roughly eight feet square. A small room. It had one small, high window, deeply recessed. A small bed. One blanket; no pillow. The only other furnishings were a cloak hook, beneath which a faded scarlet uniform item had dropped to the floor, perhaps during the murder, plus a stool that stood by the rickety bedhead. On the stool I saw one of Flora's stained wooden

66

trays with a full pitcher and a winecup that had been knocked on its side. The rich liquid gleam of the red wine in the pitcher mocked the dried and caking bloodstains everywhere else.

Military kit had been neatly stowed at the foot of the bed. To reach it meant passing close by the dead soldier, whose remains lay half sprawled on the bed. I knew Petro and his men had managed to search the kit. I, with an indictment hanging over me, had to get there and do likewise.

The man's boots were lying just under the bed; I stumbled over one of them and barely avoided contact with the corpse. I gagged, managed to recover myself, then carried on.

His boots were off; he must have been going to bed, in bed, or getting up. Someone else might have been joining him under the blanket for social reasons, but in my opinion an intruder did this. Censorinus was not dressed for company. Soldiers put their boots on before they answer a knock at the door. Soldiers always want to be able to kick out if they hate your face.

Anyway, there was only one winecup on the tray.

The rest of his stuff, as Petronius had said, appeared to be complete. I had seen it all before when I helped Censorinus pack to leave my mother's house. Sword, dagger and belt; helmet; vine staff; knapsack of the usual small tools; spare red tunic and underwear. As he was on leave, he was not carrying spears or a shield. An old mansio bill was the only document. (From the Via Appia out on the Campagna, a place I knew.)

The weapons were all stowed tidily. It confirmed my theory that he was caught completely off guard. He must have been attacked unexpectedly, making no attempt to reach his gear and defend himself. He must have died after the first ferocious blow.

Had he been robbed? At Mother's he had kept his financial arrangements from me. I could see an arm-purse on him now, unopened; that alone would not have held enough funds for his journey to Rome. The mattress looked as if somebody had pulled it askew looking for money, but that could have been Petronius. Until the body was removed there was no scope to investigate the bed properly. Censorinus would have to be lifted off first. I was desperate – but not that desperate.

With the room in such a sorry condition, I was not prepared to ferret under floorboards either. There were practical problems. I was short of time, minus a jemmy, and unable to make noise. Petro would probably come back to do it. Better for him to find anything that was there.

I tried to memorise everything so I could brood on it later. Later, something that meant nothing now might suddenly make sense.

Averting my gaze, I eased my way past the body and escaped.

I had to fight for self-control before I replaced the ropes, and when I turned round from doing that a figure standing in the gloom below frightened the wits out of me.

'Epimandos!'

We stared at one another. Even with the length of the stairs between us, I could see he looked petrified.

I descended slowly until I reached him; the horror from above came after me, fingering my neck.

He was standing in my way. He was carrying a whole earthenware pot of oysters, holding it in the crook of his arm quite easily; years of heaving great food containers from the fire to their counter-holes had given him muscle.

'Forget it, I lost my appetite.'

'Do you know who did it?' he burst out in a frightened whisper.

'I know it wasn't me!'

'No,' Epimandos said. He was high in customer loyalty.

I would have preferred time to recover, but while we were out there in the kitchen, away from other eyes and ears, I asked him about the night the soldier died. 'I told the watch captain all that.'

'You're very public-spirited. Now tell me.'

'The same as I told Petronius?'

'Only if it's true! After Censorinus and I had had our little disagreement, when did he reappear?'

'He came back in the evening.'

'By himself?'

'Yes.'

'You sure of that?'

Epimandos had been sure until I asked him; insisting he thought about it frightened him into doubts. His eyes moved rapidly as he quavered, 'He was alone when he had supper here anyway.'

'Did he stay in afterwards?'

'Yes.'

'Drinking?'

'He went upstairs.'

'Did he say anything?'

'Like what?' demanded the waiter suspiciously.

'Anything at all?'

'No.'

'Did anyone come to see him afterwards?'

'Not that I saw.'

'Were you busy that night?'

'Well . . . More than the Valerian was.' That meant normal trade.

'That evening, could anyone have gone indoors past you without you noticing?'

'It's possible.' With the tight internal arrangements, front entry would be difficult for anyone avoiding notice. But the waiter could never watch the back end of the caupona, which we locals used as our private way out if we saw debt-collectors approaching down the street. Sharp bailiffs and their bully-boys came in that way.

'Did you go out on any errands?'

'No. It was pouring with rain.'

'Were you working all night?'

'Till we closed.'

'Do you sleep here?' Epimandos nodded reluctantly. 'Show me where.'

He had a cabin on one side of the kitchen. It was a dreary burrow. The occupant slept perched on a ledge with a straw pillow and a sludge-coloured coverlet. I noted few personal possessions – just an amulet on a nail and a woollen cap. I remembered my brother had given him the amulet, probably as a pledge for an unpaid bill.

He ought to have heard anyone who got in after he closed the caupona, whether they forced the sliding doors at the front or secretly used the back entrance. But there were five empty amphorae lolling on their points against one wall: knocking back the ends of them must be the waiter's perk. I guessed he normally turned into bed dead drunk, a habit that might well be known by local villains. That night he could have been in such a stupor he failed to hear the violent struggle overhead.

69

'So did you notice any odd noises that night?'

'No, Falco.' He sounded pretty definite. Such certainty worried me.

'Are you telling me the truth?'

'Of course!'

'Yes, of course you are . . .' Did I believe him, though?

Customers were shouting for attention. Epimandos edged towards the main area of the shop, eager to get away from me.

Suddenly I sprang on him: 'Who found the body? Was it you?'

'No, the owner, going up to get his rent . . .'

So there was an owner! I was so surprised I let the waiter slip away to face the raillery in the bar.

After a moment I let myself out through the back way: a slatted stable door on rusty pins that led to an alley full of dead fish-pickle jars and olive-oil flagons. There were about fifteen years of empties, lurking below a corresponding smell.

Anyone like me who had been coming here for half a lifetime would have known about this unsecured, unsecurable exit. Any stranger could have guessed its existence too.

I paused for a moment. If I had emerged straight after seeing the body I would have thrown up drastically. Controlling myself while I questioned the waiter had helped put it off.

I turned back, looking closely at the stable door in case the killer had left bloodstains to mark his retreat. I could find none. But inside the kitchen area stood pails of water. A murderer could have washed, at least partially, before he left.

Walking slowly, I went round to the main street. As I passed the caupona heading homewards, a tall figure, plainly not a customer, hovered in the shadows outside the Valerian. I took no notice. There was no need for the usual caution. The sinister individual was neither a robber nor a marauding pimp. I recognised that bulky shape, and I knew what he was doing there. It was my friend Petronius, keeping a suspicious eye on me.

I called a mocking goodnight and kept going.

It failed. Petro's heavy footfall pounded after me. 'Not so fast!'

I had to stop.

Before I could start grumbling at him he got in first in a grim tone, 'Time's running out, Falco!'

70

'I'm dealing with the problem. What are you doing, wearing out the pavements on my tail?'

'I was looking at the caupona.' He had the tact not to ask what I had been up to there myself. We both glanced back. The usual dismal crowd were leaning on their elbows arguing about nothing, while Epimandos applied a taper to the tiny lamps that were hung above the counters at night. 'I wondered if anyone could have made a forced entry to the lodger's room from out here . . .'

I could tell from his tone he had decided that was unlikely. Looking up at the frontage of Flora's we could see that while the place was open, access would be impossible. Then once the shutters were drawn for the night there would be a blank face on the street side. Above the bar were two deeply recessed window openings, but it would take a ladder to reach them and then climbing in through such a small opening would be awkward. Censorinus would have heard anyone trying to do it well before they were on to him.

I shook my head. 'I think the killer went up the stairs.'

'And who was he?' demanded Petro.

'Don't nag me. I'm working on it.'

'You need to work fast then! Marponius has summoned me to a conference tomorrow about this stinking case, and I can tell you in advance, the conclusion will be that I have to haul you in.'

'I'll keep out of your way then,' I promised, as he growled and let me go.

Only when I had turned the corner did I remember meaning to ask him about the caupona's owner, the mystery rent-collector whom Epimandos told me had discovered the corpse.

I made it back to Mother's in a sombre mood. I seemed no further forward, though I now had some feeling for events the night the soldier died. How his death connected with Festus was a mystery. Censorinus had been killed by somebody who hated him. That depth of emotion had nothing to do with my brother; Festus had been friends with everyone.

Or had he been? Maybe somebody had a grudge against him that I wasn't aware of ? And maybe that was what had brought disaster on a man who had been known as one of my brother's associates?

71

The ghastly scene in the room still hovered on the edge of my consciousness as I went indoors.

I was already hemmed in by problems, and when I entered the apartment I discovered another: Helena Justina was waiting for me, alone.

Mother was out – probably gone to see one of my sisters. She might stay the night. I had an idea things had been arranged that way. Our driver from Germany had already taken his pay, such as it was, and left us. Helena had lent her maid to her mother. Nobody on the Aventine has a maid.

So we were alone in the apartment. It was the first time we had been on our own like this for several weeks. The atmosphere was unconducive to romance.

Helena seemed very quiet. I hated that. It took a fair amount to upset her, but I frequently managed it. When she did feel hurt I lost her, and she was hurt now. I could tell what was coming. She had been thinking all day about what Allia had told her. Now she was ready to ask me about Marina.

XVII

Things began quietly. Helena let me kiss her cheek. I washed my hands. I pulled off my boots. There was dinner, which we set about in virtual silence. I left most of mine.

We knew each other too well for preliminary skirmishes. 'Want to talk about it?'

'Yes.' Always direct, this one.

After what I had witnessed that evening, it was the wrong time for an argument, but if I tried to dodge, even temporarily, I was afraid that it could be the end of everything.

I gazed at her while I tried to clear my head.

She was wearing a long-sleeved dark blue dress, winter-weight wool, with agate jewellery. Both suited her; both went back to before I met her. I remembered them from when I first knew her in Britain; then she had been a haughtily independent young woman, recently divorced. Though her confidence had been eroded by the failed marriage, defiance and anger were what I most recalled from those days. We had clashed head-on, yet by some divine metamorphosis that had turned into laughing together, followed inevitably by love.

The blue dress and agates were significant. She may not have thought about it. Helena despised premeditated drama. But I recognised in her appearance a statement that she could be her own woman again any time she chose.

'Helena, it's best not to quarrel at night.' It was honest advice, but came out more like insolence. 'You're proud and I'm tough; it's a bad combination.'

During the day she must have withdrawn into her private self. Helena had given up a great deal to live with me, and tonight she must be as near as she would ever be to throwing that back in my face.

'I can't sleep beside you if I hate you.'

'Do you?'

'I don't know yet.'

I reached to touch her cheek; she leaned away. I snatched back my hand. 'I've never cheated you, sweetheart!'

'Good.'

'Give me a chance. You don't want to see me grovelling.'

'No. But if what I've heard is only half right, I'll be seeing you squirm soon!'

Helena's chin came up. Her brown eyes were bright. Maybe we both felt a thread of excitement, sparring like this. But Helena and I never wasted time inventing pretexts. Any accusations that were about to be flung would carry as much weight as wet sandbags.

I leaned back a little. I felt breathless. 'So what's the procedure? Are the questions to be specific, or shall I just warble cheerily?'

'You seem to be expecting a crisis, Falco.' That 'Falco' was bad.

'I do keep an eye on what you're finding out about me.'

'Have you something to say about it?'

'My darling, I've spent most of the afternoon thinking up explanations to win you round!'

'Never mind the explanations. I'm well aware you can invent wildly and phrase it like a barrister. Tell me the truth.'

'Ah that!' I always told her the truth. That was how I already knew the truth sounds more insincere than anything.

When I made no effort to respond further, Helena seemed to change the subject. 'How are you getting on with your mother's business?'

'It's my business now. I'm a murder suspect, don't forget!'

'What have you done today?' It appeared oblique, but I knew it would be relevant.

'Spoke to Maia; Mico; Allia. Got nowhere with any of them. I talked to the waiter at Flora's – and I inspected the corpse.'

I must have looked drawn. 'Did you have to do that?' Helena asked in a changed voice.

I smiled wryly. 'So you still have some heart?'

'I have always treated you reasonably!' That was a fierce dig. 'I think you have been wasting time, Marcus. It's obvious there were two people you ought to have seen immediately. You've spent a whole day dodging the issue, and contacted neither. The situation's too serious for this.'

'There is time.'

'Petronius only gave you today!'

'So you've been listening to private conversations?'

She shrugged. 'Thin walls.'

'Who are these people I'm supposed to be ignoring?'

'You know who. Your brother's old girlfriend for one. But first you should have gone straight to your father.'

I folded my arms. I said nothing; Helena fought me silently. 'Why do you hate your father?' she demanded eventually.

'He's not worth hating.'

'Is it because he left home while you were just a child?'

'Look, my childhood is none of your business.'

'It is,' snapped Helena, 'if I have to live with the results!'

Fair comment. And I could not object to her interest. Helena Justina's main criterion for living with a man was that he let her read his thoughts. After thirty years of keeping my own council, I went along with it. Being an informer is a lonely profession. Allowing Helena free access to the inner sanctum had come as a relief.

'All right. I can see I have to suffer.'

'Marcus, you're trussed up like a bird in a braising pan – '

'I'm not done for yet. Mind you don't get pecked.'

Her eyes glimmered; that was promising. 'Stop prevaricating! Tell me the truth.'

'You won't like it.'

'I realise that.'

'You win.' I faced the inevitable. I should have told her all this a long time ago. She must have half guessed it anyway, while I had nearly forfeited the right to give her my version. 'It's quite simple. I don't know what went on between my parents, but I've nothing to say to any man who walks out on his children. When my father took a stroll I was seven. Just about to assume the toga praetexta. I wanted my papa to be there watching at my first big ceremony.'

'You don't approve of ceremonial.'

'I don't now!'

Helena frowned. 'Plenty of children grow up with only one parent present. Still, I suppose the lucky ones at least get a stepfather to despise or stepmother to hate.' She was teasing, and on this subject I object to being teased. She read my face. 'That was bad taste . . . Why did your parents never divorce formally?'

75

'He was too ashamed to do it; she was, and is, too stubborn.' I used to wish I was an orphan. At least then I could have started again, without the constant hope or dread that just when everything had settled down our paterfamilias might reappear, upsetting everyone with his old blithe smile.

Helena was frowning. 'Did he leave you without money?'

I began to answer angrily, then took a deep breath. 'No, I can't say that.'

When my father ran out with his redhead we never saw him for several years; I learned afterwards that he had been in Capua. Right from the start there had been a man called Cocceius who brought money to my mother on a fairly regular basis. It was supposed to be coming from the Auctioneers' Guild. For years I accepted that story, as Mother appeared to do. But when I grew old enough to work things out I realised that the Guild was acting as agent – a polite excuse for my mother to accept my father's money without lessening her disgust for him. The main clue was that the weight of the coin bag increased with time. Charitable hand-outs tend to tail off.

Helena was looking at me for more answers. 'We just about escaped being destitute. We were barely clad and fed. But that applied to everyone we knew. It sounds bad to you, love, with your privileged upbringing, but we were the swarming mass of the great Roman poor; none of us expected any better from life.'

'You were sent to school.'

'Not by him.'

'But your family did have benefactors?'

'Yes. Maia and I had our school fees paid.'

'She told me. By the lodger. Where did he come from?'

'He was an old Melitan moneylender. My mother found space for him so the rent money would help out.' She only let him have a fold-up couch and a shelf for his clothes in a corridor. She had assumed he would hate it and leave, but he clung on and lived with us for years.

'And your father disapproved? Was the lodger a cause of arguments?'

This was all wrong. *I* was supposed to be the intruder who went round asking awkward questions, forcing long-hidden secrets to bubble to the surface of other people's ornamental ponds. 'The

Melitan did cause a lot of trouble, but not the way you mean.' The Melitan, who had no family, had wanted to adopt Maia and me. That had caused some tumultuous rows. To Helena, who came from a civilised family where they hardly seemed to wrangle over anything more serious than who beat the Senator to the best bread roll at breakfast, the riots among my own tribe must sound harsh and barbaric. 'I'll tell you about it some day. My father's disappearance was directly related to his flamboyant girlfriend, not the lodger. Times were hard and he wasn't prepared to endure the struggle with us. The Melitan was irrelevant.'

Helena wanted to argue, but accepted it. 'So your father suddenly walked out one day – '

'It seemed unexpected, but since he left with a red-haired scarf-maker, maybe we should have been prepared.'

'I've noticed you hate redheads,' she said gravely.

'Could have been worse: could have been a Macedonian; could have been a blonde.'

'Another colour you loathe! I must remember to stay dark – '

'That means you're not leaving me?' I threw in lightly.

'Even if I do, Marcus Didius, I shall always respect your prejudices!' Helena's gaze, which could be oddly charitable, met mine. A familiar spark tingled. I let myself believe that she would stay.

'Don't go!' I murmured softly, with what I hoped were pleading eyes. Her mood had changed again, however. She looked back as if she had just spotted mould on a best table napkin. I kept trying. 'Sweetheart, we haven't even started yet. Our "old times" have yet to be enjoyed. I'll give you things to look back on that you cannot even dream – '

'That's what I'm afraid of!'

'Ah Helena!'

'Ah nuts, Marcus!' I should always have spoken to her in formal Greek, and never have let her pick up my own slang. 'Stop bluffing,' commanded the love of my life. She had a sharp eye for fraud. 'So your father started a new life as an auctioneer in Capua; he eventually reappeared in Rome, the man I know as Geminus. Now he is a rich man.' She had met my father briefly. He had made sure he steamed in like Lars Porsena of Clusium to inspect the high-born madam who had picked me up. I still felt good whenever I remembered his amazement. Helena Justina was not some enamelled old baggage I was chasing for her money. He found her presentable, apparently rational, and genuinely fond of me. He never got over the shock and I never stopped gloating.

This sibyl could also be too shrewd for her own good: 'Is it his wealth you resent?'

'He can be as rich as he likes.'

'Ah! Is he still with the redhead?'

'I believe so.'

'Do they have children?'

'I believe not.'

'And he's still there twenty years later – so he does have *some* staying power!' Without intending to let her see a reaction, I ground my teeth. Helena queried thoughtfully, 'Do you think you inherited that?'

'No. I owe nothing to him. I'll be loyal to you of my own accord, princess.'

'Really?' Her light inflection belied the sharp whip in the insult. 'You know where he is, Marcus; you recommended him to my own father. Sometimes you even work with him yourself.'

'He's the best auctioneer in Rome. One of my professional specialities is recovering stolen art. I deal with him when I have to – but there are limits, lass.'

'Whereas,' she started slowly. Helena could use a word like 'whereas' not merely to shade her argument, but to add hints of moral stricture too. Her conjunctions were as piquant as anchovy. 'Whereas your brother seems to have worked with Geminus on a much more frequent footing . . . They were close, weren't they? Festus never felt the anger that obsessed you after your father left?'

'Festus never shared my anger,' I agreed bleakly.

Helena smiled slightly. She had always thought I was a broody beggar. She was right, too. 'The two of them had a long and regular partnership on a straightforward father-and-son basis?'

'It seems like it.' Festus had had no pride. Maybe I had too much – but that was the way I liked it.

'Don't you know, Marcus?'

'I am forced to that conclusion. Festus never mentioned it.' Sparing my feelings, I suppose. Mother's too. 'There was a hiatus in relations when my father was living out of Rome, but Festus must have resumed contact pretty soon afterwards.' Sometimes I wondered if they had even stayed in touch throughout the time when Father was hiding up in Capua. 'Certainly by the time Festus died they shared a lock-up in the antiques quarter, over at the Saepta Julia.' Where my mother could not see them. 'And then they were as close as two termites.'

'So your father will know about the statues and the ship that sank?'

'He should. If it was one of their joint ventures.' She had dragged the words out of me like crusted amber oozing from an old pine tree. Before Helena could capitalise on the achievement, I said sternly, 'I left him until last deliberately. I am going to see Geminus tomorrow.'

'I think you're afraid to face him.'

'Not true—but you have to understand, my father can be a very tricky customer. I wanted to assemble as many facts as possible before I tried talking to him.' She was closer to the truth than I admitted. I had never discussed family affairs with Father, and I hated the thought of starting now. 'Helena, just leave me to get on with it!'

Very manly. Asking for trouble, in fact. That glimmer in her eyes was quite dangerous now.

'All right.' I hate reasonable women. 'Don't scowl,' she complained. 'Anybody would suppose I interfered.'

'May I be eaten alive by ravens if I thought it . . . Is that the end of the marathon grilling?'

'No.'

I thought not. We still had Marina to upset our evening. The grilling had hardly started yet.

XVIII

I made one last attempt to restore peace. 'I'm in serious trouble, sweetheart. I may be under arrest soon. Don't let's spoil our evening with any more home truths.'

Helena Justina listened almost demurely, her hands lightly folded in her lap. Anyone who had never met her might suppose she was a woman of quality interviewing a cushion-stuffer who was seeking outwork. I knew her better. She looked sad, which meant she was angry – *more* angry than if she had merely looked annoyed.

Soon she would be sad too.

'Marcus, when people are so eager to tell me that you seduced your brother's girlfriend, I would like to assure them I have already heard the full story from you.'

'Thank you,' I said, pretending to assume it was a compliment. The full story posed some problems. Only Festus knew that. 'To start with, Helena, if I did seduce my brother's girlfriend, Marina did not object to it – and as for Festus, it was probably his plan.'

'Maybe she seduced you?' suggested Helena, almost hopefully.

I smiled. 'No, that's your privilege.'

Then I told her about that long and dreadful night in Rome.

My brother Festus was thirty-five years old when he died. Frankly, we had not been prepared to lose him to a hero's death. An accident during a prank seemed more his style.

Being older, he had always seemed to me to belong to another generation, though by that time the gap between us was closing. People used to say how alike we looked. That was only because we had the same rampant curls and silly grins. He was shorter and more thickset. More athletic and with a sweeter temperament. More gifted in business, luckier with women, smarter, sharper, more easily accepted as a treasure by the family. It was always pretty clear to me that both my parents and most of my sisters made Festus their favourite. (However, I had my share of being spoiled; my childhood place was as the family baby since Maia, who really owned that position, would not stand for the fuss.)

Like a good Roman citizen who saw his chance to eat, drink and fart at the Empire's expense while using its unrivalled facilities for world travel, Festus enlisted in the legions as soon as he looked old enough.

'So he *must* have been in touch with your father,' Helena commented. 'He would need the signed release from his family.'

'True. Just one aspect of public life where having a missing father causes painful embarrassment.'

'You were in the army later. What did you do about that?'

'My Great-Uncle Scaro stood in as my guardian.'

'You liked him?'

'Yes.' Uncle Scaro, a friendly old scallywag, had always given me the place in the world that my father had taken away.

Entrepreneurs do well in the army. After all, regulations exist to exploit. Whereas I had had to serve five years in the bitter Northern provinces, Festus had easily wangled himself supremely cosy billetings: a brief spell in Spain, Egypt with the Fifteenth Apollinaris, then posted East with them once the civil war broke out in Judaea. This last could have proved a miscalculation, but since the whole Empire was about to erupt then, Festus would have been fighting wherever he was. With expert precision he had placed himself under the command of the future emperor, Vespasian. His legion was led by Vespasian's own son, doubly convenient as my brother had somehow made it to centurion, so was visible to Titus Caesar daily at his war council.

In the year that the Jewish Rebellion began, when Nero sent Vespasian to deal with it and the Fifteenth Legion were posted from Alexandria to help, Festus had come home on sick leave. He had organised one of the wounds in which he specialised: it looked vicious enough to gain a pass for convalescence in Italy, though once he set foot at Ostia he seemed able to do pretty well whatever he wanted, especially if it involved girls. Other people's girls, mostly. Festus believed it was non-combatants' patriotic duty to lend home-leave centurions their women. Women went along with this.

The army was less free and easy. With the legions being so stretched out in the desert, they needed every man. After six weeks in Rome, Festus was annoyed to receive an urgent recall to Judaea.

'Festus struck us as one of life's eternal survivors. None of us imagined he was going back to be killed.'

'Festus presumably imagined it least of all,' Helena said. 'Is this where I start feeling annoyed?'

'Afraid so . . .'

On his last night in Rome, the last time I ever saw him, we went to the Circus Maximus. Festus had always been a keen attender at the Circus, mainly because of the saucy women he could sit next to in the unsegregated seats. He was a devoted frequenter of girls who frequent the few places where girls exhibit themselves accessibly. In the proximity of Festus women showed off eagerly. I used to watch with astonished fascination. It happened even when, as on that night, his long-term girlfriend Marina had been brought along.

Festus saw nothing unusual in spending the last night of home leave with both his younger brother and his girl. It made us an awkward party. He simply never noticed it. Just as he never seemed to notice me lusting after the girl.

'Was Marina attractive?'

'Distinctly.'

'Don't bother to describe her,' Helena snarled.

Festus had always liked women who drew the crowds. Even when Marina was sulking because Festus was leaving Italy heads turned as we took our bench at the Circus, and later when Festus was dragging us round a series of dimly lit bars, she made us a highly conspicuous party. She had known Festus for years. As a fixture she could rightly feel more confidence than the various kittens who succumbed to a few days of passion then found themselves airily waved goodbye. It was assumed, probably even by Festus himself, that one day he would marry her. Only Mother had doubts. She said to me once it was more likely he would outrage everyone by bringing home an exotic little doll he had only known a fortnight and announcing that he had found true love. Festus certainly had a romantic streak. However, he died before he got round to it. That saved Mother from having to train some moppet who thought herself too pretty to help in the home. It left me with the task of shocking the family with an unlikely girlfriend, and it left Marina unmarried but unassailable. She was one of the family. Because by then Marina had honoured us by producing my niece Marcia.

82

Little Marcia was assured of lifelong support from the Didius clan. If anyone ever hinted to Marina that Festus might not be Marcia's father, Marina snapped back swiftly that if Festus was not responsible, it had to be me.

Helena forced out, 'I asked you once if Marcia was yours. You denied it.'

I had hardly known her then. I had been trying to impress her. Explaining Marcia had been too difficult to tackle. Maybe I should have done it anyway. It was worse now.

'Let's say the subject carries a question mark . . .'

What had happened was that in the early hours of the morning, when Festus, Marina and I were all too drunk to be cautious, my big-hearted brother had fallen in with some sozzled artists in a down-market tavern below the Caelian Hill. His new friends were well up to standard for Festus: all badly pickled gherkins who had no cash in their frayed tunic pockets but an easy habit of joining another party's table and calling loudly for more wine. I was tired. I had been very drunk, but was recovering enough to feel sullen and foul-mouthed. By now drink seemed unattractive. Even putting up with Festus had temporarily lost its sparkle. I said I was leaving. Marina announced she had had enough too. Festus asked me to take Marina home for him.

He promised to follow immediately. He was bound to forget her. In fact I had a strong suspicion the bold brunette who had sat next to him at the Circus was now awaiting him on some balcony. Marina had noticed the brunette too. Since this was her own last chance of seeing him, Marina took it badly. When we arrived at her apartment she complained that he mistreated her. I felt hard done by too; it was *my* last chance of seeing him. He might for once have stood up some dismal strangers and stuck with us. Waiting for him to let us down while we trailed after him on the wine-bar crawl had built up a fine old head of self-righteousness.

I made the foolish comment that it was lucky for Festus that I was not the type to try and put one over on him; so Marina said, '*Why not?*'

Afterwards, Marina made it plain the occasion had given her small pleasure. There was no chance of me enjoying myself either. Drink, guilt and confusion ruined it.

Some time during the next morning, I found myself back at my apartment with no idea how or when I got there. I knew Festus would have left for the port several hours before, provided he was capable. (He was, and he did.) So we never even said goodbye.

For weeks I avoided Marina. I found excuses to leave town as much as possible. Later I heard that she was pregnant, but everyone assumed Festus had fathered the baby; it suited me to think the same.

Then a year later came the day when I returned from a visit to Great-Uncle Scaro, who lived at the family homestead on the Campagna. I went to take Mother news of her relatives. I found the whole family assembled. I remember noticing a document that lay on the table. And when none of the women wanted to speak (for once), one of my brothers-in-law threw the news at me: Festus had led a sally over a battlement at some parched town called Bethel in Galilee, and had been killed as he turned back to call his men up after him. He was awarded the Mural Crown for being the first to cross an enemy rampart, and his heroic ashes had been scattered in Judaea.

At first I could not believe it. Even now I sometimes thought it must be a dream or trickery.

It emerged that Marina and Festus had never made a habit of writing to each other, and she had seen no reason to change that simply to tell him he had acquired a daughter. Why worry him? When he came home Marina would introduce him to the gurgling child and Festus would immediately adore her. (This was correct. Apart from the fact that Marcia was a good-looking baby, my brother was a deep sentimentalist.)

Losing my brother was bad enough. It was at the same family gathering, after I came back from the Campagna, that people thrust at me Marina's sudden public declaration about our night of what is so thoughtlessly called love. She had made a wild statement announcing that I had to look after her because our misguided fling was when she had conceived little Marcia.

My family reacted to this news in their usual good-natured fashion. Not one disbelieved it. I had shown a marked fondness

84

for the new baby, and on his last visit Festus had, after all, been a wounded man.

'Was he wounded in that area?' Helena interrupted. She had been listening with a dazed expression, not entirely unsympathetic towards me.

'Look, this is about my family: it's a mad story. Festus,' I said quietly, 'had stabbed himself in the foot.'

¨Sorry. I forgot people are not logical. What happened?'

'What do you think? I was greeted with torrents of invective, and instructed to marry the girl.'

Helena looked even more numb. She thought I was telling her that I had been concealing a wife.

It had nearly occurred. Under the influence of even more guilt and confusion, and seriously drunk, I heard myself agree to do it. At that, Marina, who had a hard streak of self-preservation, counted up the lives we were about to ruin and even she panicked. She restored Festus as Marcia's father, and backed out hastily. For me it brought many more insults, though at less cost.

That left the present situation.

'What exactly is the present situation?' sneered Helena.

'Only what you think.'

'I think it's appalling.'

'Quite.'

Obviously I had to care for the child. I had to do that for my brother's sake. There was no chance of shedding my responsibility for the mother either. Conscience is a terrible thing. Marina had a hold over me that I would never break. She might have gone off and married, but why should she bother when she was free to enjoy herself with me paying the bills? Meanwhile, I had made myself a target for every kind of abuse whenever my relatives cared to exert their talent.

There was no abuse from Helena. She looked upset, though not vindictive. I would have preferred to see jugs being hurled. Understanding always makes me miserable.

Unable to bear the tension any longer, I sprang up and paced about. Helena was leaning her elbows on Ma's kitchen table; her head was bowed in both hands. Eventually I stood behind her with my hands on her shoulders. 'Helena, don't judge the present by

85

past events. You ought to know something tremendous happened to me when I met you.'

She allowed both the contact and the comment without reacting.

Helpless, I moved away. Helena got up, stretching, then left the room, evidently going to bed. I had not been invited but I tagged along anyway.

We lay in the dark for what seemed like hours, not touching. I must have dozed off for I woke again unhappily. Helena lay still. I put my hand on her arm. She ignored it. I turned away from her huffily.

After a second Helena moved too. She crept behind me, knees in the crook of mine and face pressed against my spine. I waited long enough to make some sort of point, though not so long she bounced away again. Then I turned over carefully, gathering her close. For a short period I could feel her crying. That was all right. It was my fault – but she was crying from relief that we were now in each other's arms. We were friends. We would be friends for a long time.

I held Helena until her grief subsided, then we fell deeply asleep.

XIX

It was a cold night. After the North, where they make better preparations for winter than in Mediterranean countries, we felt it all the more. Bad weather always catches Rome by surprise. With only a brazier to take the chill off the long dark hours, my brother's old room could grow bitter by dawn. Still clinging together, we both awoke.

Helena had been planning. 'If you're going to see this Marina, I think I'll come too.'

I thought it was best for everyone if I went alone. Mentioning this point of view seemed a bad idea.

Marina made a habit of being as inconvenient as possible. (She was certainly right for our family.) She lived, as she had always done, right around the curve of the Aventine, across the Via Appia and almost at the foot of the Caelian in the quaintly named Vicus Honoris et Virtutis. This irony was too obvious to be commented upon. If honour and virtue had been qualifications for living there, it would have been an empty street.

'Is she *very* good-looking?' asked Helena, as we walked there together.

'Afraid so. Festus attracted dramatic women.'

'Unlike you?'

This sounded tricky. 'I go for character . . . To find looks in addition is a bonus, of course.' I realised she was laughing at me.

The light atmosphere ended as soon as Marina let us into her two-room hutch. I had forgotten just how striking she was. I saw Helena sigh slightly. Her fierce glance at me said she felt she had been inadequately warned. Things were not going well.

Marina was a short, dark, sultry vision with immense, wide-set eyes. She manoeuvred those eyes constantly, to nerve-racking effect. With a fine nose and high cheekbones, she had a faintly Eastern appearance. This suggestion was strengthened by her manner; she thought it elegant to make gestures involving bent wrists and stagily poised fingers.

She had once been a braid-maker, but nowadays felt little need to toy with employment. Nowadays she had me. Securing an honest sucker who made no demands had left Marina free to spend her time on her appearance. Her menfriends were pretty pleased with the results. They should be. The results could have been hung up and framed. Fortune had been as generous with Marina as I was; her conquests were getting a voluptuous shape allied to a free and easy manner, attractive goods even before they discovered the permanent lien on my bank box.

She was a cracker to look at, but the air of an awe-striking goddess was wiped out as soon as she opened her mouth. She had been born common, and was making a brave attempt to remain completely faithful to her origins. 'Ah Marcus!' The voice was as coarse as hessian. Naturally she kissed me. (Well, I *was* paying the bills.) I stepped back. This only allowed more room for Helena to inspect the immaculate turnout on the breathtaking body. Marina pretended to spot Helena. 'How come you need a chaperone these days?'

'Hands off, Marina. This is Helena Justina. She thinks I'm cool and sophisticated and that my past is full of very plain girls.'

Marina became noticeably cooler herself; she must have sensed a force to be reckoned with. Helena, in the same stately blue outfit as yesterday (still registering independence), seated herself gracefully as if she had been asked. 'How do you do?' This voice was quiet, cultured, and effortlessly satirical. Marina's sense of humour was basic; basically, she didn't have one. She looked tense.

Helena made no attempt to register disapproval. It only increased the impression that she was privately sizing up the situation and intended some swift changes. Marina was known for panicking every time the sparrows cheeped; she went pale under the purplish tones of her cheek paint and flailed around for rescue. 'Have you come to see the baby, Marcus?'

There was no sign of little Marcia, so the child must be parked elsewhere. I had already had a few arguments about that habit. Marina's idea of a suitable nurse for a four-year-old was Statia, a tipsy second-hand clothes dealer married to an expelled priest. Since he had been expelled from the Temple of Isis, whose attendants had the worst reputation in Rome, his habits had to be pretty seedy. 'I'll get someone to fetch her,' Marina mumbled hastily.

'Do that!'

She rushed out. Helena sat extremely still. I managed to avoid indulging in nervous chat, and stood about looking like the man in charge.

Marina returned. 'Marcus is *so* fond of my daughter!'

'Tact has never been your strong point!' Ever since she informed my family what had gone on between us, my relationship with Marina had had formal overtones. At one point we could not afford to quarrel; now we were too remote to bother. But there was an edge.

'He loves children!' Marina gushed, this time directed even more plainly at Helena.

'So he does. And what I like,' Helena returned sweetly, 'is the way it doesn't matter whose they are.'

Marina needed time to take this in.

I watched my brother's girlfriend staring at mine: beauty in the unfamiliar presence of strong will. She looked like a puppy sniffing at a strange beetle that seemed likely to spring up and bite its nose. Helena, meanwhile, conveyed lightness, discretion and sheer class. But our hostess was right to be nervous; this was someone who could bite.

I tried to take things in hand. 'Marina, there's a problem with a dodge Festus was running. I have to talk to you.'

'Festus never told me about his dodges.'

'Everyone keeps saying that.'

'It's true. He was a tight one.'

'Not tight enough. He promised some soldiers to make them a fortune. He let them down and now they're coming on to the family to make it up to them. I wouldn't care, but one of them has been sent down to Hades and circumstantial evidence strongly points to me.'

'Oh, but surely you didn't do it!' The girl was an idiot. I used to think she was bright. (Bright enough to rook me, though she would break a logic tutor's heart.)

'Oh don't be ridiculous, Marina!' She was wearing saffron yellow, a colour so clear it hurt the eyes; even in this weather she

89

went bare-armed. She had beautiful arms. On them she wore a whole rack of bracelets that rattled continually. I found the noise highly irritating. 'Be sensible!' I commanded. Marina looked offended by this advice; I thought Helena smiled. 'What do you know about Greek statues?'

Marina crossed her legs and gave me the full eye treatment. 'Offhand, Marcus, not much that I can think of!'

'I'm not asking for a lecture on Praxiteles. What do you know about any plans Festus had for importing the stuff and flogging it to rich people?'

'It was probably with help from Geminus.'

'Do you actually know that?'

'Well it sounds right, doesn't it?'

'Nothing in the story sounds right! The whole business sounds like trouble – and we're all in it. If I go to trial for murder that's the end of my funds, Marina. Put your mind on that practical issue, take a grip on yourself and think back.'

She set herself in the pose of a very attractive, fairly thoughtful woman. As a statue she would have been high art. As a witness she remained useless. 'Honestly, I don't really know.'

'He must have talked to you about something, sometimes!'

'Why? Business was business, bed was bed.' This topic was too uncomfortable.

'Marina, I'm trying to remember things myself. Was he restless on that last visit to Rome? Preoccupied? Anxious about anything?'

She shrugged.

She could. She didn't have Petronius Longus writing her name on a certificate of arrest while Marponius hopped from one foot to another just waiting to bang his seal ring on it.

'Well you were there!' smirked Marina. The implication was pointed, and quite unnecessary.

At this point a neighbour galloped in, carrying my niece. Marina seized the child with a relieved glance of thanks, the neighbour fled, and we all prepared for trouble. Marcia looked around, assessed the audience like a professional, then threw back her head and screamed.

Marina was bluffing madly as she tried to soothe her offspring.

'See what you've done, Marcus.' She was a fond, though vague mother, who suffered unreasonably at Marcia's hands. Marcia had never been one to co-operate. She had a keen sense of occasion. She knew exactly when a tormented wail could make her mother appear like a monster. 'She was perfectly happy. She likes going to play at Statia's – '

'She's showing off as usual. Give her here!'

As Marina weakly passed the child to me, Helena intercepted. Marcia fell into her arms like a galley hitting dock, then stopped screaming and settled on Helena's lap looking blissfully good. It was a fraud, but well timed to make both her mother and uncle feel inadequate. 'Let me see what I can do with her,' Helena murmured innocently. 'Then you two can talk.' She knew Marcia. They made a fine pair of conspirators.

'She loves it at Statia's,' Marina muttered again defensively.

I was annoyed. 'You mean she loves dressing up in filthy cast-off rags, and being allowed to eat the musical bars out of the ex-priest's sistrum!'

'You don't know that they neglect her.'

'I do know I've seen Marcia do an impressive imitation of Statia falling over drunk!' She also liked singing obscene hymns to Isis and mimicking suggestive rites. The child was a natural for the low life.

Marcia gazed lovingly at Helena, as if all this was news to her. Helena kissed her curly head consolingly. 'Don't worry, darling. It's only Uncle Marcus having one of his quaint fits.'

I growled. No one was impressed.

I sank on to a stool, burying my head in my arms.

'Uncle Marcus is crying!' giggled Marcia, intrigued. Helena whispered something, then put her down so Marcia could run to me. She flung her fat arms round my neck and gave me a smacking wet kiss. A worrying smell of wine lees hung around her. 'Uncle Marcus needs a shave.' She was a frank, open-hearted child. Maybe that was why I worried about her. She would be a frank, open-hearted woman one day.

I picked her up. She always seemed tougher and heavier than I expected. Marina had hung a tawdry bead anklet on one chubby foot and let Marcia paint red spots on her cheeks. Somebody, probably at Statia's, had given her a grotesque amulet. I had to close my mind to these details or I would have really lost my temper.

Holding my brother's oddly solid child, I tried reconstructing his last night in Rome yet again. Marina had said it: I was there all right. Any clues should be apparent to me, if only I could remember them.

'I do reckon he was edgy.' I was trying to convince myself. Marina only shrugged again in her distant, disinterested way. With those shoulders and that bust, she went in for shrugs on principle. The principle was: knock 'em dead. 'Old Festus was skipping on his toes that last night. Olympus knows what caused it, though. I doubt if it was the thought of going back to Judaea. He didn't care if the arrows were flying; he thought he could duck. Marina, do you remember that gang of ghastly wall artists he picked up?'

'I remember the girl at the Circus Max!' Marina said, with force. 'I'm damned sure he picked *her* up!'

'Can't say I noticed,' I mumbled, trying to avoid a scene. Helena was watching us with the tolerant expression of an intellectual at Pompey's Theatre enduring the ghastly farce while awaiting a serious Greek tragedy. If she had had a handful of almonds, she would have been eating them one at a time with the tips of her teeth. 'Marina, think about those graffiti merchants. They were gruesome. Where did they come from? I assumed he didn't know them, but are we sure?'

'Festus knew everyone. If he didn't know them when he went into the bar, he would know them by the time he left.'

Making cronies of a barful of people was his signature. 'He had his moments, but normally he drew the line at slaves and wall painters. He was making out to us that those posers were strangers. Did you know them yourself?'

'Just some tricksters at the Virgin. Their usual ghastly clientele – '

'The *Virgin*?' I had forgotten the name. Festus would have thought it a great joke. 'Is that where we ended up?'

'It's a terrible place.'

'That part I remember.'

'I'd never seen them before.'

'It must be quite near here. Do you still hang around there?'

'Only if somebody pays me to go.' Marina was as frank as her winsome child.

'Have you ever seen those artists again?'

'Not that I recall. Mind you, if I was desperate enough to be in the Virgin, I was probably too tipsy to spot my own grandmother.'

'Or you wouldn't want your granny to spot you.' Even at eighty-four Marina's old granny would have made a good Praetorian Guard. She liked hitting first and asking questions afterwards. She was three feet high, and her right upper-cut was legendary.

'Oh no! Granny drinks at the Four Fish,' Marina solemnly put me right.

I sighed, gently.

XX

Helena could see I was growing exasperated at the way this conversation jerked about.

'What we need to ascertain,' she intervened, in a tone so reasonable I felt my left foot kick out angrily, 'is whether Didius Festus was contacting somebody in particular on his last home leave. Somebody who can tell us what his plans were. Why are you asking about the artists, Marcus? He could have been arranging business at any time during his leave. Was there really something special about his last night – and about that group?'

Suddenly Marina declared, 'There certainly was!' I started to feel hot. She was oozing indiscretion, though it did not come immediately. 'For one thing,' she said, 'Festus was jumping like a cat on a griddle. You noticed that – you just said so, Marcus. That wasn't like him. Normally he breezed into places and stirred everyone else up, but he let the excitement flow over him.'

'That's true. And he could hardly wait to drag us on from one bar to the next. Normally once he got comfortable he wouldn't shift. That night he kept dodging on to new squats every five minutes.'

'As if he was looking for someone?' suggested Helena quietly.

'For another thing,' Marina pressed on inexorably, 'there was the little matter of him sending me off with you!'

'We don't need to resurrect that,' I said. Well, I had to try.

'Don't mind me,' smiled Helena. The knives were out all round.

'Suit yourself,' sniffed Marina. 'But Marcus, if you really want to know what he was up to that evening, I think this little incident needs considering.'

'Why?' Helena asked her, bright with unhealthy interest.

'It's obvious. It was a blatant fix. He annoyed me over the brunette, then he got up sunshine's nose as well.'

'Doing what? What offended sunshine?'

'Oh I can't remember. Just Festus being himself, probably. He could behave like a short-arsed squit.'

94

I said, 'Looking back, I can see he was trying to get rid of both of us – despite the fact it was our last chance of seeing him, maybe for years.'

'You were both very fond of him?'

Marina threw up her hands elegantly. 'Oh gods, yes! We were both planning to stick to him like clams. He had no chance of keeping secrets. Even getting us to leave the Virgin was not safe enough. We would both have been back. Well, I would. If I had gone home and he hadn't turned up soon afterwards, I would have stormed out again looking for him – I knew where to look, too.'

Helena glanced at me for confirmation. 'Marina's right. Festus was often elusive, but we were used to it. She had dragged him away from drinks counters in the early hours of the morning on many occasions. It was their natural way of life.'

'What about you?'

'As it was his last night, once I sobered up a bit I might well have gone back to toast his health again. I knew his haunts as well as Marina did. If he wanted any privacy, then he had to shoot us off somewhere, and make it stick.'

'So he annoyed both of you deliberately, then threw you together?'

'Obvious!' Marina said. 'Marcus had always been jealous of Festus. This loon had been eyeing me up for years – so why did Festus suddenly present him with the goods after all that time?'

I felt surly. 'I seem to be coming out of this as weak, cheap, and sly.' They both looked at me in silence. 'Well thanks!'

Marina patted my wrist. 'Oh you're all right! Anyway, he owed you enough; no one could say otherwise. What about that business with your client?'

She genuinely puzzled me with that one. 'What client?'

'The woman who hired you to find her dog.' I had forgotten the damned dog. The female client now returned to mind quite easily – and not only because she was one of the first I ever had after I set up as an informer.

'It was a British hunting hound,' I told Helena hastily. 'Very valuable. Superb pedigree and could run like the wind. The daft creature was supposed to be guarding the woman's clothes at some bathhouse; a slave stepped on his tail accidentally and he ran off like stink down the Via Flaminia. The young lady was heart-broken . . .' It still sounded an unlikely tale.

'Well you've been in Britain!' Helena Justina said gently. She knew how to cast aspersions. 'I expect you have a special affinity with British dogs.' Oh yes. Lovely work for a professional; every informer ought to learn how to call 'Here boy!' in at least twelve languages. Five years later the jobs I was taking on seemed just as motley. 'Did you find him?' Helena pressed.

'Who?'

'The dog, Marcus.'

'Oh! Yes.'

'I bet your lady client was really grateful!' Helena understood more about my business than I liked.

'Come off it. You know I never sleep with clients.' She gave me a look; Helena had been my client once herself. Telling her she was different from all the others somehow never carried weight.

The woman in search of the lost doggie had had more money than sense and astounding looks. My professional ethics were of course unimpeachable – but I had certainly considered making a play for her. At the time big brother Festus had convinced me that tangling with the moneyed classes was a bad idea. Now Marina's words cast a subtle doubt. I gazed at her. She giggled. She obviously assumed I had known what was going on; now I finally saw the reason Festus had advised me to steer clear of the pretty dog owner: he had been bedding her himself.

'Actually,' I told Helena gloomily, 'it was Festus who found the bloody dog.'

'Of course it was,' Marina piped in. 'He had it tied up at my house all along. I was livid. Festus pinched it from the baths so he could get to know the fancy skirt.' My brother, the hero! 'Didn't you twig?'

'Ah Marcus!' Helena soothed me, at her kindest (not so kind as all that). 'I bet you never got your bill paid either?'

True.

I was feeling abused.

'Look, when you two have finished mocking, I have things to do today – '

'Of course you have,' smiled Helena, as if she was suggesting I should hide in a barrel for a few hours until my blushes cooled.

'That's right. Repolishing my grimy reputation won't be a quick job.' It was best to be straight with her, especially when she was sounding facetious but looking as if she was trying to remember where she last put the vial of rat poison.

I kissed Marcia resoundingly and gave the child back to her mother. 'Thanks for the hospitality. If you remember anything helpful, let me know at once. I'm due for the public strangler otherwise.' Helena stood up. I put my arm round her shoulders and said to Marina, 'As you see, my time should really be being taken up by this lovely girl.'

Helena permitted herself a complacent sniff.

'Are you two getting married?' Marina asked sympathetically.

'Of course!' we both chimed. As a couple we lied well.

'Oh that's nice! I wish you both every happiness.'

One thing must always be said for Marina: she had a good heart.

XXI

I informed Helena I had had enough supervision for one day and was going to my next appointment alone. Helena knew when to let me make a stand. I felt she acquiesced too graciously, but that was better than a fight in the open street.

We were virtually at her parents' house, so I took her for a daughterly visit. I made sure I escorted her to within sight of the door. Stopping for goodbyes gave me a chance to hold her hand. She could manage without consolation, but I needed it.

'Don't hate me, sweetheart.'

'No, Marcus.' She would be a fool not to view me with caution, however. Her face looked guarded. 'I always knew you had a colourful life behind you.'

'Don't judge me too harshly.'

'I think you're doing that yourself.' Maybe somebody had to. 'Marina seems a nice girl,' Helena said. I knew what that meant.

'You're hoping someone some day will snap her up.'

'I don't see why not.'

'I do. The men she hangs around with know she's not looking for a husband. It makes it easier for them – not having to worry about the fact they all have wives!'

Helena sighed.

We were standing on a corner of the great Appian Way. It was about as public as the Forum of the Romans on a quiet day. Brown-clad slaves with baskets and amphorae on their bent shoulders butted up the street in both directions trying to get in the way of five or six litters carrying ladies from refined homes. Workmen were chiselling unconvincingly at the dark bulk of the old aqueduct, the Aqua Marcia. A cart laden with marble slabs came by, struggling to mount the raised pavement as it lurched out of control. Three donkey-drovers waiting to overtake it, two old women with a goose, and the queue on a bench outside a barber's had tired of watching the cart and started to notice us.

To make the day memorable for everyone, I slid my arms

around Helena Justina and kissed her. Rome is a city of sexual frankness, but even in Rome senators' daughters are rarely grappled on street corners by creatures who are obviously only one rank up from woodlice. I had caught her off guard. There was nothing she could do to stop me, and no reason for me to stop of my own accord. A small crowd collected.

When finally I let her go Helena became aware of the crowd. She remembered we were in the refined Capena Gate sector, home of her illustrious parents. 'There are rules, Falco!' she muttered hotly.

I had heard that in patrician circles husbands had to make appointments three days ahead if they wanted to embrace their wives. 'I know the rules. I felt like changing them.'

'Do it again, and I'll jab my knee somewhere painful.'

I kissed her again, so she applied the knee, though her nerve failed and it was too gentle to do damage. The crowd applauded anyway.

Helena looked upset; she thought she had hurt me. 'Goodbye Marcus!'

'Goodbye, my darling,' I responded in a pained croak. Now she suspected me of feigning.

Helena strode to her father's house in her most frosty style. I watched her right to the door, with my arms folded. While she waited for the porter, whose attentions at the door were always haphazard, she turned back furtively to check that I was gone. I grinned and then left, knowing she was safe. Her family would lend her an escort of slaves when she wanted to go back to the Aventine.

After the tension at Marina's I felt stiff and in need of action. I made a detour for some weight training. There was plenty for a man to do at the gymnasium. I managed to linger for hours.

'We're seeing a lot of this customer lately,' Glaucus commented in his wry way.

'You guessed it; the customer is trying to avoid his family!'

Calmer, I nearly put off further investigation. But kissing Helena publicly in the street had reminded me of my preference for kissing her more privately. If Petronius decided to arrest me there would be no point struggling to rehouse us, but if I could manage to keep out of jail, new furniture for my wrecked apartment was a priority.

'Petronius was looking for you,' Glaucus warned me. My trainer had a restrained way of speaking that could play on my worst fears.

'Skip it. I'm avoiding Petro as well . . .'

I didn't care whether or not I interviewed my father, but Petronius Longus would never expect to find me in his company, so a visit to Geminus promised me some breathing-space. Besides, where my father was I might find a cheap bed. So I set off for the Saepta Julia.

With my cloak around my ears, I emerged from the bathhouse into the Forum, skulked past the Temple of Fortune below the Citadel, and furtively made for the Theatre of Marcellus, my starting-point for a hike into the Campus Martius. Everyone I passed seemed to look at me twice, as if my tunic had a foreign cut or my face was a suspicious shape.

Now that I was going to see Geminus my sour mood returned. I still felt restless. Little did I know I was heading for a chance to expend real energy.

Many public buildings have been inflicted on the Campus by men who thought they ought to be famous – all those pompously named theatres, baths, porticoes and crypts, with the occasional temple or circus to keep the tourists agape. I passed through without noticing them; I was too busy looking out for officers of the watch, in case Petronius had instructed them to look out for me.

The Saepta Julia lay between the Baths of Marcus Agrippa and a Temple of Isis; it had the Temple of Bellona at the end nearest my approach. I took a long detour round the Flaminian Circus, partly to stay unobtrusive. I was too bored to go straight up the road which reaches the Saepta the simple way. I came out near Pompey's Theatre, facing the long Porticus in front of it. I could hear a lot of noise, so I turned my boots that way.

The Porticus of Pompey was the usual impressive enclosure. Heavy architecture on four sides formed a secluded interior space where men could hang about pretending to admire works of art while they hoped something more lively would turn up: an invitation to dinner, a quarrel, an expensive boy with a body like a

100

Greek god, or at least a cheap female prostitute. Today the interior was stuffed with goods and people. No need for me to walk further: an auction was being held there, supervised by none other than my loathed papa.

The goods he was shifting looked authentic from a distance and only mildly dubious from closer to. He knew the trade.

I could hear him up on his trestle, trying to cajole bids. He had a slow, unsensational voice that carried effortlessly round the inner quadrangle. From his vantage point above the crowd I presumed he would soon see me. I made no attempt at contact. We would be face to face and quarrelling soon enough.

He was trying to rustle up interest in a mixed batch of folding stools. 'Look at this one: pure ivory; beautifully carved. Probably from Egypt. The noble Pompey himself might have sat on it – '

'Pompey had his noble head cut off in Egypt!' a heckler called out cheerfully.

'True, sir, but his noble arse was left intact – '

Pompey's stool was part of a house clearance. Someone had died and the heirs were selling up so they could divide the cash. On inspection these relics of a departed life were faintly sad: half-used flagons of ink and rolls of untouched papyrus, lidless grain jars still part full of wheat, baskets of old boots, bales of blankets, the bowl they used to feed the watchdog from. There were pans with loose handles and oil-lamps with broken noses. Lazy bidders settled their backsides against couches with chipped legs and shredded material: signs of long wear that an owner stops noticing but which stood out pathetically here.

That said, it had been a middle-class household; to me that hinted of bargains, for the family money was probably recent and the chattels had a modern air. I adopted a casual attitude, while scanning the lots eagerly.

No sign of a bed, of course; the one thing I wanted. I could see some good outdoor stoneware (I had no garden, but in Rome dreams are cheap). The outstanding piece in the sale was a pedestal table with a huge citron-wood top that must have cost thousands; even in the open air on a dull winter's day its grain shimmered lustrously. Geminus had had it polished up with oil and beeswax. I drooled, but moved on to a group of neat bronze tripods of various sizes. One, with lion's feet and a nicely scrolled lip to stop things rolling off the top, involved a fascinating device for adjusting its height. I had my head underneath, trying to work out how to move it, when one of the porters nudged me.

'Don't bother. Your old fellow's slapped a huge reserve on that. He wants it himself.'

Trust him.

I glanced at Pa on his trestle, a short but commanding figure with untidy grey curls and a straight, sneering nose. Those dark eyes of his missed nothing. He must have been watching me for some minutes. Gesturing at the tripod, he gave me a derisive wave to confirm that I would be overbid. For a wild second I would have given *anything* to get the adjustable tripod – then I remembered that is how auctioneers grow rich.

I moved on.

The heirs were determined to milk their inheritance. A pair of folding wooden doors that probably once graced a dining-room had been lifted off their pivots. The bronze dolphin from a fountain had been wrenched from its plinth, grazing the poor creature's beak. The looters had even cut handsome painted panels from interior walls, shearing them off on thick rectangles of plaster. Geminus would not approve of it. Neither did I.

Other things were not quite right today. Being a born rifler through rubbish, at first the sale goods held my attention and I hardly noticed the people or the atmosphere. Then gradually I began to suspect that I had walked in on a situation.

The auction would have been publicised for a week or so at the Saepta. Big sell-offs attracted a regular core of buyers, most of whom would be known to Geminus. Some I even recognised myself: dealers, plus one or two private collectors. There was little here for real connoisseurs, so those in search of serious art were already drifting off. The dealers were a shabby, peculiar lot, but they were there for a purpose and got on with it. A few passers-by could always be expected to wander in, and the Porticus had its daily quorum of unemployed intellectuals hanging about. Then there were various people looking embarrassed because they were auction novices; they probably included the sellers, trying to check up on Geminus, and curious neighbours of the dead man who had come to pick over his library and sneer at his old clothes.

Among the usual time-wasters in the cloisters I spotted five or six awkwardly large men who did not fit in at all. They stood about in separate places but wafted a clear smell of confederacy. They all wore one-armed tunics like labourers, but with leather accessories that could not have been cheap – wrist-guards, ponderous belts with enamelled buckles, the odd hide cap. Though they sometimes pretended to inspect the merchandise, none of them bid. Geminus had his regular cadre of porters bringing the lots to him, but they were an elderly squad, significant for their small size and meek manners. He never paid much; his labour force had stayed with him out of habit, not because they were growing fat on it.

It struck me that if thieves were planning to raid a sale in progress (which had been known), I had best hang around.

Hardly had I reached this magnanimous decision, when the trouble began.

XXII

More people were arriving to swell the crowd: ordinary men in twos and threes, wearing ordinary tunics and cloaks. Nothing to get stirred up about.

Geminus had moved on to the lamps.

'First lot in this section: an important piece, gentlemen – ' He was not a lamps man; big pots and carpentry were what grabbed his attention, so he was galloping through the lighting more rapidly than it deserved. 'A silver lampadarium, in the form of a Corinthian column, deft architectural detailing, four arms, one lamp chain is missing but could easily be replaced by a competent silversmith. An extremely nice item . . . Who'll start at a thousand?'

Bids were sluggish. Winter is a bad time for selling. The gloomy weather made everything, even deft architectural detailing, look dull. If people care for their heirs they should die when it's hot.

A yard from me a customer, one of the ordinary cloak men, pulled a plum-coloured coverlet from a basket. It had a loose end of fringe dangling; he gave it a disparaging tug, which was fair comment, but then turned to his companion with a laugh and deliberately ripped a yard more from its stitches.

A porter stepped forward adroitly and reclaimed the material. Most people noticed nothing. But I spotted two of the big lads moving disturbingly closer.

'Now a charming set,' Geminus was announcing. 'A pair of candelabra in the form of trees, one with a pine marten creeping up the stem to catch a bird in the branches – ' Someone to the left of me knocked the elbow of a porter who had been carrying a rack of condiment pots; little brown jars skittled everywhere, their gooey contents sticking sandals to the gravel as people tried to step away but found their feet welded to the pathway by old fish pickle. 'The other column has a household cat about to spring – ' A porter sprang, just in time to steady a pile of round silver scroll boxes that were teetering off balance.

Around me the atmosphere was altering. In a second, for no obvious reason, the mood became rough. I spotted the eldest porter swiping a large gilded urn from the centre of the big citron table; he threw the metalware into a chest and slammed the lid for safety. Above the heads of the crowd I spied one columnar lamp being wielded so that it tangled in the thicket of others waiting to be sold, knocking them down like pine trees in a hurricane. Two dealers, who realised what was happening, stepped back on their way out and accidentally fell among crates of kitchen gear. Cries of alarm went up as innocent viewers found themselves being jostled. Fine goods received rough treatment. Sensitive people took elbow jabs in delicate spots.

Near the auctioneer's raised platform the populace had thinned out fast as damage occurred on every side. Pottery was smashing all around and loose bronzes were bowling under foot. One of the large thugs was grappling another man, with dangerous results for Geminus; they swayed furiously against the trestle, which creaked and collapsed. I heard Geminus call a warning that changed into protest. After forty years of bellowing bids, his yell cut the air with a rasp that hurt, then he disappeared in a jumble of slats and spars.

The porters were doing what they were supposed to if a fracas arose: throwing themselves on the stuff, best pieces first, then hurling it back into the carts and crates in which it had been brought to the Porticus. As Gornia, their foreman, nipped past me gathering up valuables, he squawked, 'Show some filial piety, Marcus; give us a bloody hand with this!'

Filial piety was not my strong point, but I was prepared to join in a fight. I looked around for something useful. I seized a curtain-pole; it still had a curtain attached, so I wound that round hastily before whirling the whole heavy flagstaff to clear myself space. It marked me as trouble. As two of the big men in the hide caps ran at me, I swung the rod across their knees and cut off their rush like sickling corn.

Suddenly my father scrambled out of the wreckage of his stand. He was clutching the auction cash box and looked a nasty reddish colour. 'Not them! Not them!' I ignored him. (The traditional filial response.) 'Go for the other lot, you idiot – ' The big chaps I had been attacking must be muscle Geminus had hired. Things must be desperate if he actually paid for protection.

I grabbed his arm and pulled him upright while he still mithered on at me. 'Settle down, Pa. I haven't damaged your bouncers – ' Well, not much.

His frustrated cry was cut off as one of the supposedly innocent customers rammed him in the chest with a rolled carpet. Still breathless from his previous fall, he could not resist the blow.

One of the bouncers grabbed the 'customer' who had felled Geminus. Seizing him round the waist, he swung the fellow, carpet and all, so that he belted another troublemaker sideways with his woven load. Struggling to realign my loyalties I whammed my curtain-pole into the second man, and batted him back again. It cleared a path for my father to escape with the cash box (his main priority), while I launched myself into the midst of another fracas. Someone had a reading-couch completely up-ended on one of its sphinx-shaped ends and was turning it towards a group of bystanders. I managed to lean on him while another came at me. The end of my pole painfully settled that one, though I lost my weapon in the process. The couch crashed down, leaving one sphinx with a broken wing and several folk with badly squashed toes. Somebody came at me from behind. Applying my shoulder as I spun round, I knocked my assailant on to his back on the citron table; I gripped his belly and with a wild shove skidded him along the polished wood. His belt stud scoured out a livid white scar. My father, reappearing at exactly the wrong moment, hollered with anguish; he would rather have seen ten men butchered than witness fine wood being damaged.

The leather boys were slow learners. They still regarded me as part of the organised rumpus. I was fighting back, while I tried to remember to hit the big lads gently in order to lessen Father's compensation claim. Even so, if they charged him by the bruise, he would soon be digging deep.

It was no time for finesse. I aimed a large stone pestle at someone's neck; it missed, but the sensational crack as it hit the ground stopped him short in his tracks. I managed to shut another's man arm in a heavy box so that he screamed out with pain. I saw my father ramming someone against a column as if he were trying to demolish the whole Porticus. At this point the porters grew tired of protecting the silverware and raced in ready to break teeth. The little old chaps were tougher than they looked.

Soon wiry arms were flailing and bald heads were butting people as the auction staff took a hand. The giants had finally grasped that I was family and lined up with me. The opposition decided their hour was up and fled.

'Do we follow them?' I yelled at Gornia, the whiskery chief porter. He shook his head.

A mop of grey curls appeared again as my father brought his presence to bear on the wreckage of his sale. 'This won't encourage the buyers. I think we'll call it a day!'

'That's shrewd!' I was busy reassembling a fold-up chair that had been unfolded rather too drastically. 'Strikes me, someone else blew the trumpet on this sale . . .' When I got the chair back together, I sat down on it like a Persian king surveying a battlefield.

Geminus had clapped a consoling arm around one of the muscle-men; he was holding his eye after a particularly well-aimed blow from me early on in the fight. Several of the others had shines that would be glowing by tomorrow. I was well bruised myself, come to that. They gave me what I hoped were admiring looks; I started to feel exposed.

'Those are big lads. Do you buy them by the yard?'

'Trust you to attack the hired help!' grumbled Geminus through a split lip.

'How was I to know you had your own cohorts? I thought your old lads were on their own with it. I'd have stepped aside if I'd realised these lummoxes were being paid to get their knuckles grazed!'

Coughing with exertion, Geminus fell on to an unsold couch. He was showing his age. 'Jupiter, I could do without all this!'

I stayed silent for a while. My breathing had already stabilised, but my thoughts were running fast. Around us the toughs made a feeble show of helping the porters tidy the mess, while the old chaps worked with their usual uncomplaining zeal. If anything, the fight had perked up their spirits.

My father let them get on with it in a way that made me think this had happened before. I gazed at him, while he pointedly ignored my interest. He was a solid man, shorter and wider than I always remembered him, with a face that could pass for handsome and a nature some folk found attractive. He annoyed me – but I had been brought up by schoolmasters who declaimed that Roman fathers were stern, wise and models of humane ethics. This high-minded philosophy made no allowance for those who drink, play draughts and womanise – let alone for mine, who did most of those things sometimes, and never seemed to have read the elegant grammarians who said a Roman boy could expect his papa to spend all day thinking noble thoughts and sacrificing to the household gods. Instead of taking me down to the Basilica Julia to explain what the barristers were arguing about, mine took me to the Circus Maximus – though only when the ticket gate was being manned by his cousin, who gave us cheap rates. When I was a child, sneaking into the Games at a discount was a source of deep embarrassment to me.

It never happened to Livy.

'You were expecting trouble,' I tackled my father. 'Want to talk about what's going on?'

'All in a day's work,' replied Geminus, through his teeth.

'This was a set-up – organised disruption. Is it a racket? Who's responsible?' I had been drawn into the argument, and I wanted to know its cause.

'Somebody, no doubt.' Dear gods, he could be an awkward mule.

'Well sort it out yourself then!'

'I will, boy. I will.' Wondering how such a miserable old groucher could have fathered such a reasonable character as myself, I leaned back my head and closed my eyes. I had only just noticed I was beginning to stiffen all over, and had gone deaf in my left ear. 'Anyway,' retaliated my father, 'you took your time arriving. I expected you two hours ago.'

I opened my eyes again. 'No one knew I was on my way.'

'That right? I was told that you wanted a fatherly chat.'

'Then you were told wrong!' I worked it out. 'Helena's been here.' She was incorrigible. It was not enough to leave her outside her father's house; I should have pushed her right in through the door and told the Senator to put the bar across.

My father leered. 'Nice girl!'

'Don't bother telling me she could do better for herself.'

'All right, I won't bother to tell you . . . So how's the love life coming along?'

I grunted. 'Last time I saw her, she kneed me in the groin.'

'Ouch! Thought you'd filched a demure one!' he scoffed, wincing. 'What bad company taught her that trick?'

'Taught her myself.' He looked startled. I felt tetchy suddenly, and launched off against old grievances. 'Listen, you may live among the sleek cats now, but you must still remember what it's like to be holed up in an Aventine tenement – all men with evil thoughts and no door locks. I can't protect her all the time. Besides, if today is anything to go by, I'll never know where she is. Women are supposed to stay at home weaving,' I grumbled bitterly. 'Helena pays no attention to that.'

I had said more than I intended. My father leaned on one elbow, lolling there as if I had passed him a dish of interesting winkles but no serving spoon. 'She's still with you, anyway . . . So when is the wedding?'

'When I'm rich.'

He whistled offensively. 'Someone's expecting a long wait then!'

'That's our business.'

'Not if you make me a grandfather before you achieve the formalities.'

This was a sore point, and I reckoned he knew it. He had probably heard through the family grapevine that Helena had miscarried once, distressing us both more than either of us expected, and filling us with the usual unspoken doubts about our ability ever to produce a healthy child. Now Helena was terrified, while I was trying to delay the question for life's strongest reason: poverty. The last thing I needed was my damned father taking an interest. I knew why the old snob was so curious: he wanted us to have a family so he could boast he was related to a senator. I said angrily, 'You're a grandfather already. If you want to lavish attention where it's needed, try Victorina's orphans.'

'So what's Mico doing?'

'The usual: not much.' My father heard this without a reaction, though it was possible he would help. 'Did you go to the funeral?' I asked, more inquisitive than I wanted to appear.

'No. My assistance was deemed unnecessary.' His mood was

quiet, his manner uninvolved. I could not tell whether he was upset; I was not sure I cared.

'Victorina was your daughter,' I said formally. 'You should have been given the opportunity.'

'Don't break your heart over it.'

'If I had been here you would have been informed.' Playing the prig was not my style, but his air of resignation annoyed me. 'You can't blame anyone; you're not exactly famous as a paterfamilias!'

'Don't start!'

I hauled myself to my feet. 'Don't worry. I'm off.'

'You haven't tackled what you came to ask.'

'Helena was here; she asks my questions for me.'

'I don't talk to women.'

'Maybe you should try it for once.' Maybe he should have tried it when he was living with my mother.

It had been pointless even coming here. I could not face an argument over Festus; I really was leaving. My father, looking for something he could be awkward about, was furious. 'Right! We've entertained you with a scrap, now you run off and tell your ma you've got your tunic dirty playing on the Campus with the big rough boys.'

In the act of flinging my cloak round me, I paused. This was not helping me solve the Censorinus case. Besides, I did need a story to tell my mother, and I needed it fairly soon. She was renowned for her impatience with slackers. 'There is something I want,' I conceded.

Geminus swung his legs off the couch so he could sit up and stare at me. 'This is a novelty!'

'Wrong. I'm simply on the scrounge. Does your warehouse at the Saepta contain a cheap but decent bed?'

He looked sadly disappointed, but did rouse himself to take me there.

110

XXIII

The Saepta Julia was a large enclosed area where voting took place. It had been remodelled by the energetic Marcus Agrippa, Augustus's general and son-in-law. Since he could see he would never get a chance to be Emperor himself, he had made his mark in the next best way: by building larger and with more innovation and magnificence than anybody else. He had had a good eye for the best spots to glorify. Much of the modern Campus Martius was his work.

Agrippa had transformed the Saepta from little more than a giant sheep pen to one of the gems in his memorial complex. It now formed an architectual match with the Pantheon and the great Agrippan Baths that sprawled majestically alongside – most famous for having free public entrance. Marcus Agrippa had certainly known how to buy popularity. The space enclosed by the Saepta was big enough to be used for gladiatorial combats, and had even been flooded for mock sea fights in Nero's day, though that had proved inconvenient for the people who normally worked there. Businessmen are not impressed by having to close their premises to allow in a group of fancy triremes. The enclosing walls, two storeys high, contained a variety of shops, especially goldsmiths and bronze-founders, plus associated folk like my father, who for years had been earning a fortune from the second-hand art and antiques trade.

Because of the political connection there was another side to the place. It would have been useful for me to have my own office in the Saepta; it was where people brought my kind of work. My father's presence was the main reason I kept away from the area, though traditionally the Saepta Julia was where the informers hung out.

I mean the other informers – the ones who had given my business its bad name. Those vermin whose heyday was under Nero, skulking behind temple pillars to overhear unguarded comments from the pious, or even using conversations at private dinner parties to betray their last night's hosts. The political parasites who, before Vespasian purged public life, had put fear into the whole Senate. The slugs who had empowered bad emperors' favourites, and oiled the jealousies of worse emperors' mothers and wives. Gossips whose stock-in-trade was scandal; bastards whose very oath in court could be bought for an emerald eardrop.

Right at the start of my career I had decided that clients who went to the Saepta looking for an informer were not clients who wanted me.

I lost a lot of trade that way.

Leases in the Saepta Julia were at a premium; my father had managed to acquire two. Like Festus, he knew how things were done. I suppose having cash helped, but reputation must also have come into it. Whereas some traders struggled to fit themselves into hole-in-the-wall lock-ups, Geminus had a select suite on the upper floor, where he could stroll out on to the bacony and survey the whole enclosure below, plus a large warehouse at ground level, which was obviously more convenient for delivery of large or heavy items. His office, always stylishly fitted out, adjoined the Dolabrium, where votes were counted – throbbing with life during elections, and pleasantly quiet at other times.

We started downstairs, in his main display area. After the usual attempts to palm me off with three-legged, woodwormy frames and oddly padded couches marked with dubious sickroom stains, I persuaded my parent that if he wanted me to perpetuate the family name it ought to be done on decent equipment. He found me a bed. I refused to pay what he said it was worth, so rather than lose the chance of sharing a grandchild with the illustrious Camillus, he halved the asking price.

'Throw in the mattress, will you. Helena can't sleep on just the webs.'

'I'd like to know where you acquired your cheek!'

'Same place I learned not to sob too much when auctioneers start pretending they are facing bankruptcy.'

He grunted, still fidgeting around my purchase. 'This is pretty plain, Marcus – ' The bed had a straightforward beech frame, with boxy ends. I liked the simple scallop ornament that enlivened

112

the headboard. The mere fact it had four feet on the ground would be a luxury in my house. 'I'm having doubts. This is meant to be shoved in a wall niche,' Geminus fussed unhappily.

'I don't want silver legs and tortoiseshell. Why encourage burglars? When can you deliver?'

He looked offended. 'You know the system. Cash down, and buyer collects.'

'Stuff the system! Bring it round as soon as possible and I'll pay you when I see you. I'm still at Fountain Court.'

'That dung heap! Why don't you get a decent job and start honouring your debts? I'd like to see you install that girl of yours in a nice town house with an atrium.'

'Helena can manage without marble corridors and spare stools.'

'I doubt it!' he said. If I was honest, so did I.

'She's looking for a man of character, not libraries and a private lavatory.'

'Oh she's found that!' he sneered. 'All right, I'll have the bed taken to your flea-pit, but don't expect the favour to be repeated. It's not for you I'm doing this . . . Helena bought an item, so I'll be sending a cart up the Hill anyway.'

It gave me an odd feeling to hear my father, whom I could barely tolerate, speaking of Helena Justina with such familiarity. I had never even introduced them; not that that had stopped him presenting himself behind my back and assuming instant paternal rights. 'What item?' I growled.

He knew he had me. I could have swiped the grin off his face with the nearest besom. 'The girl has taste,' he commented. 'She pipped you on the nail . . .'

I hated to show my interest, but I had guessed. 'That tripod table! How much did you sting her for?'

He chortled annoyingly.

The porters were bringing back the unsold goods from the interrupted auction. As they hauled in the savaged wall panels I said, 'Whoever buys the house those were ripped from will need the holes repaired. You could send Mico round to offer his services to make good.'

'Make bad, you mean? All right, I'll give him the address.'

'If he's lucky the new owners won't have heard about him.

113

Anyway, his bodging can be covered up before it's noticed. The wall plaster will need painting,' I mused, trying to wheedle out information without him noticing. 'No doubt you were already thinking of a commission for suggesting a panel artist?' My father refused to bite. Like Festus, he could be secretive about business affairs. I tried again. 'I suppose you know all the hack picture painters?'

This time the twinkle in his eye that had once drawn the women appeared. Nowadays it was dry and dark and sceptical. He knew I was prodding at something specific. 'First the bed; now renovation. Are you planning to gild your filthy doss-house like a palace? Careful, Marcus! I hate to see inappropriate ornamentation . . .'

'Just a few false perspectives,' I joked back feebly. 'A landscape with satyrs for the bedroom and a set of still lifes in the kitchen. Dead pheasants and fruit bowls . . . Nothing too elaborate.' I was getting nowhere. I had to be direct. 'Helena must have told you. I want to track down a group of daubers I once saw Festus meet at a cheap bar on the lower Caelian. It was a hovel called the Virgin.'

'She told me,' he agreed, like someone refusing to enlighten a small child as to what he might be getting for a Saturnalia gift.

'So do you know them?'

'I'm not aware of it. No jury,' declared my father, 'will convict a man for being kept in ignorance of his son's friends!'

I ignored the jibe. Angrily I burst out, 'I suppose you are also going to tell me you know nothing about the scheme Festus was running just before he died?'

'That's right,' Geminus answered levelly. 'That's exactly what I'll say.'

'You're not talking to Censorinus now!' I reminded him.

'No. I'm talking to you.' This kind of conversation only occurs in families. 'It's a waste of good air,' he grumbled, then stretched abruptly. 'This is typical of you – riding the mule backwards, staring at the tail flicking flies off its arse! I thought we would have come to the soldier half an hour ago, but you do have to dally in the byways pretending you forgot what you were sent to find out – I know you were sent!' he scoffed, as I started interrupting. He knew I would not have come on my own account. 'If we have to rake over old miseries, let's start at the beginning – and let's do it respectably over a drink!'

That was when he gripped me by the elbow as if I had raised a sensitive issue too publicly, and steered me from the open frontage of his warehouse to the discreet haven of his office on the upper floor.

I felt like a man who was about to be sold a fake silver wine-heater with one foot that keeps dropping off.

XXIV

On my very occasional visits I had noticed that my father's office changed in mood and character as he sold off whatever choice pieces adorned it. To this private quarter were brought his most select customers – the ones who had to think themselves special for the next half an hour while he palmed them off with something. Here they were seated on ivory, or chased silver, or sweetly scented oriental woods, while Geminus produced exquisitely decorated cups of spicy wine and told them lies until they found themselves buying more than their budget could afford. Today he had a suite from Alexandria: delicate painted coffers and sideboards on slim legs, with horned ibis and lotus-flower patterns. To complement the Egyptian look he had dug out some tall peacock fans (permanent props, which I had seen before), and added sumptuously tasselled cushions to the odd, hard couch that had lived there for ever and was not for sale. Behind the couch hung a dark red curtain; behind that, actually bricked into the wall, was his bank box.

Before we talked, he went to the box and stashed the takings from today's auction. I knew his habits about money were methodical. He never opened the bank chest in front of the staff, let alone customers. I was treated differently – one of the few ways he acknowledged that I was family. In my presence he would quietly go to the box and unlock it with the key he kept round his neck on a thong, as if we two, like he and Festus, were in some sort of partnership. But it had only happened since my brother died.

He dropped the curtain hastily as a lad came in bringing the usual galley tray of wine and bowls of almonds. 'Hello, Falco!' grinned the youth, seeing me leaning on a wall like a spare broom. Then he looked uneasy. None of the staff knew quite what to make of me. The first few times I came here I had refused to admit to any relationship; now they all knew I was the master's son, but they could see I was not on the same easy terms as Festus. No one could blame them if they found that hard to understand; faced with my father, I felt confused myself.

Since I was not a customer the lad seemed to have second thoughts about the refreshments, but Papa grabbed at the wine flask, so he left the tray with us. 'That watch captain you know was looking for you, Falco! Some judge wants to interview you.'

Surprised, I threw nuts down my throat too rapidly, then choked. Geminus assumed that knowing look of fathers, though waited for the boy to leave before he spoke: 'Is this about the unpleasantness at Flora's?'

'Do I gather you know that dump?'

I thought he gave me a wry look. The caupona was uncomfortably close to Mother's. 'I've been there a few times.' Flora's had only existed for ten or twelve years; it postdated Pa's return from Capua. But Festus was always hanging round the place. Anyone who knew Festus was bound to have heard of it. 'Helena told me you were being fingered. Sounds as if Petronius is about to step on your tail.'

'He's given me time,' I assured him, like a man of the world who was merely threatened by a creditor who had made him a new cloak and unreasonably wanted payment.

'Oh yes? I do have some influence,' he offered.

'Don't interfere.'

'By the sound of things, you will need bail.'

'It won't come to that.'

'Right.' This was our usual happy repartee. He was hating me and I was enjoying it. 'Let me know when we all have to come to court and cheer while the bastards convict you!' We were silent while he poured wine. I left mine on the shelf where he had placed the cup. 'Oh drink up and don't be so pompous. We've been here before; you're in deep trouble, but you don't want help, especially from me – '

'Oh I want your help!' I snarled. 'I don't expect to get it, but I want to know what in Hades has been going on.'

'Sit down and calm down. You're not in some cheap drinking-house.'

I refused to sit, but forced control into my tone: 'It's obvious something happened before our famous hero speared himself at Bethel. My guess is that you were in it with him, but you hoped the affair had happened too far away to bring repercussions here.'

'It was nothing to do with me.' He made no effort to avoid self-righteousness.

117

'Then you've no reason to avoid telling me about it! We all have to face the truth,' I said grittily. 'The Fifteenth have been restationed and all the ones we apparently owe money to are making sure they snatch home leave. One man came to stir the porridge pot, and now he's dead someone else is bound to follow. This will not go away.' My father inclined his head dourly, agreeing that point at least, so I carried on. 'Whoever knifed Censorinus may have met him by accident – or they may be in on the story too. If so, I don't fancy meeting them on a dark stair. Somebody in the past must have stepped in a very nasty cow-pat, and now the stink has reached home. At the moment it's attached to me, but you won't be surprised to hear I'm planning on a good wash-down.'

'You need more than a plan.'

I felt my chest tighten. 'Is this guesswork or fact?'

'Bit of both,' said my father.

He was ready to talk. Since the winecup was handy and I hate waste, I grasped it and attached my posterior to a low stool. I had chosen a tight corner, preferring this to greater comfort. Above me a dog-headed god sneered inscrutably down his long snout from the flank of a cupboard. 'We have to discuss Festus,' I insisted in a low voice.

Our father laughed briefly, almost to himself. 'Big subject!' He stared into his wine. We were drinking from small, stupid metal cups, fancy items designed for courtesy, not serious thirst-quenching. He held his between the tips of two fingers and a thumb; he had large hands with stubby fingers, the same shape as my brother's. On his right hand he wore a grand seal ring with a haematite stone and a smaller gold one with the head of a Claudian emperor, an oddly conventional set for a man in his trade who was constantly seeing much finer jewellery. In some ways he was a conventional man, more so than either of his sons.

On his left third finger he still wore his wedding ring; I never knew why. Maybe he never thought about it.

'Marcus Didius Festus . . .' Geminus furrowed his brow. 'Everyone thought he was special. Maybe he was. Or maybe he just could have been – '

'Don't get maudlin,' I urged impatiently. 'Festus had flair and courage. Big brother thought nothing of running a business

118

venture from the army, from a thousand miles away. But he must have had a receiver at this end, and you must have been him.'

'We shared some joint investments,' he agreed.

'Like what?'

Geminus waved a hand. 'You're sitting on some of it.' The Egyptian furniture. 'Festus found this when the Fifteenth were in Alexandria. It came in a load that was shipped over just before he died.'

'I didn't see it the last time I was here.'

'No, I've just decided to get rid of it.' I knew selling could be a matter of mood. A man could lose heart extolling his dead partner's treasures; more so when the partner had also been his favourite son. 'When Festus died this just got left. Somehow I couldn't face dealing with it. But when that lag from the Fifteenth came round I took notice again. I don't know why I kept it so long; it's not my style, this lightweight stuff.'

'So where was it?'

'I had it at home.'

At this mention of the house he shared with the woman he had run off with, the atmosphere stiffened. I knew where he lived. I had never been inside, but presumably the dwelling bulged with enticing collectables. 'I thought you might still have a warehouse full of big brother's tasty imports?'

My father looked unreliable. 'There may be a few items at Scaro's old barn.' This was out on the Campagna, on Great-Uncle Scaro's farm, a place Pa had used for long-term storage after he married Ma. (Free use of her brothers' outbuildings was one obvious reason he first took to her.) My father stopped going out there when he abandoned home, but later on Festus took over the barn. 'When I got in touch with your Uncle Fabius he assured me it was virtually empty.'

'Fabius wouldn't recognise a box labelled *Bullion*! Mind if I take a look some time?'

'You'll go if you want to, whatever I say.'

'Thanks for the warrant!'

'Keep your hands off the stuff, if there is any.'

'I don't steal. Don't forget I'm big brother's executor. Anyway, I'll only go if I'm out of jail. I have a few serious questions to answer for Petronius before I can consider field trips. Look, tell

119

me about Censorinus. I know he was whinging about some project that had failed, but I have no details and I certainly don't know why he was so secretive. Was Festus importing something illegal from Greece?'

Pa looked indignant. 'Why should he? Are you saying he was robbing temples or something?' I would not have put it past him. 'Greece is stuffed with desirable art,' Father demurred. 'There was no need to raid holy shrines. Anyway, it's no secret. Festus had acquired a mixed cargo of statues, giant urns and vases. He added some conventional goods from Syria and Judaea: linen, purple dye, cedar logs.'

'You sound annoyed.'

'I'm not a bloody merchant. I hate that sort of hardware. Festus fixed it up himself. Jupiter knows how he broke into the local cartels, but you know what he was like. The Tyrian Purple Guild has been officially closed to foreigners for a thousand years, but I expect they welcomed our boy like a long-lost Phoenician prince . . . He hired a ship called the *Hypericon*; it sank off Crete.'

'You weren't involved in it?'

'No. I told you. The *Hypericon* was his own venture. He laid it on while he was out in the East. That was why he was using his comrades to provide capital. He had heard about this load; it clearly included top-rate items and there was no time to contact me.' I knew that in their partnership it was my brother who provided the entrepreneurial spirit; Pa was the financier. Festus was a finder; Pa bought and sold. That worked when they could make arrangements in advance, but posed difficulties otherwise. Corresponding with Judaea could take anything from fifteen days, if the tides and winds were right, up to half a year. Or infinity, if your ship sank.

I thought it through, to familiarise myself with the wrinkles. 'If Festus had access to good pickings, he would not allow sheer distance to inconvenience the scheme. Or lack of funds. So he involved his mess-tent cronies and they lost their cash. That's a tragedy, but what's the peculiar angle? Why the big fuss now? What was odd about this load?'

'Nothing.' Geminus spoke quietly. 'As far as I know the batch was normal. What smelled was the backing money.'

'You know that?'

'I believe it.'

'So how come?'

'Work it out.'

I considered the problem. 'What are we talking about – a few old marble gods and a bunch of blackware alabastrons?'

'Not according to Censorinus. From what he said, Festus had laid hands on enough top-quality ceramics to stock a private museum. The statuary was supposed to be outstanding. That was why he needed more cash than usual; that's why he would not risk jeopardising the deal by taking time to contact me.'

'Did you and he not have banking arrangements overseas?'

'Up to a point.' For a moment I wondered whether Pa had had limited faith in big brother's probity. He smiled slightly, seeing my doubts. But he gave me the public explanation: 'I hate investing heavily in cargoes from abroad: one bent captain, one awkward customs officer, or one big storm and it's lost. Festus found that out the hard way when the *Hypericon* foundered.'

'He was a hothead. He had good taste, but airy ideas.'

'Selling bubbles,' agreed Geminus. There was a trace of admiration in his tone. His own character was cautious, almost cynical; I had inherited that. But perhaps we both yearned to be able to take wild risks with my brother's happy bravery.

'I still don't see why the Fifteenth Apollinaris have come on our tails over it now.'

'Desperation.' My father's tone grew flat. 'Apparently the best piece in this missing cargo had the legionaries' name on it. Where would a bunch of active-service centurions get the cash to purchase a Phidias?'

'A *Phidias*?' He had handed me two shocks at once. 'This is the first I've heard about Festus cornering the market in the Seven Wonders of the World.'

'So he thought big!' shrugged our pa. Not for the first time I felt second-best in the family scheme.

'When I joked about robbing temples, I didn't have the statue of Zeus from Olympia in mind!'

'He told me it was a Poseidon,' reported my father drily. 'He did say that it was fairly small.'

'That probably meant it was huge! You knew about this?' I demanded incredulously.

'Only when it was too late to be jealous. I heard the *Hypericon* had sunk. On that last leave Festus confessed he had suffered a major loss with her, and he told me about the Poseidon.' Festus must have been bursting with it, even after his plan disintegrated.

'Did you believe the story?'

'I found it hard to take seriously. Festus was drunk most of the time on that leave – though if he *had* lost a Phidias, it's understandable. I would have been drunk myself. In fact, after he told me I soon was.'

'Well the god's appropriate, Father. If Festus had the genuine article on board the *Hypericon*, it's now at the bottom of the sea.'

'And that's where his mates in the Fifteenth may wish they were,' Geminus growled, 'if my theory of why they are so agitated holds good.'

'So what is your theory?' My sense of foreboding grew steadily.

Geminus drained his cup with an angry gesture. 'That your brother's honourable comrades had bought themselves a Phidias by robbing their legion's savings bank.'

As soon as he said it, the ghastly tale made sense.

'Dear gods. If they get found out, that's a capital offence.'

'I think we can assume,' Pa told me, with the light, wry air that my brother had not inherited, 'Censorinus was hoping you and I would pay the money back in time to save their skins. The Jewish Revolt is well in hand, the Fifteenth Apollinaris have come to a pause in their glorious military task, normal military life resumes, and – '

'Don't say it. They are now expecting a visit from the Treasury auditors!'

XXV

Things were falling into place, but they made me no happier.

The room felt cold. My corner seat had become so uncomfortable I wanted to leap up and prowl about, but was held in my place by horror.

Ma had asked me to clear my brother's name. The deeper I went, the worse things appeared. If this were true, I could not believe Festus had been unaware of the source of his funding; in fact a fear was gnawing at me that big brother might well have suggested it.

Each army legion possesses a savings bank, stored in a holy of holies under the headquarters shrine. As well as the compulsory deductions from his pay that each soldier suffers for food and equipment, and the contribution to the burial club which will give him a reverent funeral, the administration ensures that if he reaches discharge after his twenty-five years of suffering, he will go into the world with some standing: half of every imperial donative is forcibly locked up for him. These are the lavish grants paid out by new emperors on their accession, or at other times of crisis, to ensure the legions' loyalty. In a full-term career every legionary must expect to have his loyalty ensured on several occasions – and it does not come cheap.

The money is sacrosanct. A batch of clerks take care of it, and of course it represents a scandal just waiting to happen, so much cash permanently sitting about in boxes, out on the wild frontiers of the Empire. But if there had ever been such a scandal, I had never heard of it. Trust my brother to involve himself in this fabulous first!

My mind raced. If the Fifteenth did now have a large hole in their coffer, there could be reasons why it had not yet been spotted. The savings banks had been frequently topped up during the Year of the Four Emperors: four new men on the throne, during a harsh civil war, had found that pleasing the armed forces became a high priority. One reason for Galba's downfall was his reluctance to pay the customary grateful donative to the army when he came into the purple; his three successors learned from his bloody corpse in the Forum, and contributed promptly. With all these extras pounding in, the centurions of the loyal Fifteenth could have put some large rocks at the bottom of the legion's coffer, and got away with the deception.

But those uncertain days were over. Now their famous general Vespasian had become Emperor and was settling his backside on the cushioned throne for a long reign: a tax-collector's son, much given to cash-counting. The return of normality gave clerks more time to put money into piles and tick off lists on their papyrus scrolls. The bankrupt Treasury meant that auditors were Rome's coming profession. Eager accountants were out and about everywhere, looking for missing cash. It could not be long before somebody spotted a hole the size of even a smallish Phidias in a prestigious legion's money chest.

'This is not good news for the family name,' I commented.

My father had the expression you would expect of a man who is about to see his son the national hero publicly exposed, especially when his other son is taking the initiative. 'Looks like a straight choice between losing the family name, or losing the family fortune protecting it.' His comment was essentially cynical.

'That's your fortune then. It's a choice I don't have!'

'Fancy!' commented Geminus, unenthusiastically.

'We need to be braced for trouble. I don't give two peas for my reputation, but I don't relish finding angry soldiers lurking at Mother's house wanting to crack my head. Is there anything else I should be aware of in this mess?'

'Not as far as I know.' The way he said it told me there was more to be found out.

I had struggled enough for one day. I let it go, and moved on to other aspects: 'One thing puzzles me.' That was an understatement, but I had to be practical. Counting all the unknowns in this story would leave me depressed. 'Festus served in Egypt and Judaea. The missing cargo came from Greece. Would it be too pedantic to ask how come?'

'He was using an agent. He met a man in Alexandria – '

'That sounds like the beginning of a very sticky story!'

'Well you know Festus; he always had a lupin round himself. He got around the backstreets and shady bars.' My father meant Festus was always involved in numerous little enterprises, doing deals and supplying services.

'True. If there was a man selling counterfeit amulets, Festus always knew him.'

'That doesn't mean he bought the produce with the fishy smell,' Geminus argued, defending his lamented boy.

'Oh no!' I carolled facetiously. 'But sometimes he was taken in.'

'Not in this.'

'Well, let's keep the possibility in mind! Alexandria is a city with a dubious reputation to start with. Wherever he went, Festus could always be relied on to fall in with the man other people avoid. Do we have a name for the agent he was using?'

'What do you think?'

'No name!'

'Call him Nemo, like Odysseus. Nemo moved in the art world; he told Festus he could get hold of some exquisite Greek artefacts. Presumably he did it. That's all I know.'

'Did Festus at any point actually inspect this cargo?'

'Of course. Your brother had his head on,' insisted Pa. 'Festus saw it in Greece.'

'He got around!'

'Yes. Festus was a boy.'

'I thought the *Hypericon* sailed from Caesarea?'

'Was that the story from Censorinus? Presumably she went there afterwards so Festus could add his cedar wood and the dye. Maybe that was where he paid the agent for the vases and the other stuff.'

'Did the agent sail on with the ship?'

Father gave me a long look. 'Unknown quantity.'

'When his ship sank, did that have any bearing on the wound that brought big brother home?'

'Sole purpose of allowing the wound to happen, I should think.'

Festus had got himself home to sort things out. That meant the answer to at least some part of the problem lay here in Rome. So I did have a slim chance of finding it.

My next question would have been whether the events I had witnessed that day at the auction were also relevant. I never asked it. Our conversation was interrupted by a very hot, very tired child.

125

He was about twelve. His name was Gaius. He was my sister Galla's second-eldest, and an urchin of some character. Most of him was small for his age. He had the gravity of a patriarch and the manners of a lout. Gaius would probably grow up to be a man of modesty and culture, but at the moment he preferred to be difficult. He liked to wear boots that were too big for him. He had tattooed his name on his arm in Greek lettering with something that passed for blue woad; some of the letters were festering. He never washed. Once a month, on Galla's insistence, I took him to the public baths at a quiet period and cleaned him up forcibly.

Bursting into the office, he threw himself on to an empty couch, expelled a huge lungful of air, wiped his nose on the cuff of a nasty-coloured tunic and gasped, 'Jupiter, chasing you takes spunk! Don't just sit there quaking, Uncle Marcus. Give me a drink!'

XXVI

Three generations of the Didius family eyed each other warily. I ignored the plea for liquor. When I sat tight Geminus fed the urchin a small one. 'Oh Grandpa, don't be stingy!' Gaius lifted the wine jug with a deft hand and sloshed out more for himself. I retrieved the jug, then served myself a refill while there was still a chance.

Our host recaptured his jug grumpily and drained out the last trickle. 'What do you want, nipper?'

'Message for Trouble there,' he said, glaring at me.

At home he was known as 'Where's Gaius?' because no one ever knew. He roamed the city on his own in a private world of schemes and dodges: a familiar trait. He was far worse even than Festus, a complete gangster.

Still, his father was a boatman so no one could blame him. The water-flea was a womanising dead loss; even my dim sister kicked him out of their home as often as possible. In those circumstances sophistication in the children had to be ruled out.

I gazed at him benignly. Gaius was unimpressed, but gruffness would have achieved no more. There is nothing you can do, faced with a knowing sprat in an oversized and dirty tunic who behaves like a man twice your age. I felt like a pimply ten-year-old who had just heard where babies come from – and did not believe a word of it. 'Speak up, Hermes! What's the message, Gaius?'

'Petronius has offered half a denarius for the first person to find you.' I thought Petro had more sense. 'The others are all running round like bare-arsed gibbons.' Gaius prided himself on a charming vocabulary. 'Not a lead among them. I used my noddle, though!'

'How come?' twinkled Father. Gaius was acting up for him. To the grandchildren, Pa was a dangerous renegade with a deep hint of mystery. He lived amongst the glittering goldsmiths' halls of the Saepta, in a cavern full of entrancing junk; they all thought he was wonderful. The fact that my mother would go wild if she knew they came here to visit him only added to the intrigue.

'Obvious! Petro said this was one place he had covered; so I ran straight here!'

'Well done,' I observed, while my father scrutinised Galla's tricky offshoot as if he thought he might have identified a new business partner (given my own unsuitable attitude). 'You've found me. Here's a copper for bringing me the warning – now scram.'

Gaius inspected my coin in case it was counterfeit, sneered, then shoved it into a purse at his belt that looked heavier than my own. 'Don't you want the message?'

'I thought that was it?'

'There's more!' he assured me. It was meant to tantalise.

'Forget it.'

'Oh Uncle Marcus!' Robbed of his golden moment, Gaius was reduced to a child again. His thin wail filled the office as I stood up to assume my cloak. He rallied, however. 'It's about that fancy coronet you've persuaded to pay your bills for you!'

'Listen, smacker, that's the love of my life you're insulting. Don't speak of Helena Justina like a charitable foundation – and don't imply I'm hanging round the lady with a view to sequestering her cash!' I thought my father hid a grin. 'Helena Justina,' I declared, in a stately tone, 'is too shrewd to be bluffed by that sort of confidence trick.'

'She's after character!' Pa told the boy.

'So she's taken on a loser!' Gaius smirked back. 'What's the attraction, Grandpa? Is he good in bed or something?'

I pulled his ear, harder than I had meant. 'You're only jealous because Helena is fond of Larius.' Larius was his elder brother, the shy, artistic one. Gaius belched rudely at the comparison. 'Gaius, there's no need to give me the message. I'm well aware of it. Petronius wants to arrest me – and I don't want to know.'

'Wrong,' Gaius informed me, though at last he quailed somewhat. He must have known I was likely to thump him when I heard the news. His voice became much smaller as he announced rather nervously: 'Petronius Longus has arrested your Helena!'

XXVII

The judge lived in an impressive house of the type I could easily covet. Worse, his house might even convince me to aspire to his rank.

It was a detached town villa just off the Vicus Longus, not too large and not too small; it had some fine rooms for impressing public visitors, but was arranged for decent privacy. Marponius never went down to Petro's meagre guardhouse; he had felons brought here for interviews. He had a social conscience. He wanted lags like me to discover the urge to reform through seeing what could come from more legitimate types of crime. Compared to speculation and usury, mere theft and murder began to look unprofitable and quite hard work. Even being an informer seemed a dead-end job.

I presented my person at a ponderous marble portico. The elaborate studs and shiny bronze door furniture were overdone to my mind, but as an auctioneer's son I had seen that much of the world has unsubtle taste. Under the frippery, it was a solid hardwood door. The judge simply belonged to the group that likes to ruin good material.

Marponius and I would never agree on decor. I was a spare-time poet with a refined nature, whose occupation called for a sensitive, humane approach. He was a dull thug from the middle rank who had made himself rich, and therefore significant, by selling scientific encyclopaedias to New Men. By New Men I mean ex-slaves and foreign immigrants; people with overflowing coffers but no education who want to appear cultured. They could afford to buy literary works by weight – and more importantly, they could fit themselves up with ranks of literate slaves to read the works aloud. In the shifting social strata of Rome there was plenty of scope for applying gloss to upstarts. So if a treatise was Greek, incomprehensible and came in twenty scrolls, Marponius had his team of scribes copy it out. He used best-quality papyrus, black gall ink, and highly scented sandalwood for the end-pieces. Then he supplied the slaves with refined voices too. That was where the money lay. It was a neat trick. I wish I had thought of it.

I was kept waiting for some time. When I was finally let into the party, I found Marponius, Petro and Helena sitting together somewhat awkwardly. The first thing they all saw was my bruised face from the auction fight: an unimpressive start.

We were in a bright red and gold salon. The wall panels were a short series of the adventures of Aeneas, shown as rather a stodgy, bow-legged chap – the artist's diplomatic allusion to the owner's own physique. The judge's wife was dead, so Dido was spared such indignity and could appear as a highly voluptuous, handsome young piece having trouble with her drapery. The artist considered himself a dab hand at diaphanous veils.

Like his Aeneas, Marponius had a flat-topped head and a lather of light curly hair, receding each side of his rather square brow. His backside was too large, so he tended to strut like a pigeon with too much tail. As I came in he was just telling Helena he was 'a man of ideas'. A female slave was present for propriety, and she had Petro for extra protection, but Helena knew what men's ideas were like. She was listening with the usual calm expression she applied to stressful situations, though her pale face told me everything.

I crossed the room and kissed her formally on one cheek. Her eyes closed briefly, with relief. 'I'm sorry, Marcus . . .'

I sat alongside on an elaborately gilded couch, and held her hand in a light grip. 'Never apologise!'

'You don't know what I've done!'

I said to Marponius. 'Hail, Judge! I gather from the smell of new paint there is still money in scientific tomes?'

He looked torn. He wanted to slap me down, but had trouble resisting the urge to discuss business. He was proud of his efforts. Unfortunately he was also proud of being a judge. 'Pity it still leaves you time to indulge an interest in criminology. What's the charge against my wench?'

'You're both in this, Falco!' He had a sharp voice, its effect as subtle as dragging a sword across a ceramic plate.

I noticed that Petronius Longus was looking embarrassed. This depressed me. He rarely made a lot of noise, but he was perfectly capable of treating Marponius with the contempt he deserved. When Petro stayed quite so silent things must be bad.

I nodded to him as he picked up on my scrutiny. 'You owe my disreputable nephew Gaius a finder's fee But I want it on record that I came here voluntarily.' Petro's stare remained unhelpful. I tackled his glib superior. 'So what's going on, Marponius?'

'I am waiting for someone to appear as a spokesman for the lady.'

Women possess no judicial identities; they are not allowed to appear in court, but must have a male relation representing them.

'I'll do it. I act for her father.'

'A message has gone to the Senator,' Marponius fussed. Helena pursed her lips while even Petronius winced. I hoped Camillus Verus was missing at some unknown public baths.

'Falco will speak for me,' Helena said coldly, adding, 'if I must have a male mouthpiece!'

'I require your guardian,' Marponius corrected. He was a pedantic nuisance.

'We regard ourselves as married,' said Helena. I tried not to look like a husband who had just been told the household bills were three times what he thought.

The judge was shocked. I murmured, 'Socially, it's a future fixture in the calendar, though a man with your grasp of the Twelve Tables will appreciate that the mere agreement of two parties that a marriage exists brings the contract into effect – '

'Don't get clever, Falco!' Marponius knew the legal tables backwards, but rarely met women who broke the rules. He glanced at Petronius for help, though was obviously remembering he distrusted Petro's loyalties. 'What am I supposed to make of this?'

'I'm afraid it's true love,' Petronius pronounced, with the sombre air of a public works engineer reporting a cracked sewer in the vicinity.

I decided against upsetting the judge's middle-class ethics with further wit. He was more used to threats. 'Marponius, Helena Justina is an innocent party. Camillus is very public-spirited, but having his noble child wrongly arrested may offend his tolerance. Your best plan is to establish the facts before the Senator arrives, and greet him by restoring his daughter with a public apology.'

131

I could sense that the others present were sharing an awkward moment. Agitation flickered in the wondrous dark depths of Helena's eyes, and her grip on my hand felt tense. More was wrong here than I yet knew.

A slave came in and informed the judge that the messengers had failed to find Camillus Verus. People were still looking, but his current whereabouts were unknown. Good man. My future father-in-law (as it seemed best to regard him while we were pretending to be respectable) knew when to lie low in a ditch.

His sensible daughter forced herself to be gracious to the judge: 'Ask your questions. I do not object in principle to answering in the presence of Didius Falco, and that of Lucius Petronius Longus, who is a valued family friend. Ask me what you want. If they advise me to defer my response on a particular matter, we can stop until Father arrives.'

I loved her. She was hating herself for sounding so meek – and hating Marponius for swallowing the act. 'Alternatively,' I told him, 'we can all sit around a finger-bowl of honey cakes, and while we wait for her furious parent you can try to sell the lady thirteen scrolls on natural philosophy in a filigree library box.'

Helena boasted prosaically, 'If it's concerned with fiery particles, I think I've read that one.'

'Tread gently,' I teased Marponius. 'The watch captain has apprehended an educated girl!'

'I'll expect a rapid batch of injunctions!' he quipped wryly, taking a grip on himself. Marponius could be an objectionable prig – but he was no fool. If a man had any sense of humour at all, Helena was likely to bring out the best in him.

'Actually, it lets her out of the murder,' I smiled. 'She never gets into trouble; she's always curled up on all the cushions in the house, with her nose in a scroll . . .' As we joked, those eyes of hers were still sending me agonised messages. I was desperate to find out the cause. 'Sweetheart, perhaps the man you regard as your marriage partner can properly ask why you are sitting in a stranger's house with a distressed expression and somewhat lightly chaperoned?'

'This is a formal examination,' Marponius interrupted, stiffly reacting to the implied criticism. 'It is a private session of my court! The lady knows I am a judge attached to the permanent

132

tribunal relating to the Cornelian Law against assassins and drug-making –'

'Poisons, knifings and patricide,' I interpreted for Helena. The special murder tribunal had been established by the dictator Sulla. After a hundred and fifty years it had signally failed to stamp out death in the streets, but at least killers were processed efficiently, which suited Rome. The praetor had a whole panel of locally elected judges he could call on to hear cases, but Marponius had set himself up as the expert. He enjoyed his duties. (He enjoyed the status.) When he took an interest in the early stages of a particular investigation, he could rely on being chosen for the hearing afterwards if the officers of the watch ever caught someone.

Now they had caught me. Helena's distress made me attack Marponius. 'Under that legislation is there not a penalty by fire and water for inciting a judge falsely to bring a capital charge?'

'That is correct.' He had replied too calmly. He was too sure of his ground. Trouble was licking its fangs at me. 'No charge has been brought yet.'

'Then why is the lady here?'

'A charge does seem likely.'

'On what accusation?'

Helena answered me herself. 'Acting as an accessory.'

'Oh cobnuts!' I looked across at Petronius. *His* eyes, which were brown, honest and always frank, told me to believe it. I turned back to Helena. 'What's happened today? I know you went to the Saepta and visited my father.' I felt annoyed at having to mention Geminus, but making Helena sound like a girl who devoted her attentions to the family seemed a good idea. 'Did something occur afterwards?'

'I was going home to your mother's house. On the way,' she said rather guiltily, 'I happened to pass Flora's Caupona.'

I was starting to worry. 'Carry on!'

'I saw the body of Censorinus being taken away. The street was blocked temporarily, so I had to wait. I was of course in a carrying-chair,' she inserted, having grasped that some niceties were called for. 'The bearers talked to the waiter from the caupona while we were stuck there, and he happened to be bewailing the fact that he now had to tidy up the rented room.'

133

'So?'

'So I offered to help.'

I let go of her hand and folded my arms. The bad memory of that bloody room where Censorinus was murdered forced itself back into my mind. I had to repel it. Petronius knew I had been there, which was damning enough; admitting it to Marponius would be my key to a jail cell. Sending my girlfriend looked like the act of a desperate man.

I knew why she had done it. She wanted to scour the place for evidence that might clear me. But any stranger would assume she had gone there to *remove* clues that would convict. Marponius was bound to think it. Even Petro would be failing in his duty if he ignored the possibility. His deep sense of unhappiness filled the room almost like an odour. I had never before been so conscious of putting our long friendship under strain.

'It was stupid,' Helena spoke crisply. 'I offered on the spur of the moment.' I sat dumbstruck, unable to ask if she had got as far as the ghastly scene upstairs. She looked so white it seemed probable. My throat closed helplessly. 'I only reached the downstairs kitchen,' she said, as if I had transmitted my agony. 'Then I realised my presence there could only make things appear worse for you.'

'So what happened?' I managed to croak.

'The waiter seemed desperate for company. I suppose he was frightened to enter the murder room alone, even after he knew the body was no longer there. I was trying to think of an excuse to leave, without being rude to the poor man, when Petronius Longus arrived.'

I stared at him. He spoke to me at last. 'Encouraging your nicely bred girlfriend to visit the gory scene looks black, Falco.'

'Only if I'm guilty!' He must have known how closely I verged on losing my temper. 'And I did not send her.'

'A jury may not believe you,' Marponius commented.

'Juries are notoriously stupid! That's why the praetor will expect you to advise him on whether this charge is likely to stick before he lets things reach a court.'

'Oh I shall give the praetor good advice, Falco.'

'If justice is more than a dilettante hobby for you, your advice will be that this case stinks!'

'I don't think so.'

'Then you don't think – end of issue! I had no motive for killing the centurion.'

'He had a financial claim on you.' Without any formal signal, the atmosphere had shifted so that the judge was grilling me.

'No, he had a claim against my brother. But the claim was rocky. Marponius, I don't want to slander the brave centurions of the glorious Fifteenth Legion, but my private investigations already suggest it was a claim they could not pursue too openly. Anyway, where are your facts? Censorinus was seen alive, eating his dinner at the caupona, long after I had left and gone home to my own family. Petronius Longus has checked up on my movements the next day, and although there may be a period that I can't account for with witnesses, neither can you present anyone who will say they saw me at Flora's when the soldier lost his life.'

'The fact that you disagreed with him so violently – '

'Rules me out! We had a very strange quarrel, initiated by him, right in front of the very curious public. If you base your case on that, you are calling me a very stupid man.'

Marponius frowned. For a moment I had the illusion of controlling the situation, then the sensation altered. He made a gesture to Petronius. Some unpleasant challenge, previously arranged, was about to emerge.

Petronius Longus, with his air of misery deepening even further, stood up from his seat on the far side of the tasteful room and came across to me. He unwrapped a piece of cloth he had been guarding, and held out an object for me to inspect. He kept it just beyond my reach, and made sure that Marponius and Helena could both watch my face.

'Do you recognise this, Falco?'

I had a split second to reach the wrong decision. Delay would have answered for me. I took the honest option, like a fool. 'Yes,' I said. 'It appears to be one of my mother's cooking knives.'

Then Petronius Longus told me in a quiet voice, 'Helena Justina found it this morning amongst other utensils on the caupona's cooking bench.'

XXVIII

Criminals cut and run. For a second I knew why.

I stared at the knife. It was not one to excite a cutler. There was a gnarled bone handle, attached by a stout iron ring to a heavy blade that tapered to a solid point. The point had a small twist, as if at some time in its past the knife had been trapped and bent; such a nick at the end of a strong knife is impossible to straighten out.

It was like all my mother's other knives. They were not a true set, but they had all come from the Campagna when she was married. They were tough country items that she wielded with great force. Plenty of other homes in Rome must have similar gear. But I knew this was hers. Her initials were scratched on the handle: *JT*, for Junilla Tacita.

The room was quite large, but suddenly felt close and full of smoke from the braziers heating it. There were high square windows; I could hear a squall beating on the expensive glass, and one casement rattled. Squat slaves with straight-cut hair moved about constantly. Here was I, under threat of exile or far worse, while these ninnies came and went removing empty bowls and attending to the lamps. Helena dropped her hand back over mine; hers was icy cold.

Marponius was doing everything strictly now. 'Petronius Longus, have you shown this knife to Didius Falco's mother?'

'Yes, sir. She admits it must have been hers originally, but claims she lost this one at least twenty years ago.'

'How can she be sure?'

'She recognised the misshapen point.' Petro's quiet patience as he answered the judge's questions only depressed me more. 'She remembered it being caught in a cupboard door when her children were small.'

'Has she any explanation as to how it reached the caupona?'

'No, sir.'

'Describe how it was found.'

Petronius now had a set face. He gave his report with

impeccable neutrality: 'I had ordered the removal of the body this afternoon. Later I entered the caupona with a view to completing my search of the scene. The soldier's corpse had been impeding a full investigation previously. I saw Helena Justina talking to the waiter at the foot of the stairs that run up from the kitchen to the rented rooms.'

'I remember!' said Marponius importantly.

'At my approach, Helena turned towards me, and appeared to notice this knife on the work bench; she picked it up. Both of us have eaten at Falco's mother's house on many occasions. We both recognised the pattern and initials. Helena made no attempt to hide it, but handed it to me immediately. As you see, it has been washed, but is stained around the shaft junction with traces of reddish colouring.'

'You take that to be blood?'

'I am afraid so.'

'What is your interpretation?'

Petro dragged out the words slowly. 'I asked the waiter about the knife. I didn't tell him I knew where it came from. He maintained he had never seen it before; it was not one he used at Flora's.'

'Is this the weapon which killed Censorinus?'

Petronius answered reluctantly. 'It may well be. If the waiter is telling the truth, the killer may have brought his own weapon to the caupona. When he came down from the bedroom he washed it in one of the buckets of water that are always in the kitchen area; then he threw the knife among the other utensils.'

'You're looking for someone intelligent,' I said dryly. 'It was a good place to hide a domestic implement. Pity it was recognised!'

Helena murmured in anguish, 'I'm sorry, Marcus. I just saw it and picked it up.'

I shrugged. 'That's all right. I never put it there.'

'You cannot prove that you didn't,' said the judge.

'And you cannot prove that I did!'

Helena demanded of Marponius, 'Are you really convinced that knowing someone had been stabbed upstairs, the waiter would not notice a strange knife among his tools?'

'Epimandos is pretty vague,' I said. Marponius looked unhappy, knowing it was bad practice to produce a slave in court.

(Worse still if my pet theory was right and Epimandos was a runaway.)

Petronius agreed with me: 'He keeps a jumble of kitchen tools lying about at the back of the caupona. He's dreamy, untidy, and he was hysterical after the corpse's discovery. He could have missed anything.'

I was grateful for his help, but had to go on. 'Petronius, I still cannot accept unequivocally that this knife killed the centurion. Flora's is not renowned for hygienic practices; the red stains may not be blood at all, or if they are, it may be left from cutting up meat. What I'm saying is, you cannot actually prove that this is the murder knife.'

'No,' he replied levelly. 'But it's about the right size for the wounds.' It seemed too small, lying in his great hand. 'It's sharp enough,' he added. All my mother's knives were. They looked clumsy, but she used them a lot. They would slice through a cabbage stalk quite easily, taking any careless fingertip with them.

'The knife could have been anywhere since Ma lost it. It's not tied to me.'

'You are her son,' Petronius pointed out. 'Junilla Tacita is famously defensive. I cannot altogether take her word that the knife had been lost.'

'She would not lie, even for me.'

'Would she not?' Marponius asked, checking with me, Helena, Petronius. In fact none of us was sure. Attempting to appear reasonable, the judge said to me, 'If you ever brought me a suspect with this amount of evidence, you know you would expect me to order a trial.'

'I wouldn't do it. I would not be convinced myself.'

Marponius sniffed. My views were unimportant; he had too high an opinion of his own place in the world. I had my own thoughts on where he belonged: face down in a wet gulley with a rhinoceros standing on top of him.

I glanced at Petro. Slowly he said, 'Falco, I don't want to believe you did this, but no one else is a suspect, and all the circumstantial evidence indicts you.'

'Thanks!' I said.

I was feeling tired. This was hopeless. There was nothing I could say or do to extricate myself – or Helena, who looked like my accomplice in a bungled cover-up. The judge had completed his questions. He decided to hold both of us in custody.

Normally I would have appealed for assistance to Petronius. As he was the arresting officer, I had to wait for somebody else to come forward with our bail.

Somebody would. Helena Justina's family would adore the chance to berate me for getting her into this.

We were to be kept at the judge's house temporarily. He had us locked in separate rooms, but as soon as the house quietened down I picked my way out of mine and into hers. Only the fact that Helena was also trying to break her lock with a brooch pin held me up.

XXIX

I came in and leaned against the door, trying to look debonair. Helena had stepped back. Still clutching the brooch, she gazed at me. Guilt and fear were in her eyes; they were brighter than ever with anxiety now I had arrived. Mine were smiling. Probably.

'Hello, sweetheart. Are you breaking out to find me?'

'No, Marcus. I'm trying to escape before I have to face your wrath.'

'I never get angry.'

'Well you never admit it.'

I could never be angry with Helena Justina when she was fighting back with that determined glint. We were in serious trouble, however, and we both knew it. 'I am merely perplexed at how to extricate us from this mess, to which you must admit you have contributed . . .'

'Don't try being reasonable, Falco. The effort makes your ears go red.'

'Well, if you wanted to get back at me for my fling with Marina, I could have suggested less drastic ways – ' I stopped. There were tears welling in her eyes. Helena had made a terrible mistake and under the show of pride she was desolate. 'I'll get us out of this,' I said, more gently. 'Just brace yourself for some bad jokes from your father when he has to come here grovelling to Marponius while he coughs up your surety.'

'Yours has been sent for too.'

'Mine won't come.'

She would not be consoled, but we were on friendlier terms now. 'Marcus, what happened to your face?'

'It hit somebody's fist. Don't worry, fruit. Marponius hasn't enough evidence against us to name a date for a hearing in court. That means he has to release us. If I'm free on bail I shall at least be able to pursue my enquiries without constantly having to dodge Petronius.'

Helena looked rueful. 'Your best friend – who now

140

knows you're living with an idiot!'

I grinned at her. 'He knew that already. He thought you were insane to take me on.'

'He told the judge it was true love.'

'And is he wrong?' I reached for the brooch she was still holding, and pinned it back on her neatly. 'Marponius believed him enough to lock us up in separate cells to prevent collusion. Well, then – ' A tremulous smile from Helena answered my broad grin. I held out my arms to her. 'So, my darling, let's collude!'

XXX

It took so long for Helena's papa to rally round, I began to dread that he was leaving us to stew. He might have refused to pay a judicial ransom to release me, but I did think he would rescue Helena. Her mother would insist on it.

Helena's conscience was tormenting her. 'It's all my fault! I just noticed the knife and took hold of it because I wondered whatever something of your mother's could be doing there . . .'

Holding her close I soothed her. 'Hush! All the family go to Flora's. Any one of them could have decided to take their own bread-cutter to attack the week-old rolls. And they are all daft enough to leave it behind afterwards.'

'Maybe one of them will remember . . .'

My money was on Festus as the culprit, so that was out.

We were lying on a couch. (Purely for convenience; I had more tact than to seduce my girlfriend under the nose of a 'man of ideas'.) Anyway, it was a hard couch.

The room was dark, but noticeably more high-class than where I had been locked up. As a cell for a senator's daughter, it passed. There was a gilt footstool for the couch. An apple log smoked in a fire-basket. We had dim lamps, a small Eastern carpet on one wall, side-tables bearing curios, and vases on shelves. It was cosy. We had privacy. There was in fact no reason why we should rush to decamp.

'Why are you smiling, Marcus?' She had her face buried in my neck, so I was surprised she realised.

'Because I'm here with you . . .' Maybe I was smiling because we had squared the odds.

'You mean, we're in terrible trouble as usual, but this time it's my fault . . . I shall never forgive myself for this.'

'You will.'

The house had fallen quiet. Marponius was the type who dined alone then retired to his study to reread Cicero's defence of Sextus

Roscius. If ever he hired himself a dancing girl, it was so he would have an audience when he practised snippets of fine oratory.

Caressing Helena's head, I let my mind wander back over the day. Then my thoughts meandered even further, through childhood and youth, trying to make sense of the complex fiasco that had brought me here.

So far I had established that my brother, the eternal entrepreneur, had probably connived with some of his fellow centurions to rob their legion's savings bank; that he had purchased what might be a rare antique statue; and that his ship had sunk.

I had not actually established, but I strongly suspected, that the agent employed by Festus might have absconded with the statue before the ship foundered. That was good, possibly. I might be able to track down the agent and make a quick denarius from the Phidias myself.

Perhaps the agent had had nothing to do with it.

Perhaps the ship had not really sunk.

Then a more ugly possibility faced me. Maybe it had never sunk – *and maybe Festus knew that*. He could have lied about the *Hypericon*, then have sold the goods privately and run off with the money. If so, my role now was impossible. It was too late to cash in on the Phidias, I had no money to pay off the legionaries, and I could not clear my brother's name for Ma.

Almost everything I had discovered so far was dubious. It looked as if we had stumbled across the worst-ever crisis in my brother's fabled 'lupin round': his business ventures in the grey economy. Those had usually failed – usually a day after Festus himself had safely pulled out of them. He always trod a sticky path, like a wasp on the rim of a honey jar. Maybe this time he had overbalanced and fallen in.

Helena moved so she could see me. 'What are you thinking about, Marcus?'

'Oh, the Golden Age – '

'The past, you mean?'

'Correct. The long-lost, glittering, glorious past . . . Probably not so glorious as we all pretend.'

'Tell me. What aspect?'

'It's possible you have allied yourself with a highly dubious family.' Helena laughed ironically. She and I were such close

143

friends I could tell her the unthinkable: 'I am beginning to wonder if my brother the hero in fact ended his days as a thief and a candidate for cashiering.' Helena must have been expecting it, for she simply stroked my brow quietly and let me take my time. 'How can I ever say that to Ma?'

'Make quite sure of the facts first!'

'Maybe I won't tell her.'

'Maybe she already knows,' suggested Helena. 'Maybe she wants you to put the record straight.'

'No, she asked me to clear his name! On the other hand,' I argued unconvincingly, 'perhaps all this only looks like a scandal – but appearances deceive.'

Helena knew my opinion: that is not how scandals work.

She changed the subject, trying to ease my introspective mood by asking about what had happened to me earlier that day. I described the disrupted auction, then told her what I had learned from Geminus about my brother's last business scheme, including the Phidias Poseidon. I ended with how I had been summoned by that ghastly urchin Gaius and had left my father in his office, surrounded by flotsam like some old sea god in a cave.

'He sounds like you,' she commented. 'Hiding away from the world at the top of your sixth-floor apartment on the Aventine.'

'It's not the same!'

'You don't like people going there.'

'People bring trouble.'

'Even me?' she teased.

'Not you.' I grimaced at her. 'Not even today.'

'Perhaps,' Helena suggested thoughtfully, 'your elder brother also had a secret den somewhere?'

If so, it was the first I knew of it. Yet behind his open, cheery attitude, Festus had been full of secrets. He had lived with his mother; he certainly could have used a hideaway. Jupiter knew what would be waiting there if ever I discovered it.

We stopped discussing the issue because just then Marponius came in person to inform Helena that her father had arrived to free her. The judge was wearing his best toga for entertaining such splendid company, and a big grin because the surety he had demanded from the noble Camillus before he would release his dangerous daughter was extremely large. When he saw me in the same room he looked annoyed, though he said nothing about it. Instead, he enjoyed himself announcing that I too was to be set free on recognizance.

'From whom?' I demanded suspiciously.

'From your father,' grinned Marponius. He obviously knew I found the thought unbearable.

Produced for our parents as a murderer and his accessory, we managed not to giggle inanely, but felt like bad teenagers being hauled off home from the town jail after some prank in the Forum that would horrify our ancient great-aunts when they heard of it.

By the time we appeared, our two rescuers were close allies. They had met before. Now they had a disgrace in common and thanks to the judge's ingratiating wine steward, they were both slightly drunk. Geminus was down on one knee having a good look at a large urn from southern Italy that was pretending to have Athenian origins. Camillus Verus had kept slightly more control of his manners, though only by a thread. He gave me a whimsical salute, while commenting loudly to my own father, 'I suppose this makes a change from having to complain about their expensive hobbies, wild parties and shocking friends!'

'Never have children!' Pa advised Marponius. 'And by the way, Judge, your urn's cracked.'

Marponius rushed to inspect his flawed property. While he was crouching on the floor, he managed to speak a few hurried words about releasing us into family custody, the fathers' duties of supervision, et cetera. In return, Pa gave him the name of a man who could make the crack invisible (one of a horde of such dubious craftsmen known at the Saepta Julia). The judge then scrambled upright, shook hands all round like some theatrical pimp restoring long-lost twins, and let us escape.

As we struggled out into the winter night, our happy fathers were still congratulating themselves on their generosity, making jokes together about how to supervise our parole, and wrangling about which of their houses we should be dragged off to dine in.

Rome was cold and dark. It was late enough for the streets to be growing dangerous. Helena and I were hungry, but we had endured enough. I muttered that if they wanted to check up on us we would be with Ma, then we both fell into the chair they had brought for Helena and made the bearers set off at a cracking pace. I gave a loud instruction for Mother's house, then once we got around the first corner I changed the directions to Fountain Court.

Now I had an impossible mission, an indictment for murder – and two highly indignant fathers chasing me.

But at least when we reached the apartment the new bed had arrived.

XXXI

Next morning Helena was startled when I jumped out of bed at first light.

This was not easy. The new bed was successful in various ways that are private, and it had given us a most comfortable night's sleep. We awoke under a huge feather-filled coverlet which we had brought home from Germany, as warm as chicks in a nest. Beside the bed, in pride of place, stood the adjustable bronze tripod Helena had acquired from Geminus – as a present for me, apparently.

'Is this for my birthday? It's not for three weeks.'

'I remember when your birthday is!' Helena assured me. It was partly a wry joke, because of an occasion when I had somehow missed hers, and partly nostalgia. She knew the date because that was the first time I ever kissed her, before I realised the frightening fact that I was in love with her, or could believe she might be in love with me. We had been at a ghastly inn in Gaul, and I was still amazed at my bravado in approaching her – not to mention the consequences. By the way she smiled, Helena was also thinking about the occasion. 'I felt you needed cheering up.'

'Don't tell me how much he stung you for it; I don't want to be depressed.'

'All right, I won't tell you.'

I sighed. 'No, you'd better. He's my father. I feel responsible.'

'Nothing. When I said how much I liked it, he gave it to me.'

That was when I sprang out into the cold.

'Dear gods, Marcus! What's this?'

'Time is running out.'

Helena sat up, huddled in our German coverlet and staring at me from amidst a tangle of fine dark hair. 'I thought you said the enquiry would be less pressing now you didn't have to dodge Petronius?'

'This has nothing to do with the enquiry.' I was pulling on more clothes.

147

'Come back!' Helena launched herself across the bed and locked her arms around me. 'Explain the mystery!'

'No mystery.' Despite fierce resistance, I pushed her back into bed and tucked her in tenderly. 'Just an unpaid bill of four hundred thousand big ones that suddenly fell due.' She stopped struggling, so I managed to kiss her. 'First, I found out yesterday that a certain rash young lady is prepared to state in public – before a judge – that we are virtually man and wife . . . and now I've discovered my relations at large are sending us gifts to set up home! So forget the enquiry. Compared with the urgent need to assemble a dowry, a little matter of being a murder suspect fades into insignificance.'

'Fool!' Helena burst out laughing. 'For a moment I thought you were serious.'

She did have a point. When a man of my meagre standing has fallen for a senator's daughter, however much he adores her he takes a risk in hoping for something to come of it.

I let her enjoy the hilarious prospect of marriage to me, without bothering to worry her with the news that I meant what I said.

As I walked down the Aventine and towards the Emporium the warm glow of having reached a decision about Helena kept me going for about two streets. After that normality descended. Bad enough was the problem of trying to pluck four hundred thousand sesterces from thin air. If I wanted Helena I had to pay the price, but it was still far beyond my reach. Even more depressing was the next task I had set myself: seeing another of my brothers-in-law.

I tried to find him at his place of work. He was not there. I should have known. He was a bureaucrat; naturally he was on holiday.

My sister Junia, the superior one, had married a customs clerk. At seventeen, this had been her idea of moving up in society; now she was thirty-four. Gaius Baebius had progressed to supervising other clerks at the Emporium, but Junia undoubtedly had grander dreams in which a husband who merely hung around the docks collecting taxes did not feature. I sometimes wondered if Gaius Baebius ought to start testing his dinner on the dog.

They did own a dog, mainly because they wanted to have a

door-tile warning people to beware of him. Ajax was a nice dog. Well he had been once, before life's troubles got him down. Now he set about his duties as a watchdog as seriously as his master fulfilled his important role at the customs-house. Ajax's friendly greeting for tradesmen was to tear the hems off their tunics, and I knew of at least two lawsuits brought after he removed chunks of visitors' legs. I had actually given evidence for one of the plaintiffs, for which I had not yet been forgiven.

Ajax did not like me. When I appeared in his slightly smelly doorway innocently trying to gain admittance, he strained at his leash until his kennel began to slide across the floor. I managed to hop past, with his long snout an inch from my left calf, cursed the dog in an undertone, and shouted a somewhat tense welcome to whoever was inside the house.

Junia appeared. She shared Ajax's view of me. In her case it was legitimate, since my birth had supplanted her as the youngest in our family. She had maintained a thirty-year grudge against me for loss of privilege, even before I told a magistrate she kept a vicious dog.

'Oh, it's you! If you're coming in, take your boots off. They're covered with mud.' I was already unstrapping them; I had been to Junia's house before.

'Sort out your hound, will you? Good boy, Ajax! How many travelling onion-sellers has he killed today?'

My sister ignored that, but called her husband. It took two of them to drag the dog and his kennel to their proper position and calm the wild creature down.

I greeted Gaius Baebius, who had come out from his breakfast licking honey from his fingers. He looked embarrassed to be found relaxing in his second-best tunic, clearly unshaven for the past few days. Gaius and Junia only liked to be seen in public in full formal dress, with her leaning submissively on his right arm. They were spending their lives practising for their tombstone. I felt sombre every time I came within two yards of them.

They had no children. This perhaps explained their tolerance of Ajax. He ruled them like a spoiled heir. Had the law allowed it, they would have adopted him formally.

Being the only childless female among our highly fecund family had left Junia enjoying her right to bitterness. She kept herself very smart, her house so clean flies died of fear, and if asked about offspring said she had enough to do looking after Gaius Baebius. Why he caused so much work was a mystery to me. I found him about as exciting as watching a bird-bath evaporate.

'I hear you're on holiday?'

'Oh it's just a few days,' warbled Junia offhandedly.

'Of course you'll have four months at your private villa in Surrentum once the weather bucks up!' I was joking, but my sister blushed because that was what they liked to imply to people who knew them less well. 'Gaius Baebius, I need to talk to you.'

'Have some breakfast, Marcus.' My sister probably hoped I would say no, so although I had bought myself a bread roll on the way to their house, I accepted on principle. Some folk when they acquire money spend it avidly; Junia and her husband belonged to the other type, and were painfully mean in some ways. They were always changing the furniture, but hated to waste money on starving relatives.

Junia led the way to their dining-room. It was about three feet wide. Their apartment was the usual small rental, but Gaius Baebius had recently improved it with some odd partitioning. It stayed up, provided no one leaned against the walls, and enabled them to pretend they had a separate triclinium where banquets could take place. In fact people now ate squashed on stools in a row against a low table. Unfortunately, my brother-in-law's interior-design scheme meant if you had the table there was no room for even one proper eating-couch. I squeezed in without comment; he was really proud of their superior living style.

Junia served me a small chunk of loaf – making sure I got the black bits – and a sliver of pallid, tasteless cheese to help it down. Meanwhile Gaius Baebius carried on munching a mound of cold meats.

'New plates?' I asked politely, since much of mine was visible.

'Yes, we thought it was time we invested in Arretine. Such a wonderful gloss – '

'Oh these are not bad. We bought some ourselves,' I countered. 'Helena and I wanted something just a little more original. We hate to go out to dinner and find the same service we dine off at home . . . Ours was a present from a friendly potter at a little place I discovered when we were staying in Germany.'

'Really?' Junia had always been impossible to tease. She did not believe my foray into fancy dinnerware.

'I'm quite serious.' On the rare occasions when I managed to surpass these snobs I liked to make it known.

'Fancy that!' Junia rattled her bracelets and applied her gracious air. 'What did you want to ask Gaius Baebius?'

Insulting my hosts paled, so I settled down to business. 'I'm being forced to unravel a muddle our beloved Festus left behind.' I saw them exchange a glance; word of my mission had run ahead of me. Junia surveyed me as if she knew Festus was about to be exposed as a villain and she blamed me for everything. 'Did you meet the soldier who was camping out at Mother's house? He's dead – '

'And you're supposed to have done it?' Trust Junia.

'Anyone who thinks so needs a new head, sister!'

'We didn't like to say much.'

'Thanks, Junia! Leaving things unsaid until the pot boils over is a fine art in our family, but this time it won't work. I'm desperate to clear myself before I'm in court on a murder charge. It all seems to hang on Festus and his business network. Gaius, the soldier came up with some story about imports. Can you tell me this: when Festus was sending items to Italy from abroad, did his ships land at Ostia?'

'As far as I know. I expect,' offered Gaius Baebius prudishly, 'Festus thought that having a brother-in-law in customs meant that he could dodge his harbour dues.'

I grinned. 'He certainly thought it! No doubt he was wrong?'

'Of course!' exclaimed Gaius Baebius. No doubt it was sometimes true.

'Would your records show whether a particular ship landed? I'm talking about the year he died, so we have to go back a bit.'

In between large mouthfuls of breakfast, Gaius Baebius addressed the subject in his slow, pedantic way. 'Is this the ship that's supposed to be missing?' More of this story must be current than people had previously acknowledged.

'The *Hypericon*, that's right.'

'If she did land, someone would have her listed. If not, no.'

'Good!'

'If she fully unloaded at Ostia, Ostia will have the records. If her cargo went into barges and came up to be sold at the Emporium, it would be recorded here in Rome. Festus wasn't selling through official channels though, so you probably want Ostia.'

'Well, Ostia's close enough,' I replied airily. 'What if she was beached somewhere else in Italy?'

'The only way to discover that would be to visit every possible port and check their lists – if the local officials are willing to let you look at them. And always assuming,' Gaius Baebius added heavily, 'the *Hypericon* behaved in a legitimate fashion.' Something we both knew must be open to doubt. 'And paid the proper duty.'

'If not,' I agreed despondently, 'she could have slipped into land anywhere and had the cargo smuggled ashore.'

'And it was years ago.' He liked to be optimistic.

'And she may really have sunk, so I'm wasting my time.'

'Sinking was certainly the story. I remember the fuss Festus made about it.'

'At last somebody seems to know something about the problem!' I flattered him. 'I think we can assume the *Hypericon* never came into Ostia. Either she did sink – or she would have been hidden away. But would you be prepared to do something for me, old son? To help the family?'

'You mean check up on her?'

'Not only her. I want you to examine the lists for that whole year.'

'I'd have to go to Ostia.'

'I'll pay your mule hire.' He would pinch official transport anyway, if I knew him.

I could see he was prepared for the inconvenience; probably it was a good excuse to escape from Junia. As for her, she would let him go off on the trip because Festus had been her brother too. Junia must have been watching this possible scandal unfolding with more horror than the rest of us; after all, she was the one who had refined ideas.

'Let's get this straight, Falco. You want to see if Festus had any *other* commissioned vessel that came into Ostia?' Gaius Baebius loved that. 'Oho! You think he transferred the goods?'

'I've no idea. I'm simply looking into every possibility. I should have done this before, as his executor. Even if this cargo was submerged, there may be something else worth looking for. What

I'm hoping is that I may discover a cache of property belonging to Festus that I can sell to get his legion off our backs.' What I was hoping was to find more than that.

'Why don't you just tell them there is nothing?' demanded Junia angrily.

'I've already done that. Either they don't believe me, or they intend to be paid regardless of whether it ruins the whole family.' I held my tongue about the savings-bank theory. 'Gaius Baebius, are you prepared to help me? Will the lists still exist?'

'Oh they should exist all right. Have you any idea, Falco, how many vessels come into Rome in a season?'

'I'll help you look,' I volunteered quickly.

'It will still be a job and a half,' Gaius grumbled, but it was plain he would do it. 'I could go out to the coast today and see my pals at the port. I can have a look at what we're letting ourselves in for.' Gaius Baebius was a true bureaucrat; he loved to think he was so important he had to ruin his holiday by rushing back to work. Most people would baulk at a round trip of twenty miles, but he was ready to gallop off to Ostia immediately. 'I'll be back by the end of the morning.' The man was an idiot. If I carried out enquiries at such a dash, I would be worn out. 'Where can I find you later?'

'Let's have a late lunch. I'll be at a wine bar near the Caelian.'

Junia pricked up her ears. 'I trust this is not a place with a bad reputation, Marcus?' My sister kept her husband out of trouble; not that he exerted himself getting into any.

'It's not called the Virgin for nothing.' Junia looked reassured by the name of the drinking-house and told Gaius he could go.

'There may be one other problem,' I confessed. 'Any ship Festus chartered could be registered in the name of an agent he was using. Unluckily, no one I have been able to speak to – '

'He means Father!' snapped Junia.

'Is able to supply the agent's name.'

Gaius Baebius bristled. 'Well, that's a blow!'

'All right, all right! I'll sort it out somehow – '

'Gaius Baebius will have to help you,' my sister told me snootily. 'I do hope there is not going to be any unpleasantness, Marcus!'

'Thanks for the support, dearest!' I lifted a slice of veal sausage from my brother-in-law's laden plate as I took my leave.

Then I had to go back for another, to use for distracting the dog.

XXXII

My next task was trickier: I went to see my mother to ask about the knife.

She was being extremely vague on the subject. I learned no more than she had already told Petronius. 'Yes, it looked like mine. I really can't be expected to remember where something disappeared to when I probably haven't seen it for twenty years . . .'

'Somebody must have walked off with it,' I told her grimly. 'Allia's the prime candidate.'

Ma knew my sister Allia was always popping into someone else's house to borrow half a loaf or a set of loom weights. She was famous for not bothering to have her own possessions while there was anybody else she could count on to supply her needs.

Not that I was suggesting Allia was implicated in the soldier's death.

'I suppose you're right.' Whilst apparently agreeing, Ma managed to put mysterious doubts into her tone.

Under strain, I could hear myself getting annoyed. 'Well, will you ask all the family what they know about this thing? It's important, Ma!'

'So I gather! I heard you were arrested, but you let yourself be bought out!'

'Yes, my father released me,' I answered patiently.

'Last time you were in prison, *I* was good enough to bribe the jailer!'

'Don't remind me about that.'

'You ought to have more pride.'

'Last time had been a stupid mistake over nothing, Ma. This time a murder-court judge happens to have a pressing case against me. The position is rather different. If they haul me in front of a jury, your precious boy may be lost. The surety cost heavily, if that's any consolation. Geminus will be feeling the gap in his purse.'

'He'll feel it even more if you run off!' My mother clearly saw me as even more of a ruffian than Pa. 'So how are you getting on?'

'I'm not.'

Ma gave me a look as if she thought I had deliberately arranged my arrest to escape having to exert myself on my brother's behalf. 'So where are you dashing off to now?'

'A wine bar,' I said, since she already thought the worst of me. It was true, anyway.

Finding a seedy bar I had visited only once before, five years earlier, at the end of a long night's entertainment, when I was depressed and drunk, took time. I spent nearly an hour roaming alleys round the Caelian. When I finally came across the Virgin, Gaius Baebius was already there. He looked tired, but smug.

'Ho there, my travel-stained *amicus*! How did you manage to arrive so promptly? I've been wearing myself out looking everywhere. Do you know this place?'

'Never been here, Falco.'

'How did you find it so quickly then?'

'I asked someone.'

After working off his breakfast and working up another appetite with his mad gallop to Ostia, he was tucking into a substantial lunch. He had bought and paid for it; there was no offer to include me. I called for a small flagon and decided to eat later on my own.

'The records still exist,' mumbled Gaius, chewing happily. 'It will take a few months to wade through them.' He was a slow worker. I could speed him up, but I knew in advance it would frustrate me.

'I'll help if they will allow me in. Can I look at them with you?'

'Oh yes. Any citizen with a legitimate reason can inspect the shipping lists. Of course,' he said, 'you have to know the procedures.' From Gaius Baebius this was a message that he was doing me a favour, and would remind me about it in future at every opportunity.

'Fine,' I said.

My brother-in-law started making elaborate arrangements for meeting me tomorrow, while I groaned inwardly. I hate people who complicate life with unnecessary paraphernalia. And I was none too pleased at the prospect of spending days in his dreary company. Lunch was bad enough.

I was looking around. The place was as grim as I remembered. Gaius Baebius sat eating his bowlful of beef and vegetables with the impervious calm of an innocent. Maybe my eyesight was better. I was filled with unease by the dark corners and sinister clientele.

We were in a dank cellar, a hole cut half into the Caelian Hill, more a burrow than a building. Beneath its filthy arched roof stood a few battered tables lit by tapers in oily old jugs. The landlord had a lurching gait and sported a viciously scarred cheek, probably acquired in a bar fight. His wine was sour. His customers were worse.

Since my last visit one of the rough-cast walls had acquired a crudely drawn pornographic picture in wide swathes of murky paint. It involved some mightily furnished manly types and a shy female who had lost her guardian and her clothes but who was gaining some unusual experience.

I summoned mine host. 'Who did your striking art work?'

'Varga, Manlius and that mob.'

'Do they still come in here?'

'On and off.' That sounded useless. It was not a den where I wished to hang around like a critic or a collector until these flighty artists deigned to appear.

'Where can I look them up while I'm in the neighbourhood?'

He made a few desultory suggestions. 'So what do you think of our frescos?'

'Fabulous!' I lied.

Now that the wall-painting had been drawn to his attention, Gaius Baebius was staring at it so fixedly I felt embarrassed. My sister would have been seriously annoyed to see him studying it so closely, but she would be more furious if I abandoned him anywhere so dangerous. Out of brotherly regard for Junia I had to sit there fuming while Gaius slowly finished his lunch-bowl as he perused the brothel scenes.

'Very interesting!' he commented as we left.

Shedding my inane relation, I followed up the landlord's suggestions for finding the fresco painters, but had no luck. One place the

156

man had sent me was a rented room in a boarding-house. I could go back there at a different time and hope for better results. Any excuse was welcome. Needing food fairly urgently, I took myself off somewhere that by comparison was highly salubrious: back on the Aventine, to Flora's Caupona.

XXXIII

Flora's was in a greater state of misery than usual: they had the decorators in.

Epimandos was hovering outside, robbed of his kitchen but making an attempt to serve drinks and cold snippets to people who did not mind lunching in the street.

'What's this, Epimandos?'

'Falco!' He greeted me eagerly. 'I heard you had been arrested!'

I managed a grunt. 'Well I'm here. What's going on?'

'After the problem upstairs,' he whispered tactfully, 'the whole place is being done up.'

Flora's had been there for at least ten years and never seen a painter's brush before. Evidently a murder on the premises was good for trade. 'So who ordered this? Not the legendary Flora?'

Epimandos looked vague. He ignored my enquiry and burbled on. 'I've been so worried about what was happening to you – '

'So have I!'

'Are you going to be all right, Falco?'

'I've no idea. But if I ever catch up with the bastard who really did kill Censorinus, he won't be!'

'Falco – '

'Don't flap, Epimandos. A whimpering waiter kills the lively atmosphere!'

I looked for a seat. Outside they were limited. The objectionable cat, Stringy, was sprawled over one bench displaying his revolting belly fur, so I perched on a stool beside the barrel where the beggar always sat. For once it seemed necessary to nod at him.

'Afternoon, Marcus Didius.' I was still trying to think of a polite way to ask if I knew him when he introduced himself resignedly: 'Apollonius.' It still meant nothing. 'I was your schoolteacher.'

'Jupiter!' Long ago this hopeless soul had taught me geometry for six years. Now the gods had rewarded his patience by making him destitute.

Epimandos rushed up with wine for both of us, apparently

pleased that I had found a friend to take my mind off things. It was too late to leave. I had to converse politely; that meant I had to invite the ex-teacher to join my lunch. He accepted my invitation timidly while I tried not to look too closely at his rags. I sent Epimandos across the road to fetch me a hot meal from the Valerian, and another for Apollonius.

He had always been a failure. The worst kind: someone you could not help but feel sorry for, even while he was messing you about. He was a terrible teacher. He might have been a snappy mathematician, but he could not explain anything. Struggling to make sense of his long-winded diatribes, I had always felt as if he had set me a problem that needed three facts in order to solve it, but he had only remembered to tell me two of them. Definitely a man whose hypotenuse squared had never totalled the squares of his other two sides.

'What a wonderful surprise to see you!' I croaked, pretending I had not been ignoring him every time I had come to Flora's over the past five years.

'Quite a shock,' he mumbled, going along with it as he devoured the broth I had supplied.

Epimandos had nobody else to serve, so he sat down by the cat and listened in.

'So what happened to the school, Apollonius?'

He sighed. Nostalgia was making me queasy. He had had the same dreary tone when he was lamenting some stubborn child's ignorance. 'I was forced to give up. Too much political instability.'

'You mean too many unpaid fees?'

'Youth is the first to suffer in a civil war.'

'Youth suffers, full stop,' I answered gloomily.

This was an appalling encounter. I was a tough man doing a swinish job; the last thing I needed was a confrontation with a schoolmaster who had known me when I was all freckles and false confidence. Around here people believed I had a shrewd brain and a hard fist; I was not prepared for them to see me doling out free broth to this scrawny stick insect with his sparse hair and shaking, age-mottled hands while he flapped over my forgotten past.

'How's your little sister?' Apollonius enquired after a time.

'Maia? Not so little. She worked for a tailor, then she married a

159

slovenly horse vet. No discernment. He works for the Greens, trying to keep their knock-kneed nags from dropping dead on the track. He has a nasty cough himself – probably from pinching the horses' liniment.' Apollonius looked puzzled. He was not in the same world as me. 'Her husband drinks.'

'Oh.' He looked embarrassed. 'Very bright, Maia.'

'True.' Though not in her choice of husband.

'Don't let me bore you,' the schoolmaster said courteously. I cursed him in silence; it meant I would have to carry on with the chat.

'I'll tell Maia I saw you. She has four children of her own now. Nice little things. She's bringing them up properly.'

'Maia would. A good pupil; a good worker; now a good mother too.'

'She had a good education,' I forced out. Apollonius smiled as if he were thinking, *Always gracious with the rhetoric!* On an impulse I added, 'Did you teach my brother and the other girls? My eldest sister, Victorina, died recently.'

Apollonius knew he should be saying he was sorry but lost himself answering the first question. 'Some I might have done, from time to time . . .'

I helped him out: 'The elder ones had a problem getting any schooling. Times were difficult.'

'But you and Maia were always signed on every term!' he cried, almost reprovingly. He was bound to remember; we were probably the only regular attenders on the whole Aventine.

'Our fees were paid,' I acknowledged.

Apollonius nodded fiercely. 'By the old Melitan gentleman,' he insisted on reminding me.

'That's right. He thought he was going to be allowed to adopt us. He paid up every quarter in the hope he was improving two shiny-faced heirs.'

'*Did* he adopt you?'

'No. My father would not hear of it.'

This set me off reminiscing. For someone who so clearly had little interest in children once he had produced them, my father could be a ferociously jealous man. If we misbehaved he would happily threaten to sell us as gladiators, yet he took pride in rejecting the Melitan's pleading overtures. I could still hear him

160

boasting that free-born plebeians got their children as a trial for themselves, and did not breed for others' convenience.

The rows over sending Maia and me to school occurred not long before Pa lost his temper and left us. We felt it was our fault. We had the blame hanging over us; it made us a target for bullying from the rest.

After that fatal day when Papa left for an auction as usual but forgot his way home, Mother still strung the Melitan along – until even he finally twigged that no adoption would occur. He fell sick with disappointment, and died. With hindsight, it was rather sad.

'Do I sense, Marcus Didius, that all was not well?'

'Right. The Melitan caused some trouble.'

'Really? I always thought you and Maia came from such a happy family!' That just shows, teachers know nothing.

I cradled my winecup, caught up again in the anxieties the Melitan had imposed upon our house: Pa raging against him and all moneylenders (the Melitan's occupation), while Ma hissed back that she had to have the lodger's rent. Later Pa took to suggesting that the reason the old man was so keen on acquiring rights in Maia and myself was that we were his by-blows anyway. He used to roar this out in front of the Melitan as a hollow joke. (One glance at us disproved it; Maia and I had the full Didius physiognomy.) The Melitan was trapped in a stupid situation. Since he was so desperate for children, sometimes he even persuaded himself we were his.

Impossible of course. Ma, looking on like thunder, left us in no doubt.

I hated the Melitan. I convinced myself that had it not been for the anger he caused in my father, my Great-Uncle Scaro would have adopted me instead. Knowing about the quarrels that had already occurred, Scaro was far too polite to suggest it.

I wanted to be adopted. That is, if I was never claimed by my real parents. For of course I knew, as children do, that under no circumstances did I belong to the poor souls who were bringing me up temporarily at their house; someday my palace awaited me. My mother was one of the Vestal Virgins and my father was a mysterious and princely stranger who could materialise in moonbeams. I had been found on a river-bank by an honest old goatherd; my rescue from the toil and turmoil surrounding me had been foretold in a sibylline prophecy . . .

161

'You were always the dreamy one,' my old schoolmaster informed me. 'But I thought that there was hope for you . . .' I had forgotten he could be satirical.

'Still the same academic assessments: cruel, but fair!'

'You were good at geometry. You could have been a school-teacher.'

'Who wants to starve?' I retorted angrily. 'I'm an informer. It makes me just as poor, though I'm still being set puzzles, in different ways.'

'Well that's pleasing to hear. You should do work that suits you.' Nothing disturbed Apollonius. He was a man you could not insult. 'What happened to your brother?' he mused.

'Festus was killed in the Judaean War. He died a national hero, if that impresses you.'

'Ah! I always supposed that one would come to no good . . .' That dry humour again! I was expecting a long stream of anecdotes, but he lost interest. 'And now I hear you're contemplating a family of your own?'

'Word flies round! I'm not even married yet.'

'I wish you good fortune.' Once again the force of other people's premature congratulations was pushing Helena and me into a contract we had hardly discussed. Guiltily, I recognised that I was now committed both in private and in public to a plan that *she* saw quite differently.

'It may not be that simple. She's a senator's daughter, for one thing.'

'I expect your charm will win her round.' Apollonius only understood the simplicity of shapes on a slate. Social subtlety eluded him. He had never grasped why my father, a Roman citizen, should be outraged by the thought of having two of his children taken over by an immigrant. And he could not see the immense pressures that now kept me and my lady apart. 'Ah well, when you do have your own little ones, you know where to send them to learn geometry!'

He made it sound easy. His assumptions were too tempting. I was letting myself be won over by the pleasure of meeting somebody who did not see my marriage to Helena as utterly disastrous.

'I'll remember!' I promised gently, making good my escape.

XXXIV

Back at the apartment I found Helena sniffing at tunics. They were ones we had worn for travelling, just fetched back from the laundry downstairs.

'Juno, I hate winter! Things you send to be washed come back worse. Don't wear those; they smell musty. They must have been left too long in a basket while damp. I'll take them to my parents' house and rinse them out again.'

'Oh, hang mine over a door to air for a bit. I don't care. Some of the places I've been in today were not fit for pristine whites.'

I kissed her, so she took the opportunity to sniff teasingly at me.

One way and another that kept us busy until dinner-time.

According to custom in our house, I cooked. We had half a chicken, which I sizzled in oil and wine, using a rattly iron skillet over a grill on the brick cooking bench. There were no herbs, because we had been away at the time when we should have been collecting them. Helena owned an expensive collection of spices, but those needed picking up from her parents' house. All in all, things at the apartment were even more disorganised than normal. We ate sitting on stools, holding our bowls on our knees, since I still had to obtain a new table. My boast to Junia had been true: we did possess an impressive dinner service in glossy red Samian pottery. For safety I had stored it at Mother's house.

Suddenly I felt overwhelmed by despair. It was thinking about the dinnerware that did it. Problems were building up all around me, and the prospect of having our only civilised possessions packed away, perhaps for ever, was just too much to bear.

Helena noticed how I was feeling. 'What's the matter, Marcus?'

'Nothing.'

'There's something niggling you – apart from the murder.'

'Sometimes I think our whole life is buried in straw in an attic, awaiting a future we may never arrange.'

'Oh dear! It sounds as if I should fetch out your poetry tablet, so you can write a nice morbid elegy.' Helena took a mocking view of

163

the melancholy stuff I had been trying to write for years; she preferred me to write satires for some reason.

'Listen, fruit, if I did manage to acquire four hundred thousand sesterces, and if the Emperor was willing to include my name on the middle-rank scroll, would you actually be prepared to marry me?'

'Find the four hundred thousand first!' was her automatic response.

'That's me answered then!' I muttered gloomily.

'Ah . . .' Helena put her empty bowl on the floor and knelt at the side of my stool. She wrapped her arms around me, spreading her warm red stole across my knees comfortingly. She smelled clean and sweet, faintly perfumed with rosemary, which she used to rinse her hair. 'Why are you feeling so insecure?' I made no reply. 'Do you want me to say that I love you?'

'I can listen to that.'

She said it. I listened. She added some details, which cheered me up slightly. Helena Justina had a convincing grasp of rhetoric. 'So what's wrong, Marcus?'

'Maybe if we were married I would be sure you belonged to me.'

'I'm not a set of wine jugs!'

'No. I could scratch my name on a jug. And also,' I continued doggedly, 'you would then be certain that I belonged to you.'

'I know that,' she said, smiling rather. 'Here we are. We live together. You despise my rank and I deplore your past history, but we have foolishly chosen to share each other's company. What else is there, love?'

'You could leave me at any time.'

'Or you could leave me!'

I managed to grin at her. 'Maybe this is the problem, Helena. Maybe I am frightened that without a contract to honour I might storm off in a temper, then regret it all my life.'

'Contracts exist only to make arrangements for when you break them!' Every partnership needs someone sensible to keep its wheels in the right ruts. 'Besides,' Helena scoffed, 'when you do run off, I always come and fetch you back.'

That was true.

'Do you want to get drunk?'

'No.'

'Maybe,' she suggested, with a hint of asperity, 'what you do want is to sit in your shabby apartment, alone, scowling over the unfairness of life and watching a solitary beetle climb up the wall? Oh, I do understand. This is what an informer likes. To be lonely and bored while he thinks about his debts, and lack of clients, and the scores of scornful women who have trampled all over him. That makes him feel important. Your life is too soft, Marcus Didius! Here you are sharing a small but tasty dinner with your rude but affectionate sweetheart; it obviously spoils your act. Maybe I should go, my darling, so you can despair properly!'

I sighed. 'I just want four hundred thousand sesterces – which I know I cannot get!'

'Borrow it,' said Helena.

'Who from?'

'Someone else who has got it.' She thought I was too mean to pay the interest.

'We're in enough trouble. We don't need to expire under a burden of debt. That's the end of the subject.' I tightened my arm around her and stuck out my chin. 'Let's see if you're a woman of your word. You've been rude to me, princess – now how about being affectionate?'

Helena smiled. The smile itself made good her boast; the sense of well-being it brought to me was uncontrollable. She started tickling my neck, reducing me to helplessness. 'Don't issue a challenge like that, Marcus, unless you are sure you can take the consequences . . .'

'You're a terrible woman,' I groaned, bending my head as I feebly tried to avoid her teasing hand. 'You make me have hope. Hope is far too dangerous.'

'Danger is your natural element,' she replied.

There was a fold at the top of her gown which gaped slightly from her brooches; I made it wider and kissed the warm, delicate skin beneath. 'You're right; winter's dreary. When clothes come back from the laundry, people put on too many of them – ' It did provide entertainment when I tried taking some of them off her again . . .

We went to bed. In winter, in Rome, with neither hot air in wall-flues nor slaves to replenish banks of braziers, there is nothing else to do. All my questions remained unanswered; but that was nothing new.

XXXV

Gaius Baebius had not exaggerated how many records of incoming ships we would have to scrutinise. I went out with him to Ostia. I was not intending to stay there, only to provide initial encouragement, but I was horrified by the mounds of scrolls that my brother-in-law's colleagues happily produced for us.

'Jupiter, they're staggering in like Atlas under the weight of the world! How many more?'

'A few.' That meant hundreds. Gaius Baebius hated to upset people.

'How many years do you keep the records for?'

'Oh we've got them all, ever since Augustus dreamed up the import duty.'

I tried to look reverent. 'Amazing!'

'Have you found out the name of the agent Festus used?'

'No I haven't!' I barked tetchily. (I had forgotten all about it.) 'I don't want to find myself having to read this mountain twice –'

'We'll have to ignore that aspect and do the best we can.'

We settled that I would run my thumb down looking at the ships' names, while Gaius Baebius slowly perused the columns of whoever had commissioned them. I had a nasty feeling this method of splitting the details was likely to lose something.

Luckily I had left instructions with Helena that I would return home for any emergency – and to define 'emergency' liberally. Only next morning word came that I had to go back to see Geminus.

'Sorry. This is a fiendish nuisance, Gaius, but I must go. Otherwise I'll be breaking the conditions of my bail – '

'That's fine, you go.'

'Will you be all right carrying on for a while?'

'Oh yes.'

I knew Gaius Baebius had decided that I was flicking through the documents too casually. He was glad to see me depart, so he could plod on at his own dire pace. I left him playing the big man among his gruesome customs cronies while I fled back to Rome.

The request to visit Geminus was genuine. 'I would not send a false message when you were working!' cried Helena, shocked.

'No, my love . . . So what's the urgency?'

'Geminus is afraid the people who disrupted that auction are planning to strike again.'

'Don't say he's changed his mind and wants my help?'

'Just try not to get hurt!' muttered Helena, hugging me anxiously.

As soon as I reached the Saepta, I had the impression the other auctioneers were greeting my appearance with knowing looks. There was a disturbing atmosphere. People were gossiping in small groups; they fell silent as I passed.

The rumpus had happened, this time right in the warehouse. Overnight intruders had vandalised the stock. Gornia, the chief porter, found time to tell me how he had discovered the damage that morning. Most of it had already been cleared up, but I could see enough smashed couches and cabinets to guess the losses were serious. Potsherds filled several buckets on the pavement, and glass fragments were rattling under someone's broom. Bronzes stood covered in graffiti. Inside the wide doorway, what had been a garden statue of Priapus had now, as they say in the catalogues, lost its attribute.

'Where's himself?'

'In there. He should rest. Do something with him, will you?'

'Is it possible?'

I squeezed between a pile of benches and an upturned bed, stepped over some bead-rimmed copper pans, knocked my ear on a stuffed boar's head, ducked under stools hung lopsidedly from a rafter, and cursed my way to the next division in the indoor space. Pa was on his knees, meticulously collecting up pieces of ivory. His face was grey, though he applied the usual bluster once I coughed and he noticed me. He tried to stand up. Pain stopped him. I grabbed him with one arm and helped him ease his stocky frame upright.

'What's this?'

'Kicked in the ribs . . .'

167

I found two feet of free wall he could lean on and propped him there. 'Does that mean you were here when it happened?'

'Sleeping upstairs.'

'Helena said you were expecting a racket. I could have been here with you, if you had warned me earlier.'

'You have your own troubles.'

'Believe me, you're one of them!'

'What are you so angry for?'

As usual with my relatives, I had no idea.

I checked him over for ruptures and fractures. He was still too shaken to stop me, though he did protest. There was one monstrous bruise on his upper arm, a few cuts on his head, and those tender ribs. He would live, but he had taken all he could. He was too stiff to make it to the office upstairs, so we stayed there.

I had been in the store enough times before to realise that despite the clutter there was more empty space than usual. 'I see a lot of gaps, Pa. Does that mean you had the stuff smashed to ruins last night, or are you generally losing custom nowadays?'

'Both. Word gets around if you're having liveliness.'

'So there is something wrong?'

He gave me a look. 'I've called for you, haven't I?'

'Oh yes. Times must be bad! And I thought you just wanted to check that I hadn't jumped bail.'

'No chance of that,' my father grinned. 'You're the cocky sort who is bound to think he can clear himself of the charge.'

'As it's murder, I'd better.'

'And as it's my money bailing you, you'd better not skip!'

'I'll repay the damned money!' We were hard at it quarrelling again. 'I never asked you to interfere! If I'm desperate Ma will always assist with a judicial bribe – '

'I bet that stings!'

'Yes, it hurts,' I admitted. Then I threw back my head in disgust. 'Dear gods, how do I get in these messes?'

'Pure talent!' Pa assured me. He too breathed heavily and calmed down. 'So when will you be solving the murder?' I merely grimaced. He changed the subject: 'Helena sent word she had to bring you back from Ostia. Did you scavenge a bite on the journey, or can you finish off my lunch for me? I couldn't face it after the punch-up, but I don't want her-at-home to start . . .'

168

Some traditions continued, regardless of the personnel. Ma had always sent him out with his midday meal in a basket. If he was sleeping away while he guarded some particularly valuable hoard, she doggedly despatched one of us with the bread, cheese and cold meat. Now the redhead was supplying him with his daily snack – probably no longer to keep him out of expensive foodstalls, but simply because he had been trained to the routine.

I hated to be drawn into these new domestic arrangements. However, Helena had pushed me off without sustenance, and I was starving. I ate his meal. 'Thanks. Not up to Mother's standards, she'll be glad to hear.'

'You always were the charming one,' sighed Pa.

He lived in style, actually. After I had chewed through the cold kidneys rolled in bacon, with slices of must cake soaked in a piquant sauce, my father roused himself enough to say, 'You can leave me the beetroot.'

That took me back. He had always been a beet addict. 'Here, then . . . Your bacon's filled a hollow, but I could do with something to wash it down.'

'Upstairs,' said Pa. 'You'll have to go yourself.'

I made my way to the office. Here there was no evidence of the vandals, so perhaps Pa's intervention had stopped them reaching this far. Presumably they would have tried to break into the money chest. There was a possibility they would come back again for it, I reflected anxiously.

I was still poking around for a wine flask when Geminus staggered up behind me after all. He found me looking at that week's special.

It was one of the pots he loved, painted in a warm amber, with darker reliefs in several earthy tones. He had it set up on a none-too-subtle plinth. It appeared to be extremely old and Ionian, though I had seen similar at sales in Etruria. It had panache. There was a pretty striped foot, then a base decorated florally, above which the wide body carried a scene of Hercules leading the captive Cerberus to King Eurystheus, the king so terrified he had leapt into a large black cooking pot. The characters were full of life: Hercules with his lionskin and club, and Cerberus every inch a hound from Hades, his three heads distinguished by different shades of paint. Apart from his wriggly entourage of spotted

169

snakes, Cerberus reminded me of Junia's dog, Ajax. The vessel was beautiful. Yet somehow I felt dissatisfied.

Geminus had come in and caught me frowning. 'Wrong handles!'

'Ah!' The oldest story in the world of fakes. 'I knew something was odd. So your repair man needs a lesson in art history?'

'He has his uses.' The noncommittal tone warned me not to pursue this; I was intruding on the profane mysteries.

I could guess. Sometimes an article comes up for sale with an uncertain history or unconvincing provenance. Sometimes it is better to adapt the said item before it appears publicly: change a bronze palmette to an acanthus leaf; swap the head on a statue; give a silver tripod a satyr's feet instead of a lion's claws. I knew it was done. I knew some of the handy adaptors who did it. Sometimes I had been the frustrated member of an auction audience who suspected the changes but could not prove deceit.

It was part of my informing job to be aware of these procedures. I had a sideline tracing stolen art, though it never paid well. Collectors always expected a bargain, even for normal services. I grew tired of presenting an expenses bill, only to be asked if that was the best I could do on it. Most people who had treasures thieved were full of cheek, but they were novices. Giving them a ten per cent discount 'for trade' was an insult to the real connoisseurs at the Saepta.

'It's not what you're thinking,' my father told me suddenly. 'I got it for nothing. The whole top was missing. My man re-created it, but he's an idiot. With a wide neck, it should have body loops – ' He gestured to make two lugs set below the shoulders. The repair had its two handles carried up and hooked on to the throat, like an amphora. 'He can't tell a vase from a bloody jug, that's the truth of it.' Catching my sceptical look, he felt obliged to add, 'It's for sale "as seen". Naturally I'll mention what's been done – unless I really take against the customer!'

I restricted myself to saying, 'Strikes me the demigod has tied Cerberus on a rather thin piece of string!'

Then Pa produced the ritual wine tray, and we sat around with the silly cups again.

I tried to take a firm filial grip. 'Now stop behaving like a bonehead. This time you're going to tell me what is going on.'

'You're as bad as your mother for having a rant.'

'Somebody doesn't like you, Father,' I said patiently. 'Somebody other than me!'

'Someone wants some money,' sneered my honourable parent. 'Money I refuse to give.'

'Protection?'

I saw his eyes flicker. 'Not in essence. Paying up would protect me from this aggravation, certainly; but that's not the dispute.'

'Oh there is a dispute then?' I demanded.

'There was.'

'Is it not settled?'

'Temporarily.'

'So they will leave you alone for now?'

'For the time being.'

'How did you achieve that?'

'Simple,' said Geminus. 'While they were kicking seven bells out of me yesterday evening, I told them the person they really needed to argue with was you.'

XXXVI

I assumed an expression of Roman steadfastness and calm.

'What's up, son? Fly gone up your nose?'

'I'm staying detached.'

'You can't. You're in this – up to your neck.'

'I'll abdicate.'

'Afraid not,' he confessed. For once he looked guilty. 'Not possible.'

This was ridiculous. Marponius was going to be planning a new trial list soon; I should have been back at Ostia seeking to clear my name.

No, I shouldn't have been in this mess at all. I should have been living with my beloved in some peaceful villa in the country where my worst concern was whether to spend the morning catching up on my correspondence, or peel an apple for Helena, or go out and inspect the vines.

'You look upset, son.'

'Believe me, even before this news I was not exactly overflowing with Saturnalian jollity!'

'You're a Stoic.' I knew my father had no time for any flavour of philosophy. A typical Roman prejudice, based on the simple concept that thought is a threat.

I blew out my cheeks in irritation. 'Let me struggle to understand what is happening. You know some violent people who have a long-standing grievance, and they have just been told by you that I'm the person they want to tackle about their debt? So good-mannered of you to warn me, Didius Geminus! Such fatherly respect!'

'You'll dodge out of it.'

'I hope so! After I've dealt with any inconvenience from the auction-busters, I'll be looking for somebody else to attack. I advise you to start getting nippy yourself.'

'Show some piety,' complained my father. 'Show some parental reverence!'

'Cobnuts!' I said.

We were both breathing heavily. The situation felt unreal. Once, I had vowed I would never speak to my father again. Now here I was, sitting in his office with curious Egyptian gods peering over my shoulder from some inconsequential red and yellow furniture, while I let him lumber me with Hercules knows what troubles.

'Was your roughing-up arranged by the legionaries?'

'No,' said Pa. He sounded pretty definite.

'So it's unconnected with the death of Censorinus?'

'As far as I can see. Are you going to help out?'

I swore, not bothering to keep it under my breath. If I had stuck to my contempt for him, I could have avoided this. I ought to walk out now.

Yet there was only one answer to give him. 'If you're having a problem, naturally I'll help.'

'You're a good boy!' Geminus smirked complacently.

'I'm a good informer.' I kept my tone low and my temper cool. 'You need a professional for this sort of work.'

'So you'll do the job?'

'I'll do the job, but while I'm trying to save my neck on the other count I can't spare much time to dabble in auction fraud.' He must have known what was coming even before I dished it up: 'If I break into my schedule to do you a favour, you'll have to pay me at top rates.'

My father leaned back and stared at the ceiling in momentary disbelief. 'He's not mine!'

Unluckily for both of us, I certainly was.

'If you don't like it,' I mocked, 'you have a father's usual remedy. Go ahead – disinherit me!'

There was a shifty pause. In fact I had no idea what would happen, on my father's death, to the proceeds of his long auctioneering career. Knowing him, he had not addressed the issue. So that was another mess for me to sort out one day. If only to avoid it, I did my duty mentally and wished him a long life.

'I gather you're short of collateral?' he smiled, immediately all smoothness again. He passed a weary hand through those uncombed grey curls. 'Ah well, what are fathers for?' More than I ever got from this one. 'I'll hire you if that seems to be the form. What are these rates we hear so much about?' I told him, making a quick calculation and trebling them. (Well, he wanted me to get married.) He whistled in outrage. 'No wonder you never have any clients. Your charges are deplorable!'

'No worse than the auction percentage – and I work a lot harder for my wages. All you have to do is bawl loudly and bluff people. Informers need brains, bodyweight, and a gripping business sense.'

'And too much cheek!' he commented.

'So that's a contract,' I said.

Whatever it was we were clinching had yet to be revealed. That did not bother me. Shyness was usual among my clients. The inquisition of the prospective customer was the first part of any job I ever did, and usually the trickiest. Compared to that, asking questions of mere villains, cheats and bullies was easy labour.

Pa poured himself more wine. 'Drink on it?'

'I'll keep sober if I'm working.'

'You sound like a prig.'

'I sound like a man who stays alive.' I reached out and grasped his wrist, preventing him from lifting the cup. 'Now tell me what the job is.'

'You aren't going to care for it!' he assured me contentedly.

'I'll deal with my emotions. Now feel free to elaborate!'

'I should never have got you into this.'

'Agreed. You should have shown restraint when those bastards were applying their boots to the apples of your Hesperides – ' I was losing my temper (yet again). '*What's the wrinkle, Pa?*'

Finally he told me, though even then extracting the details was like squeezing olives through a jammed press.

'This is how it is. Things take time in the fine-art world. When people are commissioning creative works, they don't expect quick deliveries, so the fashion is to let problems ride.'

'How long ago did this marathon start?'

'Couple of years. I received an enquiry; I put the people off. I said it wasn't my problem; they didn't believe me. This year they must have remembered to do something about it, and they came back. More insistent.'

I was grinding my teeth. 'More aware, you mean, that they were losing cash? On whatever it is,' I added, though I knew.

174

'Exactly. They became aggressive, so I threw my javelin.'

'In a manner of speaking?'

'Well I told them to push off.'

'With spicy phraseology?'

'They might have thought so.'

'Jove! Then what?'

'It went quiet for a bit. Next the auctions were invaded. Last night it was the warehouse – and me, of course.'

'You may have been lucky last night. Read the dead sheep's liver, Pa. If these people are not soon satisfied, somebody may end up damaged even more severely. From what you mentioned earlier, these bruisers may bash me?'

'You're tough.'

'I'm not a demigod! And actually, I don't enjoy spending my life looking over one shoulder for large types with nails in their cudgels who want to practise hunt-the-decoy through the streets.'

'They don't want bloodshed.'

'Thanks for the reassurance, and tell that to your kicked ribs! I'm not convinced. There was a dead soldier at Flora's Caupona who may have inadvertently stepped in these people's way. That worries me – '

'It worries me,' cried my father. 'If you're right, there was no need for that!'

'I'd rather not have people standing round a pyre next week saying the same thing over me! In a minute I'm going to start demanding names from you – but first I have a crucial question, Father.' He looked pained at my tone, as if I were being insensitive. I forced myself to keep my voice level. 'Just tell me: does this problem of yours have anything to do with big brother Festus and his missing Phidias?'

Our father found an expression of amazement from his skilled repertoire. 'However did you realise that?'

I closed my eyes. 'Let's stop acting the farce, shall we? Just come clean!'

'It's quite simple,' Pa acquiesced. 'The people who want to talk to you are called Cassius Carus and Ummidia Servia. A couple. They don't socialise in a vulgar way, but in the trade they regard themselves as persons of influence. They have a big house with a private art gallery, nice place off the Via Flaminia. They collect statues. They had been lined up by Festus to acquire his Poseidon.'

I was already groaning. 'How closely lined up?'

'As tight as they could be.'

'And persons of influence don't like to be diddled?'

'No. Especially if they intend to go on collecting – which carries some risks, as you know. People want a reputation. They don't like their mistakes to be publicly known.'

I asked, '*Were* they diddled?'

'I reckon they think so. Carus and Servia were certainly expecting to receive the property. But then Festus lost his ship, so he failed to deliver it.'

'Had they actually paid for the goods?'

'Afraid so.'

I pulled a face. 'Then they were definitely diddled – and we are rightly being chased. How much – if it's not a saucy question – are we two honest brokers being asked to find?'

'Oh . . . call it half a million,' muttered Pa.

XXXVII

When I left the Saepta Julia, the air was thin and cold. I nearly went into the Agrippan Baths, but could not face a long walk home on a winter evening after I had let myself be made happy and warm. Better to do the heavy work, then relax.

Pa had offered me a lift in his ornamental litter back to the Thirteenth Sector, but I elected to walk. I had had enough. I needed to be alone. I needed to think.

Helena was waiting. 'Just a quick kiss, my darling, then we're going out.'

'What's happened?'

'I'm really getting grown-up work! First my mother employs me to prove Festus is *not* a criminal; now my father has hired me because Festus probably is.'

'At least your brother brings in jobs,' said my beloved, ever the optimist. 'Am I coming to help?'

'No. The irrepressible Geminus has fingered me for the Phidias. Some quick-tempered creditors may be coming here to look for me. You'll have to be stowed somewhere safer until the heat's off. I'll take you to the relation of your choice.'

She chose going back to Ma again. I took her; ducked the maternal enquiries; promised to see them both when I could; then trudged off through the gathering darkness towards the Caelian.

I was now determined to track down my brother's friends, the loathsome wall painters.

I tried the Virgin, without luck.

I tried all the other places where Varga and Manlius were supposed to hang out, but they were not there either. This was tiresome, but par for the course in my work. Investigating consists mainly of failure. You need thick boots and a strong heart, plus an infinite capacity for staying awake while parked in a draughty pergola, hoping that that strange scuttling sound is only a rat, not a man with a knife, though all the time you know that if the person you are watching for ever does turn up, they will be a dead loss.

Helena had asked, 'Why don't you go straight to the art collectors and explain?'

'I will go. I hope to have something to offer them first.'

As I stood watching an extremely nasty doss-house in the worst area of a bad district in this heartless city, it did seem unlikely that a rare old Greek statue would be standing around here with its toes as cold as mine, waiting for a lift in a waggon to a more refined environment.

I must have been there on surveillance for four hours. On a cold March Thursday, that's a long time.

The street was pitch-dark. It was short, narrow, and stinking; an easy touch for comparisons with life. The night-life was plentiful: drunks, fornicators, more drunks, cats who had learned from the fornicators, even drunker drunks. Drunken cats, probably. Everyone round here had been at an amphora, and I could understand it. Everyone was lost. The dogs; the cats; the humans. Even the fire brigade, wandering up with half-empty buckets, asked me the way to Oyster Street. I gave them correct instructions, then watched their smoky flare disappear in the wrong direction anyway. They were going to a tavern for a quick one; the fire could just blaze.

A whore offered me a quick one of the other sort, but I managed to plead poor plumbing. She cackled and launched into medical theories that made me blush. I told her I was one of the vigiles, so with a vicious curse she staggered off. Beyond the corner, where the streets were wider, even the normal night-time rumble of delivery carts seemed slack tonight. Beyond that, sharp on the frosty air, I heard the call of a Praetorian trumpet sounding the watch over their great camp. Above my head, where the stars should be, only blackness loomed.

Eventually the passers-by thinned out. My feet were frozen. My legs were too exhausted to stamp. I was wearing two cloaks and three tunics, but the chill had slid right under them. This was some way from the river, but even here the Tiber fog seeped into my lungs. There was no breeze; just that still, deceptive coldness like an animal that eats your heart while you stand.

It was a night when professional burglars would glance quickly

178

outside, then decide to stay in and annoy their wives. Heartbroken women would be hanging around the Aemilian Bridge waiting for a quiet moment to edge over the parapet and jump into oblivion. Tramps would cough to death in the gateways at the Circus. Lost children and runaway slaves would huddle against the huge black walls under the Citadel, slipping into Hades by accident when they forgot to breathe. There was no blizzard; it was not even raining. But all the same it was a bitter, baleful, dolorous night, and I hated to be out in it.

In the end I broke the rules. I strode up to the painters' lodging-house, entered by the creaking door, felt my way up five flights of stairs (fortunately I had counted the storeys when I was here before), found their room, spent half an hour trying to pick the lock, discovered the door was open anyway, and then sat in darkness waiting for them. At least I was under cover now.

XXXVIII

Manlius and Varga came swinging back home in the dead of night, arguing at the tops of their voices with a gang of other artistic delinquents as if it was broad daylight. I heard a shutter crash open and someone screamed at them; they answered with an innocent calm that hinted this was a regular occurrence. They had no sense of time. They had no sense of decency either, but having seen them cadging drinks off Festus I already knew that.

The other crowd went on, leaving my two to lurch upstairs. I sat, listening to their uneven approach. Informers dread this moment: sitting in pitch-darkness, waiting for a problem.

I already knew quite a lot about them. Anyone who broke into their room stumbled over discarded amphorae. Their room smelt sour. They owned few clothes, and paid fewer laundry bills. They lived such abnormal hours that by the time they thought of washing, even the public baths had closed. As well as their own odours, which were plentiful, they lived among a complicated waft of pigments: lead, palm resin, galls, crushed seashells and chalks, together with lime, gypsum, and borax. They ate cheap meals, full of garlic and those artichokes that make you fart.

In they fell, all paint-stains and dirty politics. The smoke from a resinous torch added itself to the other smells that lived here. It enabled me to see I was in a communal room. A small space crammed with beds for three or four people, though only these two appeared to be renting at present. The painters showed no surprise at finding me sitting there in the dark. They did not object: I had brought them an amphora. Well, I had met creative types before.

One was tall and one short, both of them bare-armed, not from bravado but because they were too poor to own cloaks. They both had beards, mainly to strike a defiant social attitude. They were aged about thirty, but their manners were adolescent and their habits puerile. Under the grime they might both have been good-looking in different ways. They preferred to make their mark

180

through personality; a kind friend should have advised them their personalities needed sprucing up.

They stuffed their torch into a narrow oil jar: some tasteful Greek's funeral urn. I guessed the Greek was still in it. That would be their idea of fun, making a lampstand out of him.

Neither of them remembered me.

'Who's this?'

'I'm Marcus – ' I began, intending full formality.

'Hey, Marcus! Wonderful to see you!'

'How's your life, Marcus?'

I refrained from saying that only select members of my family were permitted to use my personal name. Etiquette is lost on free spirits; especially ones who are habitually drunk.

Manlius was the designer. The tall, sleepy-eyed one, he wore what had once been a white tunic and had a fringe of dank black hair. Manlius squiggled and doodled in miniature. He had drawn neat little columns, swags and flower vases all around his corner of the room.

Varga's short legs were compensated for by a wide moustache. His tunic was a brownish manganese colour, with rags of purplish braid, and he wore sandals with gold thongs. Ma would have reckoned him untrustworthy. He was the one who could paint. He preferred ambitious battle scenes with bare-chested mythological giants. He had a good line in tragic centaurs; one five feet high reared up in agony above his bed, gorily speared by an Amazon.

'I'd like to meet your model!'

'The girl or the horse?'

'Oh the horse – amazing fetlocks!'

Our quips were satirical; the Amazon was startling. I pretended to admire her sensitive skin tones so we could all leer at her shape. Her body owed something to the girl who had posed for the picture, though more to Varga's fervent lust. He had improved her until she was almost deformed. I knew that. I knew his model; had seen her, anyway. His painted fighting maid was based on a luscious bundle whose proportions in real life would make a man gulp, yet not despair. The Amazon was for wild dreams.

The original model was a ripe brunette with wide-set daring eyes, eyes that had fallen on my brother once, almost certainly by design. She was the girl he had sat next to at the Circus, the night

181

he dumped Marina on me. The night, I now felt certain, when he had roamed through our city on the lookout for someone though for once, I reckoned, the girl was only a messenger.

'Who owns the body?'

'Rubinia – though I made some adaptations! She often sits for us.'

I was in the right place. That night, Rubinia must have told Festus he would see the painters at the Virgin. (She had probably told him her address too, though that was now irrelevant.)

I laughed, easily. 'I think she knew my brother.'

'More than likely!' chortled Manilus. He must be commenting on the girl; he had not asked me who my brother was.

Maybe he knew.

Probably not yet, I thought.

While I wondered how to work around to my enquiry, we lay on the beds with our boots on, drinking steadily. (Artists do not have mothers who bring them up nicely – or at least, they do not have to acknowledge them.)

My reference to Festus was forgotten. The painters were the casual type who would let you mention an acquaintance, or a relation, without further curiosity. They knew everyone. If he was carrying an amphora or sitting in a bar with a full purse on him, any stranger was their friend. Trying to remind them of one past patron among so many could prove difficult.

Our encounter tonight became as bad as I expected: they started talking about politics. Manlius was a republican. I was one myself, though wary of mentioning it in this loose-tongued company. Too serious a hope of restoring the old system implied removing the Emperor. Vespasian might be a tolerant old buffer, but treason was still a capital offence, and I try to avoid such hobbies. Being set up for a soldier's murder was unpleasant enough.

Manlius definitely wanted to dispose of Vespasian; Varga hated the entire Senate. They had a plan to turn Rome into a free public gallery, stocked by grabbing patrician collections and raiding the public porticoes, and financed from the Treasury. The plan was highly detailed – and completely impractical in their hands. These two could not have organised an orgy in a brothel.

182

'We could do it,' declaimed Varga, 'if the establishment were not protected by the mailed shirts and hidebound mentality of the Praetorian Guard.'

I decided against mentioning that I sometimes worked as an imperial agent, in case I was found decapitated in a public square. Artistic people have no sense of proportion – and drunks have no sense.

'This is a city run on fear!' Manlius slurred. 'For instance –here's a for instance, Marcus – why do slaves all wear the same clothes as the rest of us? Why do their masters make sure of that?'

'Because they work better if they're warm?'

My answer produced a huge guffaw. 'No! Because if they all wore a slave uniform, they would realise that there are *millions* of them, controlled by a mere handful of bastards they could easily overthrow if they put their minds to it – '

'Thank you, Spartacus!'

'I'm serious,' he mumbled, making serious efforts to pour himself another drink.

'Here's to the republic,' I toasted him gently. 'When every man tilled his own furrow, when every daughter was a virgin, and every son stayed at home to the age of forty-nine, saying "Yes, Father" to everything!'

'You're a cynic!' commented Varga, evidently the astute one of this rollicking pair.

I mentioned that I had a nephew who had apprenticed himself to a fresco painter on the Campanian coast. Actually Larius was on my mind now because I was thinking he might have attached himself to some useless degenerate like these two. He was embarrassingly sensible, but I should have checked before I left him there.

'Campania's a dump!' Manlius grumbled. 'We were there; it was dreadful. We went for the sun and the women and the precious grapes – plus the stupendously rich clients, of course. No luck. All snobs, Marcus. Nobody wants you unless you're a Greek or a local. We came home again.'

'Are you in work at the moment?'

'Surely. Good commission. Varga's doing The Rape of the Sabine Women for aristos to gaze at while they stuff themselves silly on peacocks in aspic. He creates a nice rape, Varga . . .'

183

'I can believe it!'

'I'm doing them a pair of rooms: one white, one black. Either side of the atrium. Balanced, see? Balance appeals to me.'

'Doubles your fee?' I grinned.

'Money means nothing to artists.'

'This generous attitude explains why you had to descend to painting rude sketches at the Virgin – settling a bill, I presume?'

Varga winced. 'That thing!'

'You were slumming,' I said, looking at the quality of what he painted for himself.

'We were, Marcus. The need to drink is a terrible thing!'

I was tired of this. My feet had warmed up enough to start hurting; the rest of me was stiff, tired and bored. I was sick of drinking; sick of holding my breath against the unsavoury atmosphere; sick of listening to drunks.

'Don't call me Marcus,' I said abruptly. 'You don't know me.'

They blinked at me blearily. They were a long way from the real world. I could have tripped them up merely by asking for their names or when their birthdays were.

'What's up, Marcus?'

'Let's go back to the beginning: I am Marcus Didius Falco,' I resumed, from an hour earlier. Thanks to the effects of my amphora their bravado was extinguished and they let me finish this time. 'You knew Marcus Didius Festus. Another name; another face; believe me, another personality.'

Manlius, the one who rescued them from trouble perhaps, waved a hand, managed to place it on the bed, and propped himself half upright. He tried to speak, but gave up. He lay down flat again.

'Festus?' quavered Varga, staring at the ceiling. Above his head, nicely positioned for gazing at while nearly insensible, he had painted a small, exquisite Aphrodite Bathing, modelled not by Rubinia but some small, exquisite blonde. If the painting was accurate, he would have done better luring the blonde to bed, but they do expect regular meals and a supply of glass-bead necklaces. No point investing in the hair dye otherwise.

'Festus,' I repeated, struggling to organise something sensible here.

'Festus . . .' Varga rolled himself sideways so he could squint at

184

me. Somewhere in those puffy eyes a new level of intelligence seemed to glimmer. 'What do you want, Falco?'

'Vargo, I want you to tell me *why*, on a certain night five years ago when I saw you with him at the Virgin, Marcus Didius Festus wanted to meet with you?'

'He can't remember who he met at the Virgin five *days* ago!' Manlius responded, gathering the shreds of his critical faculties. 'You don't want much!'

'I want to save my neck from the public strangler,' I retorted frankly. 'A soldier called Censorinus has been murdered, probably for asking just this sort of question. Unless I can shed light on events, I'll be condemned for the killing. Hear that, and understand me: I'm a desperate man!'

'I know nothing about anything,' Varga assured me.

'Well you know enough to lie about it!' I rasped good-humouredly. Then I lowered my voice. 'Festus is dead; you cannot harm him. The truth may even protect his reputation – though I'm honestly not expecting it – so don't hold back to avoid offending me.'

'It's a complete fog to me,' Varga repeated.

'I hate people who pretend to be idiots!' I spun off the bed where I was lying, and got hold of his right arm. I twisted it enough to hurt. As I sprang at him I had whipped out my knife; I laid it against his wrist so the slightest movement would make him cut himself. 'Stop messing me about. I know you met Festus and I know it's relevant! Come clean, Varga, or I'll slice off your painting hand!'

Varga went white. Too drunk to resist, and too innocent to know how to do it anyway, he stared up at me in terror, hardly able to breathe. I was so frustrated by the enquiry, I almost meant what I said. I was frightening myself, and Varga could tell. A vague sound gurgled in his throat.

'Speak up, Varga. Don't be shy!'

'I can't remember meeting your brother – '

'*I* remember you meeting him,' I declared coldly. 'And I wasn't even in on the conspiracy!'

His friend shifted anxiously. At last I was getting somewhere.

'There was no conspiracy involving us,' Manlius burst out from the other bed. 'I told that to the soldier when he came!'

XXXIX

'This is news to me!' Varga pleaded.

I pressed the knife harder against his arm, so he could feel the edge of the blade, though in fact I had it turned so it did not yet pierce the skin. 'Careful. You're very drunk, and I'm not entirely sober. One wrong move, and you've painted your last tantalising nipple . . .' I stared at Manlius. 'Carry on. I'm versatile. I can manage to threaten one man while the other does the talking!'

'Tell him,' Varga urged faintly. 'And I wouldn't mind knowing myself . . .'

'You weren't here,' Manlius explained. They had peculiar priorities. His main concern seemed to be convincing his pal that there were no secrets at the lodging-house. 'It was one of your days for taking Rubinia's measurements . . .'

'Cut the ribaldry!' I grated. 'What happened with Censorinus?'

'Laurentius,' corrected Manlius.

'Who?'

'He said his name was Laurentius.'

I released Varga, but sat back on my heels, still holding the knife where they could both see it. 'Are you certain? The soldier who died was called Censorinus Macer.'

'Laurentius was what he told me.'

If Censorinus had had a crony with him in Rome, I was very relieved to hear it; this Laurentius would be a prime suspect. Cronies fall out. They sit in a tavern having a drink, then they quarrel about money, or women, or political philosophy, or simply about whether their boat home leaves on Tuesday or Thursday. Then it's natural that somebody gets stabbed and his pal legs it . . . Or so I tried to convince myself, overlooking to some extent the violence with which the centurion had been attacked.

'So tell me about this Laurentius. What was his rank and legion, and when did he come to see you?'

'A while ago – '

'Weeks? Months?'

Being specific was not a habit here. 'A month or two . . . possibly. I don't know the other details.'

'Oh come on, you're a damned painter, aren't you? You're supposed to be observant! Did he carry a vine staff?'

'Yes.'

'Then he was a full centurion. He would have been close friends with Festus. Did he tell you that?' Manlius nodded. 'Good. Now take a deep breath and tell me what he wanted.' There was no flicker of rational thought below the painter's long untidy fringe of hair. 'Did he,' I spelled out, 'ask you about the *Hypericon*, for instance – or did he go straight to the matter of the Phidias?'

Manlius smiled finally. It was a gentle, undeceptive smile. I did not place a scruple of trust in that soft grin – but the words he uttered rang true enough: 'I don't know what you're talking about, Falco. The soldier was asking about someone. I remember,' he told me quietly, 'because it was the same person Festus was so stirred up about on that night in the Virgin.'

'Who?'

'Orontes Mediolanus.'

'The sculptor,' Varga contributed.

This was the part that did make sense.

I kept my voice as steady as possible. 'And where in Rome can I find this Orontes?'

'That's the point!' Manlius burst out, with relaxed and unvindictive triumph. 'Orontes has disappeared from Rome. In fact he vanished years ago.'

I had already guessed the sequel. 'He had vanished when Festus was after him?'

'Of course! That was why Festus came looking for us. Festus wanted to ask us where in Hades Orontes was.'

I went back a step. 'How did you know Festus?'

'He noticed models,' Varga said, convincingly. We all glanced at his Amazon and imagined Festus taking notice of Rubinia.

'And why did he think you could track down Orontes?'

'Orontes used to lodge with us,' Varga explained. 'In fact, earlier this evening, you were lying on his bed!'

I stared at it. The hard, lumpy mattress was covered with a thin blanket. Unwashed food bowls were piled underneath, and these two untidy idiots kept paint-kettles on one end, encrusted with copper oxides and enamels. Perhaps the bed had gone downhill since the sculptor lived here, but if not I could see why he might have left: maybe he was just fastidious.

'So what happened to Orontes?'

'Disappeared. One morning we went out and left him snoring; when we came back he had taken himself off. He never came back.'

'Wandering feet! Sounds like my father . . . Did you worry?'

'Why? He was grown up.'

'Were his things missing?'

I had asked the question casually. The painters half exchanged a glance before one said yes and the other no. 'We sold them,' Varga admitted. I could believe it. Their guilty expressions were right, since the property had not been theirs to sell. All the same, I sensed an atmosphere, which I noted. They could well be lying about this.

I went over all the ground a second time, confirming the facts. There was little to add. I learned only that the centurion Laurentius had gone away as dissatisfied as I was. Manlius had no information about where this soldier had been staying in Rome. Neither of them knew what Festus had wanted the sculptor for.

Or if they knew, they were not admitting it to me.

I poured what remained of the amphora into their winecups and formally saluted them.

'Farewell, boys! I'll leave you to contemplate how fine art can save the civilised world from its sterility.' From the doorway I grinned at the squalor they inhabited. 'Own up. This is just a sham, isn't it? Really, you're two hard-working citizens who love the Empire and live like lambs. I bet you say a prayer to the hearth goddess every morning and write home to your mothers twice a week?'

Manlius, who was probably the sharper one of the disreputable pair, gave me a shamefaced smile. 'Have a heart, Falco! My mother's eighty-one. I have to show devotion to such age.'

Varga, who lived among more private dreams, studied his Aphrodite mournfully, and pretended he had not heard.

XL

In Fountain Court everything lay still. That was worrying. Even in the dead of night there was usually some husband receiving brain damage from an iron pot, a pigeon being tortured by delinquent youths, or an old woman screaming that she had been robbed of her life savings (Metella, whose son regularly borrowed them; he would pay her back, if the string of prostitutes he ran worked double shifts for a fortnight).

It must be nearly dawn. I was too old for this.

As I reached the laundry, the tired trudge of my feet brought more trouble: Lenia, the drab proprietress, flung open a half-shutter. Her head flopped out, all tangles of madly hennaed hair. Her face was white; her deportment unstable. She surveyed me with eyes that needed an oculist and screeched: 'Oi, Falco! What are you doing up so late?'

'Lenia! You put the scares on me. Is Smaractus there?'

Lenia let out a pathetic wail. She would wake the whole street, and they would blame me. 'I hope he's at the bottom of the Tiber. We had a terrible row!'

'Thank the gods for that. Now kindly close up your dentistry – ' We were old friends; we could dispense with compliments. She knew I despised her fiancé. It had something to do with him being my landlord – and more with the fact he was as savoury as a pile of hot mule-dung. 'Is this goodbye to the wedding?'

'Oh no.' She calmed down immediately. 'I'm not letting him off that! Come in, come in – '

Resisting was useless. When a woman who spends her life heaving around monstrous troughs of hot water grabs your arm, you fly in the direction she pulls or lose a limb. I was dragged into the sinister cubicle where Lenia fiddled her accounts and accosted her friends, then pushed on to a stool. A beaker of cheap red wine fixed itself in my fist.

Lenia had been drinking, like the whole of Rome this wintry

189

night. She had been drinking on her own, so she was hopelessly miserable. With a cup banging against those awful teeth again, she cheered up, however. 'You look rough too, Falco!'

'Been boozing with painters. Never again!'

'Until the next time!' Lenia jibed raucously. She had known me a long while.

'So what's with Smaractus?' I tried her wine, regretting it as much as I had feared. 'Cold feet about the matrimonial benefits?'

I was joking, but of course she nodded mournfully. 'He's not sure he's ready to commit himself.'

'Poor soul! Pleading his tender youth, I suppose?' Whatever age Smaractus was, his notorious life had left him looking like some desiccated hermit half dead in a cave. 'Surely that miser can see that he'll make up for what he's losing as a bachelor by gaining a prosperous laundry?'

'And me!' Lenia retorted snootily.

'And you,' I smiled. She needed someone to be kind.

She gulped at her cup, then ground out vindictively, 'How are your own affairs moving along?'

'Perfectly, thanks.'

'I don't believe that, Falco!'

'My arrangements,' I stated pompously, 'are moving to their conclusion with efficiency and style.'

'I haven't heard about this.'

'Quite. I'm keeping clammed up. If you don't let people interfere, things don't go wrong.'

'What does Helena say?'

'Helena needn't be bothered with details.'

'Helena's your bride!'

'So she has enough worries.'

'Gods, you're a mad devil . . . Helena's a nice girl!'

'Exactly. So why warn her she's doomed? This is where you went wrong, Lenia. If Smaractus had stayed blissfully ignorant of your approach with the sacrificial pig, you could have forged his name on a contract one night when he was sleeping off a flagon and he would never have felt the pain. Instead you've put the wind up him, and given him a thousand opportunities to wriggle free.'

'He'll be back,' Lenia cracked morbidly. 'The careless prick left his beryl signet-ring.'

I managed to steer the subject away from marriage and cheap jewellery. 'If you want to upset me, try my arrest by Marponius.'

'News spreads!' Lenia agreed. 'We all heard you stabbed a soldier and ended up in manacles at a judge's house.'

'I did not stab the soldier.'

'That's right, one or two crazy types do reckon you might be innocent.'

'People are wonderful!'

'So what's this fable, Falco?'

'Bloody Festus has landed me in it as usual.'

I told her the tale. Anything to stop her drinking. Anything to stop her pouring more for me.

When I finished she hooted with her usual grating derision. 'So it's a fine-art mystery?'

'That's right. I strongly suspect that most of the statues and all of the people are fakes.'

'You do talk! Did he find you that night, then?'

'What night, Lenia?'

'This night you've been talking about. The night Festus left for his legion. He came here. I thought I told you at the time . . . Late, it was. Really late. He banged on my door, wanting to know if you had staggered home so drunk you couldn't make the stairs and were curled up in my washtub.' Since six flights do hurt after revelry, it had been known.

'I wasn't here – '

'No!' giggled Lenia, knowing about the Marina fiasco.

'He should have known where I was . . . You never told me this –' I sighed. One more in a long string of undelivered messages.

'You talking about him tonight just reminded me.'

'Five years late!' She was unbelievable. 'So what happened?'

'He flaked out in here, making a nuisance of himself.'

'He had had some.' Much like us this evening.

'Oh I can handle soaks; I get enough practice. He was broody,' complained the laundress. 'I can't stand miserable men!' Since she had elected to marry Smaractus, who was a long-faced, insensitive, humourless disaster, she was gaining practice in tolerating misery too – and with more yet to come.

'So what was Festus on about?'

'Confidential,' sneered Lenia. 'He groaned, "It's all too much; I need little brother's strong right arm", and then he shut up.'

'Well that was Festus.' Sometimes, however, my secretive brother would be gripped by a bacchic drive to talk. Once the mood was on him, once he decided to display his inner being, he would usually open up to anyone who got in the way. He would ramble for hours – all rubbish, of course. 'It's too much to hope he revealed any more?'

'No. Tight bastard! Most people find me easy to talk to,' Lenia boasted. I remembered to smile graciously.

'So then what?'

'He got fed up of waiting for his precious brother who had stayed out playing around with Marina, so he cursed me, cursed you a few times, borrowed one of my washtubs, and disappeared. He went off muttering that he had work to do. Next day I heard he had left Rome. You weren't around much afterwards yourself.'

'Guilt!' I grinned. 'I bummed off to the market garden until the heat died down.'

'Hoping Marina would have a convenient lapse of memory?'

'Maybe. What did he want a washtub for?'

'Juno, I don't know. It turned up again on the doorstep covered with mud or cement or something.'

'He must have been rinsing his smalls . . . Why did you never tell me this before?'

'No point. You would have been upset!'

I was upset now.

It was one of those pointless, tantalising events that sting you after someone dies. I would never really know what he had wanted. I could never share his problem; never help. Lenia was right. Better not to know these things.

I found an excuse to leave (yawning heavily) and staggered upstairs.

Six flights give you a lot of time for thinking, but it was not enough.

Both missing and hating my brother, I felt exhausted, dirty, cold and depressed. I could have dropped on the stairs, but the landings were freezing and stank of old urine. I was heading for my bed, knowing that all too soon I had to be up out of it again.

Despair made my feet heavy; I was chasing a hopeless puzzle, with disasters fast closing in on me. And when I reached my own apartment I groaned even more, because more trouble was waiting for me. Under the ill-fitting door a gleam of light showed. That could only mean someone was in there.

I had already made too much noise to start creeping up and springing surprises. I knew I was too drunk for an argument and too tired for a fight.

I did everything wrong. I forgot to be careful. I could not be bothered to organise a possible escape. I was too tired, and too angry to follow my own rules, so I just walked straight in and kicked the door shut after me.

I was staring at the lamp that burned on the table quite openly, when a small voice murmured from the bedroom, 'It's only me.'

'Helena!' I tried to remember that one of the reasons I loved her was her startling knack of surprising me. Then I tried to play sober.

I snuffed the light, to disguise my state. I dropped my belt and fumbled off my boots. I was icy cold, but as a gesture to civilised living I shed a few layers of clothing. As soon as I stumbled to bed Helena must have realised my condition. I had forgotten the bed was new; in the darkness it was wrongly aligned for the path my feet knew, and the wrong height. Besides, we had moved it to avoid the great hole in the roof, which Smaractus had still not repaired.

When I finally found the bed, I fell in awkwardly, almost falling out. Helena kissed me once, groaned at my foul breath, then buried her face in the safer haven of my armpit.

'Sorry . . . had to suborn some witnesses.' Warmth and comfort greeted me alluringly as I tried to be stern. 'Listen, you disobedient rascal, I left you at Mother's. What's the excuse for this?'

Helena wound herself around me more closely. She was welcome and sweet, and she knew that I was not complaining much. 'Oh Marcus, I missed you . . .'

'Missing me could get you hurt, woman! How did you get here?'

'Perfectly safely. With Maia's husband. He came right up and checked the room for me. I've spent an evening going around your sisters' houses asking about the knife from the caupona. I dragged your mother with me, though she wasn't keen. Anyway, I thought you would want to know the results,' she excused herself weakly.

'Bamboozler! So what's the good news?'

I felt a small, but obvious, belch escaping. Helena shifted further down the bed. Her voice came faintly through the coverlet. 'None, I'm afraid. Not one of your relatives can remember taking that knife from home, let alone ever using it at Flora's.'

Even in the dark I could feel my head spinning. 'The day's not a total disaster. I heard a couple of things. Censorinus had a companion in Rome – Laurentius. It's good. Petro will have to find him before he can indict me.'

'Could this be the murderer?'

'Unlikely, but possible . . .' Talking was difficult. 'And there is, or was once, a sculptor called Orestes – no, Orontes. He's disappeared, but it's given us another name . . .' In the new bed, already warmed for several hours by Helena, relaxation was seeping gloriously through my frozen limbs. I wrapped myself around her more conveniently. 'Dear gods, I love you . . .' I wanted her safe, but I was glad she was here. 'I hope Famia was sober when he brought you.'

'Maia wouldn't send me home without safe protection. If she had known it was a drunk I would be waiting for she would not have let me come at all!' I tried to think up a rejoinder, but none came. Helena stroked my cheek. 'You're weary. Go to sleep.'

I was already doing so.

Hazily I heard her saying, 'Your father sent a message. He suggests that tomorrow morning he should take you to visit Carus and Servia. He says, *Dress up*. I've put a toga out for you . . .'

I wondered who in Hades were Carus and Servia, and why I should allow these unbidden strangers to bother me with such formality. Then I knew nothing until I woke the next day with a splitting head.

XLI

It was late morning when I lurched from the apartment. I wore my favourite worn indigo tunic, since my idea of dressing up has always been to put comfort first; my heaviest boots, since the weather looked foul; a cloak, for the same reason; and a hat, to shade my eyes from painful light. My head hurt and my internal organs felt delicate. My joints ached. An upright posture seemed unnatural.

I went first to see Petronius. He was kicking his heels at the guardhouse, pretending to write reports while he sheltered from the weather. This made him glad of any excuse to wake up and hurl insults at a friend.

'Watch out, boys. A hangover on legs just found its way in. Falco, you look like a fool who has been up all night consuming cheap drink in rough company.' He had seen me do it before; I had done it with him.

'Don't start!'

'Let's have some gravity then. I assume you've come to present me with a nicely bound set of tablets detailing who killed Censorinus Macer, what their dirty motive was, and where I can find them tied to a pergola, awaiting arrest?'

'No.'

'Stupid to hope!'

'I've got a couple of leads.'

'Better than nothing,' he answered grumpily.

'What about you?

'Oh I'll stick with nothing. I like to feel safe. Why start dicing with evidence and proof?' Luckily he settled down after this frivolity and talked plainer sense. He listed the usual enquiries. He had spoken to all the people who were in Flora's the night the soldier died, but had learned nothing useful. 'Nobody saw anyone with Censorinus, or noticed anyone go up the backstairs to his room.'

'So that's a dead end.'

'Right. I grilled Epimandos a few times. I don't like the shifty

195

look in his eye. He's a strange one, though I can't prove anything against him.'

'I think he's a runaway. He looks worried because of that.'

'He's been there a few years.'

'He has.' I stretched my stiff limbs. 'He always gives the impression of looking over his shoulder.' That applied to most of Rome, so Petro received the news calmly. 'Festus knew something about his past, I think.'

'Festus would!'

'Is it worth arresting Epimandos on suspicion?'

Petronius looked prim. 'Arresting people on suspicion would mean arresting you!'

'You did!'

'Who's starting now, Falco? In the damned waiter's case, I decided against it, though I still have a man watching Flora's dump. I don't think Epimandos would conceal anything if he could clear you,' Petronius told me. 'He seems too loyal to you.'

'I don't know why that should be,' I admitted honestly.

'Neither do I,' said Petro, with his usual friendly attitude. 'Have you paid him to corroborate your story?' I scowled; he relented. 'Maybe Festus had something to do with it, if they were on good terms. Whatever it is, Epimandos is really panicking that he might have caused your brush with Marponius. I told him you were perfectly capable of getting yourself hauled up on a false charge without help from a dumb stew-doler.'

'Well that should clinch a free drink for me next time I toddle into Flora's! And how is our beloved Marponius?'

Petronius Longus growled contemptuously. 'What are these leads you promised me?'

'Not much, but I've two new names to follow up. One is a sculptor called Orontes Mediolanus who knew Festus. He disappeared several years ago.'

'That sounds a dud line.'

'Yes, leave that to me, if you like. I specialise in hopeless clues . . . Apart from him, there was a centurion called Laurentius recently in Rome, asking the same questions as Censorinus.'

Petro nodded. 'I'll take that on. It fits the form. I managed to prod your ma into remembering that Censorinus did go out a couple of evenings, saying he was seeing a friend.'

'Ma never told me!'

'You have to ask the right questions,' Petro replied smugly. 'Leave this to the professionals, eh Falco?'

'Professional bollockers! Who was the friend?'

'Your ma didn't know. He was only mentioned casually. This Laurentius is a good candidate, though. They could have deliberately planted Censorinus with your mother to harass the family, while the other man stayed elsewhere and pursued other issues.' Petro leaned back on his stool, flexing his shoulders as if he too was feeling the effects of the damp morning. He was a big, muscular character who hated drizzly weather. Except when he went home to play with his children, he needed to be out of doors; it was one reason he liked his job. 'Did you spot that Campania mansio bill?'

His eyes were half veiled, hiding any impression of collusion over me inspecting the dead man's kit at the caupona.

'I saw it,' I confirmed, also keeping my expression bland.

'Looked to me as if it was a reckoning for two.'

'I didn't notice that.'

'It was not specific, but at country prices I'd say it covered hay for two horses or mules, and more than one bed.' His voice dropped. 'Wasn't it for some place near your grandfather's farm?'

'Near enough. I would go out there, but it would be breaking my bail.'

'Why not?' Petro grinned at me suddenly. 'After all, you went to Ostia!'

How in Hades did he know? 'Are you following me, you bastard?'

He refused to say. 'Thanks for the name of Laurentius. I'll make enquiries among the military authorities, though if he was just in Rome on leave his presence may not have been registered officially.'

'If he was here with Censorinus, pretending to be innocents on holiday,' I pointed out, 'he ought to have come forward the minute he heard about the murder.'

'True,' Petro agreed. 'Suspicious, otherwise. If I have to, I'll write and query him with the Fifteenth, but that will take weeks.'

'Months, more likely. If his nose is clean with them, they won't necessarily answer a civil enquiry at all.'

'And if his nose is *not* clean with them,' Petro answered with gentle cynicism, 'they will disown him quietly, and still not answer me.' Soldiers only had to answer to military law. Petronius could certainly ask a centurion questions, and if Laurentius was shown to have killed Censorinus, Petro could report it formally – but if the murder had been committed by a fellow legionary, then the legions would deal with the culprit. (That meant the legions would hush it up.) For Marponius and Petro this new angle could be frustrating. 'There are better ways to proceed. My men can start checking the lodging-houses here; that's more likely to produce results. If Laurentius *is* implicated, it may be too late to stop him leaving Italy, but I'll have somebody watching at Ostia. If he's spotted, I can ask him politely to return to Rome and talk to me – '

'He won't come.'

'Does it matter? If he refuses, he looks guilty and you're cleared. By virtue of his non-co-operation, I can oppose any charges against you. Marponius would have to go along with it. So what are your plans, reprieved suspect?'

'I'm going out with my damned father for an educational talk on art.'

'Enjoy yourself,' smiled Petronius.

Relations between us had improved drastically. If I had known it would be so easy to retrieve our long-standing friendship. I would have invented a name for a suspect days ago and given him someone else to chase around after.

'To save you having to tail me,' I replied with my customary courtesy, 'I'm picking up Pa from the Saepta now, then spending the rest of the morning at some big house in the Seventh Sector, after which – if my parent sticks to his usual rigid habits – we'll be returning to the Saepta prompt at noon so he can devour whatever the redhead has stuffed into his lunch-satchel.'

'This is all very filial! When did you ever spend so much time in the company of Geminus?'

I grinned reluctantly. 'Since he decided he needed protection – and stupidly hired me.'

'Such a pleasure,' chuckled Petronius, 'to see the Didius family sticking together at last!'

I told him what I thought of him, without rancour, then I left.

198

XLII

Aulus Cassius Carus and his wife Ummidia Servia lived in a house whose exterior unobtrusiveness told its own tale of wealth. It was one of the few big houses built by individuals after the great fire in Nero's time; it had then managed to escape both looters and arsonists during the civil war following Nero's death. This house had been commissioned by people who flourished in hard times, and who had somehow avoided offending a half-mad emperor whose favourite subjects for execution had been anybody else who dared to proclaim artistic good taste.

Carus and Servia proved an unlikely moral: it was possible to be both Roman and discreet.

In a city where so many thousands were crammed into high-rising tenements, it always surprised me how many other folk managed to acquire large plots of land and live there in stately private homes, often virtually unknown to the general public. These two not only managed it, but did so in the classic Roman style, with blank walls apparently guarding them, yet an atmosphere of making their home available formally to anyone who produced a legitimate reason for entering. After a few words with their porter, Father and I established our business, and what had appeared from the outside to be a very private house opened all its public rooms to us.

A slave went off carrying our request for an audience. While we waited for a reaction we were left free to wander.

I had assumed my toga, but was otherwise my happy self.

'You might have combed your hair!' whispered Geminus. He eyed the toga; that had belonged to Festus, so it passed muster.

'I only comb my hair for the Emperor, or women who are *very* beautiful.'

'Dear gods, what have I brought up?'

'You didn't! But I'm a good boy, who won't ingratiate himself with thugs who kick his ancient pa in the ribs!'

'Don't cause trouble, or we'll get nowhere.'

'I know how to behave!' I sneered, subtly implying I might not draw upon the knowledge.

'No one,' decreed Didius Geminus, 'who wears a coloured tunic with his toga knows how to behave!'

So much for my indigo number.

We had passed a senatorial statue, presumably not ancestral, since our hosts were only middle rank. Also in the atrium were a couple of loyal portrait heads of the Claudian emperors, their clean-cut boyish looks at odds with the gruff and rugged features of Vespasian who ruled Rome today. The first general collection was out of doors in a peristyle garden just beyond the atrium. In March the effect was bare horticulturally, though the art showed up well. There were various columnar herms, among a rather twee gathering of hounds and hinds, winged cupids, dolphins, Pan among the reeds, and so forth. They had the inevitable Priapus (fully formed, unlike the vandalised creature at Father's warehouse), plus a gross Silenus sprawled on his back while a fountain trickled uncertainly from his wineskin. These were ordinary pieces. As a plant lover, I took more interest in the Eastern crocuses and hyacinths that were enlivening the garden.

My father, who had been here before, led me with a firm step to the art gallery. At this point I began to feel shafts of envy.

We had passed through several quiet, well-swept rooms with neutral decor. They contained a spare quantity of extremely good furniture, with one or two small but superb bronzes displayed on plinths. The entrance to the gallery was guarded by not one, but a pair of gigantic sea creatures, each bearing nereids on their threshing coils, amid fulsome waves.

We crept between the sea-nymphs and in through a majestic portal set. The alabaster door-case stood as high as my rooms at home, with huge double doors in some exotic wood studded with bronze. They were folded back, probably permanently since pushing them closed would take about ten slaves.

Inside, we were dumbstruck by a twice life-size Dying Gaul in glorious veined red porphyry. Every home should have one – and a stepladder for dusting him.

Then followed their set of Famous Greeks. Rather predictable, but these people had crisp priorities in throwing together a set of heads: Homer, Euripides, Sophocles, Demosthenes, a handsome bearded Pericles, and Solon the Law Giver. Crowding afterwards came some anonymous dancing maidens then a full-length Alexander, looking nobly sad but with a good mane of hair that should have cheered him up. These collectors preferred marble, but allowed in one or two excellent bronzes: there were Spear Carriers and Lance Bearers; Athletes, Wrestlers and Charioteers. Back with the classic Parian stone we came on a winged and sombre Eros, plainly in trouble with some mistress who had stamped her foot at him, facing a pale, even more remote Dionysus contemplating the eternal grape. The god of wine looked youthful and beautiful, but from his expression he had already realised his liver would be for it if he carried on that way.

Next came a wild jumble of delights. Plenty and Fortune; Victory and Virtue. A Minotaur on a pedestal; a caseful of miniatures. There were graceful Graces, and musing Muses; there was a colossal group of Maenads, having a ripping time with King Pentheus. There was what even I immediately recognised as a more than decent replica of one of the Charyatids from the Erechtheion at Athens. Had there been room, they would probably have imported the whole Parthenon.

The Olympian gods, as befitted their status, were lording it in a well-lit hall to themselves. Enthroned there were Jupiter, Juno and Minerva, that good old Roman triad, plus a formidable Athene, partly in ivory, with a pool to keep her humid. There was, I noted bleakly, no lord of the oceans – unless (faint hope) he was away in a workshop being cleaned.

All these pieces were astounding. We had no time to scrutinise how many were original, but any copies were so good they must be desirable in their own right.

I can only summon up a certain amount of reverence before an uncontrollable need to lighten the atmosphere sets in: 'As Ma would say, I'm glad someone else has to sponge this lot down every morning!'

'Hush! Show some refinement!' This was one of my many quarrels with Pa. Politically, he was perfectly shrewd, and as cynical as me. Move on to culture, and he became a real snob. After selling antiques to idiots for forty years, he should have been more discerning about owners of art.

We were about to leave the Hall of the Gods when the owners

thought it time to appear. They must have reasoned we would be gasping with admiration by now. On principle I tried to look too ethereal to have placed a value on the goods; no one was fooled. One of the reasons for letting folk walk around was so they could reel at the stupendous cost of what they had just seen.

The pair came in together. I already knew from Father that I was about to meet a couple where his taste and her money had made a long, successful bond. He was to speak the most, but her presence remained a force throughout. They were a firmly welded pair, welded by an inexorable interest in grabbing things. We had come to a house where the need to possess hung in the air as strong as a sickness.

Cassius Carus was a thin, mournful streak with dark curly hair. About forty-five, he had hollow cheeks, and pouched, heavy-lidded eyes. He had apparently forgotten to shave lately – too enraptured with his monumental nudes, no doubt. Ummidia Servia was perhaps ten years younger, a round, pallid woman who looked as if she could be irritable. Maybe she was tired of kissing stubble.

They both wore white, in lavishly formal folds. The man had a couple of gross signet-rings, the woman gold filigree about her, but they did not trouble much with jewellery. Their uncomfortably dignified dress was to set them up as fitting custodians of their art. Personal adornment did not come into it.

They knew Father. 'This is my son,' he said, producing a chill for a second while they worked out that I was not the fabulous Festus.

Each gave me an upsettingly limp hand.

'We've been admiring the collection.' My father liked to slaver.

'What do you think?' Carus asked me, probably sensing more reserve. He was like a cat that jumps straight on the lap of the only visitor who sneezes at fur.

In my role as the auctioneer's respectful son I said, 'I have never seen better quality.'

'You will admire our Aphrodite.' His slow, light, slightly pedantic voice made this virtually an instruction. Carus led the way for us to view the wonder, which they kept until last in the collection, in a separate courtyard garden. 'We had the water put in specially.'

Another Aphrodite. First the painter's special, now an even more suggestive little madam. I was becoming a connoisseur.

The Carus model was a Hellenistic marble whose sensuality stopped the breath. This goddess was too nearly indecent to be displayed in a temple. She stood in the middle of a circular pool, half undressed, turning to gaze back over one lithe shoulder as she admired the reflection of her own superlative rear. Light from the still water suffused her, setting up a gorgeous contrast between her nakedness and the rigid pleating of the chiton she had half removed.

'Very nice,' said my father. The Aphrodite looked even more satisfied.

Carus consulted me.

'Sheer beauty. Isn't she a copy of that very striking Venus on the great lake at Nero's Golden House?'

'Oh yes. Nero believed he had the original!' Carus said 'believed' with a flick of contemptuous malice, then he smiled. He glanced at his wife. Servia smiled too. I gathered Nero thought wrongly.

Putting one over on another collector gave them even more pleasure than possessing their incomparable piece. This was bad news. They would enjoy putting one over on us.

It was time to tackle business.

My father walked away around the path, drawing Carus with him while I murmured about nothing much to Servia. We had planned this. When two members of the Didius family go visiting there is always some fraught plan – usually an interminable dispute about what time we are going to leave the house we have not even arrived at. On this occasion Pa had suggested we should each try our wheedling skills on both parties, then we could adopt whichever approach seemed best. Not this variation, anyway. I was getting nowhere with the woman. It was like plumping a cushion that had lost half its feathers. I could see Pa going rather red, too, as he and Carus conversed.

After a while Geminus brought Carus back round the remaining half of the circle. Adroitly changing partners, he imposed what was left of his famous attraction for women on the woman of the house, while I attacked her spindly spouse. I watched Pa oozing masculine civility over Servia as she waddled at his side. She hardly seemed to notice his efforts, which made me smile.

Carus and I moved to stone benches, where we could admire the pride of the collection.

'So what do you know about marbles, young man?' He spoke as if I was eighteen and had never before seen a goddess undressing.

I had stared at more nude femininity than he owned in his whole gallery, and mine was alive, but I was a man of the world, not some boasting barbarian, so I let it pass.

In our introductory message, I had been described as a junior partner at the auction-house. So I played gauche and offered, 'I know the biggest market is in copies. We cannot shift originals these days even if we bundle them in fives and throw in a set of fish skillets.'

Carus laughed. He knew I was not referring to anything so important as a Phidias original. Anyone could shift that. Somebody probably had.

My father despaired of entrancing Servia even more quickly than I had, so they both rejoined us. These preliminaries had established the rules. Nobody wanted to be charmed. There would be no easy release from our debt. Now Pa and I sat side by side, waiting for our limpid hosts to put the pressure on us.

'Well, that's a sign of modern life,' I carried on. 'Only fakes count!' By now I knew that in chasing after Festus I was destined to expose another one.

'Nothing wrong with a decently done fake,' Pa opined. He looked calm, but I knew he was miserable. 'Some of the best current reproductions will become antiques in their own right.'

I grinned desperately. 'I'll make a note to invest in a good Roman Praxiteles, if ever I have the cash and the storage-room!' As a hint of our family poverty this was not impressing our creditors.

'A Lysippus is what you want!' Geminus advised me, tapping his nose.

'Yes, I saw the fine Alexander in the gallery here!' I turned to our hosts confidentially: 'You can always tell an auctioneer. Apart from a wandering look in his eye from taking bids off the wall – inventing non-existent calls, you know – he's the one whose ugly snout bends like a carrot that's hit a stone, after years of giving collectors his dubious investment tips . . .' We were getting nowhere. I dropped the act. 'Pa, Carus and Servia know what they want to invest in. They want a Poseidon, and they want it by Phidias.'

Cassius Carus inspected me coldly in his fussy way. But it was Servia, their financier, who smoothed down the thick white folds of her mantle and broke in. 'Oh no, it's not a future investment. That piece already belongs to us!'

XLIII

I saw my father grip his hands.

Rejecting the humble role that had been imposed on me, I hardened my attitude. 'I came to this tale rather late. Do you mind if we just run over the facts? Am I right in my understanding? My elder brother Didius Festus is said to have acquired from Greece a modest statue, alleged to be a Poseidon and thought to be by Phidias?'

'Known to be bought by us,' responded Carus, obviously thinking he had put me down wittily.

'Pardon me if I'm churlish, but do you have a receipt?'

'Naturally,' said Servia. She must have dealt with my family before.

'I have been shown it, Marcus,' murmured Pa. I ignored him.

'It was made out to you by Festus?' Carus nodded. 'Festus is dead. So what has this to do with us?'

'My point exactly!' stated Pa. He drew himself up. 'I made my son Festus independent of parental authority when he joined the armed forces.' This was probably a lie, but no outsider could refute it. It sounded straight, though I could not imagine why Pa and Festus would have gone through such a formality. Acquiring emancipation from the power of his father is something that only troubles a son who feels bound by his father's power in the first place. In the Didius family this had never applied. Any pleb on the Aventine would probably grin widely and say the same.

Carus refused to accept any disclaimer. 'I expect a parent to take responsibility for his son's debts.'

I felt a strong need for irony. 'Nice to see that some people still believe in the family as an indissoluble unit, Father!'

'Bull's testicles!' Maybe Carus and Servia took this as a reference to the mystical rites of an Eastern religious cult.

Maybe not.

'My papa's upset,' I excused him to the couple. 'When somebody says he owes them half a million, he loses his grip.'

Carus and Servia gazed at me as if what I said was incomprehensible. Their indifference to our problem astonished me. It also made me shiver.

I had been in many places where the atmosphere was more sinister. Toughs armed with knives or staves have a vivid effect; there were none of those here. Yet the mood was sour and in its way just as intimidating. The message reaching us was uncompromising. We would pay up, or we would suffer; suffer until we gave in.

'Please be reasonable,' I pressed on. 'We are a poor family. We simply cannot lay hands on so much cash.'

'You must,' said Servia.

We could talk all we wanted. But however closely we argued, we would never actually communicate. Even so, I felt compelled to struggle on: 'Let's follow through what happened. You paid Festus for the statue. In good faith he attempted to import it, but the ship sank. By then you owned the statue. It is,' I declared, more boldly than I felt, 'your loss.'

Carus tossed a new nut into the mixing bowl: 'No mention was ever made to us that the statue was still in Greece.'

That was tricky. My heart lurched. I wondered what the date was on their receipt. Trying not to look at my father, I even wondered if my impossible brother had sold the Phidias to them after he already knew it was lost. Surely Pa would have noticed this detail when he saw the receipt; surely he would have warned me?

One thing was definite: I could not draw attention to our lad's fraud by asking to see the receipt for myself now. It did not matter; if Festus had deceived them, I did not want to know.

'You mean you bought the item sight unseen?' I floundered wildly.

' "*Antique marble*," ' intoned Carus, evidently quoting from this bill of sale which I preferred not to examine. ' "*A Phidias Poseidon, heroic proportions, expression of noble placidity, wearing Greek dress, heavily coiffed and bearded, height two yards four inches, one arm raised to hurl a trident . . .*" We have our own shippers,' he informed me in a biting tone. 'The Aristedon brothers. People we trust. We would have made our own arrangements. *Then* it would have been our loss. Not this way.'

Festus could have let them take the shipping risk. He would have known that. He was always well up on customers' backgrounds. So why not? I knew without even thinking about it. Festus was bringing the statue home himself because he had some extra wrinkle up his grubby tunic-sleeve.

This was not my fault. It was not even Pa's.

That would not stop Carus and Servia.

'Are you taking us to court?'

'Litigation is not our philosophy.'

I managed not to comment, *No; only thuggery.* 'Look, I only recently came upon this problem,' I began again. 'I am trying to investigate what happened. After five years it is not easy, so I ask you to be sympathetic. I give you my word I will endeavour to illuminate the issue. I ask you to cease harassing my elderly father – '

'I'll take care of myself!' scoffed the elderly Didius, ever to the fore with a pointless quip.

'And give me time.'

'Not after five years!' Carus said.

I wanted to fight. I wanted to storm out, telling him he could do his worst and we would resist everything he did.

There was no point. I had already discussed it with Father on the way here. We could provide muscle at the auctions. We could barricade the office and the store. We could guard both our homes and never step outside without a train of armed guards.

We could not do all those things, however, every day and every night, for years.

Carus and Servia had the grim insistence of people who would persist. We would never be free of the worry, for ourselves, our property – our women. We would be smothered by the cost of it all. We would never escape the inconvenience, or the public doubt that soon attaches to people who are trailing disputed debts.

And we could never forget Festus.

They were growing tired of us. We could see they were about to have us thrown out.

My father was the first to acknowledge the deadlock. 'I cannot replace the Phidias; no similar piece is known. As for finding half a million, it would wipe out my liquidity.'

'Realise your assets,' Carus instructed him.

'I'll have an empty storehouse, and a naked house.'

Carus just shrugged.

My father stood up. With more dignity than I expected, he simply said, 'Selling everything I have, Cassius Carus, *will* take time!' He was no longer requesting favours, but laying down terms. They would be accepted; Carus and Servia wanted to be paid. 'Come along, Marcus,' Pa ordered quietly. 'We seem to have plenty of work to do. Let's go home.'

For once I abandoned my insistence on stating in public that he and I honoured different versions of 'home'.

He strode out with a set face. I followed. I was equally in despair. Half a million was more than I had already failed to assemble for my own most cherished purposes. It was more money than I really hoped to see. If I ever did see it, I wanted the cash so I could marry Helena. Well I could kiss goodbye to *that* idea for ever, if I became embroiled in this.

Yet even if it broke me for ever, I realised I could not leave my father to shoulder the whole burden of my feckless brother's debt.

XLIV

We had walked to the collectors' house. We walked back.

Well not quite: my father strode, at a ferocious pace. I hate to intrude upon another man's trouble – and when a man has just failed to escape paying out half a million sesterces, he is certainly in trouble. So I marched along beside him, and since he wanted to fume in complete silence, I joined in loyally.

As he steamed down the Via Flaminia my father's visage was as friendly as Jove's thunderbolt, and my own may well have lacked its usual winsomeness.

I was thinking hard as well.

We had almost reached the Saepta when he wheeled up to a wine-bar counter.

'I need a drink!'

I needed one too, but I still had a headache.

'I'll sit here and wait.' Monumental masons were removing my skull on a tombstone hoist. 'I spent last night oiling two painters' vocal chords.'

Pa paused in the midst of ordering, unable to decide which of the wines listed on the wall was sufficiently strong to create the oblivion he needed. 'What painters?'

'Manlius and Varga.' I paused, too, though in my case there was no real wrench to the brain cells; I had only been applying my elbow to the counter and staring vaguely round me like any son accompanying his father out of doors. 'Festus knew them.'

'*I* know them! Go on,' urged my father thoughtfully.

On I went: 'Well, there's a disappearing sculptor who used to lodge with them – '

'What's his name?' asked my father.

The barman was growing anxious. He could sense a lost sale approaching.

'Orontes Mediolanus.'

My father scoffed. 'Orontes never disappeared! I ought to

know; I use that idle bastard for copies and repairs. Orontes lodged with those loafers on the Caelian until at least last summer. They took your drink and twisted you!'

The barman lost his sale.

We raced off to find Manlius and Varga.

We spent most of the afternoon on the chase. My father dragged me round more sleepy fresco artists – and more of their burgeoning models – than I could bear to think about. We toured horrid hired rooms, freezing studios, teetering penthouses, and half-painted mansions. We went all over Rome. We even tried a suite at the Palace where Domitian Caesar had commissioned something elegant in yellow ochre for Domitia Longina, the dalliance he had snatched from her husband and installed as his wife.

'Nothing like it!' muttered Father. There was plenty like it actually; the Flavian taste was predictable. Domitian was only toying at that stage; he would have to wait for both his father and his brother to die before he could launch into his master plan for a new Palatine. I said what I thought about his decorating clichés. 'Oh you're right!' agreed Pa, grovelling to the inside knowledge of an imperial agent. 'And even adultery with the pick of the smart set is a convention nowadays. Both Augustus and that repulsive little Caligula acquired wives by pinching them.'

'That's not for me. When I grabbed a senator's daughter, I chose one who had divorced herself in readiness for my suave approach.'

'Quite right!' came a rather sardonic reply. 'You would hate to be publicly criticised . . .'

At last someone told us the address where our quarries were working. We made our way there in silence. We had no plan this time. I was angry, but saw no need to elaborate. I never enquired what Father felt, though I did find out quite soon.

The house in question was being done over completely. Scaffold hung threateningly over the entrance where old roof-tiles were flying down from the heavens into a badly placed skip. The site foreman must be a dozy swine. We clambered in, through a mess of trestles and ladders, then tripped over a tool-bag. Pa picked it up. When the watchman raised his head from a game of draughts scratched in the dusty base of a half-laid tessellated floor, I called out, 'Have you seen Titus anywhere?' and we rushed past, pretending to follow his vaguely raised arm.

There is always a carpenter called Titus. We used him several times to bluff our way around. Even a fat fusspot in a toga, who was probably the householder, let us evade questions, merely frowning fretfully when we barged past him in a corridor. His property had been in the hands of louts for months. He no longer complained when they knocked him aside, peed on his acanthus bed or took naps in their filthy tunics on his own favourite reading-couch.

'Sorry, governor!' my father beamed. He had the knack of sounding like an unskilled pleb who had just put his pick through a water-pipe and was shuffling off out of it quickly.

I knew Manlius would be working near the atrium, but there was too much going on there when we first arrived. We left him, and started working through the dining-rooms, looking for raped Sabines. It was a big house. They had three different feeding areas. Varga was touching up his Sabine ladies in the third.

The plasterer had just left him with a new section. For frescos, the trick is to work extremely fast. Varga was facing a huge new stretch of smooth wet plaster. He had a sketch, with several writhing bottoms on it. He had a kettle of flesh-tone paint already mixed. He had a badger-hair brush in his hand.

Then we came in.

'Whoa, Varga. Drop the brush! It's the Didius boys!' That harsh command, which startled both the painter and me, came from Pa.

Varga, slow on the uptake, clung on to his brush.

My father, who was a solid man, grasped the painter's arm with one hand. He gripped the painter bodily with the other, lifting him off his feet, then he swung him in a half-circle, so that a bright pink streak from the brush scraped right across three yards of plaster, just smoothed over by an extremely expensive craftsman. It had been a perfect, glistening poem.

'Mico could learn something here! Well don't just stand there, Marcus, let's fetch that door off its pinions. You nip into the kitchen alongside and pinch the rope they hang the dishrags on – '

Bemused, I complied. I never willingly take orders – but this was my first game of soldiers as one of the Didius boys. Clearly they were hard men.

I could hear Varga moaning. My father held him fast, sometimes shaking him absent-mindedly. On my return he threw the painter down, and helped me lift an ornamental folding door off its bronze fastenings. Gasping for air, Varga had hardly moved. We picked him up again, spread-eagled him, and lashed him to the door. Then we heaved the door up against the wall, opposite the one Varga was supposed to paint. I coiled the spare rope tidily, like a halyard on a ship's deck. The rope still had the damp cloths on it, which added to the unreal effect.

Varga hung there on the door. We had turned it so that he was upside down.

Good plasterwork is very expensive. It has to be painted while it's wet. A fresco painter who misses his moment has to pay from his wages for redoing the job.

Pa flung an arm across my shoulders. He addressed the face near his boots. 'Varga, this is my son. I hear you and Manlius have been singing false tunes to him!' Varga only whimpered.

Father and I walked across to the new wall. We sat down, either side of the wet patch, leaning back with our arms folded.

'Now, Varga,' Pa chivvied winningly.

I grinned through wicked teeth. 'He doesn't get it.'

'Oh he does,' murmured my father. 'You know, I think one of the saddest sights in the world is a fresco painter watching his plaster dry while he's tied up . . .' Father and I turned slowly to gaze at the drying plaster.

For five minutes Varga lasted out. He was red in the face but defiant.

'Tell us about Orontes,' I suggested. 'We know you know where he is.'

'Orontes has disappeared!' Varga spluttered.

'No, Varga,' Father told him in a pleasant tone, 'Orontes has not. Orontes was living at your dump on the Caelian quite recently. He repaired a Syrinx with a missing pipe for me only last April – his normal botched effort. I didn't pay him for it till November.' My father's business terms were the unfair ones that oppress small craftsmen who are too artistic to quibble. 'The cash was delivered to your doss!'

'We pinched it!' Varga tried brazenly.

213

'You forged the pig off his signet-ring for my invoice then – and which of you was supposed to have done my job for me?'

'Oh shove off, Geminus!'

'Well if that's his attitude – ' Pa hauled himself upright. 'I'm bored with this,' he said to me. Then he fiddled about with a pouch at his waist and pulled out a large knife.

XLV

'Oh come on, Pa,' I protested weakly. 'You'll frighten him. You know what cowards painters are!'

'I'm not going to hurt him much,' Pa assured me, with a wink. He flexed his arm as he wielded the knife. It was a stout kitchen effort, which I guessed he normally used to eat his lunch. 'If he won't talk, let's have a bit of fun – ' His eyes were dangerously bright; he was like a child at a goose fair.

Next minute my father drew back his arm, and threw the knife. It thonked into the door between the painter's legs, which we had tied apart – though not *that* far apart.

'Geminus!' screamed Varga, as his manhood was threatened.

I winced. 'Ooh! Could have been nasty . . .' Still amazed at Pa's aim, I scrambled to my feet as well, and whipped my own dagger from my boot.

Pa was inspecting his shot. 'Came a bit close to castrating the beggar . . . Maybe I'm not very good at this.'

'Maybe I'm worse!' I grinned, squaring up to the target.

Varga began to scream for help.

'Cut it out, Varga,' Pa told him benignly. 'Hold on, Marcus. We can't enjoy ourselves while he's squalling. Let me deal with him – ' In the tool-bag he had snaffled was a piece of rag. It stank, and was caked with something we could not identify. 'Probably poisonous; we'll gag him with this. Then you can really let rip – '

'Manlius knows!' wailed the fresco painter weakly. 'Orontes was his pal. Manlius knows where he is!'

We thanked him, but Pa gagged him with the oily rag anyway, and we left him hanging upside down on the door.

'Next time you're thinking of annoying the Didius boys – think twice!'

We found Manlius at the top of a scaffold. He was in the white room, painting the frieze.

'No, don't bother coming down; we'll come up to you . . .'

215

Both Father and I had nipped up his ladder before he knew what was happening. I grasped him by the hand, beaming like a friend.

'No, don't start being nice to him!' Pa instructed me curtly. 'We wasted too much time being pleasant with the other one. Give him the boot treatment!'

So much for auctioneers being civilised men of the arts. With a shrug of apology, I overpowered the painter, and pushed him to his knees.

Here there was no need to go off looking for rope; Manlius had his own for hauling up paint and other tools to his work platform. My father unwound this rapidly, hurling down the basket. Snarling horribly, he sawed through the rope. We used a short piece to tie up Manlius. Then Pa knotted the longer remaining length around his ankles. Without needing to consult one another we picked him up, and rolled him over the edge of the scaffold.

His cry as he found himself swinging in space broke off as we held him suspended on the rope. After he grew accustomed to his new situation, he just moaned.

'Where's Orontes?' He refused to say.

Pa muttered, 'Someone has either paid these nuts a fortune, or frightened them!'

'That's all right,' I answered, gazing over the edge at the painter. 'We'll have to frighten this one more!'

We climbed down to the ground. There was a plasterer's lime bath, which we dragged across the room so it was directly under Manlius. He hung about three feet above it, cursing us.

'What now, Pa? We could fill it with cement, drop him into it, let it set and then heave him into the Tiber. I think he'd sink – ' Manlius was holding out bravely. Maybe he thought that even in Rome, where the passers-by can be frivolous, it would be difficult to carry a man who was set in concrete through the streets without attracting attention from the aediles.

'There's plenty of paint; let's see what we can do with that!'

'Ever made plaster? Let's have a go . . .'

We had wonderful fun. We tipped quantities of dry plaster into the bath, poured in water, and stirred madly with a stick. Then we stiffened it with cattle hair. I found a kettle of white paint, so we tried adding that. The effect was revolting, encouraging us to experiment more wildly. We hunted through the painter's basket for colourings, whooping as we made great swirls in the mixture of gold, red, blue and black.

Plasterers use dung in their devious mysteries. We found sacks of the stuff and tipped it into our mud pie, commenting frequently on the smell.

I climbed back up on to the scaffold. Pausing only to pass a few well-informed comments on the riot of garlands, torches, vases, pigeons and bird-baths and cupids riding panthers from which Manlius had been creating his frieze, I unfastened the rope holding him. Leaning back on my heels, I let it slip slightly. Pa stood below, encouraging me.

'Down a bit! Few more inches – ' In a nerve-racking series of jerks, Manlius sank head first towards the plasterer's bath. 'Gently, this is the tricky bit – '

The painter lost his nerve and frantically tried to swing himself towards the scaffold; I paid out rope abruptly. He froze, whimpering.

'Tell us about Orontes!'

For one last second he shook his head furiously, keeping his eyes closed. Then I dunked him in the bath.

I dropped him just far enough to cover his hair. Then I pulled him out a few inches, refastened the rope, and nipped down to inspect my achievement. Pa was roaring unkindly. Manlius hung there, his once black hair now dripping a disgusting goo in white, with occasional red and blue streaks. The ghastly tide-line came up as far as his eyebrows, which were bushy enough to hold quite a weight of the thick white mess.

'Couldn't be better,' said Pa approvingly.

The painter's hair had formed itself into ludicrous spikes. Grasping his inert body, I spun him gently between my hands. He turned one way, then lazily came back. Pa halted his progress with the stirring stick.

'Now, Manlius. Just a few sensible words will get you out of this. But if you're not going to help us, I might as well let my crazy son drop you right into the bath . . .'

Manlius closed his eyes. 'Oh gods . . .'

'Tell us about Orontes,' I said, playing the quiet one of our pair.

'He's not in Rome – '

'He *was* in Rome!' Pa roared.

Manlius was cracking. 'He thought it was safe to come back. He's gone again – '

'What was he frightened of?'

'I don't know . . .' We let him swing round in another circle; being upside down must have become quite painful by now. 'Of people asking questions – '

'Who? Censorinus? Laurentius? Us?'

'All of you.'

'So *why* is he frightened? What has he done, Manlius?'

'I really don't know. Something big. He never would tell me – '

A feeling was growing. I grabbed Manlius by the ear. 'Was my brother Festus annoyed with him?'

'Probably . . .'

'Something to do with a lost statue, was it?' asked Father.

'Or a statue that was not lost at all,' I growled. 'From a ship that never sank – '

'The ship sank!' croaked Manlius. 'That's the truth of it. Orontes told me when he was getting out of Rome to avoid Festus. The ship with the statue sank; that's the honest truth!'

'What else did he tell you?'

'Nothing! Oh cut me down – '

'Why did he tell you nothing? He's your chum, isn't he?'

'Matter of trust . . .' Manlius whispered, as if he was afraid even to mention it. 'He's been paid a lot of money to keep quiet . . .' I could believe these romantic politicians would actually honour such a trust, even if the villains who bribed them were the worst kind of criminals. This lot probably lacked the moral scepticism to recognise true villainy.

'Who paid him?'

'I don't know!' His desperation told us this was almost certainly true.

'Let's get this straight,' Geminus nagged ominously. 'When Festus came to Rome looking for him, Orontes heard about it and deliberately skipped?' Manlius tried to nod. It was difficult in his position. Paint and wet plaster dribbled from his hair. He blinked his eyes fretfully. 'After Festus died, Orontes thought he could come back?'

'He likes to work . . .'

'He likes to cause a heap of shit for the Didius family! And now every time anyone else starts asking questions, your wily pal does another bunk?' Another feeble nod; more turgid drips. 'So answer me this, you pathetic runt – where does the coward run off to when he leaves Rome?'

'Capua,' groaned Manlius. 'He lives in Capua.'

'Not for long!' I said.

We left the painter hanging from his scaffold, though on our way out we did mention to the watchman that there seemed to be something odd going on in the Sabine triclinium and the white reception room. He muttered that he would go and have a look when he had finished his game of draughts.

Pa and I walked into the street, kicking pebbles morosely. There was no doubt about it; if we wanted to sort out this mystery, one of us would have to go to Capua.

'Do we believe that's where Orontes is?'

'I reckon so,' I decided. 'Manlius and Varga had already mentioned that they stayed in Campania recently – I bet they went down there to visit their pal in hiding.'

'You'd better be right, Marcus!'

In March, the long flog down to Campania just to wrench some sordid tale from a sculptor held no promise that appealed to this particular member of the rampaging Didius boys.

On the other hand, with so much at stake in my promise to Mother, I could not allow my father to go instead.

LXVI

We had been in the far north of the city; we made our way gloomily south. This time we walked at merely a brisk pace. My father was still not talking.

We reached the Saepta Julia. Pa carried on. I was so used to marching alongside him into trouble that at first I said nothing, but eventually I tackled him: 'I thought we were going back to the Saepta?'

'I'm not going to the Saepta.'

'I can see that. The Saepta's behind us.'

'I was never going to the Saepta. I told you where we were going when we were at the Carus house.'

'Home, you said.'

'That's where I'm going,' said my father. 'You can please your pompous self.'

Home! He meant where he lived with his redhead.

I did not believe this could be happening.

I had never yet been inside the house where my father lived, though I reckoned Festus had been no stranger there. My mother would never forgive me if I went now. I was not part of Pa's new life; I would never be. The only reason I kept walking was that it would be a gross discourtesy to abandon a man of his age who had had a bad shock at the Carus house, and with whom I had just shared a rumpus. He was out in Rome without his normal bodyguards. He was under threat of violence from Carus and Servia. He was paying me for protection. The least I could do was to see he reached his house safely.

He let me trudge all the way from the Saepta Julia, past the Flaminian Circus, the Porticus of Octavia and the Theatre of Marcellus. He dragged me right under the shadow of the Arx and the Capitol. He towed me on reluctantly, past the end of Tiber Island, the old Cattle Market Forum, a whole litter of temples and the Sublician and Probus Bridges.

Then he let me wait while he fumbled for his doorkey, failed to

220

find it, and banged the bell to be let in. He let me slouch after him inside his neat entrance suite. He flung off his cloak, peeled off his boots, gestured brusquely for me to do likewise – and only when I was barefoot and feeling vulnerable did he admit scornfully, 'You can relax! She's not here.'

The reprieve nearly made me faint.

Pa shot me a disgusted look. I let him know it was mutual. 'I set her up in a small business to stop her nosing into mine. On Tuesdays she always goes there to pay the wages and do the accounts.'

'It's not a Tuesday!' I pointed out grumpily.

'They had some trouble there last week and now she's having some work done to the property. Anyway, she'll be out all day.'

I sat on a coffer while he stomped off to speak to his steward. Someone brought me a pair of spare sandals and took my boots to clean the mud off them. As well as this slave, and the boy who had opened the door to us, I saw several other faces. When Pa reappeared I commented, 'Your billet's well staffed.'

'I like people round about me.' I had always thought having too many people around him was the main reason he had left us.

'These are slaves.'

'So I'm a liberal. I treat my slaves like children.'

'I'd like to riposte, and you treated your children like slaves!' Our eyes met. 'I won't. It would be unjust.'

'Don't descend to forced politeness, Marcus! Just feel free to be yourself,' he commented, with the long-practised sarcasm peculiar to families.

Pa lived in a tall, rather narrow house on the waterfront. This damp location was highly desired because of its view across the Tiber, so plots were small. The houses suffered badly from flooding; I noticed that the ground floor here was painted plainly in fairly dark colours. Left to myself, I looked into the rooms attached to the hallway. They were being used by the slaves, or were set up as offices where visitors could be interviewed. One was even stuffed with sandbags for emergency use. The only furniture comprised large stone coffers that would remain unaffected by damp.

Upstairs all that changed. Wrinkling my nose at the unfamiliar smell of a strange house, I followed my father to the first floor. Our

221

feet trampled a grand Eastern carpet. He had this luxurious item spread on the floor in regular use, not hung safely on the wall. In fact everything he had brought home – which meant plenty – was there to be used.

We marched through a series of small, crowded rooms. They were clean, but jammed with treasures. The wall paint was all elderly and fading. It had been done to a basic standard, probably twenty years ago when Pa and his woman moved here, and not touched since. It suited him. The plainish red, yellow and sea-blue rooms with conventional dados and cornices were the best foil for my father's large, ever-changing collection of furniture and vases, not to mention the curios and interesting trinkets any auctioneer obtains by the crate. It was organised chaos, however. You could live here, if you liked clutter. The impression was established and comfortable, its taste set by people who pleased themselves.

I tried not to get too interested in the artefacts; they were astonishing, but I knew they were now doomed. As Pa walked ahead of me, sometimes glancing at a piece as he passed it, I had the impression he was secure, in a way I did not remember from when he lived with us. He knew where everything was. Everything was here because he wanted it – which extended to the scarf-maker, presumably.

He brought me to a room that could be either his private den or where he sat with his woman conversing. (He had bills and invoices scattered about and a dismantled lamp he was mending, but I noticed a small spindle poking out from under a cushion.) Thick woollen rugs rumpled underfoot. There were two couches, side-tables, various quaint bronze miniatures, lamps and log baskets. On the wall hung a set of theatrical masks – possibly not my father's choice. On a shelf stood an extremely good blue-glass cameo vase, over which he did sigh briefly.

'Losing that one is going to hurt! Wine?' He produced the inevitable flagon from a shelf near his couch. Alongside the couch he had an elegant yard-high gilded fawn, positioned so he could pat its head like a pet.

'No thanks. I'll go on tending the hangover.'

He stayed his hand, without pouring for himself. For a moment he gazed at me. 'You don't give an inch, do you?' I understood, and glared back silently. 'I've managed to get you inside the door –

but you're as friendly as a bailiff. Less,' he added. 'I never knew a bailiff refuse a cup of wine.'

I said nothing. It would be a striking irony if I set out to find my dead brother, only to end up making friends with my father instead. I don't believe in that kind of irony. We had had a good day getting ourselves into all sorts of trouble – and that was the end of it.

My father put down the flagon and his empty cup.

'Come and see my garden, then!' he ordered me.

We walked back through all the rooms until we reached the stairs. To my surprise, he led me up another flight; I assumed I was about to partake in some perverse joke. But we came to a low arch, closed by an oak door. Pa shot open the bolts, and stood back for me to duck my head and step out first.

It was a roof-garden. It had troughs filled with plants, bulbs, even small trees. Shaped trellises were curtained with roses and ivy. At the parapet more roses were trained along chains like garlands. There, between tubs of box trees, stood two lion-ended seats, providing a vista right across the water to Caesar's Gardens, the Transtiberina, the whale-backed ridge of the Ianiculan.

'Oh this is not fair,' I managed to grin feebly.

'Got you!' he scoffed. He must have known I had inherited a deep love of greenery from Ma's side of the family.

He made to steer me to a seat, but I was already at the parapet drinking in the panorama. 'Oh you lucky old bastard! So who does the garden?'

'I planned it. I had to have the roof strengthened. Now you know why I keep so many slaves; it's no joke carrying water and soil up three flights in buckets. I spend a lot of my spare time up here . . .'

He would. I would have done the same.

We took a bench each. It was companionable, yet we remained distinct. I could cope with that.

'Right,' he said. 'Capua!'

'I'll go.'

'I'm coming with you.'

'Don't bother. I can rough up a sculptor, however devious. At least we know that he's devious before I start.'

223

'Sculptors are all devious! There are a lot of them in Capua. You don't even know what he looks like. I'm coming, so don't argue. I know Orontes, and what's more, I know Capua.' Of course, he had lived there for years.

'I can find my way round some two-mule Campanian village,' I snarled disparagingly.

'Oh no. Helena Justina doesn't want you being robbed by every low-season pickpocket and picking up floozies – '

I was about to ask if that was what had happened when he went there, but of course when Pa ran off to Capua, he took his own floozie.

'What about leaving the business?'

'Mine is a well-run outfit, thanks; it can stand a few days without me. Besides,' he said, 'madam can make decisions if any snags arise.'

I was surprised to learn the scarf-maker commanded so much trust, or even that she involved herself. For some reason I had always viewed her as a negative figure. My father seemed the type whose views on women's social role were stiff and traditional. Still, it did not follow that the scarf-maker agreed with him.

We heard the door open behind us. Thinking about Father's redhead, I looked round quickly, afraid I should see her. A slave edged out with a large tray, no doubt as a result of Pa's talk with his steward. The tray went on to a bird-bath, creating a makeshift table. 'Have some lunch, Marcus.'

It was mid-afternoon, but we had missed other refreshment. Pa helped himself. He left me to make my own decision, so on that basis I conceded the issue and tucked in.

It was nothing elaborate, just a snack someone had thrown together for the master when he came home unexpectedly. But as snacks go, it was tasty. 'What's the fish?'

'Smoked eel.'

'Very nice.'

'Try it with a drop of damson sauce.'

'Is this what they call Alexandrine?'

'Probably. I just call it bloody good. Am I winning you round?' my father asked evilly.

'No, but pass the rolls, will you.'

There were two strips of eel left; we jabbed at them with our knives, like children fighting over titbits.

224

'A man called Hirrius had an eel-farm,' Pa began obliquely, though somehow I knew he would be working around to discussing our own precarious position. 'Hirrius sold his eel-farm for four million sesterces. It was a famous sale; I wish I had handled it! Now you and I could do with just one pool like that.'

I breathed slowly, licking sauce from my fingers. 'Half a million . . . I'll come in with you, but that's not much of an offer. I've been trying to raise four hundred thousand. I suppose I may have collected ten per cent so far.' That was optimistic. 'I refrained from pricing up your lovely chattels, but the picture's bleak for both of us.'

'True.' My father seemed surprisingly unworried, however.

'Don't you care? You have obviously assembled a wealth of good things here – yet you told Carus and Servia you would sell.'

'Selling things is my trade,' he answered tersely. Then he confirmed, 'You're right. To cover the debt means stripping the house. Most of the stuff at the Saepta belongs to other people; selling for customers is what auctioneering is about.'

'Your personal investment is all in this house?'

'Yes. The house itself is freehold. That cost me – and I'm not intending to mortgage it now. I don't keep much cash with bankers; it's vulnerable.'

'So how healthy are you on the sesterces front?'

'Not as healthy as you think.' If he could seriously talk of finding half a million, he was filthy rich by my standards. Like all men who don't have to worry, he liked grousing. 'There are plenty of demands. Bribes and easements required at the Saepta; I pay my whack to the Guild for our dinners and the funeral fund. Since the store was raided, I've some big losses to cover, not to mention compensating the people whose auction was knocked apart that time you were there.' He could have added, *I still give your mother an annuity*. I knew he did. I also knew she spent his money on her grandchildren; I paid her rent myself. 'I'll have a bare house when I finish with Carus,' he sighed. 'But I've had that before. I'll come back.'

'You're too old to have to start again.' He must be too old to feel sure he could manage it. By rights, he should now have been able to retire to some country farm. 'Why are you doing it? For big brother's reputation?'

'My own, more likely. I'd rather sneer at a stick like Carus than let Carus sneer at me. What about you?' he challenged.

'I was the hero's executor.'

'Well I was his partner.'

'In this?'

'No, but does it matter, Marcus? If he'd asked me to come in on a Phidias I would have leapt at it. Let me handle the debt. I've had my life. You don't need to ruin your chance of making things legal with your senator's daughter.'

'Maybe I never had any chance,' I admitted dismally.

Another of the discreet house slaves paddled up, this time bringing us a steaming jug of honey and wine. He poured for us both without asking, so I accepted the cup. The drink was headily laced with Indian spikenard. My father had come a long way from the days when all we drank at home was old wine lees, well watered down, with the odd vervain leaf to disguise the taste.

Light clung to the distant sky with a fragile grip as the afternoon drew in. In the grey haze across the river I could just see the Ianiculan Hill running away to the right. There was a house over there which I once dreamed of owning, a house where I had wanted to live with Helena.

'Will she leave you?' Pa must have read my thoughts.

'She should.'

'I didn't ask what she *ought* to do!'

I smiled. 'She won't ask it either, knowing her.'

He sat quiet for a time. He liked Helena, I knew that.

Suddenly I leaned forward, resting my elbows on my knees, cradling my cup. Something had struck me. 'What did Festus do with the money?'

'The half-million?' Pa rubbed his nose. He had the same nose as me: straight down from the forehead without a bump between the eyebrows. 'Olympus knows!'

'I never found it.'

'And I never saw it either.'

'So what did he tell you about it when he was mentioning the Phidias?'

'Festus,' drawled my father, with some exasperation, 'never gave me any idea the Phidias had been paid for by the collectors! That I only learned from Carus and Servia well afterwards.'

I sat back again. 'They really did pay him? Is there any chance this receipt of theirs is forged?'

Pa sighed. 'I wanted to think so. I looked at it very hard, believe me. It was convincing. Go and see it – '

I shook my head. I hate to pile up misery.

I could think up no new queries. Now Orontes Mediolanus was our only lead.

We spent some time (it felt about two hours) arguing about arrangements for getting to Capua. By Didius standards this was fairly refined. Even so, all my sensible plans for lessening the agony of a long, tiring journey were overturned. I wanted to ride down there at the fastest speed possible, do the business, then pelt home. Pa insisted his old bones were no longer able to endure a horse. He decided to arrange a carriage, from some stable he vaguely specified as a meeting-place. We came near to agreeing terms for sharing expenses. There was some discussion about a departure time, though this remained unclear. The Didius family hates to upset itself by settling practicalities.

Yet another servant appeared, on the excuse of collecting the tray. He and Pa exchanged a glance that could have been a signal. 'You'll be wanting to leave soon,' hinted my father.

Nobody mentioned the woman he lived with, but her presence in the house had become tangible.

He was right. If she was there, I wanted to disappear. He took me downstairs. I pulled on my cloak and boots hurriedly, then fled.

Luck was against me as usual. The last thing I felt able to cope with happened: not two streets from Father's house, while still feeling like a traitor, I ran into Ma.

XLVII

Guilt settled on me like an extra cloak.

'Where are you sneaking from?'

We stood on a corner. Every passer-by must have been able to tell I was a son in deep trouble. Every lax villain on the Aventine would be chuckling all the way to the next drinking-house, glad it was not him.

Honesty pays, people tell you. 'I've been enjoying the entertainments of my father's smart town house.'

'I thought you looked sick!' sniffed Ma. 'I brought you up to avoid places where you might catch a disease!'

'It was clean,' I said wearily.

'What about the little job I asked you to help sort out for me?' From the way she spoke, I was thought to have forgotten it.

'Your "little job" was what got me arrested the other day – Helena, too. I'm working on it. That's why I had to go to Pa's. I've been running around on your commission all today, and tomorrow I have to go to Capua – '

'Why Capua?' she demanded. For obvious reasons Capua had long been a dirty word in our circle. That pleasant town was a byword for immorality and deceit, though apart from having once played host to my absconding father, all Capua ever did was to overcharge holidaying tourists on their way to Oplontis and Baiae, and grow lettuce.

'A sculptor lives there. He was involved with Festus. I'm going to talk to him about that business deal.'

'On your own?'

'No. Pa insists on coming with me,' I admitted. Ma let out a terrible wail. 'Mother, I cannot help it if your estranged husband starts claiming his paternal rights belatedly.'

'So you're going together!' She made it sound like the deepest treachery. 'I would have thought you'd want to avoid that!'

I wanted to avoid the whole journey. 'At least he can identify the sculptor. The man is now our only hope of sorting out this

228

business – which I warn you, is likely to prove expensive in every way.'

'I can lend you a few sesterces – '

'A few sesterces are nowhere near enough. The price of extracting our family from this problem is about half a million.'

'Oh Marcus, you always did exaggerate!'

'Fact, Ma.' She was trembling. I would be trembling myself if I said 'half a million' too many more times. 'Don't worry. This is men's business. Geminus and I will deal with it – but you have to accept the consequences. Finding so much to clear up my brother's problem puts paid to any hope in Hades that I can marry Helena. Just so you know. I don't want any nagging on the subject. It's out of my hands – and we have our beloved Festus to blame for everything.'

'You never liked your poor brother!'

'I loved him, Ma – but I certainly don't like what he has done to me now.'

I saw my mother lift her chin. 'Perhaps the whole business would be better left alone . . .'

'Ma, that is impossible.' I felt tired and cold. 'Other people will not let us forget it. Look, I'm going home. I need to see Helena.'

'If you're going to Capua with that man,' advised my mother, 'take Helena to look after you!'

'Helena's just returned from one long journey; the last thing she wants is a trip to deepest Campania.' Not, anyway, with a raddled old auctioneer and a hangdog informer who had never in his life been so depressed.

My mother reached up and tidied my hair. 'Helena will manage. She won't want you on your own in bad company.' I wanted to say, '*Ma, I'm thirty, not five years old!*' but arguing never got me anywhere with Mother.

Most people would think that a senator's daughter who abandoned herself to a low-life informer *was* bad company.

But the thought of taking Helena on one last fling before I was bankrupt did cheer me up.

At home, Helena Justina was waiting for me.

Dinner was eel again. A vast consignment must have wriggled

into market that morning. The whole of Rome was sitting down to the same menu.

Dinner was normally my province. Since I reckoned my beloved had been brought up merely to behave chastely and look decorative, I had laid down a rule that I would buy and cook our food. Helena accepted the rule, but sometimes when she knew I was busy and was afraid of not getting fed that night, out she would rush to provide us with an unscheduled treat. My ramshackle kitchen made her nervous, but she was perfectly competent at following the recipes she had once read out to her servants. Tonight she had poached her offering in a saffron sauce. It was delicious. I munched it down gallantly while she watched me eat every mouthful, searching for signs of approval.

I sat back and surveyed her. She was beautiful. I was going to lose her. Somehow I had to tell her the news.

'How was your day with your father?'

'Wonderful! We played about with some collecting snobs, had fun picking on some artists, and now we're planning a bad boys' outing. Would you like to go to Capua?'

'I may not like it, but I'll tag along.'

'I warn you, Pa and I are established as the fabulous Didius muckers – a rough pair whose very name can clear a street. You'll be coming to impose some sobriety.'

'That's a pity,' Helena told me, with a glint in her eye. 'I was hoping I could be a loose woman who keeps a gold piece down her cleavage and swears horrendously at ferrymen.'

'Maybe I like that idea better,' I grinned.

False jollity gave me away. Seeing I needed consolation she sat on my lap and tickled my chin. In the hope of this kind of mistreatment, I had been barbered in Fountain Court before I came up. 'What's the matter, Marcus?'

I told her.

Helena said she could dispense with being middle-class and married. I suppose that meant she had never expected it to happen anyway.

I said I was sorry.

She said she could see that.

I held her tight, knowing that I ought to send her back to her father, and knowing I was glad that she would never agree to go.

230

'I'll wait for you, Marcus.'

'You'll wait for ever then.'

'Ah well!' She amused herself making small plaits in my hair. 'Tell me what happened today?'

'Oh . . . my father and I just proved that if different members of the Didius family combine efforts to solve a problem – '

Helena Justina was already laughing. 'What?'

'Two of us can make even more of a mess of it than one!'

XLVIII

Horace once took a journey down the Via Appia. He describes it as a farrago of crooked landlords, potholes, house fires, gritty bread and infected eyes; of being packed into a ferry to cross the Pontine Marshes, then without explanation being left motionless for hours; of staying awake half the night all keyed up for an assignation with a girl who never bothered to turn up . . .

Compared to us, Horace had it soft. Horace was travelling as minutes secretary to a summit conference of Triumvirs. He had rich patrons and intellectual company; Virgil, no less, to pick the burs off his riding-cloak. He stayed in private houses where they burned pans of sweet oil to welcome him. We stayed in public inns (when they were not closed up for winter). In place of Virgil I took my father, whose conversation fell several hexameters short of epic poetry.

However, unlike Horace, I had a hamper thrust upon me by my mother with not only good Roman bread but enough smoked Lucanian sausage to last a month. And I took my own girl. So I had the comfort of knowing that had I not been completely exhausted by travel, she would have been smilingly available any night of my choice.

One thing Horace did not have to do on his trip to Tarentum was visit his Great-Auntie Phoebe and a host of morose country relatives. (If he did, he left it right out of the *Satire*; and if his relatives were like mine, I don't blame him for that.)

There were three reasons for visiting the market garden. First: Phoebe herself, who would have heard about Helena and who was overdue for an introduction if I ever wanted a bowl of her rocket soup again. Second: so we could leave Geminus at the nearby mansio where the dead Censorinus, and possibly his centurion pal Laurentius, had stayed. Pa could not nowadays visit the market garden due to what passes for tact in our family; instead he was instructed to make himself at home at the inn, buy the landlord a

232

large one, and find out what the soldier (or perhaps two soldiers) had been up to. The third reason for going was to investigate my brother's store.

Much is made of the Great Roman country estates staffed by thousands of slaves for the benefit of absentee senators. You hear less about subsistence farms like the one my mother's brothers ran, but they are there. Outside Rome itself and many another town, poor people scrape a living for large families who swallow any profit, slogging away, year after year, with little more than bad tempers to show for it. At least on the Campania there was decent soil, with fast roads to a voracious market when anything grew.

That had been how my parents met. On a trip to Rome, Ma had sold Pa some doubtful brassicas, then when he went back to complain, she coyly let him take her for a cup of wine. Three weeks later, with what must have seemed at the time like country acumen, she married him.

I tried to explain the set-up to Helena as we drove down the track. 'My grandfather and Great-Uncle Scaro originally shared the farm; now at various times one or two of Ma's brothers run the place. They are a raggedy set of characters, and I can't say which we'll find here. They are always going off for a foreign love affair, or to recover from a fit of remorse because their cart ran over a grass-cutter. Then, just when someone is delivering twins on the kitchen table and the radish crop has failed, they arrive home unexpectedly, all eager to rape the goatherd's teenage daughter and full of mad ideas for horticultural change. Be prepared. There's bound to have been at least one ferocious quarrel, some adultery, a dead ox poisoned by a neighbour, and a fatal accident in the nuttery since I last came. Unless Uncle Fabius discovers he had an illegitimate son by a woman with a weak heart who is threatening a lawsuit, he counts the day lost.'

'Isn't it rather inconvenient on a farm with work to do?'

'Farms are lively places!' I warned.

'True! We must expect people who spend all day dealing with Nature's bounty of life and death and growth to have seething emotions to match.'

'Don't mock, woman! I spent half my childhood on this farm. Whenever there was trouble at home we were sent here to recuperate.'

233

'It sounds the wrong place for a rest!'

'People on farms can handle trouble as easily as pulling salad leaves . . . Let me continue with the briefing, or we'll arrive before I've done. At the centre of all this strife, Great-Auntie Phoebe occupies the hearth like a rock, making polenta that would halt an epidemic and holding everyone together.'

'Your grandfather's sister?'

'No, she's his unmarried second wife. My grandmother died early – '

'Worn out by the excitement?' suggested Helena.

'Don't be romantic! Worn out by childbearing. Phoebe was a slave originally, then Grandpa's comfort for years. It happens all the time. For as long as I can remember they shared one bed, one table, and all the hard work my uncles had no time for because of their fascinating social lives. Grandpa made her a freedwoman and was always intending to marry her, but never got around to it –'

'I see nothing wrong with that, if they were happy,' said Helena, in a stern voice.

'Neither do I,' I replied, suavely deleting any tone of criticism. 'Except Phoebe is ashamed of it. You'll find her very diffident.'

Helena thought all my stories a joke until we got there.

Great-Auntie Phoebe was spinning imperturbably beside the hearth. She was a small, sweet, round-cheeked woman who looked as frail as grass but had more strength than three grown men. This was just as well, since while the others were being introspective about their personal lives she had to harvest cabbage and turn a fork in the manure heap. Not so much lately. She was probably eighty, and had decreed that delivering a calf was now beyond her dignity.

She had a passionate interest in our entire family, based on the fact she had nursed most of us through colic and adolescence. Festus had been her favourite, needless to say. ('That limb!')

Uncle Fabius was away from home for dark reasons no one would specify.

'Same trouble again?' I grinned at Phoebe.

'He never learns!' she whispered, shaking her head.

Uncle Junius was here, spending his time complaining about the absent Fabius. Well, his free time anyway. His main energy was taken up with a rapidly failing carp-farm and his efforts to seduce a woman called Armilla, wife of a neighbouring, much more prosperous, landowner.

'Leading him on?' I demanded, showing Helena how to read the code.

'How did you know?' clucked Phoebe, breaking off her thread.

'Heard it before.'

'Ah well!'

There had been a third brother once – but we were not allowed to mention him at all.

All the time we appeared to be talking about my uncles, the real subject under scrutiny was my new girlfriend. It was the first time I had brought anyone other than Petronius Longus (mainly because I used to come on holiday when both the grapes and the girls were ripe, with obvious intentions to enjoy both).

Helena Justina sat, dark-eyed and gracious, accepting the ritual scrutiny. She was an educated girl, who knew when to curb her ferocious temperament or else condemn us to thirty years of the family accusation that she had never wanted to fit in.

'Marcus has never brought one of his Roman friends to see the farm before,' commented Great-Auntie Phoebe, letting it be understood that she was referring to my female acquaintances, that she knew there had been many, and that she was relieved I had finally found one who must have displayed an interest in growing leeks. I grinned amiably. There was nothing else to do.

'I'm very honoured,' said Helena. 'I've heard a lot about you all.'

Auntie Phoebe looked embarrassed, thinking this must be a disapproving reference to her unsanctioned relationship with my free and easy grandpapa.

'I hope you don't mind if I mention this,' Helena went on. 'About sleeping arrangements. Marcus and I usually share a room, though we are not married, I'm afraid. I hope you're not shocked. It's not his fault, but I've always believed a woman should keep her independence if no children are involved . . .'

'That's a new one on me!' cackled Phoebe, who apparently liked the idea.

'It's new to me,' I replied, more nervously. 'I was hoping for the safety of respectability!'

Helena and my great-aunt exchanged a witty glance.

'That's men for you – they have to pretend!' Phoebe exclaimed. She was a wise old lady whom I held in great affection, even though we were not related (or more likely because of it).

Uncle Junius grumpily agreed to take me to the store. On the way out, I noticed Helena staring curiously at the little semi-circular niche where the household gods were displayed. There was also a ceramic head of Fabius, with flowers reverently laid before it by Phoebe, who always honoured the memory of any absent uncle (except, of course, the one who was not talked about). She had another bust of Junius on a nearby shelf, ready for the honorific treatment the next time *he* flitted. Back in the niche, between the conventional bronze statues of dancing Lares bearing their horns of plenty, lay a dusty set of teeth.

'Still got those then?' I chivvied, trying to make light of it.

'It's where he always kept them overnight,' replied Uncle Junius. 'Phoebe put them there before the funeral, and no one has the heart to remove them now.'

I had to explain to Helena. 'Great-Uncle Scaro, one of life's eccentrics, once had his mouth attended to by an Etruscan dentist. Thereafter he became a passionate devotee of Etruscan bridge-work – which is a high art form, if you can afford the gold wire. Eventually poor Scaro had no teeth left to attach the wires to, and no money, come to that. So he tried to invent his own false teeth.'

'Are those them?' Helena enquired politely.

'Yup!' said Junius.

'Goodness. Did they work?'

'Yup!' Junius was plainly wondering if the senator's daughter might be a candidate for his doleful attentions. Helena, who had a fine sense of discretion, kept close to me.

'These were model four,' I reminisced. Uncle Scaro thought a lot of me; he always kept me informed on the progress of his inventive schemes. I thought best to omit that some teeth on model four had come from a dead dog. 'They worked perfectly. You could chew an ox bone with them. You could tackle nuts, or fruit with pips. Unfortunately, Scaro choked on them.'

Helena looked heartbroken.

'Don't worry,' said Uncle Junius kindly. 'He would have seen it

236

as part of his research. Swallowing them by accident was just how the old beggar would have wanted to go.'

Uncle Scaro's teeth smiled gently from the lararium as if he were still wearing them.

He would have liked my new girlfriend. I wished he were here to see her. It gave me a pang to leave Helena standing there, solemnly dusting his teeth with the end of her stole.

There was very little of interest in the store. Just a few broken wicker chairs, a chest with its lid staved in, a dented bucket and some straw-dust.

Also, standing at the back like a row of gloomy tombstones for Cyclops, four huge rectangular blocks of quarried stone.

'What are those, Junius?'

My uncle shrugged. A life of confusion and intrigue had made him wary of asking questions. He was afraid he might discover a long-lost heir with a claim on his land, or the taint of a witch's prophecy that could blight his efforts with the neighbour's luscious wife or get him into a ten-year feud with the ox-cart mender. 'Something Festus must have left,' he mumbled nervously.

'Did he say anything about them?'

'I wasn't here then.'

'Off with a woman?'

He gave me a nasty look. 'Bloody Fabius might know.'

If Fabius knew, Phoebe knew as well. We walked thoughtfully back to the house.

Great-Auntie Phoebe was telling Helena about the time a crazy horseman whom we later discovered might have been the Emperor Nero fleeing from Rome to commit suicide (a minor aspect, the way Phoebe told it), galloped too fast past the market garden and killed half her chickens in the road. She did not know what the stone blocks were, but told me Festus had brought them on that famous last leave of his. I did find out from her, however, that two men who must have been Censorinus and Laurentius had come to the farm asking questions some months ago.

'They wanted to know if Festus had left anything here.'

'Did they mention the stone blocks?'

'No. They were very secretive.'

'Did you show them the store?'

237

'No. You know Fabius – ' I did. He was a suspicious bastard at the best of times. 'He just took them out to an old barn we have full of ploughing equipment, then he played the country idiot.'

'So what happened?'

'It was down to me as usual.' Great-Auntie Phoebe liked to be seen as a woman of character.

'How did you get rid of them?'

'I showed them Scaro's teeth on the lararium and said those were all we had left of the last unwanted stranger – then I set the dogs on them.'

Next day we set off south again. I told Pa about the four blocks of stone. We both pondered the mystery without comment, but I was starting to have ideas, and if I knew him he was too.

He told me Censorinus and another soldier had stayed at the mansio.

'Old news!' Helena and I relayed Phoebe's tale.

'So I wasted my time! It was a lousy inn,' moaned my father. 'I suppose you two were being pampered in the lap of luxury?'

'We were!' I assured him. 'If you can stand hearing about Phoebe's chickens, and listening to Junius complaining about his brother, then it's a grand place to stay!' Pa knew that.

'I expect Junius had his eye on your girl?' he hinted, trying to annoy me in return. Helena raised the elegant curves of her eyebrows.

'He was thinking about it. I nearly took him on one side and had a quiet word – but if I know Junius, warning him against it is the certain way to make him do something.'

Pa agreed. 'It's as pointless as shouting "He's behind you!" when the Spook starts looming at the Honest Old Father in an Atellan farce . . . Where was drippy Fabius?'

'Off with his old trouble.'

'I can never remember what his trouble is.'

'Neither can I,' I confessed. 'Either gambling or boils, I think. He ran away to be a gladiator once, but that was only a passing aberration when he wanted to avoid the lupin harvest.'

'Phoebe asked after you, Didius Geminus,' said Helena in a stern voice. She seemed to think we were being frivolous in our discussion of the family news.

238

'I suppose the actual enquiry was, "How's that useless city mollock who fathered you?" ' grunted Pa to me. He knew what they all thought.

He had always known. Being constantly despised by my mother's peculiar relatives must have been one of the trials that had eventually proved too dreary to endure.

IXL

Capua.

Capua, Queen of the central plain (and home of smart fleas).

Capua, the most spendidly flourishing city in rich Campania (if you listen to the Capuans) or even in Italy (if you get stuck with one of those who has never seen Rome).

Do not fail to view the grand Augustan amphitheatre, which stands four storeys high with its eighty great arches all capped with marble deities – though it is more recent than Spartacus, so don't get romantic political ideas. Also, while viewing this splendid edifice, keep your eyes in the back of your head and your hand on your purse. The people of Capua earn their livelihood from visitors, and they do not always ask before claiming it. Never forget: they are so flourishing because we are so stupid. What's yours can become theirs very rapidly in Capua.

When Capua opened its doors and its heart to Hannibal, it is said that its luxury sapped his men so much that he never won another battle. We could have endured some luxury of this disgraceful quality, but things have changed since then.

We drove into Capua on a wet Monday evening, in time to find all the eateries closing up. One carriage-horse went lame just as we reached the forum, giving us an uneasy sensation that it might not be possible to drive home when we wanted to escape. My father, who had come to protect us with his special knowledge of this area, had his money pinched within two minutes. Luckily, our main cash was hidden under the floor of our carriage, with Helena's sensible feet guarding it.

'I'm out of practice,' grumbled Pa.

'That's all right. I always make a mess of choosing my travelling companions and end up nursemaiding incompetents.'

'Thanks!' muttered Helena.

'You were not included.'

'My hero!'

After ten days of misery, which ought to have been a bare

week of mild pain, we were all on the edge of rebellion.

I found us a lodging-house in the usual hurried rush when darkness is descending so fast you close your eyes to the drawbacks. It was right next to the market so there would be a racket in the morning, not to mention cats yowling on the rubbish and ladies of the night plying their trade under the empty stalls. The fleas were lying in wait with little smiling faces, though they at least had some tact and stayed invisible at first. The ladies of the night were out and about already: they stood in a line silently watching us unload the coach.

Looking for cash boxes their pimps could come and lift, no doubt.

Helena wrapped our money in a cloak and carried it into the boarding-house in a bundle over her shoulder like a tired child.

'Marcus, I don't like this . . .'

'I'm here to take care of you.' She was not reassured. 'Father and I will chalk up a message on the basilica saying, "*Anyone who rapes, robs or kidnaps Helena Justina, will have to answer to the ferocious Didius boys!*" '

'Wonderful,' she said. 'I hope your fame has reached this far.'

'Indubitably!' responded Pa. Long words had always been a form of bluff in the Didius family.

It was an uncomfortable night. Luckily by the time we went to bed, having failed to find an edible dinner, we were prepared for the worst.

Next day we moved to another boarding-house, providing more easy silver for another cheating landlord, and delight to another pack of fleas.

We started to visit artists' studios. All claimed they had never heard of Orontes. All of them had to be lying. Capua thought a great deal of itself but it was, frankly, not that big. Orontes must have been going round for weeks glueing up mouths on the off chance that someone or other might follow him here.

We stopped asking.

We moved to yet another lodging-house and kept our heads down, while Father and I started to watch the forum from doorways and arches where we could not be seen.

Hanging around the forum of a strange town, in the middle of winter, when there is a gap in the local festivals, can make a man depressed.

Helena told us on our return to the current doss-house that there were no fleas, but she had definitely found bedbugs and an ostler had tried to get into the room with her when we left her on her own.

He tried again that night when both Pa and I were sitting there. Afterwards we argued for hours about whether he knew there were three of us and had come hoping for a full orgy. One thing was definite; he would not try again. Pa and I had made it plain we did not welcome friendly overtures.

Next day we moved again, just to be safe.

Finally we had some luck.

Our new rooms were above a caupona. Ever one for a risk, I popped down for three platefuls of their green beans in mustard sauce, with a side order of seafood dumplings, some bread, pork titbits for Helena, olives, wine and hot water, honey . . . the usual complicated list when your friends send you out to pick up what they gaily describe as 'a quick bite'. I was staggering under an immense tray, so heavy I could barely lift the thing, let alone open the door to carry it upstairs without spillage.

A girl held the door for me.

I took up the tray, grinned at my darling, stuffed some titbits between my jaws, and grabbed my cloak. Helena and my father stared, then fell on the food tray and let me get on with it. I ran back downstairs.

She was a lovely girl. She had a body you would walk ten miles to grapple, with a carriage that said she knew *exactly* what she was offering. Her face was older than first impressions, but had only gained in character from extra years. When I sauntered back, she was still at the caupona, buying spare ribs in a parcel to take out. She was leaning on the counter as if she needed extra support for her abundant figure. Her bold expression had silenced all the street trade, while her dancing brown eyes were doing things to the waiter that his mother must have warned him not to allow in public; he didn't care. She was a brunette, if it's of interest.

I settled down out of sight, and when she left I did what every man in the place was wanting to do: I followed her.

L

Don't even think it.

I never follow strange women with that idea.

Anyway, the darling brunette was not entirely a stranger to me. I had seen her undressed (though she was unaware of it). And I had seen her at the Circus sitting next to Festus. I could have called out her name and tried to get to know her by saying, 'Excuse me, but I think I saw you with my brother once' (*that* old line!).

Her name, had I wanted to play around like a barboy, was Rubinia.

I did the decent thing. I trailed her to the love-nest she shared with the sculptor Orontes. They lived four miles outside the city and must have thought themselves safe from discovery, especially during the hours of darkness. The gorgeous model had been quite unaware that expert feet were silently slipping along after her.

I waited until they had had time to eat their ribs and quaff their liquor and knot themselves together in an intimate arrangement. Then I went in without knocking.

They were very surprised.

And I could tell they were not pleased.

LI

Nudity does not affront me. Fighting it, especially in the female version, can be disconcerting for anyone.

The outraged model came at me with a dinner knife. As she ran across the sculptor's studio she was breasting the air with the formidable panache of the famous Winged Victory of Samothrace, though less formally clad. Luckily it was a large studio. I had a good view of her provocative features – and time to defend myself.

I was unarmed and short of ideas. But a pail of cold water stood near at hand. Brought in from a well I had seen in the garden, it was the best resource available. I grabbed it and hurled the icy contents straight at the screeching girl. She let out a louder, even higher-pitched scream, and dropped the knife.

I ripped a stiff cloth from the nearest statue and flung the unwieldy material around her, pinioning her arms.

'Excuse me, madam; you seem to be lacking a stole – ' She took this badly, but I clung on to her. We swung round in a wild dance, while the lovely Rubinia called me some names I was surprised a woman knew.

The studio was in a high barn of a building, dimly lit by one taper at the far end. Dark stone shapes loomed on all sides, casting huge, peculiar shadows. Stepladders and other equipment lay everywhere, dangerous traps for a stranger with his mind on other things. Artists are not tidy people (too much time wasted on dreaming, for one thing; and in between the creative processes, too much drink).

I shook the girl angrily, trying to keep her still.

By this time a large man who must be the missing sculptor had struggled upright from the tangle of their bed in the far corner of the place. He too was completely naked, and recently aroused for a different kind of combat. He was broad-chested, no longer young, bald, with a bushy beard as long as my forearm. He cut an impressive dash as he powered across the dusty floor yelling abuse.

These artistic types were noisy swine. No wonder they lived in the country, with no neighbours to annoy.

Rubinia was still screaming, and wriggling so frantically I did not immediately notice that her lover had snatched up a chisel and a mallet. But his first wild swing missed, and his mallet hissed past my left ear. As he feinted, this time with the chisel, I turned sharply, so the girl was in front of me. Rubinia bit my wrist. I lost any inhibitions about using her as a shield.

Still dragging the girl, I dodged behind a statue as Orontes lashed out. His chisel zinged off a half-formed nymph, modelled by someone more slender than the solid wench I was trying to subdue. Rubinia's feet scrabbled on the floor as she tried to lock her legs around the nymph's haunches. I jerked sideways preventing it, though I was losing my grip on the dust-sheet and its astonishing contents. She had slithered lower; any minute I should lose Rubinia too.

The sculptor popped out from behind a marble group. I hurled myself backwards, just missing a ladder. He was taller than me, but made clumsy by drink and agitation; his domed forehead knocked into the obstruction. As he cursed, I seized what might be my only chance. I was losing my grip on the girl, so I flung her as far from me as I could, aiding the process painfully with my boot on her expansive rear. She crashed into a pediment, letting loose another mouthful of barracks invective.

I grabbed the dazed sculptor. He was strong, but before he realised what I was up to I had whirled him in a half-circle. Then I pressed him into a sarcophagus that was standing on its end as if made to receive visitors. Seizing its massive lid, I slid the thing sideways and attempted to close the coffin on the man who was supposed to be mending it.

The stone lid's weight surprised me and I only managed to jam the thing halfway across before Rubinia came at me again, hurling herself on to me from behind and trying to tear out my hair. Dear gods, she was a stayer. As I squirmed around to face her she let go of my shoulders and grabbed the mallet. Frantic blows rained all around me, though her idea of how to hit a target was fortunately hazy. Landing a blow was made more difficult by the fact she was springing about like a maddened polecat, jabbing kicks at the part of me I prefer not to have attacked.

With two of them to overpower, things were becoming desperate. I managed to lean against the sarcophagus lid to keep Orontes trapped behind me, and at the same time fastened Rubinia's hammer wrist in my hardest grip. It must have hurt her badly. For a few seconds she went on trying to murder me, while I tried to prevent it happening. Finally I broke her hold on the weapon, gave her a clout on the temple, and grappled her.

At that moment the door crashed open. In raced a familiar short sturdy shape, topped by frenetic grey curls.

'Cerberus!' exploded my father, with what I hoped was admiration. 'I only let you out on your own for a moment, then I find you wrestling with a naked nymph!'

LII

'Don't just stand there cracking witticisms,' I gasped. 'Lend me a hand!'

Pa sauntered across the studio, grinning like Festus would have done. 'Is this some new form of excitement, Marcus? Having your end away on a coffin lid?' Then he added, with glee, 'The high and mighty Helena Justina is not going to like *this*!'

'Helena's not going to know,' I said tersely – then I threw the naked model at him. He caught her and held on with rather more relish than necessary. 'Now you've got the problem, and I've got the scenery!'

'Cover your eyes, boy!' growled Geminus cheerfully. 'You're too young . . .' He himself seemed to be coping, but I supposed he was used to fine art at close quarters. Holding Rubinia's wrists together and ignoring her passionate attempts to unman him, he catalogued her attractions with a deeply appreciative leer.

I fell prey to some tetchiness. 'How in Hades did you get here?'

'Helena,' he said, enjoying the emphasis, 'felt worried when she noticed you sloping off with that nasty smirk on your face. And now I see why!' he jibed. 'Does she know what you're like when you go off amusing yourself?'

I scowled. 'How did you find me?'

'Not difficult. I was fifteen yards behind you all the way.' That would teach me to congratulate myself on my expert tracking; all that time I was hoofing after Rubinia, so pleased with myself for doing it discreetly, someone had been tailing me. I was lucky the whole of Capua had not come to see the show. Father went on, 'When you sat down on the well-head for your watchdog session, I nipped up the road for a flagon – '

Now I was furious. 'You went off for a *drink*? And are you saying that even after the ostler incident you left Helena Justina all on her own at a lodging-house?'

'Well this is no place to bring her!' minced my pa, at his most annoying. 'She's a game girl, but believe me, son, she would not like this!' His eyes wandered salaciously over both of our naked companions, pausing on the coffined Orontes with a harder glare. 'I'm glad you've put that nasty piece of work in a suitable place! Now calm down, Marcus. With three bowls of beans inside her, Helena will be a match for anyone.'

'Let's get on with this!' My voice was clipped.

'Right. Release the corpse from the stoneware, and we'll tell the nice people why we've come visiting.'

I turned round, though still applying my full weight to the carved lid of the sarcophagus. It was a dreary thing to see an inch from your nose – all badly proportioned heroes, leaning askew as if they were marching up a ship's deck.

'I don't know about releasing him,' I mused, curling my lip at Orontes. 'He can hear us from where he's standing. I think I'll find out everything we want before I let him hop out of it . . .'

My father latched on to the idea eagerly. 'That's good! If he won't talk, we can leave him there permanently.'

'He won't last long in that thing!' I commented.

My father, whose lurid sense of humour was rapidly reasserting itself, dragged Rubinia to a statue of a particularly lewd satyr, and used his belt to tie her to its hairy hindquarters in a suggestive position.

'Ah Marcus, she's started crying!'

'She likes to make an effort. Take no notice. A girl who was prepared to kick me in the privates gets no sympathy from me.'

My father told her *he* was on her side – but she had to stay there. Rubinia demonstrated more of her vivid vocabulary. Next Geminus helped me wedge a large lump of stone against the coffin lid, so it was held fast, still half covering the opening, with Orontes peering out. I was leaning on a ladder that was tilted against a wall opposite, while Pa climbed up a large enthroned goddess and settled demurely in her lap.

I stared at Orontes, who had caused us so much trouble. He was, though I did not know it yet, to cause us rather more.

With his bald top and his great curly, bushy beard he had once been handsome and still had the dramatic authority of some old Greek philosopher. Wrap him in a blanket and sit him in a portico and folk might flock to hear him straining his brain. So far he had had nothing to say to us. I would have to cure that.

248

'Right!' I tried to sound menacing. 'I have had no dinner, I'm worried about my girlfriend, and even though your sultry model is a glad eyeful I'm in no mood to let this take all night.'

The sculptor finally found his voice. 'Go and jump in the Phlaegraean Marsh!' It was a deep, sombre voice, made raspy by drink and debauchery.

'Show some respect, cumin-breath!' Pa shouted down. I liked to proceed with dignity; he loved to lower the tone.

I carried on patiently. 'So you are Orontes Mediolanus – and you're a lying runt!'

'I'm not saying anything to you.' He braced himself against the inside of his stone prison, managed to shove one knee through the opening, and tried to grapple off the lid. Working with stone had given him muscle, but not enough.

I went over and kicked the sarcophagus unexpectedly. 'You'll just tire yourself out, Orontes. Now be reasonable. I can lock you in the dark in this rather heavy sarcophagus and come once a day to ask if you've changed your mind yet – or if I decide you're not worth my trouble, I can lock you in there and just not bother to come back.' He stopped struggling. 'We've not met,' I went on, politely resuming the introductions as if we were lying on marble slabs in some elegant bathhouse. 'My name is Didius Falco. This is my father, Marcus Didius Favonius, also known as Geminus. You must recognise him. Another relation of ours was called Didius Festus; you knew him too.'

Rubinia emitted a high-pitched noise. It could be terror or annoyance. 'What's that squeak for?' growled my father, gazing down at her with salty curiosity. 'Hey, Marcus, do you think I should take her out the back and ask her some questions privately?' The innuendo was obvious.

'Wait a bit,' I restrained him. I hoped he was bluffing, though I was not entirely certain. Ma had always called him a womaniser. He certainly seemed to throw himself into any available form of fun.

'Let her brew, you mean . . .' I saw Father grin evilly at Orontes. Maybe the sculptor remembered Festus; anyway, he did not look keen to see his glamorous accomplice leaving with yet another rampant Didius.

'Think on,' I murmured to him. 'Rubinia looks like a girl who may be easily swayed!'

'Leave me out of it!' she caterwauled.

I pushed myself off the ladder and ambled over to where Rubinia was tied up. Beautiful eyes, brimful of malice, sparkled at me. 'But you're in it, sweetheart! Tell me, were you swayed by Didius Festus the night I saw you at the Circus?' Whether she remembered the occasion, she coloured slightly at my brother's name and my heavy innuendo. If nothing else, I was storing up domestic strife between Rubinia and Orontes when they reminisced about our visit after we had left. I turned back to the sculptor. 'Festus was madly trying to find you. Your girlfriend here passed him on to your friends Manlius and Varga and they bamboozled him nicely . . . Did he ever find you that night?'

Inside the sarcophagus Orontes shook his head.

'Pity,' said Pa, in a clipped voice. 'Festus had his methods with traitors!'

Orontes proved as great a coward as his friends the two painters had been. All the fight was going out of him before our eyes. He groaned, 'In the name of the gods, why don't you all just leave me alone! I never asked to get into this, and what happened was not my fault!'

'What did happen?' both Pa and I demanded simultaneously. I glared at my father angrily. This would never occur with my old pal Petronius; we had a well-established routine for doing a dual interrogation. (By which I mean Petro knew when to let me take the lead.)

But as it turned out, shouting at Orontes from two directions worked the required effect. He whimpered pathetically, 'Let me out of here; I can't stand confined spaces . . .'

'Shut the lid a bit more, Marcus!' commanded Pa. I strode towards the stone coffin, looking determined.

The sculptor screamed. His girlfriend yelled at him: 'Oh tell the bastards what they want and let's get back to bed!'

'A woman with the right priorities!' I commented quietly, a foot from her entombed lover. 'Are you ready to talk then?'

He nodded miserably. I let him out. Immediately he made a dash for freedom. Expecting it, Father had slid gracelessly down the front of the vast matron who was forming his armchair. He landed in front of Orontes and punched up the sculptor's chin with a mighty blow that knocked him out.

I caught him under the hot hairy armpits. 'Oh brilliant, Pa. Now he's unconscious! This way he'll tell us a lot!'

'Well what else did you want? To see the bastard escape?'

We got him laid neatly on the floor, then threw a jug of cold water over him. He came to, to find the pair of us lolling against the statuary while I complained to my father. 'You do have to overdo everything! Settle down, will you? We want him alive at least until he's talked . . .'

'I should have hit the girl harder,' mumbled Pa, like some demented thug who liked torturing people.

'Oh she's all right – so far.'

Orontes stared around wildly, looking for Rubinia. There was no sign of her in the studio. 'What have you done with her?'

'Not too much – yet,' smiled Father.

'Missed his vocation!' I commented. 'Don't worry; she's just a bit frightened. I've managed to hold him back so far, but I can't go on doing it. Now talk, Orontes, or you get a chisel somewhere you may not expect and Jupiter only knows what this maniac will inflict upon your bit of decorative womanhood!'

'I want to see Rubinia!'

I shrugged. Ignoring his frantic gaze, I carefully examined the statue I had chosen to lean on. It had the body of a Greek athlete in tiptop condition, but the head of a Roman countryman aged about sixty, with a lined face and very big ears. 'Ovonius Pulcher', according to its plinth. There were half a score of these monstrosities scattered through the studio, all with identical bodies but different heads. They were the latest craze; everyone who was anyone in Campania must have ordered one.

'These are horrible!' I said frankly. 'Mass-produced muscle with entirely the wrong faces.'

'He does a good head,' Pa disagreed. 'And there are some nice reproductions around us here. He's a damn good copyist.'

'Where do the youthful torsos come from?'

'Greece,' croaked Orontes, trying to humour us. Pa and I turned to each other and exchanged a slow, significant glance.

'Greece! Really?'

'He goes to Greece,' my father informed me. 'Now I wonder if he used to go there and find things for our Festus to sell?'

251

I whistled through my teeth. 'Treasure-hunting! So this is the clod-brained agent Festus used to employ! The legendary man he met in Alexandria . . . Greece, eh? I bet he wishes he'd stayed there sunbathing on the Attic Plain!'

'I need a drink!' interrupted the sculptor desperately.

'Don't give him any,' snapped Pa. 'I know him of old. He's a drunken sot. He'll drain it and pass out on you.'

'Is that how you spent the bribe, Orontes?'

'I never had a bribe!'

'Don't lie! Somebody doled out a lot of money for you to do them a favour. Now you're going to tell us who paid you the money – and you're going to tell us why!'

'Bloody Cassius Carus paid the money!' my father suddenly shouted out. I knew he was guessing. I also realised he was probably right.

'That true, Orontes?' Orontes groaned in feeble assent. We had found some wine while he was unconscious. Pa nodded to me, and I offered the sculptor the wineskin, pulling it back after Orontes had taken one thirsty swig. 'Now tell us the full story.'

'I can't!' he wailed.

'You can. It's easy.'

'Where's Rubinia?' he tried again. He didn't care much about the girl; he was playing for time.

'Where she can't help you.' Actually we had shut her up somewhere to keep her quiet.

Pa swung closer and grasped the wineskin. 'Maybe he's frightened of the girl. Maybe she'll give him an earful if she finds out he's talked.' He took several deep swigs, then offered me a turn. I shook my head with distaste. 'Wise boy! For the heart of a wine-producing area this is dreadful vinegar. Orontes never drank for the flavour, just the effect.'

Orontes looked at his wineskin yearningly, but Pa held on to the dreadful prize. 'Tell us about the Phidias,' I urged. 'Tell us now – or Pa and I are going to hurt you much more than anyone else who's threatened you before!'

I must have sounded convincing, because to my surprise Orontes then confessed.

'I go to Greece whenever I can, looking out for bargains – ' We groaned and sneered at his hybrid statues again, to show what we thought of that. 'Festus had an arrangement with me. I had heard where there might be this Phidias. I thought we could get hold of it. Some run-down temple on an island wanted to have a clear-out; I don't think they really appreciated what they were turfing on to the market. Even so, it wasn't cheap. Festus and some other people managed to put the money together, and he also lined up Carus and Servia as eventual purchasers. When his legion left Alexandria to fight in the Jewish Rebellion, Festus wangled himself a journey to Greece as an escort for some despatches; that was how he came with me to view the Phidias. He liked what he saw and bought it, but there was no time to make other arrangements so it had to go on with him to Tyre. After that he was stuck in Judaea with the army, so I was supposed to supervise bringing it back to Italy.'

'You were to escort it in person?' Pa queried. I guessed that was the usual system he and Festus had imposed to protect an item of large value. Either one of them, or an agent they really trusted, would have stuck with it every mile of its journey.

'That was what I promised Festus. He was sending a whole load of other stuff – nice goods, but minor quality by comparison – in a ship called the *Hypericon*.'

I poked him with the toe of my boot. The sculptor closed his eyes. 'Since the *Hypericon* sank while carrying the Phidias, and you're lying here annoying us, the rest is obvious. You broke your promise to Festus, and bunked off elsewhere!'

'That's about right,' he confessed uncertainly.

'I don't believe I'm hearing this! You let a statue worth half a million travel alone?' Pa was incredulous.

'Not exactly – '

'So *what* exactly?' menaced Pa.

Orontes groaned hopelessly and curled up, hugging his knees as if he was in some terrible pain. A bad conscience hurts some folk that way. 'The ship with the statue sank,' he whispered.

'We know that!' My father lost his temper. He hurled the wineskin at a Coy Nymph; it burst with a horrible squelching sound. Red wine trickled down her scanty drapes like blood. 'The *Hypericon* – '

'No, Geminus.' Orontes took a deep breath. Then he told us what we had come to find out: 'The Phidias that Festus bought was never on the *Hypericon*.'

LIII

I ran the fingers of both hands deep into my hair, massaging my scalp. Somehow this shock was not the surprise it ought to have been. Everyone had been telling us the *Hypericon* was carrying the statue; readjusting to another story took an effort. But some things which had made no sense before might now fall into place.

'Tell us what happened,' I commanded the sculptor wearily.

'There had been some mix-up. Festus and I took the Phidias to Tyre, but the rest of his stuff, things he had fixed up on his own account, had gone to Caesarea. Festus then told me he had to make himself look a bit official – '

'You don't say!' Pa was getting rattled. 'There was a war on in that region!'

'Well that's it!' Orontes exclaimed gratefully. He appeared to lack any grasp of world events. Perhaps this was understandable, when he saw my brother behaving as if the Jewish Rebellion had been arranged solely to further his own business commissions. 'Anyway, he went down to Caesarea to supervise his other stuff and to fix up a ship – what turned out to be the *Hypericon*.'

'So you were not using her before this?' I asked.

'Oh no. We were in military transports up to then.' Bloody Festus! 'I was left in charge of the statue. Festus told me before I brought it south to let one of the Aristedon brothers inspect it.' The name was familiar; I remembered Carus and Servia mentioning they used these people to ship goods for them. 'They were to verify it for the new owners, and until they did, Festus could not clear the banker's order.'

'So Festus was paid by Carus through a banker in Syria?'

'More convenient,' Pa muttered. 'He wouldn't have wanted to carry that kind of sum with him from Rome. And if his mates in Judaea had put up the stake money, he could pay them their profits straight away with less risk to the cash.'

'I see. But before Carus would cough up so much money, he

wanted an agent of his own to see the goods? So how did you lose our statue, Orontes?'

He was really squirming now. 'Oh gods . . . I thought it was for the best . . . Aristedon, their agent, turned up in Tyre and approved the statue. I was supposed to take it by road to Caesarea, but with soldiers barging about on all the highways, I was not looking forward to the trip. It seemed a godsend when the Aristedon brother suggested that his clients would prefer him to ship the Phidias in his own boat, the *Pride of Perga*.'

'Did you go along with that?' demanded Pa contemptuously.

'I assume Aristedon gave you some form of receipt?' I added dangerously.

'Oh yes . . .' Something was not right there. He had gone pale, and his eyes were wandering.

'So you let him take it?'

'Why not? It meant I could stop worrying about it. And I could forget about coming home on the *Hypericon*. I wanted to go back to Greece. That way I could spend my commission from Festus buying stuff for myself.'

I weighed in: 'So you handed over the Phidias, let the rest of my brother's cargo take its chance with the *Hypericon*, flitted off to Achaea, then wandered back to Italy in your own good time?'

'That's right, Falco. And since it meant I escaped drowning, I'm not going to apologise!' It seemed a reasonable attitude – unless this clown had lost your family a small fortune. 'After I got home I discovered the *Hypericon* had sunk and Festus had lost all his gear.'

'So where in Hades is the Phidias?' grated Pa.

'I was just congratulating myself on having saved it, when I heard that the *Pride of Perga* had miscarried too.'

'Oh come on!' roared my father. 'This is too much of a coincidence!'

'It was a bad time of year. Dreadful storms everywhere.'

'So then what happened?' I put in.

'I found myself in trouble. I was visited by Carus. He made me swear I would not tell Festus about the statue swap – '

'He paid you for this deception?'

'Well . . .' The sculptor looked more shifty than usual. 'He bought something I had.'

255

'It can't have been one of your pieces,' my father said pleasantly. 'Carus is a shit, but he is a connoisseur!'

Orontes spoke before he could help himself. 'He bought the receipt.'

Both Father and I had to try very hard to restrain ourselves.

'How much for?' I asked, with feigned lightness of tone – my only way to avoid a burst blood vessel.

'Five thousand.' The admission was almost inaudible.

'*Is that all*? The bloody statue was worth half a million!'

'I was hard up . . . I took what I could get.'

'But whatever did you think you were doing to Festus?'

'It didn't seem so bad,' wailed Orontes. Clearly he belonged to the amoral class of artists. 'If I had not changed the arrangements, Festus would have lost the statue anyway, in the *Hypericon*. I don't see any difference!'

'*All* the difference!' my father raged. 'Half a million nice bright shiny ones that Carus now thinks he can force us to pay!'

'He was trying to squeeze Festus too,' Orontes conceded dismally. 'That was why I didn't want to meet him when he came back to Rome. I reckoned Festus knew what I had done, and was coming after me.'

Father and I looked at each other. We were both reminiscing about my brother, and we were both perturbed. Simple rage did not explain the agitation Festus had been showing on that last trip home. If he had known that this worm Orontes had cheated him, he would simply have enlisted help, either from me or from Father, to blast the fool. Instead, he had been running in circles trying to organise one of his secret plans. It could only mean he really believed that Cassius Carus had a grievance, and needed to be squared.

Orontes misinterpreted our silence. Giving his all, he went on in anguish, 'Carus must have been putting terrible pressure on Festus by then, and Carus is known as a dangerous character.'

'Too dangerous for a fool like you to meddle with!' my father told him brutally.

'Oh don't go on – ' He had no grasp of priorities. 'I'm sorry about what happened, but there seemed no way for me to get out of it. The way Carus first put it, he made me feel I had done wrong to let the statue go. He said everybody would feel better if we pretended it had never happened.'

'I cannot believe this character!' Pa muttered to me in despair. 'Can we get the five thousand off him?'

'I've spent it,' Orontes whispered. By then I was prepared for that. Nothing useful or good would ever come out of this studio. 'I spent everything. I always do. Money seems to shrivel up the minute I appear . . .' I gave him a glare that should have shrivelled something else. 'Look, I know you have a lot to blame me for. I never thought it would end the way it did – '

A bad feeling was creeping over me. Both my father and I were very still. A man with more astuteness would have shut up rapidly. But Orontes lacked any sensitivity to atmosphere. He went straight on: 'I left Rome and kept right out of the way as long as I knew Festus was prowling about. When Manlius told me he had left, I hoped he had managed to sort something out about the cash, and I just tried not to think about it. So how do you imagine I felt when I heard what had happened to him, and realised it was all my fault?' His question was almost indignant. 'I knew Carus and Servia hate to be done down, and I realised their methods could be harsh. But I never thought,' Orontes wailed, 'Carus would put the frighteners out so badly that Festus would do what he did!'

'What did Festus do?' I demanded in a low voice.

Suddenly Orontes realised he had caused himself an unnecessary predicament. It was too late. The reply came dragging out of him irresistibly: 'I suppose he had come under so much pressure, he chose to die in battle so that he could get away from it!'

LIV

When I returned to the inn where we were currently staying, Helena was in bed. She stopped there, grumbling occasionally, while I spent half an hour trying to force the door-catch: my father's idea of keeping her safe had been to lock her in. Unfortunately, he had remained at the studio to keep an eye on Orontes. I had walked the four miles back to Capua, in the dark, getting more and more cold, footsore and miserable – only to find that my aggravating father still had the key to our room stuffed down his tunic somewhere.

My efforts to break in quietly failed dismally. In the end I abandoned caution and took a run at the door with my shoulder. The lock held, but the hinges gave. There was a terrible noise. It must have been obvious throughout the building that a Roman lady of status was having her room broken into, yet nobody came to investigate. Nice place, Capua. I could not wait to get out of it.

I squeezed inside. Unable to find a tinder-box, I bruised myself squeezing back out again to fetch a lamp from the corridor. Then I puffed my way back in a second time, cursing harshly.

Helena had eaten her own bowl of beans and all the side orders. I devoured my own cold portion, plus half of Father's, while I started to tell her what had happened. Cold beans can be fine in a salad in summer, though as a main course in winter they lack panache. Oil had gelled on them unpleasantly.

'Is there any bread?'

'You forgot to bring it. Too busy,' Helena informed me from beneath the blankets, 'ogling big-busted customers.'

I carried on talking, putting in all the details about Rubinia's unclothed bust.

Helena could always be won over by a story, especially if it featured me. At first barely the tip of her nose was visible above the bedcovers, but gradually more emerged as the tale of the silly antics and hard questioning caught her interest. By the time I had finished she was sitting up and holding out her arms for me.

I climbed into bed and we wrapped ourselves together for warmth.

'So what happens now, Marcus?'

'We've told Orontes he has to come back to Rome with us. He knows he is in real danger from either Carus or us, so he's happy to wilt under whichever option lets him return where he really wants to be. The man's an idiot!' I complained restlessly. 'He has no concept that there now has to be a confrontation – and that whatever happens, it will turn out unpleasantly for him. He's just happy to stop running.'

'But have you escaped paying all that money to Carus?'

I sighed. 'This is a problem. Carus does have written evidence that he paid Festus for the statue, whereas we ourselves have nothing to prove that Orontes handed the thing over to his representative in Tyre. Aristedon and the ship's crew drowned when the *Pride of Perga* sank. There are no other substantial witnesses.'

'And as for the bribe Carus subsequently paid to the sculptor, naturally an extortionist does not give a receipt to his collaborator?'

'No, love – so we cannot prove the fraud. It's Orontes's word against Carus's.'

'Orontes could appear as a witness, though?'

'Oh yes!' I agreed gloomily. 'He can appear. If we can keep him alive, sober, and willing to testify – which Carus will try to prevent. If we can keep him more frightened of us than he is of Carus, so that when we haul him into court he tells our story. And if we can make this limp, lying, unreliable character look believable to a jury!'

'Carus will probably bribe the jury.' Helena kissed my ear. 'Orontes is a bad witness,' she added. 'He ignored your brother's instructions, then sold the receipt without a quiver. The opposing barrister only has to accuse him of perennial bad faith, and you've lost your case.'

By now I was ranting moodily. 'Orontes is completely flabby. Carus is rich and single-minded. In court he would come over as an honest citizen while our man would be quickly discredited . . . But we're not giving this to the barristers. Why pay fees on top, when you're already up to your nostrils in dung? Pa and I are determined to do something, however.'

259

'What can you do?' Her hands were wandering pleasantly in places that liked wandering hands.

'We haven't decided. But it has to be big.'

We both fell silent. Exacting revenge from the collectors needed time and careful thought. Tonight was not the moment. But even if my own ingenuity failed me, I half hoped to lure Helena into contributing some devious invention. Something had to be done. She would understand that. She hated injustice.

She had become completely still in my arms, though I could sense busy thoughts working in that needle brain.

Suddenly she exclaimed, 'Trust you to leave a gap in the story!' I started, afraid I had passed over something significant. 'The luscious nude model went missing from the scene halfway through!'

I laughed awkwardly. 'Oh her! She was there all the time. While the sculptor was unconscious we gave her the choice of shutting up and promising to stop kicking, or being tucked out of the way while we woke him up and questioned him. She preferred to stay volatile, so we penned her in the sarcophagus.'

'Dear gods, the poor thing! I hope Orontes will be allowed to let her out of it?'

'Hmm! I don't want to make sordid suggestions,' I mumbled, 'but I strongly suspect that when my ghastly parent gets bored with discussing theories of art, he will arrange that Orontes has enough wine to knock him senseless – then Geminus may surreptitiously let out the model himself.'

Helena pretended she had no idea what sordid suggestions I meant.

'So what next, Marcus?'

'Next,' I promised her with intense relief, 'you and I and my happy father, and the sculptor, and his luscious model if he wants to bring her, are all going home . . . I wonder if Smaractus will have bothered to fix the roof?'

Helena was silent again. Maybe she was contemplating sharing a trip home with Rubinia. Maybe she was worrying about our roof.

I had plenty to think about as well, and none of it was cheerful. Somehow I had to devise a scheme to punish Carus and Servia. Somehow I had to avoid us paying out to them half a million sesterces which we had never owed them anyway. To keep myself from exile I had to solve a murder that was beginning to look inexplicable. And somehow I had to explain to my mother that her beloved son the national hero may have been no more than a failed entrepreneur who took a long stride into oblivion simply because the pressure of his bungled business commitments was growing too much for him.

'What time is it?' asked Helena.

'Jupiter, I don't know! The middle of the night – tomorrow, probably.'

She smiled at me. It had nothing to do with anything we had been discussing. I knew that, even before she said gently, 'Happy birthday, then!'

My birthday.

I had known it was coming. I thought no one else here with me had realised. Ma would be thinking about me with her own scornful reverence, but she was in Rome, so I had escaped the nostalgia and damson cake. Pa had probably never known his children's anniversaries. And Helena . . . well. A year ago, Helena had been with me on my birthday. We had been strangers then, resisting any hint of attraction between us. All the same, I had given myself a brief birthday treat and kissed her, with unexpected results for both of us. From that moment I had wanted more of her; I had wanted it all. I had started the sequence that ended with me falling in love with her, while a small, dark, dangerous voice began whispering that it might be a challenge to make this unattainable creature love me.

It was a year since the first time I held her in my arms, assuming then that it would be the only occasion she ever let me come near her. A year since I saw that look in her eyes when I risked it. A year since I fled from her, stunned by my own feelings and misunderstanding hers, yet knowing that somehow I would have to hold this woman in my arms again.

'Remember?'

'I remember!'

I took a long slow breath against her hair, absorbing the sweet natural scent of her. Without moving, I enjoyed the now familiar shape of her body, cosseted against mine. Her fingers moved

261

against my shoulder, tracing patterns that raised goose-pimples. 'Here we are in another stinking inn . . . I could never have dreamed I would still have you near me.'

'Oh Marcus, you were so angry with me.'

'I had to get angry before I dared touch you.'

She laughed. I could always make her laugh. 'You laughed me into adoring you!' she commented, as if I had spoken.

'Not that night! You locked yourself in your room, and refused to speak to me.'

'I was too terrified.'

'Of me?' I was amazed.

'Oh no! I knew that when you stopped playing iron-jawed demigods you would be a complete sweetheart . . . Of myself,' confessed Helena. 'Frightened of how much I wanted to be in your arms, how much I wanted you to go on kissing me, how much I wanted more than that – '

I could have kissed her then. Her dark eyes were soft and inviting; she was willing me to do it. But it was more fun to lean back so I could see her, and just think about it while she smiled at me.

No year of my life would ever bring me so much change. No trick of fate would ever give me anything so precious.

I put out the light so I could forget our dismal surroundings; then I ignored all the debts and disasters that were oppressing me. A man must have some comfort in his life. I said, 'I love you. I should have told you that right at the start a year ago – and this is what I should have done about it straight away . . .'

Then I let my thirty-first birthday begin with a celebration in the noblest Roman style.

LV

Our carriage-horse was still lame, so we hired a couple of litters, went across to the coast and took a ship home from Puteoli. I will pass over it briskly, though the journey seemed interminable. I spent most of it lying under a leather sail. The only times I poked my head out were when I needed to be ill.

That was often enough.

I believe the others found the weather fair, the sea air invigorating, and their various fellow passengers an enthralling mixture of types. Helena and my father got to know each other better, while they had the tact to keep the cheating sculptor and his blowzy mistress well away from me.

Even though I knew my taxes had paid for it, no sight was ever so welcome to me as the great lighthouse at Portus, the new complex at Ostia, unless it was the colossal statue of Neptune. When we sailed under Neptune's knees I knew our ship was inside the basin, and about to berth. We had to wait about before disembarking while the usual nautical business took precedence over passengers' eagerness to land. I managed to send a message ashore to the customs post, so the first sight that greeted us when our feet hit the quay was Gaius Baebius, my brother-in-law.

'You might have spared us!' muttered Father under his breath.

'I'm hoping to cadge a free ride home in official transport if we tag along with him.'

'Oh smart boy! *Gaius Baebius*! Just the man we were hoping to see . . .'

My brother-in-law was full of something – something and nothing, needless to say. He was reticent in front of strangers – and even before Helena, since a customs-clerks supervisor's attitude to women tends to be traditional, and Gaius Baebius had had seventeen years of living with my sister Junia to teach him to keep his mouth shut. Junia had the strong-willed woman's traditional attitude to men: she thought we were there to be told we were

263

idiots and made to keep quiet.

Leaving Helena disconsolately guarding the baggage (which was *our* idea of what women were for), Father and I got Gaius on his own in a wine bar and set about grilling him. Freed from female supervision, out it poured: 'Listen, listen, I've had some luck!'

'Won at the races, Gaius?' Pa chivvied. 'Don't tell the wife then! Junia will whip it out of your hand before you can take breath.'

'Olympus, Marcus, he's worse than you for looking on the dark side . . . No. I've found something you were looking for – '

'Not a trace of the *Hypericon*?'

'No, not that. I'm sure she really sank.'

'Don't you keep a list of lost vessels?' Pa demanded.

'Why should we?' Gaius Baebius gave him a scornful look. 'There's no money for the state in seaweed and silt.'

'That's a pity,' Father carried on. 'I'd like to know for certain that the *Pride of Perga* really hit bottom – '

'So what have you discovered, Gaius?' I insisted, as patiently as I could while I was tossed between this squabbling pair.

'Festus!'

I felt a sickly qualm. I was not yet ready to talk to any member of the family on that subject. Even Pa fell silent.

Gaius Baebius noticed I had lost my appetite; he lunged eagerly to grab my bowl.

'Give!' urged my father, trying not to sound subdued. 'What about Festus?' His eyes had fallen on a second spoon, with which he fought Gaius Baebius for what was left of my food.

'I found – ' Gaius had his damned mouth too full of my snack to talk. We waited for him to masticate with the ponderous thoroughness that characterised his life. I could have kicked him. Rather than have to endure his pained reproach if I attacked him, I restrained myself, though the restraint was precarious. 'I found,' he let out meticulously after a long wait, 'the note of what Festus paid in excise dues when he came ashore.'

'When? On his last leave?'

'Exactly!'

My father's eyebrows, which had retained more blackness than his rampant hair, shot up his brow. He looked down that long,

264

straight nose of his. 'Festus came home on a stretcher in a military supply ship!'

'Yes, he came home on a stretcher, but he damned soon hopped off it!' Gaius Baebius risked a slightly critical note. All my sisters' husbands had looked askance at my brother, as in fact they still did at me. Gaius Baebius would be full of himself if he ever found out that Festus had thrown himself into his heroic death in order to escape some bullying creditors – not to mention the messy detail that unknown to my brother the creditors were criminally fraudulent.

Having to face people like my brothers-in-law with this depressing tale was the main trial ahead.

'So Festus, despite being wounded, managed to bring something home with him on which duty was payable?' I sounded as pedantic as Gaius himself; it was the only way to squeeze sense from him.

'You're with me!' cried Gaius triumphantly. 'You're not so dumb!' The man was unbearable.

Father rescued me before I exploded. 'Come on, Gaius! Don't keep us in suspense. What was he importing?'

'Ballast,' said Gaius Baebius.

He sat back, satisfied that he had baffled us.

'Hardly seems to rate paying duty,' I commented.

'No. The tax was a small debit.'

'Sounds to me as if Festus may have made a payment to somebody at the customs post in order to get his item described as valueless!'

'That's a slur on the service!' said Gaius.

'But it makes sense,' answered Pa.

My father had a way of sounding sure of himself that could be intensely irritating. I only endured it because I thought he must be holding out on Gaius Baebius, who annoyed me even more. 'Father, we can't even guess what this import was – '

'I think we know.'

I assumed Geminus was bluffing, but he looked too calm. 'Pa, you've lost me – and Gaius Baebius is a thousand miles behind!'

'If this "ballast" is what I reckon it might be, then you've seen the stuff, Marcus.'

'I take it we don't mean a load of fancy gravel for rich people's garden paths?'

'Bigger,' said Father.

Another mystery that had long been lying at the back of my memory found its moment to rush to the fore. 'Not those blocks of stone I was shown in the store by drippy Uncle Junius?'

'I guess so.'

'Have you seen old Junius? How is he?' flapped Gaius Baebius, with his normal fine grasp of priorities.

'So what are these blocks?' I asked my father, ignoring the interruption.

'I have some ideas.'

That was all he would say, so I sprang the thrill for him: 'I'm not short of ideas myself. I bet the ship that Festus came home in discovered a sudden need to call at Paros, the Marble Isle.'

Pa chortled. He agreed with me. 'I wonder how our canny lad persuaded the captain to stop off for him?'

Gaius Baebius was squirming like a child left out of adult secrets. 'Are you talking about Festus? What would he want marble for?'

'Having something made, no doubt,' I replied offhandedly.

'Could have been anything,' Father murmured, smiling to himself. 'Copies of statues, for instance . . .'

My own thoughts exactly. Festus would reason, *Why sell only one half-million Phidias, when a sculptor like Orontes could be making you quadruplets?*

'Oh that reminds me!' uttered my sister's bright spark. 'The ballast was not all he had to pay duty on. I nearly forgot to mention – there was some sort of statue as well.'

LVI

We came up from Ostia by river. It was a cold, slow trip. We made a silent party, all lost in contemplating the mystery that Gaius Baebius had handed us.

It had stopped raining, but when we reached Rome the sky was full of unshed showers. The roads were glistening. Pools of water lapped over the pavements where careless stall-holders and frontagers had let cabbage leaves and old brick-ends block gullies. Roofs dripped occasionally. The air was damp with Tiber fog, through which our breath wreathed extra moisture trails.

As we disembarked, one of Petro's men who had been keeping an eye on the river barges came up. 'Falco!' he coughed. 'Petronius has us all looking for you.'

'I haven't skipped bail. I was with my surety – ' My laughter died. 'Problem?'

'He wants a word. Says it's urgent.'

'Mars Ultor! What's up?'

'That other centurion who's connected with the stabbed legionary made himself known. The boss interviewed him once, but he deferred a final judgement while we checked the man's story.'

'Am I cleared, or did he come up with an alibi?'

'Don't they always? Better hear it from Petro. I'll run up to the guardhouse and say you're back.'

'Thanks. I'll be at Fountain Court. Any time Petronius wants me, I'll make myself available.'

'You sound like one of his women!' remarked the trooper mysteriously.

We met at Flora's. I found Petronius Longus sitting over his lunch while he talked to the waiter and one of his own men, Martinus. Martinus stepped outside when I turned up. Another meal, previously ordered by my courteous friend, appeared at once in front of me. Epimandos served us with great diffidence, a mark of respect for Petronius, presumably.

267

I noticed that alongside Petro his thick brown cloak lay folded neatly on a pile of gear that I recognised as the dead soldier's kit. I ignored it politely for the time being. Epimandos, who may also have recognised the stuff, walked around that part of our bench as if the watch captain had brought a witch's cauldron into the bar.

Petronius was as placid and unperturbed as usual. 'You look depressed, Falco. Do I blame the caupona broth?'

'Blame Festus,' I confessed. He laughed briefly.

I had known Petronius long enough to tell him the worst. He listened with his usual impassivity. He had a low opinion of people with artistic interests, so the Carus deceit came as no surprise. He had a low opinion of heroics too; hearing that my brother's demise might not have been so glorious as we had all been pretending left Petro equally unmoved.

'So when were the civic crowns ever awarded to the right men? I'd sooner your Festus snapped one up than some bugger who happened to know the faces in a war council.'

'I suppose you have a poor opinion of the Didius family anyway?'

'Oh, some of you can be all right!' he replied with a faint smile.

'Thanks for the recommendation!' We had covered enough formalities. I could broach business now. 'So what's with the centurion?'

Petronius stretched his long legs. 'Laurentius? Seems a straight sucker who happened to have palled up with an unlucky one. He came to the guardhouse, saying he had only just heard the news, what could I tell him about it, and could he take charge of Censorinus's effects?' Petro patted the kitbag in acknowledgement.

'You've arranged to meet him here? What's the idea?'

'Well, probably nothing. A vague hope of unnerving him with the scene of the crime,' Petro grinned. 'It might work if he did it – if not, you and I are poisoning ourselves with Epimandos's broth for nothing, as usual!'

'You don't think he did do it.' I had deduced this from his tone. 'What's his story?'

'They both had leave. Censorinus was supposed to be staying with a "friend's family". I haven't let on so far that I know you all. Laurentius is Roman-born, so he was at his own sister's house.'

'You checked that?'

'Of course. It matched.'

'And where was Laurentius when the murder occurred?'

'Laurentius, plus sister, plus sister's four children, were all staying with an aunt at Lavinium. They went for a month.'

'And you've now been to Lavinium?' I asked him gloomily.

'Would I fail you? I did my best, Falco! But everyone at Lavinium from the town magistrate downwards confirms the tale. The actual night in question was somebody's wedding, and I can't even make out that the centurion could have slipped away unnoticed and come back to Rome secretly. He was much in evidence at the festivities, and until halfway through the next morning he was lying in a kitchen, nicely drunk. The whole wedding party can vouch for him – except the bridegroom, whose mind was on other things. Laurentius didn't do it,' Petro confirmed in his steady voice. He picked his teeth with a fingernail. 'Actually, having met him, he is just not the type.'

'Who is?'

'Well . . .' Petronius graciously accepted that hard and fast theories, like instinctive judgements, only exist to be disproved. But I knew what he was saying. He had liked the centurion. That meant I would probably like him too – though his easily proven innocence unfortunately left me the much harder task of proving my own. I was starting to feel gloomy again – once more a suspect under threat.

I leaned my chin in my hands, staring at the filthy table. Stringy the cat jumped up onto it, but walked around my patch as if its greasy condition was too disgusting for an animal to tolerate. Petronius stroked him absently, while signalling Epimandos to bring more wine.

'Something will turn up, Falco.'

I refused to be consoled.

We were drinking in silence when Laurentius arrived.

As soon as he leaned on the outdoor counter I could see what Petro meant. He may well have killed in his professional capacity, but this was no casual murderer. He was about fifty, a calm, wry, sensible type with a small-featured, intelligent face and neat strong hands that were used to practical work. His uniform was

269

well cared-for, though the bronze studs were not ostentatiously buffed. His manner was rational and quiet.

He looked for us then ordered a drink, in that order. He came over without fuss, politely bringing his flagon with him.

Then he gave me a second look, so I would notice it, and said, 'You must be related to Didius Festus?' People who had known my brother always spotted the likeness.

I acknowledged the relationship. Petronius introduced us both, without commenting on why I was there.

'I checked your story,' Petronius told the centurion. 'Regarding your whereabouts when the murder was committed, you're in the clear.' The man moved his head, accepting that Petronius had a job to do, and that it had been done fairly. 'I've brought you your crony's kit; there's nothing we need as evidence. You gave us an affidavit. If you want to leave Rome to return to your unit, I have no objections. But I do have a few other questions,' Petro said, throwing it in unexpectedly as the centurion prepared to leave us. Laurentius sat down again.

His eyes went to me and I said, 'Censorinus had been staying with my mother.' Again he acknowledged the situation with a small turn of the head. I added quietly, 'Before he moved out to here.'

Laurentius glanced around the bar swiftly. If there was alarm in his eyes, it seemed the right sort of shock. 'Is this where . . . ?'

Petronius nodded, staring at him steadily. Realising what was going on, the centurion returned his gaze with a cool, almost angry expression. 'I have never been here before.'

We believed him.

Released from the test, he looked around again. He was simply a man whose friend had died there, showing the natural sad interest. 'What a place to go . . .' His eyes fell on Epimandos, who jumped and darted away somewhere into the back room. 'Did that waiter find him?'

'The owner discovered him,' said Petro. 'A woman called Flora. She went in to ask for his rent.'

'*Flora?*' It was the first I had heard of this detail. 'I thought "Flora" was a myth!'

Petronius said nothing, though he seemed to give me an odd look.

Laurentius was now becoming more upset. 'This trip of ours has all turned into a horror – I'm regretting we ever bothered.'

'Long leave?' asked Petro politely.

'I'm taking a break. I've asked for a new posting. The Fifteenth has been reassigned to Pannonia – I can't stand a tour in that tedious backwater.'

'Will you get a new legion?'

'Should do. I'm looking for action. I've asked for Britain.'

Petro and I, who had served there, exchanged a wry look. 'You seem confident.'

'Oh yes. The chance of a move is a bonus for those of us who held the fort in Judaea while the rest came home with Titus for his official Triumph.' Laurentius glanced at me with a slight smile. 'The Festus principle, you know – never volunteer for anything, unless you're volunteering to be left out!'

'I can see you knew my brother!' I grinned.

The military chat had relaxed the tense atmosphere. Laurentius turned back to Petro, asking confidentially, 'Have you no idea what happened to Censorinus?'

'None,' Petro said slowly. 'I'm beginning to think it must have been just one of those casual encounters that go wrong sometimes. We may solve it one day. If so, it's most likely to be solved by accident.'

'Pity. He seemed a good man.'

'Had you known him long?'

'On and off. He wasn't from my own century.'

'But you were in the same investment club?' There was no change in Petro's tone as he asked, and he appeared to be looking at his wine. But once again, Laurentius knew what was happening.

'This is about that?' He glanced from Petronius to me.

Petronius Longus adopted the frank approach: 'I asked Falco to be here because he needs the same answers as I do. Your pal had a fine old row with him, and we would like to know why. Falco *needs* to know, because the quarrel implicates him in the death.'

'Wrongly?' the centurion asked me in a light, easy tone.

'Wrongly,' I said.

'Nice to be sure of these things!' Laurentius folded his hands calmly on the table. 'Anything you want to know, Watch Captain,' he said. 'If it will help find the killer.'

'Right.' Then Petronius raised a hand so his trooper Martinus, who had been hanging about at the counter, came back into the caupona and sat down with us. Laurentius and I exchanged half a smile. Petronius Longus was doing things properly. Not only was he making sure he had a witness to his own procedure when he interviewed two suspects (one of them known to him), but Martinus brought out a waxed tablet and openly took notes. 'This is Martinus, my second in command. He'll be keeping a record, if the two of you don't mind. If what we talk about is shown to be a private matter which has no bearing on the murder, then the notes will be destroyed.'

Petro skewed round to ask the waiter to step out and give us some privacy, but for once Epimandos had discreetly disappeared.

LVII

Petronius asked the questions; at first I sat tight.

'Centurion, are you now prepared to volunteer what it was you and the dead man wanted from the Didius family?' Laurentius nodded slowly, though made no reply. 'You were trying to recover your stake money from an investment which Didius Festus had organised?'

'In effect.'

'Am I allowed to ask where the money came from?'

'None of your business,' Laurentius answered pleasantly.

'Well,' said Petronius, at his most reasonable, 'let me put it this way: the dead man's quarrel with Falco over this money has been cited as a possible motive for Falco stabbing him. I know Falco personally, and I don't believe he did it. I do know that we are talking about the price of a statue by Phidias, and it could be suggested that a group of centurions on active service in the desert might have found it difficult to come up with so much ready cash?'

'It was not difficult,' Laurentius informed him laconically.

'Resourceful fellows!' smiled Petronius. This was all extremely civilised – and it did not help.

The centurion had enjoyed dodging but was not, in fact, trying to be difficult. 'The money we are trying to replace now we had gained on a previous flutter; it would have been doubled by another sale which Festus was hoping to make. I came to Rome to ascertain what happened about that second sale. If Festus went ahead, we're well in profit. If he didn't, we're back level; we'll just have to give it the gambler's shrug and start again.'

I felt obliged to intervene. 'You sound nicely philosophical! If that is your attitude, why was Censorinus so desperate when he tackled me?'

'It was different for him.'

'Why?'

Laurentius looked embarrassed. 'When he first came into the syndicate, he was only an optio – not one of us.'

273

The trooper Martinus was grimacing at Petro, not understanding the reference. Unlike us, he had never been in the army. Petro quietly explained to his man. 'An optio is a soldier who has been nominated as suitable for promotion to centurion, but who is still waiting for a vacancy. It can take a long time for one to come up. He spends the waiting period acting as second in command in the century – much like yourself.' There was a slight edge in Petro's voice. I knew he had long suspected that Martinus was trying to encroach on his position – though he did not think Martinus was a good enough officer to push him aside.

'I'd better come clean on the whole story,' said Laurentius. If he had noticed the personal atmosphere, it was one he understood.

'Clarification would be appreciated,' I agreed, as mildly as I could.

'A group of friends,' Laurentius explained, 'found the money for an investment – never mind how – ' I avoided looking at Petronius; this was almost certainly a reference to raiding the legionary savings bank.

'Don't write this down,' Petronius instructed Martinus. Martinus awkwardly lowered his stylus.

'We made the investment successfully – '

'And I hope you replaced your capital?' Deliberately I let him know I had guessed where they had taken it from.

Laurentius smiled demurely. 'Relax. We did! Censorinus was not part of our syndicate then, incidentally. On that first scheme we made something like a quarter of a million profit, between ten of us. We were happy men, and Festus was already a hero in our eyes. There was no way to spend the money in the desert, so we sank it into *another* investment, knowing that if we came unstuck we could now just thank the Fates for being vindictive, and we'd lost nothing overall – though if we made our sale, we could all retire.'

'Censorinus then came in with you?'

'Yes. We had never talked about our winnings, but when people have a windfall word always gets out. Censorinus was already being considered as a candidate for promotion. He was becoming friendly with our group in anticipation of his co-option. Somehow he must have heard we were on to a good investment. He approached us, and asked to come in on it.'

Petro showed an interest: 'The rest of you were risking your profit – but he had to draw on his savings?'

'Must have,' shrugged Laurentius. Again he was revealing embarrassment. 'Obviously we expected him to match what we put into the kitty.' Since their kitty was founded on an illegal loan from the savings bank, this was wondrously unfair of them. They had pulled off a scam – and immediately overlooked their good fortune in getting away with it. 'Actually, I now realise he put in everything he had and then borrowed some, but at the time the rest of us were pretty offhand about where he was finding the cash.' Petro and I could imagine how cocky the others would have been; how insensitive to a newcomer. 'Look, there was no pressure on him to join us. It was his choice.'

'But when your project fell through it hit him much harder than the rest of you?' I asked.

'Yes. So that's why,' Laurentius said to me with a hint of apology, 'he did tend to become hysterical. He was a bit of a jumpy beggar anyway, in my opinion – ' That was shorthand for saying Laurentius himself would not have promoted him. 'I'm sorry. With hindsight, I ought to have handled the whole thing myself.'

'It might have helped,' I said.

'Did he explain?'

'Not properly. He was very evasive.'

'People like to be suspicious,' Laurentius commented.

I drained my winecup with a wry smile. 'And your syndicate is suspicious of me?'

'Festus always said he had a very sharp brother.' That was news. I set the cup down again carefully. Laurentius murmured, 'Our second investment seems to be mislaid. We did wonder if it might have been found by you?'

'I don't even know what it is,' I corrected him gently – although by then I thought I did know.

'It's a statue.'

'*Not* the drowned Poseidon?' asked Petronius. His man Martinus made a jump towards his stylus again, but Petro's great paw clamped over his wrist.

'No, not the Poseidon.' Laurentius was watching me. I think he was still wondering whether I might have found this second piece, perhaps when Festus died.

275

Meanwhile I myself was wondering if Festus had disposed of it deliberately, and diddled his mates.

'Everyone's keeping secrets!' I told the centurion levelly. 'You'll be glad to hear I live in squalor. The watch captain will assure you I'm not soaking in luxury with profits that should have been yours.'

'He lives in a pit!' Petro grinned, confirming it.

'This special item seems to be lost,' I said. 'I searched my brother's property after he died, and I've looked in his store since, but I haven't found your treasure. My father, who was my brother's business partner, never heard tell of a second statue. And as far as we can see, even the agent Festus was using for your business never knew it existed.'

'Festus thought the agent was an idiot.'

I was pleased to hear that. I thought so too. 'So where did this statue come from?'

'The same island as the other,' said Laurentius. 'When Festus went to Greece to inspect the Poseidon, he found out that the temple actually owned two they might sell.' I could imagine my brother giving Orontes the slip, and getting talking to the priests on his own. Festus never took agents on trust. His winning style could easily have uncovered further information that the sellers had withheld from Orontes, who lacked all my brother's charm, as I knew well. 'We only had enough cash to buy the Poseidon at first. We had to sell on – '

'To Carus and Servia?'

'Those were the names. What we got from them replaced our original stake money, and enabled your brother to go back to Greece with our profit – '

'But *without* Orontes?'

'Without Orontes.'

'And he bought?'

Laurentius smiled with resignation. 'That time he bought a Zeus.'

LVIII

Later the same day, for the first time in history, my father had himself brought over to Fountain Court. When he arrived Helena was wrapped in a blanket, reading, while I scrubbed a bucket of mussels. He expected her to vanish so we could enjoy a manly chat, as happens in normal households, but she waved to him graciously and stayed where she was. He then expected me to shove the bucket away shyly under the table, but I carried on.

'Gods! I'm killed by the stairs . . . She's got you hard at it then?'

'This is how we live. No one asked you to turn up and criticise.'

'Marcus is the cook,' said Helena. 'He likes to feel he's supervising my domestic education. But I would be allowed to make you some hot honey if you want?'

'Got any wine?'

'Only for those who are stopping to dinner,' I snapped. My father was incorrigible. 'We're nearly out. I can't feed casual inebriates; I want it for the sauce.'

'I can't stop. Expected at home. You're a hard-hearted host.'

'Have the honey. She does it with cinnamon. You'll have sweet breath, a pleasant temper, and it will ease your poor old chest after the stairs.'

'You're living with a bloody apothecary, girl!' Pa grumbled at Helena.

'Yes, isn't he wonderful? Like a human encyclopaedia,' she answered, with evil insincerity. 'I'm going to lease him to Marponius . . .' Then she smiled and made sensible drinks for all of us.

My father gazed slowly around our outer room, deduced there was another just as awful behind the curtain, dismissed the balcony as a disaster waiting to send us to an early death, and turned up his nose at our furniture. I had acquired a pine table. We liked the fact it had all four legs and very little woodworm, but by his standards it was plain and pitiful. Apart from that we owned the mean stool I was sitting on, the chair Helena gave up for him, another she fetched from the bedroom for herself, three beakers, two bowls, one stew-pot, some cheap lamps, and a mixed set of scrolls containing Greek plays and Latin poetry.

He was looking for ornaments; I realised that we had none. Perhaps he would send us a chestful next time he did a house clearance.

'Olympus! Is this it then?'

'Well in the next room there's the scallop-end bed you sold me, and a rather nice movable tripod Helena picked up from somewhere. Of course our summer villa at Baiae is a haven of unconfined luxury. We keep our glass collection and the peacocks there . . . So what do you think?'

'It's even worse than I feared! I admire your courage,' he said to Helena, visibly moved.

'I admire your son,' she answered quietly.

Pa still looked wounded. The horror of my living quarters seemed a personal affront to him. 'But this is awful! Can't you get him to do something?'

'He's trying his best.' Helena sounded terse.

I went out and peed off the balcony to avoid any need to contribute. An angry shout arose from the street below, cheering me up.

When I came back in, I told my father what I had learned from the centurion about the statue of Zeus. 'It makes things neat, anyway. First we have one statue and one ship – now there are two ships and two statues.'

'But it's not quite symmetrical,' Helena commented. 'One of the statues was lost in one of the ships, but the Zeus came ashore with Festus and presumably still exists somewhere.'

'That's good,' I said. 'This one is lost, but we can find it.'

'Are you going to try?'

'Of course.'

'You've had no luck so far!' remarked my father gloomily.

'I wasn't looking until now. I'll find the Zeus – and when I do find it, even if we repay the centurions' syndicate their share of the investment, there's still a chance for the rest of us to get rich. In addition to big brother's agreed percentage of the proceeds, we have four blocks of genuine Parian marble. We can do what Festus must have been planning, and have four copies made.'

'Oh surely you wouldn't sell fakes, Marcus!' Helena felt shocked. (At least I assume she did.) Pa gazed at me with a whimsical expression, waiting for me to answer her.

'Never entered my mind! Good copies can fetch a wonderful price in their own right.' It sounded almost sincere.

Helena smiled. 'Who would make your copies?'

'Orontes – who else? We were clambering all over his stuff at the studio; he has a sure touch with replicas. It's my belief that was all Festus wanted to ask him the night he was looking for the bastard so urgently. Orontes was petrified that Festus wanted a fight with him, when in fact my het-up brother was quite innocent of the Carus fraud, and was just offering Orontes work. Festus had received his military orders. He had to go back to Judaea. It was his last chance to fix the deal.'

'And is Orontes really good?'

Pa and I consulted each other, remembering again what we had seen of his work at Capua. 'Yes; he's good.'

'And after the trick he pulled on Festus, he owes us a free commission or two!'

Helena tried it out: 'So Festus was simply wanting to say to him, "Come and look at this Phidias Zeus I've just brought home, and make me four more of them" . . .' She jumped in her seat. 'So Marcus, this means the original must have been somewhere it could be viewed! Somewhere Festus could have shown it to the sculptor that very night – somewhere here in Rome!'

She must be right. It was here. It was worth half a million, and as my brother's heir and executor, part of it belonged to me. It was here, and I would find it if it took me twenty years.

'If you can find it,' said Helena quietly, 'I have an idea how you two could get your own back on Cassius Carus and Ummidia Servia.'

Father and I pulled our seats closer, and gazed at her like attentive acolytes at a shrine.

'Tell us, my darling!'

'To make my idea work properly, you will have to pretend you believe they really did lose their money on the Poseidon. That means you will have to put together the half-million sesterces and actually pay over the cash – '

We both groaned. 'Must we?'

279

'Yes. You have to convince them that they've beaten you. You have to lull them into a false sense of security. Then when they are full of themselves for cheating you, we can make them over-reach and fall for this proposal of mine . . .'

That was when Helena, my father and I sat together around my table, and hatched the scheme that would give us our revenge. Father and I put forward some refinements, but the basic plan belonged to Helena.

'Isn't she bright?' I asked, hugging her with delight as she explained it.

'She's beautiful,' agreed my pa. 'If we bring this off, maybe you'll use the proceeds to let her live somewhere more appropriate.'

'We have to find the missing statue first.'

We were nearer to that than we thought, though it took a tragedy to bring us near enough.

It was a good afternoon. We were all friends together. We had schemed, and laughed, and congratulated ourselves on how clever we were and how skilfully we were planning to turn the tables on our opponents. I had given in over the wine, which we poured into beakers for toasting each other and our scheme of revenge. With it we ate winter pears, laughing again as the juice ran down our chins and wrists. When Helena took a fruit that was going brown, my father reached for a dinner knife and cut off the bruised portion for her. Watching him hold the fruit in one sturdy hand while he pared off the bad part, stopping the knife-blade against his blunt thumb, a pang of reminiscence took me back a quarter of a century to another table, with a group of small children clamouring to have their father peel their fruit.

I still did not know what we had done to drive him away from us. I would never know. He had never wanted to explain. For me that had always been the worst part. But perhaps he simply could not do it.

Helena touched my cheek, her eyes quiet and understanding.

Pa gave her the pear, cut in slices, popping the first piece into her mouth as if she was a little girl.

'He's a demon with a blade!' I exclaimed. Then we laughed some more, as my father and I recalled how we had rampaged against the painters as the dangerous Didius boys.

It was a good afternoon. But you should never relax. Laughter is the first step on the road to betrayal.

After Father had gone, normality resumed. Life reasserted its usual grim messages.

I was lighting a lamp. I wanted to trim off the burnt wick. I was thinking about nothing as I tried to find the knife I normally used. It was missing.

Pa must have walked off with it.

Then I remembered the knife that had stabbed Censorinus. Suddenly I understood how a knife which had once been my mother's had arrived at the caupona. I knew how my mother, who was so careful, could have lost one of her tools. Why when Petronius Longus had asked her about it, she had chosen to seem so vague – and why when Helena tried to question members of the family, Ma had almost feigned disinterest. I had seen her being vague and unresponsive on the same subject scores of times. Ma knew exactly where that 'lost' knife had gone twenty years ago. Its discovery must have placed her in a terrible dilemma – wanting to protect me, and yet aware that the truth itself would not spare our family. She must have put the knife in my father's lunch-basket, on the day he left home. Either that, or he had simply picked it up for some job or other and carried it away with him the way he had mine today.

My father had been in possession of the murder weapon.

Which meant that the main suspect for killing Censorinus would now appear to be Didius Geminus.

LIX

It was a wild idea. Those are the ones that always seem the most believable once they strike you.

This was one thing I could not say to Helena. Not wanting to let her see my face, I stepped on to the balcony threshold. Ten minutes ago, he had been here, joking with the two of us, more friendly than he and I had ever been. Now I knew this.

He could have lost that knife, or even thrown it away, a long time ago. I did not believe he had. Pa was famous for collecting cutlery. When he lived with us, the decreed system was that every day he was given a knife in his lunch-basket; he usually pinched the daily knife. It was one of the irritating habits by which he made his presence felt. He was always in trouble about it, one of the endless wrangles that colour family life. Sometimes he needed a sharp blade to prod a suspect piece of furniture, testing for worm. Sometimes he had to swipe through the cords tied around a bale of new stock. Sometimes he palmed an apple from a fruit stall in passing, then wanted to cut slices as he walked. We children bought him a fruit-knife for a Saturnalia present once; he just hung it on the wall of his office, and went on exasperating Mother by filching the picnic tools.

He must still do it. I would bet he was driving the redhead to distraction with the same little game – still on purpose, probably. And the day Censorinus died, maybe the knife in his pouch had been that old one.

So my father could have killed the soldier. Why? I could guess: Festus again. Rightly or wrongly, Geminus must have been trying to protect his precious boy.

I was still standing there, lost in desperate thoughts, when we had another visitor. It was so close to my father's departure, and Geminus was so much on my mind, that when I heard feet on the stairs I thought it must be him again, coming back for a forgotten cloak or hat.

They were old feet, but they belonged to someone lighter and more fragile than my hefty pa. I had just worked that out, with great relief, when the new arrival staggered in. Out of context, it took me a moment to recognise his troubled voice as he asked for me. As I came in from the balcony I saw Helena, who had been full of concern for the old man, grow suddenly still as she noticed my own frowning face. The light I had meant to attend to was flaming up madly; she strode across and blew it out.

'Oh it's Apollonius! Helena Justina, this is the man I was telling you about the other day; my old teacher. You look terrible, Apollonius. Whatever's wrong?'

'I'm not sure,' he gasped. It was a bad day for elderly folk at Fountain Court. First my father had arrived whey-faced and coughing. Now the six flights of stairs had nearly finished Apollonius as well. 'Can you come, Marcus Didius?'

'Get your breath! Come where?'

'Flora's. Something has happened at the caupona; I am sure of it. I sent a message to Petronius Longus, but he hasn't appeared, so I thought you might advise me what to do. You know about crises – '

Oh I knew about those! I was up to my neck in them.

Helena had already fetched my cloak from the bedroom. She stood holding it, staring hard at me but keeping her questions to herself.

'Stay calm, old friend.' I felt a strange, deep, gentle care for other people who were in trouble. 'Tell me what has disturbed you.'

'The place has been shuttered since just after lunch-time – ' Flora's never closed in the afternoon. So long as there was a chance of extracting a copper from the public for a lukewarm stuffed vine leaf, Flora's never closed at all. 'There is no sign of life. The cat is scratching at the door, crying horribly. People have been beating on the shutters, then just walking away.' Apollonius himself probably had nowhere else to go. If he found the caupona unexpectedly closed he would just sit outside on his barrel hopefully. 'Oh please come, if you can, young Marcus. I feel something is dreadfully wrong at that place!'

I kissed Helena, grabbed my cloak and went with him. The old man could only go slowly, so when Helena decided not to be left out, she soon caught up with us.

We saw Petronius arrive at Flora's just ahead of us. I was glad of it, although I would have gone in on my own otherwise. But Apollonius was not alert to the sensitivities. I was still under suspicion for what had happened to Censorinus. If there was some new upset at the scene of his murder, it was better to have official company.

The caupona was as the old man had described. Both huge shutters had been drawn across the wide entrances in front of the counters; both were securely locked from inside. It looked as I had rarely seen it except at the dead of night. Standing in the street, Petronius and I tossed up pebbles at the two small windows in the upper rooms, but nobody responded.

Stringy was gnawing at one doorpost miserably. He rushed up to us, hoping we might give him some dinner. A caupona cat does not expect to find himself hungry; he was thoroughly indignant. Petronius picked him up and fussed him while he stared at the locked building thoughtfully.

Across the street at the Valerian there were more customers than usual. People, some of whom would normally have been wasting a few hours at Flora's, turned on their elbows to watch us, while eagerly discussing the unusual activity.

We told Apollonius to wait outside. He sat down on his barrel; Helena stopped with him. Petronius gave her the cat, but she put it down fairly swiftly. Even though the poor girl had fallen for an informer, she did have some principles.

Petro and I walked round to the back alley. There was the usual stink of kitchen rubbish; the usual seedy atmosphere. The stable door was locked – the first time I had ever seen that. It was of flimsy construction; the lower portion was weaker and gave way to a hard shove from Petronius. He reached in and fiddled with the bolts on the upper half, eventually giving up and simply ducking underneath. I followed. We emerged inside the kitchen area. Everywhere was completely still.

We stood, trying to see in the dark. We recognised that silence. We knew what we were looking for. Petronius always carried a tinder-box; after several attempts he struck sparks, then managed to find a lamp to light.

As he held up the little lamp he was standing ahead of me, his bulk blocking my view. His shadow, that great head and the raised arm, sprang up to the side of me, flickering alarmingly on the rough caupona wall.

'Oh shit, he's dead!'

I assumed it was another murder. Still locked in my own preoccupations, I thought drably, *Geminus must have come here and killed the waiter just before he turned up at Fountain Court so full of concern for us, so full of laughter and fun* . . .

But I was wrong. I had hardly begun to feel angry with my father when Petronius Longus moved aside for me.

I noticed another shadow. By the single flame of the feeble lamp, its slow motion attracted attention as a long, dark, slanted shape turned slightly with some changing air current.

In the well of the stairs was Epimandos. He had hanged himself.

LX

Petronius had the longer reach. He cut the body down, not even needing the stool Epimandos had used. We were far too late; the corpse was cold. We carried him into the deep dark of the interior, and laid him on a counter. I fetched the thin blanket from his bed and covered him. Petronius unlocked and partly pushed open a shutter. He called in the others.

'You were right, Apollonius. The waiter's topped himself. It's all right; don't be afraid to look. He's decent now.'

The old teacher came into the caupona, showing no excitement. He looked at the covered body with compassion. He shook his head. 'Saw it coming. Only a matter of time.'

'I must talk to you,' Petronius said. 'But first we all need a drink – '

We looked around, but then gave up. It seemed tactless to raid Flora's. We all went over to the Valerian. Petronius told the other customers to make themselves scarce, so they wandered across to Flora's and stood outside in huddles. Rumours had spread. A crowd collected, though there was nothing to see. We had locked up after us. Petronius, who had his soft side, even brought away the distressed cat.

The Valerian had a quiet atmosphere and quite good wine. The waiter allowed Petro to feed Stringy, which was sensible because Petronius was looking for an excuse to start a fight over nothing just to ease his feelings. He always hated unnatural death.

'This is a tragedy. What can you tell me?' Petro asked the teacher wearily. He was stroking the cat and sounded as if he was still looking for trouble. Apollonius blanched.

'I know a little about him. I'm at the caupona frequently . . .' Apollonius left a small, tactful pause. 'His name was Epimandos; he had been a waiter there for five or six years. Your brother,' he said, turning to me, 'arranged the job for him.'

I shrugged. 'I never knew that.'

'There was some secrecy surrounding it.'

'What secrecy?' demanded Petronius. Apollonius looked shy. 'You can speak freely. Was he a runaway?'

'Yes, he had been a slave, I believe,' agreed my old geometrist.

'Where did he come from?'

'Egypt, I think.'

'*Egypt?*'

Apollonius sighed. 'This was told to me in confidence, but I suppose now the man is dead . . .'

'Tell me what you know!' Petro commanded bluntly. 'That's an order. This is a murder enquiry.'

'What? I thought the waiter had committed suicide?'

'I don't mean the waiter.'

Petro's angry manner was making Apollonius clam up. It was Helena who reassured him, asking gently, 'Please tell us. How did a slave from Egypt end his days serving in a caupona here?'

For once my terrible teacher managed to be concise. 'He had had a bad master. I understand the person was notorious for his cruelty. When Epimandos ran away, Didius Festus found him. He helped him come to Italy, and to obtain work. That was why Epimandos had a special regard, Marcus, for members of your family, and for you.'

I asked, 'And do you know why Epimandos killed himself today?'

'I think so,' Apollonius responded slowly. 'His cruel master was the medical officer in your brother's legion.'

'This all happened when Festus and the Fifteenth Legion were stationed at Alexandria?'

'Yes. Epimandos worked in the infirmary, so everybody knew him. After he escaped and came to Rome he was terrified that one day somebody would walk into Flora's, recognise him, and send him back to that life of torment. I know there was an occasion recently when he thought he had been noticed – he told me so one evening. He was in great distress and had got himself extremely drunk.'

'Was that Censorinus?'

'This he did not actually say,' Apollonius replied carefully.

Petronius had been listening in his fatalistic way. 'Why have you never mentioned this before?'

'Nobody asked.'

Well he was only the beggar.

Petro stared at him, then muttered to me, 'Censorinus was not the only one who noticed the waiter. Epimandos probably killed himself because he guessed he had also been recognised by Laurentius. It happened when we ourselves invited the centurion to Flora's earlier today.'

Remembering how the waiter had shot out of sight when Laurentius looked at him, I believed it and was appalled. 'Do you know this for certain?'

'Afraid so. After we all left the place, Laurentius was puzzling over why the waiter had seemed familiar. He finally remembered where he had seen Epimandos before, then realised its implication regarding the death of Censorinus. He came straight to see me. That was one reason why I was delayed when Apollonius sent his message.'

I had been feeling grey before this news, which was deeply depressing. It did solve some of my problems. For one thing, it showed my brother Festus in a better light (if you approve of helping slaves escape). It also meant I could stop panicking over Geminus. This reprieve for my father had hardly sunk in; I must still have looked dreadful. I was coming to terms with just how relieved I felt.

I suddenly realised that Helena Justina was gripping my hand fiercely. Saving me mattered to her so desperately she could no longer hold back: 'Petronius, are you saying that the waiter must have been the soldier's murderer?'

Petronius nodded. 'I reckon so. You're cleared, Falco. I shall tell Marponius I am no longer looking for a suspect in the Censorinus case.'

Nobody gloated.

Helena had to be certain about all this. 'So what happened the night he died? Censorinus must have recognised the waiter, possibly while he was in the midst of quarrelling with Marcus. Later perhaps he had a confrontation with the waiter. When Epimandos realised the trouble he was in, the poor soul must have been in despair. If Censorinus was spiteful, maybe he threatened Epimandos with returning him to his master, and then – '

She was so unhappy Petro finished it for her. 'Epimandos took him up a drink. Censorinus obviously failed to realise the danger he was in. We can never know if he really did threaten the waiter – and if so, whether the threats were serious. But Epimandos was clearly terrified, with fatal results. Desperate, and more than likely drunk, he stabbed the soldier with a kitchen knife which he snatched on his way upstairs. His terror of being returned to the medical orderly explains the ferocity of the attack.'

'Why did he not run away afterwards?' Apollonius asked thoughtfully.

'Nowhere to run,' I answered. 'No one to help him this time. He tried to discuss it with me.' Remembering Epimandos's pathetic attempts to get my attention I was furious with myself. 'I dismissed him as just curious – the usual sensation-seeker who hangs around after a murder. All I did was brush him aside and threaten vengeance on whoever had committed the crime.'

'You were in a difficult position personally,' Apollonius consoled me.

'Not as bad as his. I should have noticed his hysteria. After he killed the soldier he must have frozen. I've seen it before. He just acted as if it had never happened, trying to blot the event right out of his mind. But he was almost begging to be discovered. I should have recognised that he was appealing for my help.'

'There was nothing to be done!' Petro pointed out harshly. 'He was a runaway slave, and he had murdered a legionary: nobody could have saved him, Marcus. If he hadn't taken this action today, he would have been crucified or sent to the arena. No judge could have done otherwise.'

'It was very nearly me who ended up in the dock!' I answered hollowly.

'Never! He would have stopped it,' Apollonius broke in. 'His loyalty to your family was too strong to let you suffer. What your brother had done for him meant everything. He was desperate when he heard they had arrested you. He must have been in anguish, hoping you would clear yourself and yet not discover his own guilt. But from the start his position was hopeless.'

'He seems a very sad character,' Helena sighed.

'After what he had suffered in Alexandria, his quiet life here was a revelation. That was why he exploded at the thought of losing it.'

289

'Yet to kill someone!' protested Helena.

Again it was Apollonius who answered her: 'The caupona looks dreadful to you, maybe. But nobody beat or whipped him, or subjected him to worse abuse. He had food and drink. The work was easy and people talked to him like a human being. He had a cat to fondle – even me at the door to look down on. Within this small world at the crossroads, Epimandos had status, dignity and peace.' From a man in beggar's rags himself the speech was heartbreaking.

We all fell silent. Then I had to ask Petronius. 'What's your theory about that knife?'

Helena Justina glanced at me quickly. Petro had an unfathomable expression as he said, 'Epimandos lied when he claimed he had never seen it. He must have used it often. I have just managed to trace the knife to the caupona,' he admitted, surprising me.

'How?'

'Leave it alone.' He sounded embarrassed. He could see I wanted to argue. 'I am satisfied, Falco!'

I said quietly, 'No, we ought to get this sorted out. I think the knife left my mother's house with my father – '

Petro cursed under his breath. 'Exactly!' he told me. 'I know it did. I didn't want to mention it; you're such a touchy beggar on some subjects – '

'What are you saying, Petro?'

'Nothing.' He was trying to hide something; that was obvious. It was ridiculous. We had solved the murder – yet we seemed to be plunging deeper into mystery. 'Look, Falco, the knife was always part of the caupona's equipment. It's been there ever since the place first opened ten years ago.' He looked shiftier than ever.

'How do you know?'

'I asked the owner.'

'Flora?'

'Flora,' said Petronius, as if that ended everything.

'I didn't think Flora existed.'

'Flora exists.' Petronius stood up. He was leaving the Valerian.

'How,' I demanded emphatically, 'did this Flora acquire the knife if Pa had it?'

'Don't worry about it,' said Petro. 'I'm the investigating officer, and I know all about the knife.'

'I have a right to know how it got there.'

'Not if I'm happy.'

'Blow you, Petro! I was damned nearly sent to trial because of that implement.'

'Tough,' he said.

Petronius Longus could be an absolute bastard when he chose. Official posts go to people's heads. I told him what I thought of him, but he simply ignored my rage.

'I must go, Falco. I'll have to advise the owner that the waiter's dead and the caupona's empty. That crowd outside is looking for an excuse to break in and smash up the furniture while they help themselves to free wine.'

'We'll stay there,' Helena volunteered quietly. 'Marcus will keep the thieves and looters out until a watchman can be sent.'

Petro glanced at me for confirmation. 'I'll do it,' I said. 'I owe Epimandos something.'

Petronius shrugged and smiled. I did not know the reason, and I was so annoyed with him I did not care.

LXI

I told Helena to go home; rebelliously she came with me.

'I don't need supervision.'

'I disagree!' she snapped.

The waiter's body still lay where we had left it in the main part of the building so we hovered about in the back. Helena marched into the little cubicle Epimandos had slept in, and sat on his bed. I stood in the doorway. I could see she was furious.

'Why do you hate your father so much, Falco?'

'What's all this about?'

'You can't hide from me. I do know!' she rampaged. 'I understand you, Marcus. I can see what perverted suspicions you were harbouring about who had used your mother's knife!'

'Petronius was right. Forget the knife.'

'Yes, he's right – but it took a long argument to convince you. You and your stubborn prejudices – you're hopeless! I really did think that after Capua and your meetings with Geminus in Rome these past few weeks, you and he had at last reached an accommodation. I wanted to believe you two were friends again,' she wailed.

'Some things don't change.'

'Well you don't, obviously!' I had not seen Helena so angry for a long time. 'Marcus, your father loves you!'

'Settle down. He doesn't want me, or any of the rest of us. Festus was his boy, but that was different. Festus could win anybody over.'

'You are so wrong,' Helena disagreed miserably. 'You just won't see the truth, Marcus. Marriages do fail.' She knew that; she had been married. 'If things had been different between your parents, your father would have had just as strong a grip on you and all the others as your mother has today. He stands back – but that doesn't mean he wants to. He still worries and watches over what you all do – '

'Believe that if it pleases you. But don't ask me to alter.

I learned to live without him when I had to – and that suits me now.'

'Oh you're so stubborn! Marcus, this could have been your chance to put things right between you, maybe your only chance . . .' Helena rounded on me pleadingly: 'Listen, do you know why he gave me that bronze table as a gift?'

'Because he likes your spirit and you're a pretty girl.'

'Oh Marcus! Don't always be so sour! He took me to see it. He said, "Look at this. I had my eye on it for Marcus, but he'll never accept it from me".'

I still saw no reason to change my own attitude because these two had palled up. 'Helena, if you have come to an arrangement, that's charming and I'm delighted you get on so well – but it's between you and him.' I did not even object to Helena and Pa manipulating me, if that thrilled them. 'I don't want to hear any more.'

I left her sitting on the waiter's bed, below the amulet Festus had once given Epimandos. It had not done the waiter much good.

I stalked away. The main bar, with its sad contents, still repelled me, so I lit another lamp and stomped upstairs.

I looked in the two small rooms that lay above the kitchen area. They were furnished for thin dwarves with no luggage who might be prepared to spend their free time at Flora's sitting on rickety beds staring at spiders' webs.

Gruesome fascination drew me to the other room again.

It had been scrubbed and rearranged. The walls had been washed over with a dark red paint, the only colour that would hide what had been underneath. The bed was now below the window, instead of by the door. It had a different blanket. The stool where the soldier's wine tray had been placed by Epimandos on that fatal night had been changed for a pine box. As a gesture to decor, a large Greek pot with a lively octopus design now stood on a mat on the box.

The pot used to be in the bar downstairs. I remembered it there; it was a fine item. I had always thought that. However, when I went to have a closer look, I noticed that the far-side rim was badly chipped. The pot would not repay mending. All the owner could do with the thing was shove it somewhere and admire the octopus.

293

I was thinking like Pa.

I always would.

I lay on the bed gloomily.

Helena could no longer bear to be at odds with me, so she came upstairs too. Now it was her turn to stand in the doorway. I held out my hand to her.

'Friends?'

'If you like.' She stayed by the door. Friends we might be, but she still despised my attitude. However, I was not intending to change it; not even for her.

She looked around, realising this was where the soldier died. I watched her quietly. Women are not supposed to think, but mine could and did, and I liked to watch the process. Helena's strong face changed imperceptibly as she considered everything here, trying to imagine the last minutes of the soldier's life, trying to comprehend the waiter's demented attack. This was no place for her. I would have to take her downstairs again, but too soon a move would offend her.

I was watching Helena, judging my moment, so the puzzled thought caught me unawares: 'There's something wrong about this room.' I stared about me, wondering what had worried me. 'The size is odd.'

I did not need Apollonius to draw me a geometric sketch. As soon as I thought about it, I realised the floor plan here upstairs was much smaller than the ground-floor area. I swung myself upright and went out on to the landing to check. The other two guest rooms, which were so tiny they hardly counted, occupied the space above the kitchen and the waiter's cubicle. The staircase used up a few more feet. But this eight-foot-square room where Censorinus had died was only about half the size of the caupona's main room downstairs.

Behind me Helena had entered the soldier's room. 'There's only one window here.' She was acutely observant. As soon as I went back to her I understood what she meant. When Petronius and I stood in the street throwing pebbles up, there had been two square openings above our heads. Only one lit this room. 'There must be another bedroom up here, Marcus – but there's no door into it.'

'It's been blocked up,' I decided. Then a possible reason struck me. 'Dear gods, Helena, there may be something hidden up here – another body, for instance!'

'Oh really! You always have to dramatise!' Helena Justina was a sensible young woman. Every informer should have one as his associate. 'Why should there be a body?'

Trying to withdraw from the ridicule, I defended myself. 'Epimandos used to be terrified of people asking questions about these rooms.' I heard my voice drop, as if I were afraid of being overheard. There was nobody here – or if there was, they had been sealed up for years. I was remembering a conversation I must have misconstrued at the time. 'There is something here, Helena. I once joked about hidden secrets and Epimandos nearly had a fit.'

'Something hidden by him?'

'No.' I was drowning in a familiar sense of the inevitable. 'Someone else. But someone Epimandos respected enough to keep the secret – '

'Festus!' she exclaimed quietly. 'Festus hid something here that he did not tell even you about – '

'Ah well. Not trusted, apparently.'

Not for the first time I fought off a wild pang of jealousy as I faced the fact that Festus and I had never been as close as I had convinced myself. Maybe nobody had known him properly. Maybe even our father only touched him in passing. Not even Pa knew about this hiding-place, I was sure of that.

But now I knew. And I was going to find whatever my brother had left in it.

LXII

I ran downstairs, looking for tools. As I went, I checked again the layout of the small landing. If there was indeed another room, it had never been accessible from the corridor; the stairs were in the way where its door ought to be.

Bringing a cleaver and a meat-hammer from the kitchen, I ran back. I felt mad-eyed, like a butcher who had run amok in the August heat. 'People must have entered through this room here . . .' In Rome, that was common. Thousands of folk reached their bedrooms through at least one other living area, sometimes a whole string of them. Ours was not a culture that valued domestic privacy.

Feeling the wall with my open hand, I tried to forget how it had been splashed with the soldier's blood. The construction was rough lath and plaster, so rough it could have been my brother-in-law Mico's work. Maybe it was. Now I remember Mico telling me that Festus had arranged work for him . . . But I doubted whether Mico had ever seen what was bricked up in the missing room. Somebody else must have filled in the doorway secretly – almost certainly someone I knew.

'Festus!' I muttered. Festus, on his last night in Rome . . . Festus, rolling away from Lenia's laundry in the dead of night, saying he had a job to do.

That must have been why he wanted me; he needed my help with the heavy work. Now I was here without him, and about to undo his labours. It gave me an odd feeling, which was not entirely affectionate.

A few inches from the cloak hook I found a change in the surface. I walked the width of the wall, tapping it with a knuckle. Sure enough, the sound altered, as if I was passing a hollow area, slightly more than two feet wide. It could have been a doorway once.

'Marcus, what are you going to do?'

'Take a risk.' Demolition always worries me. The caupona was

296

so badly built, one wrong move could bring the whole place crashing down. Doorways are strong, I told myself. I bounced on my heels, testing the floor, but it felt safe enough. I just hoped the roof stayed up.

I felt for a crack, applied the cleaver like a chisel, and tapped it gently with the meat-hammer. Plaster shattered and dropped to the floor, but I had not been fierce enough. I had to use more force, though I was trying to be neat. I did not want to crash into the hidden room in a great shower of rubble. What was there might be delicate.

By pulling off the upper skim of plaster, I managed to trace the edge of the lintel and frame. The doorway had been blocked with fireclay bricks. The infill had been poorly done, hurriedly no doubt. The mortar was a weak mix, most of which crumbled easily. Starting from near the top, I tried to remove the bricks. It was dusty work. After much effort I freed one, then lifted out more, bringing them towards me, one at a time. Helena helped pile them to the side.

There certainly was another room. It had a window, matching the one where we were, but was pitch-black, unlit and filling with dust. Peering through the hole, I could make out nothing. Patiently I cleared a space in the old doorway that would be wide enough and tall enough to step through.

I stood back, recovering, while the dust settled a little. Helena hugged my damp shoulders, waiting quietly for me to act. Covered with dirt, I grinned at her excitedly.

I took the pottery lamp. Holding it ahead of me, I squeezed an arm through the narrow gap and stepped sideways into the tomblike stillness of the next room.

I had half hoped to find it full of treasure. It was empty, apart from its single occupant. As I pulled my shoulders through the gap and straightened up, I met the man's eyes. He was standing by the wall exactly opposite, and staring straight at me.

LXIII

'Oh Jupiter!'

He was not a man. He was a god. The lord of all the other gods, unmistakably.

Five hundred years ago a sculptor with divine talent had breathed life into a massive marble block, creating this. The sculptor who was later to ornament the Parthenon had, in the days before his greatest fame, made for some small anonymous island temple a Zeus that must have excelled all expectations. Five hundred years later, a gang of cheap priests had sold it off to my brother. Now it stood here.

It must have been an awesome task hauling this upstairs. Some of the tackle my brother had used lay abandoned in a corner. I wondered if Epimandos had helped him. Probably.

Helena had ventured into the room after me. Clutching my arm, she gasped, then stood with me staring in rapture.

'Nice piece!' I whispered, aping Geminus.

Helena had learned the patter: 'Hmm! Rather large for domestic consumption, but it does have possibilities . . .'

Zeus, naked and heavily bearded, surveyed us with nobility and calm. His right arm was raised in the act of hurling a thunderbolt. Set on a pedestal in the darkened inner sanctum of some high Ionic temple, he would have been astonishing. Here, in the silent gloom of my brother's abandoned glory hole, he quelled even me.

We were still standing there, lost in admiration, when I heard noises.

Guilt and panic struck us both. Somebody had come into the caupona below us. We became aware of furtive movements in the kitchen area, then feet approaching up the stairs. Someone looked into the soldier's room, saw the mess and exclaimed. I dragged my attention from the statue. We were trapped. I was trying to decide whether there was more to be gained by extinguishing the lamp or keeping it, when another light was thrust through the gap in the brickwork, with an arm already following.

The arm wriggled frantically, as a broad shoulder jammed in the narrow space. Someone cursed, in a voice I recognised. The next minute loose bricks tumbled inward as a sturdy figure forced its passage, and my father burst through into the hiding-place.

He looked at us. He looked at the Zeus.

He said, as if I had just produced a bag of apples, 'I see you've found it then!'

LXIV

His eyes devoured the Phidias.

I asked quietly, 'What are you doing here?' Pa let out a small groan of ecstasy, ignoring my question as he lost himself in admiration of the Zeus. 'Did you know this was here, Pa?'

For an instant Geminus blinked unreliably. But he cannot have known for much longer than I had, or the statue would not have been left here. He must have been starting to guess as he came up the stairs. I tried not to believe he had run into the caupona at top speed, intent on breaking down the wall himself.

He walked around the Zeus, admiring it from all sides. I amused myself wondering whether, if he had found the statue first, he would ever have told me.

My father's expression was inscrutable. I realised he looked just like Festus, and that meant I shouldn't trust him.

'We should have known, Marcus.'

'Yes. Festus was always hanging around this place.'

'Oh he treated it like home!' agreed Pa, in a dry tone. 'We should have guessed. And what's more,' he declared, 'this won't be the end of it. Your precious brother must have had hideaways packed with treasure everywhere he ever went. We can find them,' he added.

'Or we can tire ourselves out looking!' I commented. Euphoria dies very quickly. I felt tired already.

'He will have had a list,' said father, hanging his lamp on the statue's thunderbolt and coming back round to us.

I laughed. 'That would be madness! If it was me, the details would be locked only in my own head!'

'Oh me too!' agreed Pa. 'But Festus was not like us.'

I saw Helena smile, as if she enjoyed thinking that my father and I were alike. With half a million sesterces' worth of Phidias standing opposite, I allowed myself to smile back at her.

We all stood about for as long as possible, gazing at the Zeus. Then, when it became ridiculous to stay in that dark empty space any longer, we squeezed back to the comparative luxury of the furnished room beyond.

Pa surveyed the rubble from my demolition work. 'You made a right mess here, Marcus!'

'I was as tidy as I could be, in a hurry and without proper tools –' While the others gawped and marvelled, I had been planning. 'Look, we need to move fast. We'll have to cover up this rubble as best we can. It would be better to remove the statue before anybody sees it. Horrible – but we must shift it. *We* are sure it belonged to Festus, but explaining that to the owner of the building may not be so easy –'

'Relax,' interrupted my father graciously. 'Nobody's coming here tonight.'

'That's where you're wrong. Will you listen to me? I've been left here on guard while the owner is informed by Petronius that the waiter's dead. Any moment we're expecting to be joined by the mysterious Flora, and she won't be pleased to discover this great hole in her wall –'

Something made me stop. Nobody else was coming. Pa had said it in a flat voice. Even without a reason given, I understood.

'Thanks for looking after things,' my father chirruped wryly. I was still trying to ignore the implications, though already aghast. He reassumed his shifty look. 'Flora's not coming. Acting as watchman is man's work; I volunteered.'

Then I groaned as I realised what I should have worked out weeks before. I knew why my brother had always treated this place as if he owned it; why he had found jobs here for runaways; why he had made free with the rooms. It was all in the family.

Petronius was right. Flora existed. And right, too, that I would have preferred not to discover it. Flora's Caupona was the business my father had bought for the woman who now lived with him, to stop her interfering in his own. *Flora* was Pa's ladyfriend.

LXV

The first part of our plot against Carus and Servia was the most painful: my father raised half a million sesterces by auctioning his chattels. A friend of his called the bids on the day, with Gornia from the office supervising the rest of the sale. Father went to Tibur for a couple of days while it happened, presumably taking the redhead. I had gone to the Campagna, to fetch one of our blocks of Parian stone.

We closed the caupona, on the excuse of Epimandos's death. We made a space in the kitchen area, installed the marble block, brought Orontes over from his lodging with the painters on the Caelian, and set him to work.

'Can you do it?'

'If it will get you awkward beggars off my back . . . Oh I'll do it; just leave me in peace to get on with it!'

Using the Zeus as a copy, together with his memory of its brother the Poseidon, Orontes was to redeem his betrayal of Festus by making us a new Phidias.

While this was in hand, we lulled the collectors into a false sense of security by paying off our supposed debt.

It was just before dawn.

We drove up the Via Flaminia in an open cart, during the last hour that wheeled vehicles were allowed into Rome. Mist hung above the Campus Martius, clothing all the silent public buildings with a wintry chill. We passed the grey stone of the Pantheon and the Saepta, heading towards the elegant gardens and mansions up in the north of the city.

All the streets were still. The revellers had gone home; the robbers were busy hiding their swag under floorboards; the prostitutes were sleeping; the fire brigade were snoring. Door-porters were so deeply asleep visitors could have banged for half an hour and still been left out on the step.

We were ready for that.

When we reached the peaceful middle-class lane where Cassius Carus dwelt with his lady, we backed our cart up against their front portal. As if on cue, one of our oxen lowed. My father sat up on the cart, blurred in the light of smoking torches, and solemnly began to bang an enormous copper bell. A great cloud of starlings rose like a dark curtain from the pantiled roofs and circled anxiously. I and two helpers walked along the street pounding massive gongs.

It was a refined middle-class area where the inhabitants liked to keep their heads down on their pillows whatever excesses were going on outside, but we roused them. We kept up the noise until everyone took notice. Shutters flew open. Watchdogs were barking. Tousled heads appeared everywhere while we carried on banging in a slow, deliberate manner as if it were some dread religious rite.

Finally Carus and Servia burst from their front door.

'At last!' roared my father. The helpers and I gravely made our way back to him. 'The vultures appear for the reckoning!' Pa informed the audience. 'Now hear me: Aulus Cassius Carus and Ummidia Servia maintain that my son Didius Festus – who died a national hero, in possession of the Mural Crown – owed them half a million sesterces. Never let it be said that the Didius family reneged!' It was brilliant. After years of observing puzzled punters in the auction ring, he had the knack of sounding like a man who believed he had probably been cheated, though he could not quite see how. 'Here's the cash then! I call on all those present to be my witnesses.'

He walked to the edge of the cart. I joined him there.

'Here's your money, Carus! It's been counted!'

We raised the first lid together, up-ended the chest on the edge of the wagon, and let its contents spill out on to the roadway. The first consignment of our half-million tumbled at the collectors' feet. With an anguished cry they fell on it, vainly trying to catch up the cash as the coins bounced and spun over pavement and gutter. We shoved aside the empty chest and heaved forward another. Helped by our companions we continued this until a mound of twinkling coinage filled the entrance to the Carus home, chest-high, like a great pile of winter grit left beside a steep road.

303

It was all in small change. Box after box of mixed coppers, ancient bronze bits and silver fell like the mica chips that spangle the sand in the Circus Maximus. We emptied the entire amount into the road. We had no need of a receipt: the whole street could bear witness to our delivery. In fact, as we turned the cart and drove away, many of the collectors' extremely helpful neighbours were rushing up, still in their slippers and nightwear, eager to help gather up the money from the road.

'Enjoy it, Carus,' was my father's parting shot. 'That little lot should see you all right at a few public latrines!'

LXVI

Some weeks later, the fine-art world was humming with news of a forthcoming private sale.

At the gallery of Cocceius stood an interesting marble.

'I can make *no* claims,' said Cocceius, who was an honest kind of dealer, 'for its artist, or its antiquity.'

Collectors soon heard about the statue's striking features, and flocked to gawp. It was a Poseidon: nude, one arm poised and throwing a trident, and with a rich curly beard. Very Greek – and quite magnificent.

'It has an intriguing history,' Cocceius informed enquirers in his comfortable way. He was a quiet, reassuring man, a pillar of the Auctioneers' Guild. 'The illustrious Senator Camillus Verus found this rather nice piece in the attic when going through his late brother's house . . .'

That old tale!

People all over Rome went rushing home to look in their attics.

Nobody else had one.

Two people, a man and a woman heavily wrapped in cloaks and veils, came to view the statue incognito. Cocceius gave them a familiar nod.

'What's the provenance, Cocceius?'

'None, I fear. We can make no guesses. Though it's certainly Parian marble, as you can see.' That was evident. This was no Roman copy in limestone. Even fine Carrara would be noticeably more grey in the vein . . .

'What's the reason for selling?'

'It seems a convincing story. I understand the Senator is trying to raise cash to put his second son into the Senate. I dare say you can ask around their neighbours for confirmation. The bright young thing has made an unexpected name for himself, and with Daddy having Vespasian's ear, his path is now clear to the top.

Finance is their only problem. So offers are invited for this rather handsome sea god, though you'll have to use your judgement as to what it is . . .'

'Where did it come from?'

'Absolutely no idea. The noble Senator's brother imported things. But he's dead, so we can't ask him.'

'Where did he trade?'

'All over. North Africa. Europe. Greece and the East, I believe . . .'

'Greece, you say?'

'There does appear to be some minor damage to one shoulder . . .' Cocceius was completely open, a model of neutrality.

'It's excellent. But you make no claims?'

'I make no claims.' Cocceius was certainly honest; such a refreshing change.

There are many ways of making claims – and not all of them involve direct lies.

The closely swaddled collectors went away to think about it.

Next time they came, the owner was apparently considering withdrawing the statue from sale. Alarmed by this news, the cloaked man and woman stood in the shadows and listened. Maybe other people were in other shadows, but if so they were invisible.

The Senator's noble daughter was explaining to Cocceius that her father might be having doubts. 'Of course we do need the money. But it's such a lovely thing. If it commands a large price, that's wonderful. But we're tempted to keep it and enjoy it at home ourselves. Oh dear! Father doesn't know what he should do for the best . . . Could we ask an expert to have a look at it?'

'Certainly.' Cocceius never pushed his clients to sell against their will. 'I can arrange for an art historian to give you an authoritative opinion. How much are you prepared to pay?'

'What can I get?' asked the noble Helena Justina.

Cocceius was honest, but a humorist. 'Well, for a small fee I can get you a man who will close his eyes and say the first thing that comes into his head.'

'Forget the small fee,' she answered.

'For a little bit more I can get you a *proper* expert.'

'That's better.'

'Which sort would you like?'

Helena looked surprised – though not so surprised as she might have looked before she met me. 'Which sorts can I have?'

'Either Arion, who will tell you it's genuine – or Pavoninus, who will maintain it's a fake.'

'But they haven't seen it yet!'

'That's what they always say.'

Apparently Helena Justina was now growing tense. 'How much,' she demanded at her most crisp (which was about as crisp as toasted bread when you answer the door and forget it until you smell smoke), 'how much would we have to pay for the very best?' Cocceius told her. Helena drew a sharp breath. 'And what will we get for that exorbitant amount?'

Cocceius looked embarrassed. 'You will get a man in a slightly peculiar tunic who stares at the statue for a very long time, drinks some herb tea in a thoughtful manner, then tells you both of the possible verdicts and says that frankly he cannot say for certain which is correct.'

'Ah I see! He,' said Helena, collapsing with a smile, 'is the really clever one.'

'Why is that?' asked Cocceius, though he knew all along.

'Because without putting his own reputation at risk, he leaves people to convince themselves of what they want to hear.' The noble Helena reached a decision in her usual swift manner. 'Let's save our cash! I can speak for Papa.' Obviously they were a free-thinking, liberal family. (And the women were *very* forceful.) 'If we can establish my brother's career the sale will be worth it. People will recognise quality. If anybody offers a good figure, Papa will sell.'

The collectors in the cloaks hurriedly sent both Arion and Pavoninus to look at the Poseidon; then they also paid for the man in the odd tunic, who had very peculiar diction too, and who said that they must make up their own minds.

They decided their need for the Poseidon was desperate.

The question of money was discreetly raised.

Apparently, in order to put young Justinus into the Senate, the illustrious Camillus would need a very large amount. 'The figure which has been mentioned,' said Cocceius in a hushed voice, like a doctor announcing a fatal disease, 'is six hundred thousand.'

Naturally the collectors offered four hundred. To which the owner replied that that was an outrage; he could not possibly settle for less than five. The deal was struck. Half a million in gold aurei (plus the commission to Cocceius) was exchanged for the unknown statue.

Two hours later people were being invited to a viewing at the private house of Cassius Carus and Ummidia Servia, who had acquired a Poseidon by Phidias.

We were even. We had got them off our backs, then retrieved our money. We had fooled them: we had sold them our fake.

We still had the Zeus. We were rich.

Father and I bought an amphora of the best well-aged Falernian. Then we bought two more.

After that, before we touched a drop but knowing we were on the verge of becoming extremely drunk, we went along together to the caupona for a fond look at our Zeus.

We went in through the back lane. The stable door had been properly locked by Orontes when he left. We opened up, amid happy exclamations. We banged the door behind us and lit lamps. Then slowly our celebrations died.

In the cleared space where I had placed the marble block for Orontes to carve still stood – a marble block. A chunk of it was missing, however. Clean stone gleamed with Parian whiteness where this piece had been removed: a neat rectangle, taken off the top. Most of the marble that was supposed to have been transformed into the Poseidon remained untouched.

We walked upstairs. By then we both knew what had happened, but we had to see the proof.

In the room where our Phidias Zeus had been left for Orontes, all that remained now was a severed arm holding a thunderbolt.

'I'm dreaming this . . .'

'That lazy, cheating, dissolute bastard! If I catch him – '

'Oh he'll be far away . . .'

Instead of bothering to carve a whole new statue, Orontes Mediolanus had simply adapted the existing one, giving it a new right arm. Now the Zeus had a trident instead of a thunderbolt.

Instead of a fake, we had sold Carus and Servia our genuine Phidias.

LXVII

It was April, and not as far as I knew an official black day in the Roman calendar, though it would be for ever in mine. In the old republican period New Year began on the Ides of March, so this was the first month of the year. The Senate went into recess to brace itself. To tackle April, you needed to be fit. April was packed with celebrations: the Megalensis and the Floral Games, the Games and Festival of Ceres, the Vinalia, the Robigalia and the Parilia, which was the birthday of Rome itself.

I was not sure I could sustain so much civic joy. In fact, at the moment I hated the thought of any jollity.

I walked through the Forum. At his request I had taken my father to the Saepta and dumped him in his office, stunned, though sober at that point. He wanted to be alone. I, too, could not face seeing anyone. My entire family would be gathering at Mother's, including Helena. Being greeted with garlands, when in fact I was bringing them nothing but my own stupidity, would be unbearable.

I should have checked up. Orontes had told me he preferred to work uninterrupted. I had been taken in by that simple lie.

Creation is a delicate process. Deceit is a fine art.

The Fates had a fine way of deflating our arrogance. I walked through Rome, driving myself on until I could accept what I had done, the chances I had lost. I needed occupation, or I would lose my sanity.

There were still questions to pursue. In all this, I had not forgotten the original commission from my mother. We had solved a murder, and almost pulled off a vengeful coup on behalf of the whole family, but one subject remained open even now: my elder brother's reputation.

Maybe his had been a flawed judgement. Carus, with the aid of Orontes, had defrauded him. I could hardly blame Festus for that any longer, since Orontes had done the same to me. One

309

commercial transaction had gone awry, the only one I knew about. Even without possession of the facts, Festus had been taking steps to put it right. Only his death had intervened. Only the fact that he had trusted no one – not even Father, not even me – had prevented his plans from being followed through.

Was Festus a hero?

I did not believe in heroics. I did not believe he had made some glorious, selfless sacrifice for Rome. Being honest, I had never believed it. He was romantic – but if he had ever, for some unimaginable reason, *chosen* that path, then he would have clinched his deals first. Festus could not have borne the thought of leaving an unfinished scheme. That Phidias, bricked up in Rome where it might never have been found; those blocks of marble abandoned on my sleepy uncles' farm; they told me absolutely: he was expecting to come back.

Did he think I would finish the business? No. I was his executor, but only because the army had forced him to make a will. It was a joke. There was nothing to bequeath formally. There had never been plans for me to adopt those transactions that were my brother's pride and joy. He had wanted to do it; he had intended to complete them himself.

My only legacy was to decide, now, what kind of name I should allow him to keep.

How could I decide?

All I could do was miss him. There was nobody like him. Anything I had ever done that was bad had had its origin in his encouragement. The same went for anything affectionate or generous. I might not believe he was a hero, but that still left plenty to believe in: that great heart, that great colourful, complicated character which even three years after he had died still dominated all of us.

I had continued for too long simply wondering. Tonight, if it existed anywhere, I was going to find the truth.

I had entered the Forum down the Gemonian Steps from the Capitol. I walked from the Rostra and the Golden Milestone, the whole length of the Basilica Julia to the Temple of Castor, where I thought about attending the baths, then abandoned the thought. I was in no mood for the attentions of slaves and conversation with

310

friends. I passed the Vestals' House and Temple, emerging into the area the republicans called the Velia.

All of the district around me, from the Palatine behind me to the Esquiline ahead, taking in both the Oppian and Caelian hills, had been destroyed by fire and then taken over by Nero for the abomination he called his Golden House.

House was the wrong word. What he had created here was even more than a palace. Its lofty structures leapt between the crags, a feast of fabulous architecture. The interior decor was unbelievable, its richness and imagination surpassing anything artists had previously created. In the grounds, he had achieved another wonder. If the architecture was amazing, despite representing such blatant megalomania, even more dramatic was this entire landscape surrounding the halls and colonnades: a natural countryside within the city walls. Here there were parks and woodlands where wild and tame animals had roamed, all dominated by the famous Great Lake. It had been the tyrant's private world, but Vespasian, in a calculated propaganda coup, had thrown it open to everyone as a vast public park.

Smart move, Flavians! Now we had an emperor who treated his own divinity as an irony. He talked of pulling down the Golden House, though he and his sons were currently living there. The lake, however, had already been drained. It was the best-placed site in Rome, right at the end of the Sacred Way, on the main approach to the Forum. There Vespasian intended to use the cavern left by the drained lake to build the foundations and substructures of an immense new arena that would bear his family name.

It was the glory of the city long before the Emperor laid the first stone with his golden trowel. Sightseers regularly came and stood around it. This was the place in Rome to spend a peaceful hour, or several, watching someone else at work. The site of the Flavian Arena had to be the biggest- and best-ever hole in the ground.

I had last stood here looking at it in the company of the centurion Laurentius. After the waiter's death at Flora's Caupona, Petronius and I had sought him out. Rather than talk at his sister's house, amidst the clamour of her young children, we had walked through Rome until we ended up at this building site.

311

Here we had told Laurentius what had happened to Epimandos, and of our belief that Epimandos must have murdered Censorinus.

Laurentius had been prepared for it. Recognising the runaway had already suggested the whole story. Nevertheless, its confirmation, and hearing about the waiter's lonely end, had made us all dispirited.

Laurentius was a sensible type, but even he began to philosophise gloomily.

'Look at those, for instance!' he had exclaimed, as we passed a group of Eastern prisoners. They were digging foundations, though not very busily. Construction sites have their moments of frantic activity, but this had not been one of them. 'We legionaries flog ourselves in the burning sun with our brains boiling in our helmets,' Laurentius complained bitterly, 'while this lot calmly get captured and take their ease in Rome . . . What's it all for?' he demanded. The old cry.

That was when I had asked him about Festus. He had not been present at Bethel. 'I was off with a detachment under Cerialis, in bandit country further south. We were clearing the ground around Jerusalem in preparation for the siege, while the old man himself tackled the towns in the hills − ' He was referring to Vespasian. 'Is there a problem, Falco?'

'Not really.' I felt obliged to show some diffidence. To criticise a campaign hero is to take issue with the whole conduct of the campaign; nailing Festus as less than glorious would diminish the survivors too. 'I did wonder what exactly happened.'

'Did you not receive a report?'

'Who believes reports? Remember, I've been in the army myself!'

'So what are you thinking?'

Somehow I had laughed, almost dismissively. 'Knowing what I do now, I wonder whether when Festus overstretched himself commercially, your own syndicate might have chucked him off the ramparts in disgust at their financial loss?'

'Not an issue!' replied the centurion. He was terse. 'Trust the report . . .' There was nothing else I would learn from him.

Yet as he turned away, in the act of leaving us, he threw back over his shoulder, 'Believe the story, Falco.' Those hard bright eyes glared at me from that quiet, trustworthy face. 'You know what happens. These things are all the same when you get down to it – what took Festus off was probably some stupid accident.'

He was right, and if so, he was right that we all had to forget it. I could believe that angle. Yet it was not enough. For my mother there had to be more than mere belief.

I could go to Pannonia. I could find people who had been present – the men from my brother's own century who had followed him on to the battlement. I already knew what they would tell me. They would say what the army had said.

I could get them very drunk, and they would then tell me another story, but that would be because drunken soldiers all hate the army, and while they are drunk they blame the army for a lot of lies; those lies become truths again as soon as they sober up. His comrades had a vested interest in my brother's official fate. Dead men have to be heroes. Nothing else applies.

Dead officers even more so.

The Judaean campaign was now famous: it had produced an emperor. That was an accident which nobody had expected in the months when Festus died. Festus was lost in March or April; Vespasian was not hailed emperor anywhere until July, and it had taken him a great deal longer than that to complete the process of gaining the throne. Until then, the Jewish Rebellion was nothing. Just another political foul-up in a terrible spot where we pretended to be taking the gifts of civilisation to the wild men, in order to keep a toe-hold in a lucrative trade arena. Unlike most of his colleagues, Festus at least knew at firsthand about the dyes and the glass and the cedar wood, and the links with the silk and spice routes which we needed to protect for ourselves. But even with that knowledge, nobody would fight there – not for a baking desert full of nothing but goats and squabbling religious zealots – unless they could believe at least the promise that their corpse would achieve some glory. Being first man over the battlement of some faded hill town had to count.

It had to count for the mother he had left behind in Rome too.

So since she had asked me, I did what I could. This niggle had been dogging us all for three years now, and the time had come to settle it.

313

The Flavian Arena was to be built by a workforce which the conquests of Vespasian and Titus had conveniently provided: captured Judaean slaves.

I had come to see them.

LXVIII

It was late afternoon when I started my search. I had to tackle one after another of the grisly gang foremen, whose demeanour was worse than the prisoners they guarded. Each passed me on to some other filthy lout with a whip. Some expected money just for saying no. Most were drunk and all of them were nasty. When I finally found the right group of prisoners, talking to them was quite pleasant by comparison.

We spoke in Greek. Thank the gods for Greek – always there to help an informer dodge paying the price of an interpreter.

'I want you to tell me a story.' They stared at me, anticipating violence. It was giving me bad memories of a time I once disguised myself as a hard-labour slave. I found myself scratching reminiscently.

These were prisoners of war, nothing like the millions of nice, clean, cultured fellows Manlius and Varga had ranted about, the secretaries, stewards, toga-folders and wine-mixers who filled the streets of Rome looking just the same as their kempt masters. These were the few male survivors of various Judaean massacres, hand-picked to look good in Titus Caesar's Triumph. Most of the thousands of prisoners had been sent to forced labour in Egypt, the imperial province, but these shaven-headed, dirty, sullen youths had been carried off to Rome first to be paraded as a spectacle, then to rebuild the city in Vespasian's '*Roma Resurgans*' campaign.

They were fed, but thin. Building sites start work at dawn and pack up early. It was late afternoon. They were sitting around braziers now, outside their crowded bivouacs, their faces dark and hollow in the firelight as the winter darkness fell. To me they looked foreign, though I dare say I myself was being regarded by them as an exotic from a culture where everyone had dark jowls, unsavoury religious beliefs, strange culinary habits and a big hooked nose.

'Bear up,' I consoled them. 'You're slaves, but you're in Rome.

315

It may seem hard for hill-farmers to find themselves brought here for endless mud-shovelling, but if you survive this hard labour through to the stonecutting and construction work, you're in the best place in the world. We Romans were hill-farmers once. The reason we clustered here among our theatres, baths and public venues is quite simple – we noticed that hill-farming stinks. You're alive, you're here – and you have access to a better life.'

Jests were not required. Even well-meant stoicism failed. They were desolate and dreaming of their goats.

They let me talk, however. Anything different is welcome to men on a chain-gang.

I knew from their foreman that these hailed from the right area. I explained what I wanted. 'It happened about this time of year, and about three years ago. There had been a hiatus since the autumn before, after Nero died; you may remember a period of uncertainty when hostilities ceased. Then came spring. Vespasian decided to revive his campaign. He climbed into the hills – where you come from – and he occupied your towns.'

They stared at me. They said they did not remember. They said it like men who would lie to me even if they did.

'What are you?' they asked me. Even prisoners of war are curious.

'An informer. I find things for people. Lost things – and lost truths. The mother of this soldier has asked me to tell her how he died.'

'Does she pay you for this?'

'No.'

'Why do you do it?'

'He matters to me too.'

'Why?'

'I am her other son.'

It was as pleasing circuitous as a riddle. The slight shock drew a dry cackle of laughter from these demoralised men whose days were confined to digging foreign mud from a giant foreign hole.

A prisoner rose from his haunches. I never knew his name. 'I remember,' he said. Maybe he was lying. Maybe he just felt I had earned some sort of tale. 'Vespasian was placing garrisons in all the towns. He took Gophna and Acrabata. Bethel and Ephraim came next.'

'Were you at Bethel?' He swore that he was. Maybe he was lying now. There was no way I could really tell. 'Was it a stiff fight?'

'To us, yes – but probably, no.'

'Not much resistance?'

'Little. But we were going to fight,' he added. 'We gave up when we saw the fierceness of the Roman charge.'

Evidently he thought this was what I was wanting to hear. 'That's gracious of you,' I said politely. 'Did you see the centurion?'

'The centurion?'

'The officer. Mailed shirt, metal on his legs, fancy crest, vine stick – '

'The officer who led the charge?'

'He led it?'

'From the front!' smiled the prisoner, certain I would like that. Maybe he had been a soldier too.

'But he fell?'

'He was unlucky.'

'How?'

'An arrow squeezed in somehow between his helmet and his head.'

I believed that. This man had seen our boy.

Helmet not strapped properly. Trust him. Always unlaced, unhooked, half-belted. He hated feeling trapped. Loved sauntering into battle with his chin-strap waving free, as if he had just paused to dint the enemy on his way to somewhere else. Jupiter knows how that man got promoted.

Well I knew how. He was bloody good. Our Festus, with even only half his mind on a problem, could outstrip most of the dull plodders he was up against. Festus was the charismatic kind who soars to the top on talent that is genuine, easy and abundant. He was made for the army; the army knew its man. Stupid enough to show he did have that talent. Placid enough not to offend the establishment. Bright enough, once he was in position, to hold his own against anyone.

Yet still dumb enough to leave his helmet loose.

'Is this satisfactory?'

It was what I had come to hear.

Before I left they gathered around me with more questions about my work. What did I do, and who did I act for? I repaid their description of Bethel with some tales of my own. They were starving for stories, and I had plenty. They were fascinated by the fact that anybody from the Emperor down could hire me and send me out into the world as an agent; they even wanted to take me on for a commission of their own. (They had no money, but we were on good terms by then and I had mentioned that half my 'respectable' clients forgot to pay.)

'So what's your quest?'

'A retrieval.'

They began a long rambling saga involving a sacred item.

I had to break in. 'Look, if this involves the treasures that the conquering Titus lifted from your Temple at Jerusalem and dedicated on the Capitol, I'll stop you there! Robbing trophies from Rome's most sacred altar lies outside my sphere of activity.'

They exchanged furtive glances. I had stumbled on some much older mystery. Intrigued, I pressed for details. What they had lost was a large ship-like box of great antiquity, surmounted by two winged figures and supported on two carrying-poles. The Judaeans wanted to find it because it had magical properties which they believed would help them overthrow their enemies. Ignoring the fact that I didn't want my fellow Romans struck by lightning or smitten with fatal diseases (well not many of them), I was tempted. I love ridiculous stories. But explaining such a peculiar commission to Helena was more than I could face.

I grinned. 'Sounds as if you need a real daredevil for this job! I do divorces, which are hard enough, but I don't think I can undertake to find Lost Arks . . .'

I repaid their information about Festus with hard currency, and we parted friends.

As I picked my way from the bivouac, the unknown prisoner called out after me, 'He was heroic. His whole heart was in the matter. Let his mother be told, the man you seek – your brother – was a true warrior!'

I didn't believe a word of it. But I felt prepared to tell the lie.

LXIX

I can't say I was feeling happy, but I did feel sufficiently improved to give myself a minor treat: I walked from the Forum up the Via Flaminia to the collectors' house. Then I joined the throng who were congregating in their gallery, viewing the Phidias.

Smart people were standing around with that air of constipated fright people have when gazing at great art without a proper catalogue. The women were wearing gold sandals that hurt their feet. The men were all wondering how soon they could politely leave. Silver salvers with very small pieces of almond cake were handed round to reward those who had come to do reverence. As usual on these occasions there had been wine earlier, but by the time I arrived the waiter with the tray had disappeared.

Poseidon looked good. Among the other marble gods, ours held his own. I felt a certain glow of pride. I felt even better when Carus wafted up, his mournful face almost happy for once, with Servia bundling along on his arm.

'Looks impressive.' I popped in an almond slice. 'What's the provenance?'

They dwelt lightly on the tale of the illustrious senator and his brother who imported from the East. I listened thoughtfully. 'A brother of Camillus? Not the one with the cloud attached to his name? I've heard a few shady stories about that one – wasn't he a merchant who handled dubious commodities, and died in mysterious circumstances?' I stared back at the statue. 'Well, I'm sure you know what you're doing!' I remarked. And then I left.

Behind me, I had left an insidious worm of distrust already gnawing morbidly.

LXX

The party at my mother's house which I had wanted to avoid was over. 'We heard about your disaster so I sent them home.' Ma sounded gruff.

'Geminus sent a message about what happened,' Helena explained in an undertone.

'Thank you, Papa!'

'Don't grouch. The message was mainly to warn us to look after you. When you didn't turn up we were worried sick. I've been looking for you everywhere – '

'That makes you sound like Marina drag-netting the bars for my brother.'

'The bars were where I looked,' she confirmed, smiling. She could see I was not drunk.

I sat down at Ma's kitchen table. My women surveyed me as if I were something they ought to catch in a beaker and put out on the back steps. 'I had a job to do, remember. A certain party commissioned me to investigate Didius Festus.'

'And what did you find out?' Mother demanded. 'Nothing good, I dare say!' She seemed to be her old self.

'Do you want to know?'

She thought about it. 'No,' she said. 'Let's leave it alone, shall we?'

I sighed gently. That was clients for you. They come pleading with you to save their skins, then when you've given up weeks of hard effort for some pitiful reward, you take them the answer and they stare at you as if you're mad to bother them with these puny facts. A case that was all in the family made things no better, though at least I knew the parties from the start, so I was prepared for it.

A bowl of food appeared before me. Ma ruffled my hair. She knew I hated that, but she did it anyway. 'Is it all sorted out?' This was a purely rhetorical question, meant to soothe me by pretending to show an interest.

I took a stand. 'All except the knife!'

'Eat your dinner,' said my mother.

Helena muttered to Ma apologetically, 'I'm afraid Marcus has a fixation with tracing your old cooking knife – '

'Oh really!' snapped my mother. 'I don't see the problem.'

'I think Pa took it.'

'Of course he did.' She was perfectly calm.

I choked. 'You could have said that in the first place!'

'Oh I thought I did . . .' I would get nowhere trying to pin her down. Now everything was my fault. 'What are you making so much fuss for?'

I must have been exhausted, because I came straight out with the question everyone had been too sensitive to pose to her: 'If Pa pinched the knife when he left home, how did it reach the caupona?'

My mother appeared to be offended she had reared such a fool. 'Surely it's obvious! It was a good knife; you wouldn't throw it out. But that woman of his wouldn't want someone else's equipment in amongst her own kitchen tools. First chance she got, she gave it a decent home somewhere else. I would have done the same,' said Ma, without vindictiveness.

Helena Justina looked as if she were trying not to laugh.

After a silence it was Helena who risked an even braver question: 'Junilla Tacita, what went wrong between you and Geminus, all those years ago?'

'Favonius,' replied my mother, rather shirtily. 'His name was Favonius!' She had always said that changing his name and pretending to become someone else was ridiculous. My father (said my mother) would never change.

'What was the reason he left?'

Helena was right. My mother was tough. There was no real need to tiptoe around these dainty issues which she must have faced squarely in her time. Mother answered Helena quite freely: 'No special reason. Too many people crammed in too small a space. Too many quarrels and too many mouths to feed. Then people give up on each other sometimes.'

I said, 'I never heard you tell anyone that before!'

'You never asked.' I had never dared.

I ate my dinner, keeping my head down. Coping with family, a man needs to build up his strength.

Helena Justina was seizing her chance to explore. She should have been an informer; she had no inhibitions about asking tactless questions. 'So what made you marry him? I imagine he must have been very good-looking in his younger days.'

'He thought so!' Ma chuckled, implying otherwise. 'Since you ask, he seemed like a good prospect, with his own business and no hangers-on. He ate well; I liked the way he cleaned up a dinner-bowl.' A rare nostalgic haze came over her. 'He had a smile that could crack nuts.'

'What does that mean?' I scowled.

'I know!' Helena Justina was laughing, probably at me.

'Well, he must have caught me in a weak moment,' decided Ma.

I did tell her what the prisoners had said about her famous son. She listened, but what she thought or whether she was pleased to know it was impossible to tell.

She must have had another weak moment after that, because she suddenly exclaimed, 'Did you leave him at the Saepta then?'

'Who? Geminus?'

'Somebody ought to get him out of there.' I felt the familiar formidable sense of pressure as once again my mother was planning an unwelcome job for me. 'He shouldn't be left there all on his own, brooding and getting drunk. It's Tuesday!' Ma informed me. 'He'll have nobody at his place.' Quite right. Pa had told me his red-headed fancy piece, Flora, would be over at the caupona, on her weekly visit, going through the accounts. 'There's a new waiter at that food stall; she'll be wanting to supervise.'

I could hardly believe what I was hearing. In connection with the family, my mother knew everything. You could never escape it; not even if you left home for twenty years.

'I'm not going to be responsible – ' I mumbled weakly.

Then, needless to say, I left for the Saepta Julia.

LXXI

The Saepta was supposed to close in the evening, but rarely did. Jewellery stalls do most of their trade at night. I always enjoyed the atmosphere after dinner. Streamers of small lamps were lit around the porticoes. People relaxed. There were faint odours of spiced meat and fried fish from itinerants selling hot food from trays. The small shops looked like glittering caverns of treasure as the lights gleamed off the metalware and gems. Trash you would never look at by day turned into highly desirable curios.

My father's office had lost its Egyptian furniture but had gained, courtesy of a forthcoming sale, an elephant's foot, some African war gear with a funny smell, a stone throne that could convert into a personal lavatory, two copper cauldrons, three tall stools, a small obelisk (suitable for a garden ornament) and a rather nice set of glass jugs.

'I see you're back on target to make a fortune out of junk! The mulberry glass could turn into a real sale.'

'Right. You should come into partnership; you could be good at this.' My father appeared to be sober: quite a surprise.

'No thanks.' We stared at each other, each thinking over the failed statue scam. The mood between us prickled savagely. 'I've done my best, Pa. I went to the Carus house tonight and planted the thought that they bought a fake. They may have the Phidias, but they'll never enjoy it.'

'This is really good!' rasped my father sarcastically. 'Some people convince the customers that fakes are real. *We* have to live the hard way – we pretend that the genuine article is a fraud!' He launched into the normal family flattery: 'This is your fault!'

'I admit it. End of subject.'

'I left you in charge,' he roared at me bitterly.

'Orontes was your contact! I'll trace him, don't worry,' I threatened, enjoying the prospect of knocking out the sculptor's brains.

'No point. He'll be miles away with that frowsty whore

Rubinia.' My father was as angry as I was. 'I've not been idle either; I've been to see Varga and Manlius. He's left Rome all right.'

'I'll get him back!' I insisted. 'We still have four blocks of good Parian marble – '

'It won't work,' Pa answered rebelliously. 'You cannot force an artist to produce on command. We'd risk him splitting the stone or turning it into some crass cupid with a dimpled bum that you wouldn't stick on a bird-bath. Or a boudoir nymph!' (His worst insult.) 'Leave it with me. I'll find someone.'

'Oh that's rich. One of your hacks, I suppose. We're back in the world of putting false noses on damaged busts, distressing brand-new carpentry, adding Greek handles to Etruscan urns – '

'I'll find somebody else, I said! Someone who can do us a decent copy.'

'Nice Lysippus?' I sneered.

'A nice Lysippus,' my father agreed, not turning a hair. 'Better still, four of them. Wrestlers would be popular.'

'I've lost interest,' I complained bitterly. 'I'm not cut out for this. I know nothing about sculpture. I can never remember whether the canon of perfect proportion is supposed to be illustrated by the Spear Carrier of Polyclitus and the Discus Thrower of Lysippus – '

'Wrong way round,' said my father. Actually I knew I had it right. He was trying to unnerve me. 'And it's the Scraper, not the Discobolos, who illuminates the rule.'

'Four wrestlers then.' Defeated by his tireless villainy, I calmed down. A new sculptor would have to be paid his commission, but four good copies of fashionable originals would still bring us in a birthday present and a half.

'You want to learn how to stay peaceful,' advised Pa. 'You'll do yourself damage blowing off like that every time the Fates hand you a small reverse.' He was the world's most blatant hypocrite.

I noticed we both had our arms folded as we both seethed. With the same wild hair and our chests thrust out, we must have looked like a pair of antique warriors squaring up under the beaded rim of a cinerary vase. He remembered to ask what I had come for.

'Rumour had it you were drunk. I've been sent to shove your head under a fountain and drag you off home safely.'

'I'm sober – but I'll get drunk with you now if you like,' Pa offered. I shook my head, though I knew it was a kind of truce.

He sat back on the old couch, considering me. I stared back. Since he was perfectly sober and not visibly brooding, it seemed time to put an end to my pointless trip. Something was delaying me. There was something I had been thinking about sub-consciously.

'So what are you hanging about for, Marcus? Want to have a talk?'

'There's no more to say.' There was only one chance for this sort of submission, so I waded straight in: 'I could ask you a favour, though.'

My father was startled, but managed to rally: 'Don't strain a gut!'

'I'll ask you once, and if you say no we'll forget it.'

'Let's not make a Pythian dance out of it.'

'All right. You've got five hundred thousand sesterces bricked into the wall chest behind you, am I right?'

Father looked guarded. He dropped his voice carefully. In-voluntarily he glanced towards the gloomy red curtain behind his couch. 'Well yes, that's where it is – at the moment,' he added, as if he suspected me of planning to steal it. His suspicion reassured me. Some things remained beautifully normal, even though I felt sick and light-headed.

'Consider this then, Father. If we had never found the Zeus, you were so sick of having auctions disrupted we would have paid the money to Carus, with no prospect of recouping it. Your money chest and my bank box in the Forum would both be empty now.'

'If you want your contribution back – '

'I want more than that,' I apologised.

My father sighed. 'I think I know what's coming.'

'I promise this is the first and only time in my life I'll lean on you.' I took a deep breath. There was no need to think about Helena; I had been thinking about her for the past twelve months. 'I'm asking for a loan.'

'Well, what are fathers for?' My father could not decide whether to mock me or to groan. There was no suggestion of refusing, even for a joke.

Asking the question had made me feel nervous myself. I grinned at him. 'I'll let you see the grandchildren!'

'What more can I ask!' quipped Geminus. 'Four hundred thousand was it? Carus paid up in big gold ones. At four sesterces to the denarius and twenty-five denarii to the aureus, that will be four thousand – '

'It has to be invested in Italian land.'

'Land then. I dare say I can find an agent to buy us a bog in Latium or a bit of Alban scrub . . .' He rose from the old couch and pulled back the curtain, fetching out the key on its greasy thong. 'You'll want to have a look at it.'

We stood side by side as he unlocked the chest. Even before the lid came up completely I could see the soft gleam of the aurei sparkling under the heavy woodwork. The money chest was full. I had never seen so much gold. The sight was both soothing and terrible.

'I'll pay you back.'

'Take your time,' said my father gently. He knew what this had cost me. I would be in hock to him for the rest of my life – and that had nothing to do with the money. The four hundred thousand was only the start of this debt.

He closed down the lid and locked the chest. We shook hands. Then I went straight to the Palatine and asked to see Vespasian.

LXXII

Under the Flavian emperors the imperial palace was being run with an atmosphere so professional it was positively staid. Sufficient Neronian flimflam remained here to make their serious efforts appear almost ridiculous by contrast. Beneath the exquisite painted panels, stuccoed ceilings with frivolous arabesques, extravagant carved ivory and massed beaten gold, sober teams of bureaucrats now toiled to drag the Empire back from bankruptcy and make us all proud to belong to Rome. Rome itself was to be rebuilt, its most famous monuments meticulously restored while carefully chosen additions to the national heritage would be positioned at suitable spots: a Temple of Peace, nicely balancing a Temple of Mars; the Flavian Arena; an arch here; a forum there; with a tasteful number of fountains, statues, public libraries and baths.

The Palace had its quiet times, and this was one of them. Banquets were held, since a cheerful and well-run banquet is the most popular form of diplomacy. The Flavian regime was neither mean nor cold. It valued teachers and jurists. It rewarded entertainers. With luck, it would even reward me.

In normal circumstances personal petitions for social advancement would be left with the Palace chamberlains to await a decision in maybe months' time, although reviewing the Senatorial and Equestrian Lists was a Flavian priority. One of Vespasian's first acts had been to appoint himself Censor, with the aims of conducting a headcount for taxation purposes and bringing new blood to the two Orders from which public posts were filled. He had his own ideas about suitable people, but never despised the noble Roman art of putting oneself forward. How could he, after he, a rather despised member of the Senate, had put himself forward successfully for the post of emperor?

Adding my scroll to the mountain in a chamberlain's office did not suit the Falco temperament. Since I was known as an Imperial agent I walked in, looking as if I had some sinister affair of state on my mind, and jumped the queue.

I was hoping to find the old Emperor in jovial mood after his dinner. He worked early and late; his most redeeming country virtue was simply getting things done. Evenings were when he was in good spirits, and when favours should be asked. Evening was therefore when I turned up in my toga and best boots, barbered neatly but not effeminately, aiming to remind him of successful missions on my part and old promises on his.

As usual, I left my luck with the Guard on the door. Vespasian was out of Rome.

The Flavians were famous as a family team. Having two grown sons to offer long-term stability had been Vespasian's chief qualification. He and his elder son Titus were virtually partners now; even the younger, Domitian, took a full part in public duties. The night I came to beg for advancement both imperial sons were working; the chamberlain, who knew me, told me to choose which Caesar I wanted to see. Even before I had made up my mind I knew the best choice was to walk away. But I was geared up for action, and could not back down.

Not even I could ask Titus, who had once cast interested eyes on Helena, to give me promotion so I could snatch the girl myself. There had been nothing between them (as far as I could ascertain), but without my presence there might have been. He had a pleasant mentality, but I hate to push a man beyond reasonable limits. Tact necessarily intervened.

'I'll take Domitian.'

'Best thing. He's doing the public appointments nowadays!' The Palace staff laughed. Domitian's fervour in handing out postings left and right had caused even his mild father to criticise.

Despite jumping the queue, I had to wait about. I ended up wishing I had brought one of the judge's encyclopaedias to read or my will to write. But finally it was my turn, and in I went.

Domitian Caesar was twenty-two. Handsome; solid as a bullock; curly-topped, though hammer-toed. Brought up among women while his father and Titus were away on public duties, instead of his elder brother's sweet disposition he now had the introverted, obstinate air that is more often found in an only child. In his first acts in the Senate he had made mistakes; as a result he had been demoted to organising poetry competitions and festivals. Now he conducted himself well in public, yet I distrusted him.

There were reasons for that. I knew things about Domitian that he would not want repeated. His reputation as a plotter had foundation: I was in a position to indict him for a serious crime. I had promised his father and brother they could rely on my discretion – but my knowledge was what had prompted me to choose him of the two young Caesars, and I walked into his presence tonight full of confidence.

'Didius Falco!' I had been announced by officials. It was impossible to tell from his greeting whether the young prince remembered me.

He wore purple; that was his privilege. His wreath was fairly plain and reposing on a cushion. There were no mounds of grapes or jewel-encrusted goblets, very few garlands and certainly no sinuous dancers writhing around the floor. He was attending to public business with the same seriousness as Vespasian and Titus. This was no debauched, paranoid Julio-Claudian. Yet I knew he was dangerous. He was dangerous – and I could prove it. But after so many years in the business, I should have known that did not make my own position safe.

The room was of course full of attendants. Slaves who looked as though they had work to do were, as always in the Flavian audience chamber, quietly proceeding with their business, apparently unsupervised. There was someone else there too. Domitian gestured to a figure on the sidelines.

'I have asked Anacrites to join us.' My request for an audience would have been relayed long before I was actually summoned; during the tedium of my long wait, this disaster had been arranged. Domitian thought I was there as an agent. He had sent for support. Anacrites was the Palace's official Chief Spy.

He was tight-lipped and tense; pale-eyed; obsessively neat; a man who had brought the undercover arts of suspicion and jealousy to new depths.

Of all the petty tyrants in the Palace secretariat he was the meanest, and of all the enemies I could have picked in Rome I hated him the most.

'Thanks, Caesar. We need not detain him. My business is personal.' Nobody reacted. Anacrites stayed.

'And your business is?'

329

I took a deep breath. My palms were sweating unaccountably. I kept my voice low and even. 'Some time ago your father made me a wager that if I could produce the financial qualifications, he would make me a member of the middle class. I have recently returned from Germany where I completed various actions on the state's behalf. I now wish to marry and settle to a quieter life. My elderly father agrees with this decision. He has deposited four hundred thousand sesterces with a land agent, for investment in my name. I have come to beg the honour which your father promised me.'

Very neat. So restrained. Domitian was even more restrained. He merely asked me, 'You are an informer, I believe?'

So much for polite rhetoric. I should have said, *'You're a rat and I can prove it. Sign this scroll, Caesar, or I'll spew the dirt from the Rostrum and finish you!'*

His Caesarship did not look at Anacrites. Anacrites did not need to speak to him. Apart from the fact that everything must have been settled between them before I had even crossed the threshold for my fatal audience, the rules were quite clear. Domitian Caesar stated them: 'In reforming the Senatorial and Equestrian Orders, my father is concerned to provide reputable, meritworthy groups from whom he can draw future candidates for public posts. Are you,' he asked, in that measured tone with which I could not quarrel, 'proposing that *informers* should be regarded as reputable and meritworthy men?'

I opted for the worst kind of salvage: telling the truth. 'No, Caesar. It's a seedy, disgusting occupation, picking over secrets at the worst end of society. Informers trade in betrayal and misery. Informers live off other people's death and loss.'

Domitian stared. He had a tendency to be morose. 'Nevertheless, you have been useful to the state?'

'I hope so, Caesar.'

But the upshot was inevitable. He said, 'That may be. But I do not feel able to grant this request.'

I said, 'You have been most courteous. Thank you for your time.'

He added, with the diffidence that characterised the Flavians, 'If you feel an injustice has been done, you may wish to ask my brother or the Emperor to re-examine your case.'

330

I smiled bitterly. 'Caesar, you have given me a reasoned adjudication which conforms with the highest social principles.' Once Domitian had stacked the odds against me there was no point in exclaiming. Titus would probably refuse to interest himself. I knew without exposing myself to more sorrow that Vespasian would support his boy. As my own would say, what are fathers for?

I scoffed, 'Injustice I cannot accuse you of, Caesar – merely ingratitude. No doubt you will inform your father of my views, the next time he wants me for some stinking mission that exceeds the capabilities of your normal diplomats?'

We inclined heads politely, and I left the audience.

Anacrites followed me out. He seemed shocked. He even seemed to be calling upon some brotherhood of our trade. Well, he was a spy; he lied well. 'Falco, this had nothing to do with me!'

'That's good.'

'Domitian Caesar called for me because he thought you wanted to talk about your work in Germany – '

'Oh I do like that,' I snarled. 'Since you had nothing at all to do with my achievements in Germany!'

The spy was still protesting. 'Even freed slaves can buy their way into the middle rank! Are you accepting this?' Spies are simple people.

'How can I quibble? He followed the rules. In his place, Anacrites, I would have done the same.' Then, knowing that Anacrites was probably a freedman, I added, 'Besides, who wants to rank with slaves?'

I walked from the Palace like a prisoner with a life sentence who had just heard he was to benefit from a national amnesty. I kept telling myself the decision was a relief.

Only as I plodded to collect Helena from Mother's did I gradually allow my spirits to sink under the knowledge that my losses today, which already included dignity and pride, now had to include ambition, trust and hope.

331

LXXIII

Not knowing how to face Helena Justina, I went to get drunk. At Flora's Caupona there were lamps along both counters. The new waiter was presiding with a care and attention which must already have lost several of the old lackadaisical customers. Not a crumb marred the mock-marble counters, which he flicked every few seconds with a cloth, while waiting eagerly for requests to serve the few nervous inebriates. What the caupona had gained in cleanliness it now lacked in atmosphere.

Still, that would change. The old dismal standards were too ingrained to stay under for long. After ten years, mediocrity would reassert itself.

I was pleased to see this new waiter was a man I recognised.

'Apollonius! Just filling in until you get the call back to education?'

'On the house!' he said proudly, placing a cup two inches from my elbow and following it with a neat little dish of exactly twenty nuts.

There was no way I could get drunk in such a pristine environment. Good manners forbade forcing this enraptured soul to hear my pathetic ramblings, let alone mop up after me. I managed a minute of small talk, then drained my cup. I was just leaving when a woman came in from the back room with her sleeves rolled up, drying her hands on a towel.

For a moment I thought it was Mother. She was small, tidy, and unexpectedly grey-haired. Her face was sharp, her eyes tired and suspicious of men.

I could have left even though she had seen me. Instead, I took a deep breath. 'You must be Flora.' She made no reply. 'I'm Falco.'

'Favonius's younger son.' I had to smile at the irony of my preposterous father running away to a 'new life' when even the woman he took with him insisted on using his old name.

She must be wondering whether I posed some sort of threat.

332

Probably Festus when he was around had worried her; possibly she understood that I was different.

'May I ask you to give a message to my father? It's bad news, I'm afraid. Tell him I went to the Palace, but was turned down. I'm grateful, but his loan won't be required.'

'He will be very disappointed,' the redhead, who was no longer a redhead, commented. I fought off my anger at the thought of the two of them discussing me.

''We'll all survive,' I told her. Speaking as if we were one glorious united family.

'Perhaps you will have another opportunity,' Flora offered me quietly, like any distant female relation consoling a young man who had come to announce a failure on the worst day of his life.

I thanked Apollonius for the drink, and went home to my mother's house.

Too many voices greeted me; I could not go in.

Helena must have been waiting. As I reached the foot of the stairs again, heading off by myself, her voice called out, 'Marcus, I'm coming – wait for me!'

I waited while she seized a cloak, then she ran down: a tall, strong-willed girl in a blue dress and an amber necklace, who knew what I had come to tell her well before I spoke. I did tell her, as we walked through Rome. Then I gave her the other dreary news: that whatever I had said to Anacrites, I did not intend to stay in a city which broke its promises.

'Wherever you go, I'll come with you!' She was wonderful.

We went up on the Embankment – the great ancient rampart built by the republicans to enclose the original city. Rome had long outgrown these battlements, which remained now as a memorial to our forefathers and a place to climb to view the modern city. Helena and I came here in times of trouble, to feel the night air blowing around us while we walked above the world.

From the Gardens of Mycaenas on the slopes of the Esquiline arose a soft springtime odour of damp soil stirring with new life. Dark, powerful clouds were thrusting across the skies. In one direction we could see the stark crag of the Capitol, still lacking the Temple of Jupiter, lost to fire in the civil wars. Curving round it, outlined by small lights on the wharves, the river took its meandering course. Behind us we heard a trumpet from the Praetorian barracks, causing a raucous surge of drunken noise from a drinking-house near the Tiburtina Gate. Below, monkeys chattered among the disreputable booths where fortune-tellers and puppeteers entertained the cheap end of society who even in winter took their fun out of doors. The streets were full of waggons and donkeys, the air rent with shouting and harness-bells. Exotic cymbals and chanting announced the begging priests and acolytes of some unsavoury cult.

'Where shall we go?' demanded Helena as we walked. Respectable girls are excited so easily. Brought up to be chaste, staid and sensible, naturally Helena Justina now kicked up her heels at the first promise of a jape. Knowing me spelt ruin for her parents' dreams of curbing her, just as knowing her spelt disaster for my own occasional plans to reform into a sober citizen.

'Give me a chance! I have just reached a wild decision in a moment of despondency; I don't expect to be taken up on it.'

'We have the whole Empire to choose from – '

'Or we can stay at home!'

Suddenly she stopped in her tracks, laughing. 'Whatever you want, Marcus. I don't mind.'

I threw back my head, breathing slowly and deeply. Soon the damp winter odours of the soot from a million oil-lamps would be giving way to summer's scents of flower festivals and spicy food taken in the open air. Soon Rome would be warm again, and life would seem easy, and taking a stand would become just too much agony.

'I want you,' I said. 'And whatever life we can make for ourselves.'

Helena leaned against my side, her heavy mantle wrapping itself around my legs. 'Can you be happy as we are?'

'I suppose so.' We had paused, somewhere above the Golden House, near the Caelimontana Gate. 'What about you, sweetheart?'

'You know what I think,' said Helena quietly. 'We reached the decision that mattered when I first came to live with you. What is marriage but the voluntary union of two souls? Ceremony is irrelevant. When I married Pertinax . . .' She very rarely referred to this. 'We had the veils, nuts and the slaughtered

334

pig. After the ceremony,' said Helena baldly, 'we had nothing else.'

'So if you marry again,' I replied gently, 'you want to be like Cato Uticensis when he married Marcia?'

'How was that?'

'Without witnesses or guests. Without contracts or speeches. Brutus was present to take the auguries – though maybe you and I should dispense even with that. Who wants their failures to be prophesied in advance?' With me, she could be certain there would be failures. 'They simply joined hands, communing in silence, while they gave their pledge – '

Romantic moments with a girl who is well read can be difficult. 'Cato and Marcia? Oh that's a touching story. He divorced her!' Helena remembered angrily. 'He gave her away to his very rich best friend – while she was *pregnant*, mark you – then when the lucrative second spouse dropped dead, Cato took her back, acquiring the fortune. Very convenient! I see why you admire Cato.'

Gamely I tried to laugh it off. 'Forget it. He was full of weird ideas. He banned husbands from kissing their wives in public – '

'That was his grandfather. Anyway, I don't suppose anyone noticed,' Helena snapped. 'Husbands ignore their wives in public; everyone knows that.'

I was still living with a mass of prejudice derived from Helena Justina's ex-husband. Maybe one day I would dispel her bad memories. At least I was willing to try. 'I won't ignore you, love.'

'Is that a promise?'

'You'll see to it!' I said, holding off a moment of panic.

Helena chuckled. 'Well I'm not the incomparable Marcia – and you're certainly not Cato!' Her voice dropped more tenderly. 'But I gave you my heart a long time ago, so I may as well add my pledge . . .'

She turned towards me, grasping my right hand in hers. Her left hand lay upon my shoulder, as always with that plain band of British silver which she wore on her third finger to mark her love for me. Helena made a good stab at the pose of adoring submissiveness, though I am not sure whether I quite pulled off the frozen look of caution which is often seen in married men on tombstones. But there we were, on that April night on the

Embankment, with nobody to see us, yet the whole city assembled around us had we wanted the presence of witnesses. We were standing in the formal Roman matrimonial pose. And whatever communing in silence entails, we were doing it.

Personally I have always thought that Cato Uticensis has a lot to answer for.